The Watcher and The Watched

MICHAEL CRAWLEY

A NEON PAPERBACK

This paperback edition published in 2006 by Neon
The Orion Publishing Group Ltd.
Orion House, 5 Upper Saint Martin's Lane
London WC2H 9EA

A CIP catalogue record for this book is available
from the British Library.

Printed and bound in Great Britain by
Mackays of Chatham.

ISBN 978-1-905-61930-6

I

Petra

My name is Petra, and I like to watch.

It is *because* I like to watch that I bought my condominium apartment on the twenty-fifth floor of Crystal Towers North. It has a wonderful view. From my windows I can see almost the entire interiors of three one-bedroom suites — peer into three bedrooms, three living/dining rooms and three solarium/dens.

I can also glimpse inside, to a greater or lesser extent, twelve more rooms, belonging to eight more apartments — three more bedrooms, three more solarium/dens and two more living/dining rooms.

For a voyeur like me, Crystal Towers is paradise.

Crystal Towers South — the high rise twin to my building, is exactly forty feet away. The apartments in the North Building, that face south, sold for a few thousand dollars less than those that have an uninterrupted view north. I'd have paid a premium to have *my* view, into other apartments, instead of one of the scenic ones. Looking north, from the North building, the view is of mountains. From the South building, looking south, you overlook the Ocean.

I didn't want either. What I craved was what I got — a clear view into other people's lives — particularly their love-lives.

Make that 'sex-lives'. I didn't care whether they loved each other or not.

My windows — all of the windows in both buildings — were designed to take the fullest advantage of the views. They are floor-to-ceiling, and they are wall-to-wall, and they are each made up of two sheets of clear non-reflective plate glass, set at ninety degrees, enclosing a triangular section of Italian-tiled floor.

Standing in one of those triangles, looking out through the invisible glass, it almost feels as if you are on the outside of the building, in the open air, with nothing between you and the drop — twenty-four floors, in my case.

No one who has any fear of heights buys into Crystal Towers.

When I'd paid and tipped the movers, and they'd left, the first things I unpacked were my new cameras. I'd bought three of them, one for each window. I was very self-disciplined. I simply set the Nikon SLRs up on their tripods, one in the triangle in my living/dining room, one in my bedroom, and one in my solarium/den, loaded them with 400-speed Kodak, and adjusted the focus of their 500mm telescopic lenses, in case any 'photo-op' arose.

I was satisfied. The magnification was sufficient that I could read the signature on a painting that hung on the far wall of the living/dining that was directly opposite my bedroom. With that sort of resolution I'd be able to distinguish individual pubic hairs, once there were pubic hairs to focus on. There would be. I was sure of that. People who live two hundred and fifty feet above the ground grow careless about drawing blinds.

I turned to my other chores. It took the rest of the day to unpack and set up the remainder of my things, although I live a Spartan life, and have very little furniture. I live alone, you see, and had no intention of ever inviting guests. Most of the furniture that I own is props, for my work.

What took time was my computers, my equipment, my dark-room-in-a-closet, my mirrors, and my wardrobe. They had all been packed very carefully. By the time I was done I had a dozen large cartons, several of them still half-full with the Styrofoam beads and forms that had protected all my precious things.

I called the concierge before piling all my discards in the hallway outside my door. The service is very good, and I'd already spread a few hundred in tips, to make it even better.

It's worth paying, to preserve my privacy. I never furnish the way other people furnish. If I'd let the building's staff into my home, there might have been gossip, about that 'weird woman in 2510'.

I protect my own privacy, as only one who makes her living by stealing the privacy of others will.

It *is* stealing — what I do. I wouldn't count it as theft if I was a voyeur simply for the thrills, but it is also how I make my livelihood. Isn't it nice? I earn my living from doing what I love to do best — being a 'Peeping Tom', or, in my case, a 'Peeping Thomassina'.

And it's a good living. In some circles, 'Petra, no last name', is famous. I'm considered something of an artist, by those who know my work. It's all a sham, of course. I don't consider what

I do to be 'art', but simply a 'craft'. Nevertheless, my works sell for tens of thousands, or sometimes more. I get less for the 'photographs', and more for the 'paintings'. Neither are genuine 'art'.

What I do is very simple. I take photographs of people. For *my* work, I mainly take photographs of people in 'compromising situations'. I don't hire models. I use real people, in real situations, secretly. I steal their images.

And I use myself.

I'm 'self-created'. What I am — what I look like — is all artificial. My body is nice, but not spectacular. I have reasonable breasts, I suppose, but my hips are much too slim. Perhaps my legs are my best feature, being overlong for my proportions. An old friend used to call them 'wrap-around' legs.

My face is pretty, in an 'elfin' sort of way, but definitely not beautiful. About all it has going for it is the size of my eyes — and their almond shape — but certainly not their colour.

My eyes are... I suppose 'pale and nondescript' would be the best description. That's me all over — the original me. I'm not an albino, but I *am* colourless. My hair, which I keep cropped as short as an otter's pelt, is fair — not 'blonde'. 'Blonde' has colour, and life.

My skin is white — almost to the point of translucency. Kind people have called it 'alabaster', or 'egg-shell'. My lips, and even my nipples are the palest pink. What little body hair I once had has been removed, permanently.

None of that matters, not now. In fact, my lack of colour is an advantage. I own sixteen pairs of contact lenses, tinted in shades from light blue to jet black, and even two pairs in metallic finishes, gold and silver, plus a pair in glittering demonic red.

My eyes are whatever colour I choose them to be, natural or unnatural. My preference is for the 'unnatural', in eye colour as in most things. 'Natural' is where we started, right? Since then we've been making improvements.

I have a wardrobe of wigs. Some are real hair, and some are 'wild', in greens and blues and tinsel tones. I can make my eyes and hair match — which is something you don't see that often.

My cosmetic case can give me a pink glow, a deep tan, or even that beautiful golden olive that you only see on a few very young Greek girls from the villages high in the Pindus Mountains.

My cosmetics give me *definition*. I am a canvas. I paint myself *on* myself, fresh and different, at least once a day.

That too, that, 'self-delineation', is both my pleasure, and part of my profession.

And my computers bring it all together.

I photograph people, both male and female, while they are performing acts of love, or even when they are not, provided they are either scantily clad, or nude. My computer feeds on these photographs. With a little help from me, my computers strip off garments, and... improve? Alter? Adjust?

A delicate bra fades away, leaving breasts that are invisibly supported. Blemishes disappear. A few pounds of excess weight melts. Breasts are lifted. Ugly hair dissolves. Penises enlarge. Poses are rearranged. Bodies are juxtaposed.

One expanded pixel at a time, composites appear. An hour at my screen melds that kneeling girl with that standing man — and although they have never met — she is performing fellatio on him.

Perhaps 'she' is me. I am my own best model. I have made love, electronically, with hundreds of people who have never met me or even seen me, and never will.

Those who see my work never recognise a subject as 'me'. That's vital. Nor would my unwitting models recognise themselves. *My* people, the ones I create from the raw materials of too-human flawed bodies, are all idealised, incredibly beautiful, each one perfect, in its own way.

That is my craft. I require no 'inspiration'. Real sex is my 'divine impulse'. I am simply the distiller. I skim off the dross. In life, a couple making love may be, to my mind, contaminated by non-erotic influences. She may be planning a menu; he might be at the office, mentally. That inattention shows. My computers boil it off, leaving just the quintessential lust.

Just as my computers have the power to make her thighs more slender, and his more muscular, so do they bring *focus*. In my work, the couples, the trios, the foursomes, are all intent on one thing only. Pure Sex.

I am the purifier.

You won't see my work in public galleries. I am collected, by special people, wealthy people, with rarefied tastes. My coffee-table book, *Gods and Goddesses*, was distributed privately, by a company that has offices in Hamburg and Hong Kong. I could have retired on what I was paid for those thirty-six computer-enhanced photographs.

My favourite composition was 'Circe at Night'. It took a lot of work. I, of course, was the basis of Circe herself, and that part was easy. It was the animals that were arduous to create. Circe was shown kneeling, and performing cunnilingus on a creature that was half panther, half woman. She was, at the same time, being sodomised by a Minotaur, and being suckled on by an asp and a racoon. In the background, pigs and wolves, tigers and antelopes, all coupled in a variety of imaginative ways, while the near foreground hinted that the lion had, indeed, laid down with the lamb.

It took two hundred and forty hours to complete, not counting research and the gathering of materials. A full forty of those hours were spent just in getting the shadows right.

Other pictures in the book portrayed the obvious myths, Leda and her Swan, Europa and her Bull, Venus and Apollo, but some were more creative — Pan and Aphrodite; Orpheus, Euridice and Pluto, lit by hellfire, in triple embrace; and Arachne, spider-goddess, spinning a bondage-web around a rampant Hercules.

If people still believed in those old Gods, I'd likely be hunted down for heresy.

I'm working on another book of photographs, right now. It will be based on those tales from the Arabian Nights that don't make it into children's books.

I prefer to work on paintings, though. Perhaps I shouldn't dignify what I do with the word 'painting'? I use my computers again, you see. With modern technology it is simplicity itself to transfer the composite photographs that I produce, onto canvas. They only appear as shadows, of course — the colours don't come out true. That's when I take up my palette, and do my 'paint-by-numbers' thing.

It takes me perhaps a month of long days to transform an erotic photograph into a 'work of erotic art', which I can then sell for a hundred times what I would have been paid for the original computer-photograph.

I should concentrate my efforts on that, if I was greedy, but the problem is *time*. My library of raw-material illicit photos grows faster than I can use it up. You see, when my camera captures an erotic image, I find myself consumed with a lust, a lust to redefine, purify, turn lead into gold. I have to work quickly, or those lenses will freeze yet another pair, or more, of human forms, that *demand* I turn them into immortal images of undiluted sensual ecstasy, abandoning the previous project.

I can't keep up. My supply of images is ample. The demand for my work seems to be insatiable. It is my production that causes a bottleneck. I shall die, one day, with ten thousand potential creations yet unborn. That is the tragedy of my life. I suppose it is the tragedy of any creative life.

By the time I had done unpacking and arranging, it was dark, and I was dirty.

I showered, quickly and efficiently, without lingering, covered my body with a brief cotton wrap, and poured myself a sipping drink — a champagne flute, half Cointreau, half orange juice that has been chilled until crystals of ice formed. My eyes skipped over my many mirrors. I am not fond of looking at myself in my natural state. Petra is not beautiful until she has been created anew.

My cameras beckoned. There was a light on in the room directly opposite my window. It was a living/dining room, which is better for me than a bedroom. So many people turn off the lights, and crawl under covers, when they make love in bedrooms. People who make love in living rooms leave the lights on, and are generally more imaginative in their sexual activities.

I pulled up a stool, perched, and put the viewfinder to my eye. A moment of fine-adjusting the focus brought me the image of a man, alone. He was tall, rangy, with greying hair that was tied at his nape in a pony-tail. His face had a sardonic cast — almost like a pirate.

He was naked.

He had the shoulders of a gladiator, sloped, and heavy. His waist was trim for a man who had to be in his late forties, and his bottom, turned towards me, was lean, hard, and looked as if it had been cleft by the upward stroke of an axe.

He was doing something with a television set — no — the VCR sitting above the set. He turned towards me as he walked back to his seat — a black leather recliner, sculpted and modern. There was a matching sofa against the other wall, oversized in every dimension. The rest of the furniture looked to be antique. Like the man, the apartment was a combination of old elegance and modern functional.

The plates of his pectorals were solid slabs, punctuated by small crisp nipples; his ribcage was full, and strong; he had a flat belly, and beneath it, his sex was as curved as a scimitar, so arced that its head wagged against his belly an inch above his navel.

I squeezed the camera's button, capturing him.

He sank into his chair. The arms obscured my view of his private parts, but then he pressed back, and rose on the seat.

I squeezed once more.

The man's long artistic fingers pointed a remote. The screen flickered with light. My angle was wrong. I couldn't see what it was that he was watching, but it had to be erotic. The mere anticipation of viewing it had engorged him to full quivering erection.

A man, naked, alone, with a full erection, watching a video? It was easy for me to guess what sort of tape it was. My surmise was confirmed when the man took himself in hand, and began to stroke, slowly, lovingly.

I squeezed, and squeezed.

He had a beautiful penis. When I used these stolen images, I would leave it as it was, unretouched. Sometimes nature is kind.

He moved. It almost startled me. I had been expecting him

to stay the way he was, slowly pumping, watching the screen's images, until his lust overcame him, and he gathered speed in the sprint towards his climax. I was ready for that. My film is fast. With luck, I might have captured his milky fountain as it squirted. Somehow I was sure that it would be a real spurting, not some dribble, and I was equally sure that it would be a proud jetting, not smothered in a convulsive folding of his body and cut off by a gripping fist. No — this was a man who would gush, arrogant and proud.

But he moved. I held my breath... and exhaled slowly. He wasn't deserting me, leaving my camera unfulfilled. No — he simply hitched his legs, one over each leather arm, spreading his thighs wide. He braced, and straightened his limbs, lifting himself higher, making his body into a bridge of taut lust.

If only I'd had another camera, there with him, pointing up from the floor in front of his chair! What a magnificent image I could have captured then!

His hand was moving faster. If wasn't that frantic pace that signals that the end is close, just a gradual quickening of the rhythm, as if the erotic content of what he was watching had intensified, and he was reacting to its urge.

I squeezed, with one hand, and smoothed my beaded glass under my wrap, across my left breast, icy on its nipple. Perhaps..? Perhaps I should join that stranger, in spirit? I let my thighs part, and laid my glass aside.

I *do* masturbate, but rarely when I am just 'me'. My preference is to prepare myself, lovingly, creating out of my banal body and insipid face some special form, transforming myself into an erotic image, fully worthy of giving, and receiving, love. Then I adore my own creation, in mirrors.

My fingers found the warmth between my thighs. No one could see me. My room was dark. There was no one there to see how unworthy I was, so why didn't I..?

I wanted to, but I couldn't.

Was it possible for me to dash to my cosmetics and prepare myself, swiftly, and get back to my position in time to join him, when his time of joy came?

Ambivalent, I hesitated for a long moment, and then made up my mind. It took just a few minutes to give myself the minimum — burgundy lips and nipples, two quick smears of Bordeaux eye-shadow — but when I returned to my stool, I was too late. That room, that lust-filled room opposite, was in darkness.

I washed my wasted beauty away, and went to my solitary bed, unfulfilled.

II

Millie

My husband, Hugh, is a true romantic. He never forgets birthdays, or anniversaries. Between the fixed celebrations, he creates more. Scarce a month passes that he doesn't find some excuse for a 'special occasion'.

He is my husband, my friend, and my lover. Especially 'my lover'.

Hugh believes that love — physical love — should be an endless adventure. So do I. We both do our best to surprise each other, as often as possible, with some new variation of the way that we show each other how we feel.

The excitement never dies, so our love will last forever.

Hugh surprised me that evening.

I was late back from my bridge game, and feeling good. We girls only play for a penny a point — just for fun — but I'd managed to finish the game fifty-some dollars up. That was a first, for me. Usually I'm ten or twenty dollars down. It's my lack of concentration.

How the other girls can spend an entire evening, sitting still, and not let their minds wander to thoughts of sex, I don't know. Every time one of the others had complained about 'going down' in her contract, I'd had to suppress a fit of giggles.

Somehow, that night, I'd managed to win consistently, and I'd still enjoyed a fantasy or two. Penny, our hostess, is quite attractive, even if she *is* ten pounds overweight. Between bids, I'd done things to her plump little body, in my mind, that would have shocked the modest cotton panties that I was sure she wore, off her, had she known. And *still* I'd won.

I drove home hoping that Hugh was still up, and awake. I planned to relate to him exactly what I'd been thinking about, and to have him pleasure me, very slowly, with his mouth, as I told him my fantasy tale about binding Penny's breasts with thin twine, and the things I'd thought of doing to her nipples. We both of us, Hugh and I, have rich fantasy lives, and always share them, for our mutual pleasure.

I opened the door to our apartment, on the twenty-fifth floor of Crystal Towers, South Tower, hung my coat in the closet, and slipped out of my demure go-to-bridge blue and white polka dot dress. That left me in bra and panties — *much* skimpier that Penny would dare wear, and my garter-belt, hose, and heels. I'd have liked to have changed into something more exotic, but I was in too much of a hurry to get my thighs wrapped around Hugh's face. I needed the magic of his tongue, and when I need, it can get to be quite urgent.

I fluffed up my marmalade hair, stepped into the living room, and froze. Hugh *was* up, very much so. The darling man was stark naked, spread wide-legged on his recliner, watching TV, and playing with himself. I was touched. My sweetheart had arranged the 'tableau vivant' especially for me,

I knew. Not only that, the video he was watching was one he'd made about two years before — of me — when he'd snuck into the bathroom and caught me masturbating in the shower.

He's *such* a romantic! Hugh had arranged to have me catch him masturbating, watching *me,* as I'd been when *he'd* taped me, masturbating. You can't affirm your mutual sexuality much better than that, can you!

What could I do but complete the chain?

Silently, as if he didn't know I was there, I hooked my thumbs into my panties, and eased them over my hips and down my thighs. Watching his lovely strong fingers manipulate his own sweet strong flesh, I, as Hugh puts it, "fondled my petals until my orchid bloomed and my stamen was stiff." Once I was open, and wet, I folded three fingers together and slid them in — up — deep — deeper — deepest.

My fingers' rhythm soon matched that of Hugh's hands pumping. As his penis stroked *through* his hand, my fingers slid *up*, inside me. His upstroke was my downstroke. Fifteen feet apart, we were making synchronised love to each other, through our hands, our lust, and our love.

Hugh knows that video well. He knows *precisely* when I reach my first climax, on it. I could tell by the speed of his hand that he planned to join the video-me, in simultaneous orgasm. From where I stood I could see both Hugh, and the screen. I was doubly stimulated. Watching myself, and remembering that night, turned me on tremendously.

Watching Hugh being aroused by that same electronic *souvenir d'amour*, intensified my pleasure. He had started before me, but I had come home with lust fizzing in my veins, so my level of arousal was able to catch up with his quite quickly. I paced myself, and...

...and we loving three came together, Hugh, video-me, and real me, in a triple gush of joy.

"Shall we continue in the bedroom?" Hugh asked as he wiped himself.

And we did.

III

Petra

I woke ready to throw myself into my work. Sexual
frustration does that for me. Sex is my power-source,
after all.

I bathed, and dressed. I made my face up in flawless
translucent pink. My lips became cupid's bows. I put on a
shortish black wig, a page-boy, that curled immaculately to
the nape of my neck. The pale blue suit that I buttoned was
circa 1955, a vintage Dior. It had a full skirt, over a dozen
frilly white underskirts, and a fitted waist-length jacket, with
tight sleeves and a high Peter-Pan collar. My hose were beige,
'fully fashioned', with seams, and my shoes were black patent,
with small neat heels. Finally, I pulled on lacy white wrist-
length gloves and topped myself with a perky pill-box hat
that had a brief white veil.

I was a picture-perfect 1950's glossy-magazine version of a
housewife, a more glamorous June Cleaver, perhaps, or a

young Jackie Kennedy.

The pose was an easy one. I just had to lean forwards from my hips, one arm extended, stiff as a Barbie doll, my fingers curled loosely around nothing, and press down on the remote trigger on the floor with my shiny toe.

When I'd fed the shot to my computer, and touched up my face slightly, I'd add a stallion, with a pizzle that I'd exaggerate. My empty fingers would curl around the beast's scarlet-tipped penis, as if masturbating him. It would make one of my commissioned pictures for *Depravité du Monde*, a Danish monthly that is published in four fractured languages.

I should have got on with my next project, but I was edgy. I could still see that beautiful man, with his so-masculine body arched high above that chair in a rigour of lust. I could still see the curved prong of his sex. Its arc was branded on my cortex. I decided to take a day off my scheduled work, and simply concentrate on exploring my neighbours. *That* too, was part of my work, wasn't it?

This time I was determined not to be caught unawares. I really *needed* an orgasm. I would dress properly for the occasion. If my peeking proved unfruitful, I could always play 'charades'.

That's what I do, when my body demands release, and I have no one to spy on as I satisfy it. For 'charades', I dress up, take a few pictures of myself, and always end up in front of a mirror, spying on whoever it is I've painted on myself, as *she* masturbates, the slut. I've tried masturbating with no visual component, but it never works.

Why on earth do people have sex in the dark?

I stripped off my 1950's perfection, washed her face down my vanity sink, and walked into my closet.

The man I was hoping to spy on was an 'older man', and

obviously highly sexed. That made my choice of 'me' very easy. I laid out my costume ready, and went back into the main bathroom, where I'd had then add extra mirrors and Hollywood lighting. There was plenty of room for the extras. The bathrooms are oversized, with Jacuzzi tubs big enough for two, and separate glass showers, quarter circular, in a corner.

My make-up was to be 'natural', to look as if I had no make-up on at all, just a pretty face, with a trace of pink to its lips, and a few freckles. The wig was honey-blonde, with braids that reached down to my waist. I applied just enough nipple-rouge to define my nipples, no more.

I debated whether or not to wear any underthings, and decided yes, I would. It'd be more in character. I pulled on a pair of dark blue cotton panties, with elastic at the waist and legs, and a pleated tartan kilt, very short. My shirt was white cotton, and thin, but the pockets over my breasts made it just thick enough not let my pale-pink nipples show through unless someone looked very closely. I added white knee-socks, flat 'Mary-Jane' shoes, and a blue-and-gold stripped tie, knotted more than tied.

When I was done I was back in the fifties once again, as a cute schoolgirl, maybe fourteen or fifteen — the kind that boys' mothers approved of, and boys' fathers looked at from the corners of their eyes, and directed into deep-seated armchairs, the better to view the careless sprawl of slender young thighs. I'd become the sort of babysitter divorces are made of.

'Depraved innocence' is one of my favourite things.

Skipping, and humming 'Why do Fools Fall in Love', I went to my stool and camera, and settled down.

There was no sign of life in the apartment directly opposite — 'his' apartment.

I trained my telescopic lens into every apartment it could

reach, and drew blanks on all. I even tried two floors up, where all I could glimpse was the ceilings, before I remembered that it was the floor with the common rooms — with a pool table and card tables, etcetera.

Still, it was early. I frisked to my kitchen, made myself a plate of peanut-butter and blackberry jelly sandwiches, and poured a tall glass of cold milk.

By five, my plate just held crumbs, and I was still searching in vain. I'd just about decided to go to a mirror and seduce my juvenile self, when my eye caught a movement in a bedroom one floor down, and to my right. It was likely nothing, but I rushed into my solarium, where the viewing into that room would be better.

I was in luck.

Their bedroom was crowded with furniture. It looked as if they'd inherited from two sets of Victorian parents, and had crammed their place with oversized ornate mahogany. There was barely two feet between the foot of a carved bed and the front of a serpentine dressing table, with three mirrors.

I appreciate people who decorate with mirrors. My telescopic lenses can't see around corners, but if there are mirrors...

Those ancient wooden-framed looking glasses showed me parts of a young blonde woman leaving her bathroom. What I saw was a towel being rubbed on a face, and a naked torso, to just below a trim waist. The towel's rubbing vibrated a pair of full breasts before it was draped casually around a swan-like neck.

She sat herself on the foot of the bed. I could see her three times over, then. From my side I got a profile view of her bosom, tip-tilted, and with a delightful heft. Her navel folded as she leaned forward.

I could see what she was wearing below her waist — white hose, with matching panties and garter belt. In her largest mirror I saw both staring-nippled breasts as she raised her arms to pin her hair back. The furthest mirror framed her other profile, the side of her other breast.

She bent closer to the mirror. Her breasts swayed. She pursed her lips, and picked up a pot of cream.

The naughty teen on my stool, spying on the older lady, pulled up her skirt and slid a cool hand between the elastic at the waist of her panties and her warm belly.

A movement caught my eye. I panned my lens. A young man entered the bedroom, dressed in just a shirt and tie, bare-legged. It looked as if the couple were getting ready to go out for the evening.

The man looked at the woman, in the mirror. His eyes changed, clouding, the way men's eyes do. He looked at his watch. Apparently they had time to spare, because he crossed the room, slid on his bottom across the bed, and straddled the woman's rear, from behind, bracketing her hips with his thighs. He folded his arms around her waist and nuzzled her naked back. I zoomed in, to watch the play of his tongue on the ridge of her spine, and then I pulled back out again, for the 'big picture'.

She ignored him. Her make-up was more important than he was.

His hands cupped her breasts. She smiled into the mirror, and reached for foundation. He jiggled her. She did that 'purr' thing with her shoulders, leaning back on him for a moment, and continued with her face.

I — the schoolgirl on the stool — was moistening.

The man's fingers found the woman's nipples. What he was doing to them must have distracted her, because she tried to brush his hands away. He said something, and she replied. He argued. So did she. His fingers kept working, plucking, twisting.

Perhaps the persuasion of his fingers proved more potent than that of his words, or it could be that she just decided to humour him. She leaned up and forward, lifting her rear high, but still working on her face. He pushed her panties down to her thighs and shimmied closer to the foot of the bed, beneath her naked hips. With his palms steering her bottom, she sunk back down. His face went slack. He lay back, flat on the bed, with her sitting on him, obviously impaled to the hilt.

With her elbows on the dressing table, applying mascara with deft little upwards strokes, she held perfectly still from her waist up, but her hips rotated, and ground, very slowly.

I zoomed back, for a fuller picture, tracked, and then zoomed in, close on his face. It was screwed up in an agony of ecstasy. I panned, to her hips, where they swivelled in small controlled circles. And *still* she worked on her face.

There was a bruise low on her left buttock, as if she'd bumped a desk. A blue vein emphasised the pure whiteness of her inner thigh, the one furthest from me. Muscles flexed under her skin.

His hands cupped and rubbed at her bottom, squeezing and stroking alternately, lifting her and lowering her on his palms.

She finished her face. Leaning forward once more, she took her weight on her arms. Her rear went into a shaking judder, fast and furious, and then... either he said something, or she knew him very well, for she pulled up, and off him, leaving his flesh straining up and his hips jittery with lust. She turned, took his penis in her hand, and pumped, hard, twice.

He rolled to his side as the second pump pulled him into completion. I squeezed twice on my camera's trigger as white cream frothed from him, seemingly straight at my lens, but really just onto the rumpled bedcovers.

Some people, like me I guess, are sponges when it comes to blame. My first thoughts, on seeing that man reach his orgasm, were of guilt. I'd been watching him, mainly with the intention of discharging my own pent-up sexual tension. He'd come, and I hadn't, and ergo — it was all my fault. I had an irrational feeling I'd somehow let him down. He'd strived for, and reached, his orgasm, but he'd had to do it alone. The woman had been the instrument, but hadn't really been a full participant. I found that sad. Self-love is one thing, but if two people are involved, they should both be *involved*.

I hadn't failed him, of course. If he'd been able to delay his reaction to the blonde's gyrating hips for just a minute longer, I'd have reached my own release, and been able to get back to my work. It was *his* fault for being so fast, if anyone's.

I licked my fingers clean, and shimmied out of those ugly panties. I was too horny to play 'innocent' any more. If I was to be a teenybopper, I wanted to be one who was more 'depraved', and less 'innocent'.

I tore the tie from my neck and hooked a hand to rip the buttons of my shirt open, leaving it agape, showing one breast. By the time I got to the mirror in my studio — that had been the 'den' — I looked as if I had just been thoroughly ravished, and had enjoyed every moment.

Standing spread-legged and bent-kneed before the glass, I pulled my skirt up at the front to tuck its hem into its waist-band, thrust my naked bald pubes forward, and rammed three fingers deep... but it didn't work.

My lust couldn't focus on that depraved schoolgirl. It was aimed elsewhere — at an older man with a pony tail.

When I got back to the camera in my living room there was

a light on in the room opposite. The man — *my man* — was having his supper, at a small table at the other end of the room. He wasn't naked this time. He was wearing a plum velvet jacket that, combined with his full grey locks and pony tail, made him even more of a swashbuckler from a past century than he'd seemed before.

He wasn't alone. Sitting opposite him was a woman with a tumbling mass of auburn-and-tawny, silver-streaked blonde-tipped hair. She was in forest green. Even when I zoomed in close I couldn't be sure whether her dress was a dull-finish fine-ribbed jersey, or perhaps a textured Ultrasuede. Whatever, it clung. It was backless, sleeveless, and left her shoulders bare, but fit her high at the throat. The fabric was thin enough that the prominence of her nipples cast shadows on it.

She stood and went to the buffet to pour wine, so I had the opportunity to see her from head to foot. She too, like the man, seemed out of some past era.

The shape of femininity today is more streamlined. This woman wasn't svelte. She was voluptuous. Her waist had to be less than twenty-four inches, but her hips were a fanfare of vibrant curves. Her legs were long, and tapered. I couldn't see them directly, because the dress reached the floor, but it concealed nothing of her thighs' shape. It lay on them like a thin coat of green snow.

She suited him. They were a matched pair. He was magnificently masculine, and she was gloriously feminine. Their mating would be like that of a satyr with a wood nymph. I took three quick shots of them, even though they were fully clothed and doing nothing sexual at all.

That's wrong. They lived. They breathed. With them, those were sensual acts.

I chewed the end of my wig's blonde braid, and lifted my skirt again, ready to accompany them into pleasure. This time there would be no delay. The moment one of them touched the other, I would start fondling myself.

Their meal continued. Although I couldn't hear a word, I knew that they were flirting. His lifted eyebrow brought a smile to her lips. Her shrug, sinuous despite the weight of her breasts, made his nostrils flare. There was repartee, there had to be, and innuendo, and suggestions, insinuations, hints conveyed by looks and grins. They were sitting there, those two, eating supper, and stroking each other verbally. Their meal was foreplay.

The heat in his eyes was matched by the flame in hers.

I checked my camera, and reloaded swiftly, even though there were a dozen frames left unshot. The erotic tension *had* to break. When it did, I didn't want to miss capturing a single moment.

He said something that made her laugh. She reached both hands to the back of her neck, and unhooked. The front of her dress fell to her waist. Her breasts were magnificent — full and proud, with halos the colour of milky coffee and espresso nipples the size of demi-tasses.

He sipped wine. Their conversation continued.

He wasn't indifferent to her wanton display — I could see that in his eyes. He was just... controlled? Savouring the teasing that her body was inflicting on him?

I wriggled on my stool. This was going to get *very* interesting, I was sure.

They'd been eating lobster. There were dishes of melted butter over short candles. Keeping her eyes on his, without changing her expression, she dipped two fingers into clear warm liquid, and drew circles around one nipple, on its halo at first, but then spiralling in towards its peak.

The nipple gleamed. I zoomed in just in time to catch a close-up of one drop of butter-dew, trembling as it hung from dark engorged flesh.

She moved. I had to zoom back quickly to get the picture again.

The man stood, and took his jacket off. Still chatting, he rounded the table, took a dish of butter, and used *his* finger — just one — to make her second nipple match the first.

She took his hands in hers, tucked in his fingers so that just the index one on each hand was still unfolded, guided them to the butter, and then back to her nipples. Once his fingertips were rotating on her glistening points, she turned towards him, twisting on her chair.

I remembered to part my thighs and moisten the balls of two fingers and my thumb in my own seepings.

I could see by the movements of the woman's arms that she was opening the fly of his dark pants, but I couldn't — *dammit* — see more. I *did* see her reach for the second container of butter, but when she turned to him again, to *use* it, her lovely naked back blocked my view.

"Turn around!" I demanded, my slippery fingers gripping the shaft of my clit, ready to start, but they couldn't hear me. My imagination had to suffice.

I was tempted to make a dash to my kitchen, to fetch butter for *me*, but I'd learned my lesson.

Her back curved. She was bent low enough that her mouth had to be... his face changed then, as men's faces will.

Visualising the view that I was being denied, I spread my own thighs even further apart, found my core with the trembling fingers of my other hand, and then... then he took her shoulders and pulled her from her chair. The two of them sank to the floor — *behind the damned table.*

My fingers ceased their stroking. I waited, and waited.

I must have been half-dozing when they stood up and brought me to my senses. He was naked, and all she had left on was a pair of glossy black hose, a lacy black garter belt, and stiletto sandals.

I fumbled for the trigger of my camera as they turned away from me to the doorway, his hand light on her nape, her soft hip rubbing his hard thigh. My greasy thumb slipped on the camera's button, and they were gone.

I hadn't even got a picture to show for my patience, let alone an orgasm. My bed was very lonely that night.

IV

Millie

My right leg was numb when I woke. I eased the weight of Hugh's hard thigh off it, and rubbed it back to tingling life. The bedclothes had disappeared to the floor, except for the sheet that tangled our feet. My garter-belt and my other stocking had to be somewhere in that heap, because I found that I was wearing just one.

I smoothed that single stocking up my thigh again from where it had rumpled down to my knee and stretched my legs out straight, parallel and pointy-toed. The visual effect is rather nice — when one leg is sheathed in black nylon and the other is pure-white naked. It doesn't feel bad, either, when you rub them together. I could understand why Hugh liked me to wear hose to bed and rub the insides of *my* thighs up and down the outsides of his.

He was still sprawled on his belly, asleep, even though it had been me who had been pretzeled the night before.

I tiptoed to the vanity and quickly repaired my face. I don't usually do that. Hugh is quite used to seeing my naked face in the morning, and claims that all the enhancement it ever needs is the lustful look that I seem to wear whenever I'm near him.

If he hadn't been going out for the day, I'd have left my face bare, at least until after I'd showered, perhaps till noon. As he *was* going out, I was determined that he'd leave our apartment wanting me — a lot.

It's a game we play, when we are going to be apart for a while. Each of us does their best to stir the other, so that when we see each other again, we are both already desperate to tangle limbs.

I phone him at his office, as well, from time to time, to add a few coals to his fire.

A double layer of lipstick and a touch of eyeshadow had to do. If I took too long he might wake up on his own. I wanted to wake him *my* way. Rouse him? Same thing.

He was still laying on his face when I got back to him. His penis was trapped under his belly, out of my reach. Still, there are other ways.

I untangled the bedclothes from around his feet. A gentle touch on his ankles moved his legs wide apart without waking him. My Hugh is a total slut, even asleep.

I laid down between his thighs. My hands stroked his buttocks, too softly for him to feel my touch, but *I* could feel the tiny hairs, tickling the tips of my fingers. Although he was completely relaxed, I could feel the muscles twitch a response under his skin as my caresses grew stronger. One hand on each cheek, I parted him gently, easing him wide enough that his sphincter was exposed to me, and then wider, opening the tiny pucker. I moistened my tongue, extended it into a stiff lance of hot wet flesh, rimmed his knot once, and stabbed.

"Um?" He stirred.

My tongue squirmed, a slippery little fish, swimming up a tight stream, as deep into him as it could wriggle.

"Morning."

I didn't answer him. I couldn't very well, could I?

"Yes," he said, softly. "Oh yes, my slut-love."

My hands were kneading now. Squeezing.

There was pressure on my cheeks as he pushed back at me — back and up. I let him lift his hips from the bed without withdrawing my tongue. Once he was on all fours I released his right cheek and groped around him. His flesh was fevered already, and hard as silk-sheathed marble.

Hugh hasn't been circumcised. I prefer him with his full foreskin. I've been told that the nakedness of circumcision leads to a desensitising of a man's glans. Some women like that, claiming it makes a man last longer. I feel differently. I want my Hugh just as sensitive as possible. Anyway, when *I* make love to a man, he comes when I want him to, not a second sooner, not a moment later.

I know that I'd find it uncomfortable to have the head of my clitoris exposed all the time, and I *certainly* wouldn't want it to lose any feeling.

On the other hand, Toby, who I'd lived with for a little over a year, had been circumcised, and I'd liked his penis — a lot. Perhaps it's just my temperament, to like what I've got.

My hand explored Hugh as I licked. I tickled that special spot just behind his scrotum, played with the springiness of his curly hairs, and stroked slowly, with just the pads of my fingers, along the underside of his shaft.

My mouth started to make gobbling sounds. Hugh loves it when I make a noise when my mouth is working on him. I let myself slobber a little. Drops of my saliva ran down his crease.

He made to turn around. I stopped him by circling his shaft and gripping.

I paused long enough to hiss, "Stay still!" nipped him once, quickly, and slid my tongue back into his rectum.

"But..."

I pumped, slowly, one stroke the full length of his shaft, right to its head. Hugh's foreskin had retracted. His glans was bare and wet. I smoothed my palm over it, and returned to his shaft. That shut him up. He was frozen, not wishing to miss one second of the sensations I was bestowing on his flesh.

My shoulders felt the backs of his thighs harden. I pumped some more, once lingering, twice fast, and then once slow again. Hugh can't climax when I do it in that broken rhythm. He gets harder, and closer, but it isn't until I relent and 'gallop him home' that he's allowed his orgasm.

That wasn't my intention. I had one eye on the bedside clock. It was three minutes to eight. My hand tightened, but still held him back. Two minutes, one... I accelerated, just a touch. I raked the nails of my free hand down the back of his thigh at the precise moment that the alarm went off.

I took my mouth and tongue from his bum, my hand from his heat, and said, "You've a board meeting in ninety minutes. That means you've exactly half an hour to have breakfast and get ready."

"Sod breakfast!" he said. "Open your mouth you teasing bitch, and I'll give *you* breakfast."

I was off the bed before he could roll over and grab me. "I'll make toast. You jump in the shower."

"Shower with me?"

"No — and no fair playing with yourself, either. What *I* start, *I* finish. Them's Millie's rules."

"You'll finish — when?"

"We'll see. Hold the thought."

"All damned day?"

"All damned day. I want you to be thinking about *me* when that cute secretary of yours wiggles past you in her slit-sided miniskirt."

"Perhaps I'll bring her home with me tonight."

"Promises, promises. Go shave and shower."

I stayed just as naked as I was, except for slipping into mules, and brushed my teeth as he showered. Dripping wet, and still fully erect, he climbed out, wrapped his arms around me from behind, bent me forward over the sink, and slid into me with one long strong stroke.

I squirmed in his arms. "You'll be late!"

"No I won't." He withdrew, leaving me with an empty feeling. "I just wanted tit-for-tat. Now *you* can spend the day horny, just like me. What have you got planned for today, anyway?"

I turned to face him, knelt squidged down between him and the vanity, and told his erection, "*I'll* be fine. If anyone comes to the door, I'll seduce them. If no one comes, I'll simply be forced to masturbate."

Hugh towelled his hair, just as if my breath wasn't hot on the head of his sex. "Who are you expecting to drop by?"

"You never know. Maybe a Jehovah's Witness, or perhaps a nice pair of clean-cut Mormons." I took his shaft in my hand, opened my lips into a big 'O', and wobbled his plum in circles inside the loose wet ring of my lips, making gurgling noises deep in my throat at the same time.

He called me his 'bitch-whore', which is his favourite term of endearment for me when he's desperate with lust.

My mouth mumbled down his shaft an inch at a time, to its

base. There I worked my lips, deliberately marking him with a thickly smeared ring of lipstick. He'd be aware of that crimson circle, all day. It would serve as a constant reminder of what was waiting for him when he got home. I call it 'marking my place'.

I withdrew, stood up, and gave him a chaste peck on the cheek. "Go eat — it's on the kitchen counter. I'll lay your things out."

"You'll suffer for this, tonight," he threatened me as he left the bathroom.

I whispered to his still-damp, broad-shouldered tapered back, "That's exactly what I was hoping for."

Once he was out the apartment door I cleaned away the supper things and showered. My breasts were feeling delightfully heavy, my nipples were pebbles, the lips of my sex were fizzing, my clit throbbed loneliness, and I could still feel the empty place inside me where Hugh had distended me with that one crafty thrust.

As horny as that, it took every effort for me to restrict my shower-play to the loofah's brisk caresses. I managed though, somehow. There was a plan in my head, for lunchtime, that would work much better if I was really needy.

I had three hours to wait.

The CD played Eartha Kitt's 'Sugar Daddy', and the 'Arabian Song', the two sexiest things she's recorded, over and over. I put on a tiny black vinyl thong — just a triangular scrap on strings — and strapped my feet into a pair of five and a half inch-heeled pumps.

Eartha's voice, alone, can make me feel sexy. That thong can do the same. Hugh bought it for me at the sex-shop. It has a thick raised seam inside, with rubber bobbles on it, that fit between my lips so that when I walk...

The shoes — when I'm tottering around on tip-toe, insteps bent taut, bum clenched tight and thighs straining to maintain my balance — those can do it as well. The triple combination had my sex dripping wet in no time.

I danced through my chores, even dusting all my ornaments, my thighs slithering against each other and my buttocks flexing in time to the throb of Eartha's voice.

Everything was done by eleven. There are only three rooms, a kitchen, and two baths. That doesn't take long, even though the rooms are large. Idleness would have found work for my fingers — between my legs — so I filled a pail with hot water and vinegar and did the living room windows.

They were so clean by the time I finished that when I rubbed my naked breasts against one that was still vinegary-wet, they squeaked. The coolness felt good. I tried the same again, delicately, with just the tips of my nipples. That felt good, as well.

It felt so good that I slipped my thong off, spread wide, shimmied up to the glass, and slithered the front of my sex against it.

Then I broke into a giggling fit. It was a good job we were so high up. If anyone had seen me, from outside..?

The thought made me repeat my sex-slide, more slowly, lasciviously, eyes closed, imagining what some passing bird might have seen, hovering level with my groin.

I had to wipe the window again, after that. I'd left smears.

It was twelve-fifteen. Hugh would be through with his meeting by twelve-thirty, and back in his office. Still daydreaming about being spied on, I dragged Hugh's black leather recliner to the window, facing it and close, got the cordless phone from the kitchen and fetched a bottle of that nice aromatic oil that makes your skin glow when you rub it in, from beside our bed.

Sprawled on the chair in exactly the same pose as Hugh had held when he'd arranged to have me 'catch' him masturbating — legs spread and hooked over the arms — I held the phone to my ear, my thumb poised over the buttons, and started to play with myself.

I did my nipples first. I teased them with slow finger-tip spirals, in from the rims of their haloes, *almost* to my tips, and then slowly back out again. A few minutes of that had me arching my back and purring. I gave each nipple a nice tweak, as a reward for being so patient, gripped the phone between my chin and shoulder, and poured oil onto my right palm.

My hand cupped my sex. My fingers dabbled between my lips as the heel of my hand ground down on my mound. Pretty soon I was humping up at my hand and moaning.

It was twelve twenty-six.

The oil was working. My entire pubic area was tingling and hot. The oil, mixed with the juices I was seeping, became twice as slippery.

I experimented. With the heel of my hand pressing down, squeezing tight on my throbbing clit, I fanned my fingers over my sex's pouting swollen lips. It made a 'fripping' sound. I was breathing hard, and fast. My chest was heaving.

It was twelve twenty-nine and forty seconds.

My hand went faster. Frip-frip, frip frip, fripfripfrip. I thumbed the telephone's 'on' button, and 'speed-dial one'. As I listened to the ringing at the other end, my hips came up off my seat. My thighs strained apart until their tendons creaked.

Hugh said, "Hello?"

"I'm — I'm..."

"You sound as if you're close to coming."

"Yes. Listen to..." I heard myself make an animal grunt.

"...me. Listen to *this!*"

I snatched the phone down to where my fingers were frantic on my sex. I knew he could hear the wet noises it was making. *I* could hear them, and that was over the roaring of blood in my ears.

My flickering fingers moved. Their tips were flipping my sex's lips, *and* the protruding head of my clit. It was knowing that my Hugh was listening that tipped me over the edge, though.

I *screamed* a strangled orgasm up from somewhere deep inside the tangle of knots that were writhing in my belly. I screamed it loud enough that he had to be able to hear it even over the sweet sloppy splashing sounds my dabbling fingers were making in the shallows of my sex.

V

Petra

It was a wonderful day. My camera and I got our first really detailed look at all the intricacies of her body, and it was the first time I watched *them* making love. At least — I guess it qualified as 'making love'.

*****

I sing to myself as I get ready in the mornings. It's not that I'm proud of my four-note voice. I sing because I often spend a week or more without talking to another human being. When I do that, and I don't sing, when the time comes that I have to speak, I make a funny croaking noise. Singing to myself oils my vocal chords, I suppose.

I had Manitas del Platas on the stereo, and skatted to some Spanish folk music that I couldn't name. That put me in a 'Spanish' mood, so I dressed appropriately.

I have a 'suit of lights'. It isn't exactly what a toreador would wear. Peggy, the little woman who makes my costumes, ran it up for me.

The pants are made from satin-finish gold Spandex, intricately embroidered with thousands of red sequins. Even though the fabric stretches, those pants still fit so tightly that they have invisible zippers that run down the backs of their legs, to let me get into them.

First, I set a pair of patent-leather Cuban-heeled shoes, with diamanté buckles, side by side on the floor. Once I have those pants on I can't bend, so the shoes have to be waiting for me.

I went into the bathroom and gave myself an olive complexion, down to my waist. The contacts I slipped in were jet black. I did my eyelids dramatically, using two tones of blue and some blended-in silver. I painted my lips and nipples a deep carmine, and fitted a glossy black wig with a short 'queue' on my head.

I'm very organised. The head and foot of my bed are made of scrolled brass. In my dresser I have a short cord with a hook at one end and a ring at the other. I hung the ring over one scroll at the foot of my bed.

With the zippers undone, it doesn't take me long to work myself into the torso part of those Spanish pants. Once I'd smoothed the fabric to coat every curve and crease of my body, I pulled the zippers down as far as I could unaided — down the backs of my thighs to behind my knees. Then I laid down on my bed, lifted one leg up, hooked the tab of the zipper to my dangling cord, and shimmied back away from it, dragging the zipper closed all the way to my ankle.

Repeat for the other leg — and I was sealed in, from waist to ankle.

That little gadget isn't just for those pants, of course. I have some vinyl and some rubber garments that need the same treatment, to get into solo.

I rolled stiff-legged off my bed and stepped into my shoes.

My costume was completed by a black felt tricorn that perched on top of my wig, and a bolero jacket. That jacket matches the pants, but it is made of stiff brocade. It is short — to just below my breasts, and shaped to cup them from the sides, like clam-shells. It *just* covers my nipples, when my arms hang loose.

My sword isn't an authentic bull-fighter's one. It's a light-weight cavalry sword, with a basket hilt. That didn't matter. I'd change the sword's appearance in my computer.

In front of a mirror and a camera, I posed. I lifted the hilt of my sword high, its point angled down, as if ready to thrust between a charging bull's horns, through the muscles of its thick neck and into its heart. My swordless hand, also raised, curled its fingers as if they were wearing castanets and Manitas del Platas was about to strum something wild.

When my arms lifted high, the clam-shell of my bolero parted, baring my breasts. I arched my back, slightly, to bring the fan of my ribcage into relief. My tummy sucked tight, hollowing below my ribs. Sequins glistened over the subtle thrust of my pubic mound and on the quivering tautness of my slender thighs.

The woman in the mirror looked *gorgeous*.

My toe pressed the floor-trigger, capturing her.

I turned my back to the mirror for the next shot, so that the camera would see how tightly, and *separately*, sheathed my buns were, but I was twisted at the waist sharply enough that the curved profile of my breast would be punctuated by one peaked nipple.

I like that 'half-turned' pose. It makes a slim waist look even narrower.

After an hour of toreador poses I was ready to go and change into a full black Spanish lace skirt and mantilla. I had it in mind to complete the Spanish set of photographs with a veiled senorita, some poses bare-breasted and some with my breasts lightly draped with see-through lace. Perhaps I could do something sexy with a lace fan, as well?

But first I'd just take a quick peek at my neighbours, 'just in case', even though it was early.

I was glad I did.

She — the man's woman, was doing her housework. At first glance I thought she was shod but naked. She was bending over at her hips, her legs held straight enough to tauten the skin behind her knees. She was dusting the nick-nacks on the bottom shelf of a rather fine Louis Quinze étagère. As she straightened up I saw that a thin cord circled her waist, and ran down her back to disappear between her buttocks. When she turned it confirmed that she was wearing a minute glossy *cache-sex*.

I zoomed in for a closer look, but she was moving, and it's almost impossible to hold on a moving object that small, at that distance. I was sure though, that a few springy little hairs had escaped around the edges. So — she didn't depilate her pubes, like I'd had done. She had to trim there, though. Most women's pubic hair covers a larger area than that skimpy garment did.

I pulled back to get her entirely in frame. She was working her way up, one shelf at a time, jiggling some, and rubbing her thighs together, as if she had music playing.

I wondered what it might be? People's choice in music tells you a lot about them. Perhaps it was better I didn't know. If it had been 'rap' or the like, I could have fallen out of lust with her.

I counted seven shelves. As she was just on her second, she'd likely be standing there with her back to me for some time. I took one quick shot of her full-length, and then focused in and panned down, filling my viewfinder with half of her, from her feet to her waist. It was an ideal opportunity for me to get detailed pictures of every inch of her, from the back. If I got really lucky, perhaps she'd find a chore that turned her to face me, so that I'd have a complete record of her from both sides. With that much data I could computerise her into any position I liked, later, solo or in combination with any of the other bodies I had trapped in my records.

Including mine.

That thought made me squirm, nicely. I didn't try do anything about quenching my rising lust, though. Pictures come first.

My first shot covered what I had in frame, from her feet to the small of her back, and then I went in closer for just feet-to-calves.

I knew *exactly* how she felt, standing on those tall and slender heels. I have heels just like them, on a couple of dozen pairs of shoes, sandals and boots.

One of her feet was turned slightly. I focused on it as sharply as I could and shot it. The shoe was black patent — what there was of it. There was a toe-cap, just, and then nothing until her elevated heel, where a strip of leather rose to an ankle strap. She'd need the strap, to hold it on.

The heel was somewhere between five and six inches of delicate shiny tapered black rod, and that was all.

Those heels did incredible things to her legs, as my heels do to mine. I have an album of photographs to prove it. The slightest change in weight, as she worked, rippled the muscles in the backs of her calves, and, as I panned slowly up, clicking all the way, the long muscles in her thighs were alternately flexing and relaxing, to maintain her balance, even when she was almost still.

Heels like that restrain — strain and restrain — your feet.

Your insteps become the tethers to lines of electric tension that run from the balls of your feet, up through the entire lengths of your legs to join together at some magic nexus up inside your body.

Where those lines meet depends on how you stand. If you lean back a touch, they run together somewhere inside your vagina, perhaps immediately behind your pubic bone, or deeper and higher, until you feel sure the knot that joins them must be at the very mouth of your womb.

Then, if you rock forwards a few inches, that mystic junction moves. It moves back through your belly until it stimulates you high inside your rectum, clenching muscles that you don't usually think about.

Swaying, you can move the lines of force, massaging yourself internally.

The woman's buttocks were tightly bunched when I got to them. Then one relaxed, as she leaned sideways, and then that one knotted and the other one relaxed. Then, when she worked on the middle of the shelf, she flexed them alternately, perhaps in time to the beat of her music.

It was fascinating to watch. Her bum was rounded, but not overly plump. I could see the muscles play beneath her skin, so her cheeks definitely weren't layered with fat. Her rear was a hard peach, maybe, but divided deeper than any peach would be.

I wondered what it would feel like, beneath my fingertips. Not uniform, I didn't think. The muscles would be closer to the surface in some places, so those areas would be firmer, but the undersides of her cheeks now — those would give to the touch, just a little. Enough to make your fingers want to pinch, perhaps.

An inch above where the cleft between her buttocks joined, at the base of her spine, there was a pad of muscle. 'The love muscle', I've heard it called, because it is exercised when a woman lifts her hips up off a bed, to meet a man's downwards thrust.

Hers was well developed.

Something fluttered down, almost out of frame. She'd dropped her duster. I pulled back my focus just a tad, quickly, just in time for her to part her legs slightly and bend over again, away from me. I was ready this time. I got a lovely chiaroscuro black-and-white composition of the softly bulging *cache-sex* as it protruded backwards between her thighs, glossy enough to catch pin-points of light, as if it was soaking wet, and framed by the stark whiteness of her skin.

Perhaps that scrap of shiny fabric *was* wet. Could it be that the lady was enjoying some naughty thoughts as she did her chores? Of course it could. Dressed like that, for housework? She was fantasising sex as she worked. She had to be.

I felt a warm wash of love flood through me. She was *another,* just like me. We were sisters-in-lust.

I wondered what, exactly, she was thinking about. That lovely man of hers? His tongue, doing squirmy things inside her sex? Or was it *her* mouth, doing nice things to him? If I could have seen her face, would her mouth have been slack with lust, and wet?

She stretched for an upper shelf. Her waist was tiny. The curves, where her hips narrowed to her waist, became almost horizontal before they turned upwards, slender for the elongated length of her midsection, and then tapering out where her ribs were.

I watched her back muscles play for a long while — the lift and slide of her shoulder blades under her skin — the sway of her slender neck, half-concealed beneath a tumble of curls. Each tiny movement she made raised the level of my lust.

I wanted to *taste* her.

My need grew too great to resist any longer. I reloaded the camera, in haste. Once I started my self-love, I didn't want to have to stop.

When I put my eye to the viewfinder again, I'd lost her.

In panic, I took my eye from my camera and tried to spot where she'd gone, with unaided vision.

She was coming back into the living area, weighed down on one side by a pail of something. I had a full-front view of her now, and she was walking straight towards me.

Oops! She was going to wash her windows!

I grabbed my tripod and backed into my room, far enough that I was cloaked in shadow.

Safely concealed again, I returned to my spying — and it was incredible.

She was ten feet closer to me now — as close as she *could* be. As she washed, stretching and bending in a way that was driving me delirious, I had a quarter-front profile, because of the angle of the windows. She bent. Her waist, on the inside of the bend, creased. On the other side, it stretched. Her breasts swayed. She stretched up, and her breasts lifted. She wiped, and they jiggled. It was incredibly erotic — this simple chore.

Her belly was softly rounded, not flat. Her navel was deep. If she had been laying flat on her back you could have filled that dimple with a fine cognac, and lapped...

When I went in close I could see the lines that ran from her groin to the hollows inside her hipbones. The cords that joined the one around her waist to the *cache-sex* ran parallel to them, inside. Her garment was smaller than her mound, so that softness bulged deliciously to either side.

Her body twisted. One of those delicate groin-lines became a fold; the other just a strip of paler white, with a tracery of blue of veins showing through the translucent pallor of her skin.

Those lines would be very sensitive. The tip of a tongue, or the point of a fingernail, could have traced their lengths, drawing erotic fire on her skin.

I shivered, feeling what she would have felt. My hand went to my mound... ...and felt sequins.

Double damn, *triple* damn! I couldn't get out of those pants without going into my bedroom and rolling on the bed and it would take all of six or seven minutes and by then...

Furious with myself, I hooked my thumbs into my waistband and rolled, forcing Spandex down, over my belly, to the tops of my thighs, and... and they wouldn't go any lower. Not only that, but the roll of fabric gripped me like a straightjacket. I couldn't get my pants down, and I couldn't part my legs.

Still watching the woman's dance, I felt my way blindly across my pubic mound. Ah! The pants were just low enough that I could push down, and insinuate one finger, slotting it between the stretched fabric below and my own flesh above, until I could, at least, get it to my clitoris. Just. It would have to do.

I rotated on my button. It was *frustrating*. My finger was so constricted, it could barely twitch. It would take *forever* for me to reach an orgasm that way — but I had no choice. Best to enjoy what I *could* do.

She completed the window that turned her partly away from me, and then started on the other, facing almost straight at my camera. If I hadn't been back inside my room a bit, she'd certainly have seen me.

For a fleeting moment I *wanted* her to see me — to know what the beauty — no, not 'beauty' — what the *sexiness* of her body was making me do.

I squashed the thought. I'm a watcher, not a 'watched'.

My finger was aching, but I couldn't stop. I especially couldn't stop when she squatted down, legs splayed, to clean the bottom of the window. I got three crisp shots right into the 'v' of her thighs, tight on her mound. If only she'd been completely naked! My God! Down like that, her lips would have been pulled apart. I could have photographed their inside surfaces, where I just *knew* she'd be incredibly pink, and glistening, perhaps even dripping, wet.

My finger was cramping. Hard as it worked, it kept me so damn *close,* on the very edge, but it couldn't quite... I held it still, and stiff, and let my hips do the work, grinding and bumping on it, driving my soft wet heat onto it, just a fraction, and dragging back off it so that it crushed on the head of my clitoris.

The windows were done. The woman drew a finger across the glass, 'squeaking' it, I supposed. And then — it was *gorgeous* — she stood straight, pressed her breasts to the glass, and *dragged* them across it. Her breasts were flattened against the pane, white circles with dark centres, distorted out of shape, skewed sideways with the friction.

She leaned back, away from the glass, her belly pressed to it, and lifted her breasts in her palms, each nipple pinched between two fingers. Manipulating herself delicately, she drew little circles on the glass with the tips of her nipples. Or was it circles? Perhaps she was writing me a message? *I lust for you?*

My hips bucked at my finger, furiously. What I was watching was so incredibly sexy, and it had to be the climax, because what else could she do?

It wasn't the climax. She, lovely inventive she, found another game. She tugged at her side, pulled loose the string of her *cache-sex*, plucked it from the soft grip of her sex's lips, and let it drop to the floor. She pressed her whole body against the glass. Her thighs parted slowly, incredibly wide. Her waist folded, lifting her sex, lifting it until the top of her sex's 'v' parted, and was pressed to kiss cold glass.

I had to hold my hips still for long enough to tighten my focus as close as it would go. Yes, her pubic hair *was* trimmed, down to a small neat triangular patch, an arrow head on her clit's shaft. Yes, she *was* an incredible livid pink, inside, but that wasn't all. It was that shaft — her clitoris — that froze me. It was long, and thick — as long and thick as two joints of my little finger. Its tip was totally exposed, just as pink as her inner lips, and the size of a small grape. A pink juicy peeled grape! And she was squashing it against the glass!

I shuddered, and teetered on the edge of an orgasm, but somehow I couldn't quite *get there*.

And then she turned away from the window. I could have sobbed. Perhaps I would have, but she came back, dragging that black leather recliner. She disappeared again, but I wasn't worried that time. She hadn't set the chair directly facing me for nothing.

Yes, she was back with a portable phone and a bottle of something. My finger began its slow rotation again. She was going to do *something*. I had faith in her. *This* time I'd make it.

Was she making a call? It looked as if she was. She was holding the phone to her ear as if she was, but she hadn't dialled and she wasn't speaking. No — she was playing with her nipples. If I'd had a hand free I'd have played with mine, just to keep her company.

That didn't last more than a few minutes. She gripped the phone under her chin, opened the bottle, and poured something into her hand. That hand, the oily one, went to her sex.

My legs were trembling. My belly convulsed with lust. She massaged oil over, and *into* her sex. She caressed the shaft of that over-sized clitoris of hers. She rubbed its head with her thumb, and then between thumb and fingers, and then she used her whole hand, spread-fingered, rubbing and flickering and delving, covering her entire pubic region with a gloss of oil, or perhaps oil mixed with her own sweet juices.

Her fingers became a frantic blur, and *then* she did something to the buttons on the phone, and they blurred again, and she spoke, and rammed the phone down between her thighs, still frotting wildly, and arched her back clean off her seat, and a rictus grin twisted her mouth, and I *knew* she was screaming her orgasm.

And *I* convulsed with mine. Simultaneous orgasms, at forty feet.

When I recovered, my first thought was to wonder who it had been she'd called, to share that special moment with. I wished it had been me.

One thing was sure. Whoever had been on the other end of that line, whether it was the pony-tail man or not, was going to come visiting, soon. No one could resist a summons like that.

I hobbled to my bedroom to get out of my toreador pants, and to prepare myself for *her* visitor. My lovely day wasn't over yet.

I showered, quickly, and dashed back to my camera still dripping. There was no sign of her. The camera in my den could see into her bedroom. I still couldn't find her, but at the far side of the room her bathroom door stood open, and steam had clouded the mirror over her vanity.

She was either in the shower or taking a bath. I thought it would be a bath. Her breasts were most likely floating now, amid perfumed bubbles. She'd be preparing herself for her man. A woman like that would take her time, getting ready for love. She'd savour every moment, drawing out the pleasure of anticipation.

That meant I had time to complete *my* preparations.

I have an antique barber's chair that has been fitted with castors. I wheeled it from my work-area into the living room and set it in place in front of the window. It reclines. I'd be half-sitting, half-laying, as I watched. The show promised to be a long one. I'd be comfortable.

I'd need refreshments.

I mixed a pitcher — eight ounces of one-fifty proof vodka, six ounces of clam-and-tomato juice, a dash of celery salt, a squeeze of lemon, and two spoonfuls of the really powerful sauce that Rebecca had brought me back from Mexico. It's like a Bloody Caesar, but *hot*. I call it a 'Bloody Hell'.

Beside the pitcher — on a side-table beside my barber's chair, I put two crisp cool Russet apples. When your mouth is burning they make a delicious contrast in tastes.

Next to the apples — my Lady Remmington massage kit, plugged in and already fitted with my favourite head — the one with plastic fingers that are as fine as hairs.

From back in my den I checked her bathroom again. She was standing, naked, in front of her bathroom vanity. She was making herself beautiful for her man. That meant that *I* had time to make myself beautiful enough to be worthy of watching them.

I'd be beautiful enough that I'd want to watch myself, as well. Two of my full length mirrors are on stands. I arranged one to the side of where I'd be sprawled.

What to wear? What would be appropriate to the mood? I decided that 'absolute depravity' was the only look that would be suitable.

I did my face first. My eyes changed shape. I drew them more slanted, in iridescent green, extending their corners up and wide, almost to my hairline. Green contacts. Eyebrows that paralleled the lines from the corners of my eyes, and then zoomed even higher. A touch of blush beneath each cheekbone, to give them emphasis. Lips like fresh blood and nipples to match. A fine dusting of eggshell powder, white-on-white.

The wig that I chose was almost as short as my own pale hair, but black — as close on my scalp as the pelt on an otter.

I talced my arms and legs.

The boots were thin black rubber, almost stockings. I unrolled them up my legs all the way to the creases of my groin. Their heels were a full five inches, and forced me walk 'en pointe'.

My gloves were of matching black rubber — shoulder length. They fit my fingers close enough that you could see the cuticles of my nails through them. I added a matching choker.

With all four limbs sheathed in clinging blackest matte black, my neck snugly circled by the same and the alabaster skin of my torso whiter than ever, by contrast, I needed just one last garment to complete this version of myself.

The belt was also black rubber, seven inches wide, with three buckles that are set one above the other. Buckled, it nips my waist down to twenty-two inches, and compresses my midriff in its second-skin grip from just beneath my breasts to below my waist, almost to my navel.

I was *almost* the image of total depravity. One last touch? I'm not a smoker, except when I need a cigarette as a prop. One pack of cigarettes lasts me a month, or more. Still, looking the way I did, lounging in that chair, a long ebony cigarette holder and a gold-tipped Sobranie Black Russian would complete the picture. I fetched the cedar-inlaid box and the gold Dunhill lighter Paul had given me for Christmas two years before.

Then I was ready. I settled into my chair, pulled my tripod over, and waited.

VI
Millie

I did my face and made myself a cup of coffee while I decided what to wear.

I fancy myself as an amateur student of sexual psychology. What you wear for sex should suit your mood. That's a basic. It should also compliment the mood of your lover, or lovers.

I sipped, and thought about how Hugh would be feeling. Sex and power are interwoven. That morning, I'd demonstrated my power. I'd shown it by rousing poor darling Hugh, and then denying him. He'd retaliated, some, with that quick slide into my body when I'd been bent over the vanity, but there could be no doubt as to who had been in charge.

I had to restore his confidence in himself.

Lust has to be a two-way street. If you lust after someone, and feel that the lust isn't equally reciprocated, that lust can turn sour. I'd shown him that I could drive him crazy with wanting me, and still control myself enough to deny him. It'd been fun. We'd both enjoyed it. Even so, it was time for me to show him that I wanted him just as badly as he wanted me. I nurture our relationship, in my way.

I tried to imagine what it would be like to want someone, all the time, but they only wanted you back once a week, or once a month. You'd feel degraded, wouldn't you? The lust would have to die, wouldn't it? Lust feeds on lust. Deny it that nourishment, and it starves. The strain, and the shame of wanting and not having your lust returned in equal measure would kill it.

That's our secret, Hugh and me. We both want it about the same — a lot.

So — what to wear?

I thought about something submissive. Perhaps something gauzy and white and floating? Something he could rip off my trembling body, and so demonstrate his mastery?

Hugh likes me in 'off-the-shoulder'. I have a number of peasant blouses that I can wear low enough and loose enough to get *exactly* the response from Hugh that I crave.

When I wear one at dinner, his eyes can't leave my breasts. He thinks I don't feel his gaze, but it burns. I'd know where his eyes were even if I had my eyes closed. Sooner or later he gets up, walks round behind me, stands looking down into my cleavage, and then his hands follow his eyes, pushing the blouse down and freeing my breasts.

When that happens he'll spend endless minutes, caressing me until my nipples ache from it, driving me slowly crazy with lust, and then I can't help but turn to him, and drag his mouth down to where it can finish the task that his fingers have started.

I've had orgasms that way, still fully dressed to up to my

waist, my sex untouched.

But he'd threatened me with his revenge. *Any* initiative on my part — such as showing him that it was my breasts that needed his attentions the most — might interfere with his plans.

No — I had to be available to him to in that every way — but the way I was dressed mustn't prompt him to think that I expected any particular style of loving.

If I was simply naked? But he enjoyed disrobing me. Naked, I'd be denying him that pleasure, and it was vital that I denied him *nothing*, that night.

I settled for high-heeled mules, black hose with garters that nipped my thighs, a simple gold chain around my waist, and my black and gold kimono, loosely sashed.

I had a pitcher of very dry vodka martinis, a dish of blue-point oysters sitting in ice, and Chicago-style fillet mignons on beds of thinly sliced sin-black Portobello mushrooms waiting when he got home.

He put a small parcel, wrapped in crimson and tied with a silver ribbon, on the counter. He had a present for me, but didn't intend to give it to me yet. That told me what he had in mind. I'd teased him, in the morning. He was going to tease me, in the evening.

I liked that.

As we sat eating, opposite each other, I let my kimono slip down my shoulders and part until only the points of my breasts held it together. When I let my shoulder droop seductively, my nipple winked at him. He noticed, but he didn't say a word.

Okay. He didn't seem to want me to be sophisticated and seductive. Perhaps that wouldn't have been enough to salve his male ego. It seemed he wanted me to be more direct in the way I showed I wanted him — raunchy even. That was fine. I can do 'raunchy'.

I put one hand inside my robe and pinched myself. "My nipples are very hard," I told him.

"Really?" He didn't ask me to show him how hard.

"I'm wet, between my legs, you know, from wanting you all day."

"Are you?" He dabbed his plate with hot French bread, soaking up mushroom-juice.

"What did you have planned for the evening?" I asked, moving my breast on my palm, under satin, knowing that my nipple was visible through the fine fabric.

He stood. "I need a shower, first. Then I have a report to read."

I cleared away while he showered. When he came back in his robe I could smell his cologne and his chin was smooth. He *did* have something in mind, but he was making me wait for it. He's such a divine *bastard*.

He sat, and read. I brought him a fresh drink and sat on a stool, close by — close enough that his long arm could reach out to me, if he wished.

He didn't though. Just in case he was watching me, secretly, I stretched my legs out straight and let my kimono fall apart far enough that my thighs, stark white above my stocking-tops, were exposed.

He read on, but his robe twitched, at his groin. I allowed myself a small smile. If he wanted me to show him how much I wanted him, before he made his move, well, I could do that. I'm not proud.

That's not true. I'm *not* too proud to show Hugh how I feel about him, and his loving. I *am* proud of the effect I have on him.

I stood and stretched, parting my kimono all the way down. "I'm horny for you," I told him.

He glanced up. His eyes widened, but he controlled himself. "Are you?"

"Yes. I can't wait any longer." I pulled my sash untied. With my kimono tucked behind my back, I lifted one muled foot onto the arm of his chair and pushed my pubes at him. The lips of my sex parted, showing pink. "See? My clit is throbbing and I'm wet. Can you smell me?"

He sniffed, and grunted. His eyes went back to his report.

My free hand opened my lips even wider. "I really need something long and hard inside there," I said. My finger hooked and slid in.

"I'm sure you'll find something," he said.

I pushed my belly even closer to his face. "Watch!" I ran my fingertips down the shaft of my clit, and then pulled back on its hood, popping its pink head.

"Yes," he said. "It certainly looks as if you are aroused."

"Then I'll just have to find something to play with."

"I suppose you will."

I gave my clit's shaft a long slow caress as I thought. Hugh's free hand was laying along the arm of his recliner. I *was* having an effect. He'd made a tight fist. His thumb was poking up, rigid as...

"I'll be right back," I promised.

He grunted again.

I returned with some oil and my manicure set. Squatting on the stool by his side, I took his thumb and trimmed his nail. He had to be curious, but his game demanded that he ignore what I was doing.

When I'd trimmed, and filed, I opened the oil and set it aside, handy. My two small hands enfolded his big fist. I leaned over, made an 'o', and slowly sucked his thumb into the wet heat of my mouth.

He shifted in his seat.

My tongue played. I bobbed my head, sucking the ball of his thumb from my lips to the back of my throat, and then slurping off it again. When it was thoroughly wet, and I could see his robe was tented, I poured oil over his thumb and massaged until it was thoroughly coated with a mix of aromatic oil and my saliva.

Two loose fingers circled his thumb and caressed it from base to tip, masturbating it. The tendons in Hugh's neck stood out, but he read on.

"Yes," I said. "I think I've found just the thing." I stood, still holding his hand, made a long leg over the arm of his chair, set one foot on his seat, beside his thigh, and lowered myself.

His thumb stayed stiff, though he could have folded it and denied me. I found it with the softness of my sex's lips, wriggled down, and impaled myself.

"It's smaller than what I want," I gritted through my teeth, "but it will just, have, to do." I raised, and lowered, and rotated. As my lust grew, and my clit elongated, I found that if I leaned over I could get its head on the ridge of muscle at the base of Hugh's thumb. That's where I ground down. Bending over him like that, my breast was inches from his face. I shook my shoulders, flicking the tip of my nipple across his cheek.

I know his mouth was watering, because he licked his lips, but that was the only reaction I got from him.

I went into a hip-judder, and came — really wet — soaking Hugh's hand.

"Are you done?" he asked me as I dismounted.

"For the moment."

He paused for a moment, looking past my shoulder. His

eyebrow lifted and he shrugged. I was about to ask him what the distraction was when he said, "No, you aren't done yet," writhed to his feet, and scooped me up. I thought he was taking me to our bed, but it was the bathroom he had in mind. He set me down, pulled my kimono off, and bent me forwards with my face over the sink.

His big strong hands arranged me exactly the way he wanted me. I *love* it when he does that. I adore being his toy.

I was leaning with my hands gripping the edge of the vanity, my legs straight and stiff and parted. My back was parallel with the tiled floor. Like that, my breasts look their very best, I think. There's nothing that shows a woman's breasts off as well as when she's on all fours, or in any position that lets them dangle, unsupported. In those positions, small breasts look bigger and sagging breasts don't droop. Even perfect breasts, as Hugh claims mine are, are enhanced.

"Watch," he ordered. "Watch your own eyes, in the mirror."

I looked. He was right. I'd just had an orgasm, but my lids were hooded and my pupils dilated. I was very much in lust, with a wonderful man.

His robe followed my kimono to the floor. He squatted down. One of his hands parted my lips, from behind, while the other stretched between my thighs to reach my breasts. His tongue licked the backs of my thighs. His fingers tweaked one nipple, and then the other. Satisfied that they were hard and sharp, he flattened his palm just beneath one, and rotated it, barely touching my aching peak.

Hugh nibbled at the base of my spine.

"I want you so bad," I sobbed.

"Wait!" He licked down, down the crease of my bum, lightly across my sphincter, making it twitch, and to the 'v' at the back of my sex.

I thought he was going to put his tongue inside me, but he lapped sideways, back to my inner thigh, and slid an open-mouthed wet kiss down to my stocking top.

"Do it to me, darling," I begged. "I can't stand to wait any longer."

"Watch her eyes."

I did, and her breasts as they swayed, barely grazing the skin of his teasing palm, but my attention focused on his torturing tongue. It explored my legs again, to the crease where my bum meets my thighs, and then darted between my lips, slithering into me. I thrust back, arching my back and lifting my rear to give him easier access. My sex's lips were loose and swollen, parted for him. He sucked one into his mouth, nibbled on it, and turned to the other.

"My clit?"

"This?" He buried his chin into my sex and ground it. Even when he's clean shaven, there is a roughness to his chin. It prickled me in a way that I found incredibly tantalising.

His mouth opened wide enough that I could feel his breath heating me. Hugh stretched his tongue out to its fullest extent, curled it, and found my pearl with its tip. He sucked harder, drawing my clit down and into his mouth. His lips clamped on it as his tongue did that magic flickering dance and I got so *close*.

He knew. He always does. Just as I was on the brink, he stopped.

I moaned, "No, no, no."

"Yes!" He stood up. "Keep still for a moment."

I felt hard smooth heat press against my lips. They were ready to welcome him into their folds — more than ready. Hugh moved a fraction, nesting his solid egg in my melting nest, and paused.

"You want it?" he asked my reflection in the mirror.

"Please?" I nudged a little, not pushing, just inviting.

He pulled back. "Ask me nicely." Back into the nest, no deeper than before, just enough to make my sex ravenous.

"Pretty please? Hugh, I need it, baby. Give it to me hard, huh?"

A wet finger stroked upwards between my cheeks. I forced my sphincter to dilate, trying to catch its tip, but it glided past.

"What do you need?"

"You. In me. Deep inside."

"This deep?" He gave me half an inch.

"Deeper!"

"More?" He grinned at me. "This much more?" Another inch.

"Go deep, please?"

"But this is nice, isn't it?" He rocked, in an inch, and out again.

It *was* nice, deliriously nice, but it wasn't what I *needed*.

"Give it to me," I begged, "and I'll be your sex-slave for three full hours, tomorrow. Four even. Anything you want, you'll get."

"I thought you *were* my sex-slave," he gloated. "What was it you said that first day, in the park? 'Any where, any time, any how'?"

"Yes, yes, yes. I *am* your slave. I was born to serve you, Master — to be used by you. Now *use* me, damn you, you bastard!"

"Like this?" He slid another two slow inches into me.

I'd have jerked back on him, but he'd spread one hand on the small of my back and the other cupped my bum. He was strong enough to hold me immobile without any effort.

"If I go in another little way," he teased, "you'll use those nice strong muscles that you've got inside you, right?"

"Yes!" It wasn't what I wanted. What I needed at that moment, more than any sort of preliminary, was a good hard pounding, but *anything* would have been better than that slow torture.

Very slowly, with infinite control, he slid *in* two more inches, back an inch, in again, even deeper, and eventually, after all those long quivering minutes, my bum was nestled against his firm flat belly, and he was in all the way, distending me.

He held rigid. "Now you may squeeze."

It was like I had a smooth hot rock buried in me. I clamped down on it, relaxed, clamped, relaxed.

"Yes," he said. "That's nice. You want an orgasm?"

I was getting into a nice rhythm of contractions. If I'd let the tempo build, I could have made it to a climax on that alone, but he needed my need, so I asked him, "Give me one, lover."

"Please?"

"Please, you bastard!"

He leaned over me. One arm wrapped around my waist. His hand smoothed down my belly. I tensed, waiting to see whether he was going to touch me properly, or just tease me some more.

Two of his fingers bracketed the sheath of my clit and pulled it back, hard — so hard that it felt as if my clit's head curled up to meet the ball of his thumb.

His other hand found my right breast, milked down on it once to get a grip on the point of my nipple, and tugged on it with loving cruelty.

His thumb rotated on my clit's head. I pulled up a little, elongating my nipple even more, dragging on it until I could feel the pull at its root.

"*You* do it," he commanded me. "Go for it, bitch-whore!"

I let the juddering start in my hips, building up faster and faster, bucking back on his rigid bulbous-headed stalk, jerking and rotating, and just *let go!*

This was for me, not for him. He wanted to feel my climax. I knew that was what he wanted, and that's what I gave him. With his fingers and his thumb urging me, I was over the top in a few moments of delirium.

The juice flooded from of me, scalding hot, coating the insides of my thighs and soaking into my stocking-tops.

Hugh withdrew, almost out, still totally stiff. "Now we start over," he said, and began that devilishly shallow in-and-out rocking again.

VII

Petra

I'd had two soft little orgasms while she'd ridden his thumb, and then he'd carried her away. I slid off my barber's chair and ran to the camera that looked into their bedroom just in time to see their bathroom door close behind them.

Two soft little orgasms hadn't been enough. When I'm a touch tipsy, as I'd been then, I like a whole series of small climaxes, building, and then one good hard one that turns me inside out before going back to the minor ones again.

I went back to my chair and knelt up on its padded arms with my bum raised to the mirror. With my head down on the seat, I could see backwards between a spread of black rubber legs.

Watching the depraved slut in the mirror do it to herself, with a flat rubber hand knifing deep into her sex from behind and the head of her massager purring between her thighs, I gave myself a good strong stomach-twisting climax.

By that time I was past tipsy. I was drunk on booze and lust and the sweet smell of my own sex. I felt ready for half a dozen more major orgasms, in rapid succession.

I only managed the one, courtesy of Miss Fist and Lady Remmington. After that, even though I tried, it felt that something was missing. For once, watching my recreated-self in the mirror wasn't enough visual stimulus. I felt cheated that I hadn't been able to watch *them*, to their finish.

I was still feeling sulky the next morning. I'd slept in. That much booze does that to me. After my shower I slipped into a wrap, toed into mules, and noodled around for a while, trying to find work that would interest me.

Work? I couldn't kid myself. The only chores that I could bring myself to were those that related to that damned couple.

I developed and printed the photos I had of them. My scanner fed the images to my computer. I played, letting the program do most of the work. As usual, when I'm too lazy to do the job properly, my subjects came out looking like cartoons with pasted-on human heads.

I punched up a close-up of the woman's groin and edited out the strings of her *cache sex*, and then the triangle of fabric itself. The idea was to patch-in the close shot I had of her sex, but the best picture of it in my file had been taken when she was squatting, and it was open-mouthed, so it wouldn't fit. I drew in her pubes instead, from imagination and memory, but somehow it didn't look right. I needed either a better picture, or even just a close-up look, with my unaided eyes.

I enlarged the first picture again, larger than life. That close, I could see tiny droplets of perspiration on the crease-line of her groin.

My mouth watered.

If I'd had a picture of the pony-tail man's tongue, fully extended, I'd have overlaid it, to show him licking the sweat from her skin. I didn't have one. Still — my computer had lots of shots of my own outstretched tongue in its memory.

I pulled one and married it to the groin-picture. Yes, that was nice. I filed the composite and brought up a shot of her sex when it had been stretched open. The same image of me — the 'tongue-shot' — suited it well. I edited out the tip of my tongue so that it looked to be lapping inside the woman's cleft.

Why was I breathing so fast?

As the man and the woman were a 'pair', I pulled the best shot I had of his penis, overlaid and retouched it, and got a composite that showed *his* penis, *and* my tongue, both probing her sex, side by side.

I was damned well panting, and I hadn't painted myself to look like a desirable woman yet.

Using an animation program, I made his penis slide in and out between her lips, while the tip of my tongue lapped at the head of her clitoris.

It was no use. I saved and switched off. I really *needed* to get my face painted on and my body dressed up as somebody sexy.

Who? Who should I be. My problem was my lust. It was clouding my brain. I needed more sex, soon.

Sex is always within reach, of course. I could think of five available people, three men and two women, off the top of my head. Any one of them would have come to my call, ready and eager. But they would have expected 'relationships'. I wasn't desperate enough to make that sacrifice.

The easy way would be to paint someone on me, and make love to her. When I was done I could be rid of her as fast as I could wash my face.

That was what I did for sex, mainly. For some reason it didn't appeal right then. My desire had acquired a focus. Two focuses, foci? A man and a woman, and I didn't even know their names.

I assured myself that the infatuation would pass. All I had to do was spy on them, and masturbate as I did it, frequently, and the novelty would wear off.

Perhaps there was someone else I could spy on?

I checked the too-much-furniture people, and caught the tail-end of their lovemaking. I hadn't missed much. They'd been doing it under the bedclothes, spoon-fashion. After they were finished she pushed her covers down. Hot from all that effort, I guess. I got a shot of her naked breasts, just for the file. You never know when you'll need two quite-nice breasts, lolling a little.

They were late getting up. I booted my small computer and checked day/date/time. It was a little before noon, on a Saturday. That could mean my couple would be staying home.

They were. I didn't rush to dress myself though. He was sprawled on that recliner, and she was on the sofa. Both were reading. Both were in thick long robes. There were newspapers on the floor between them. I could see the remains of breakfast on their table. It was a very domestic scene, damn it!

They started to talk. She went to the pass-through from the kitchen and opened something while her back was towards me. Back in the living room she gave him a peck. He gave her a pat. I thought maybe... but then they talked some more. She glanced towards the window and away again. They talked some more, again. He got up, went through to the bedroom, and pulled the blinds.

What did he do that for? Something private? But I'd seen about as 'private' as it gets, through their window.

I was just about to give up on them when she stood up, stretched, and yawned. The way she extended her arms and opened her robe to her waist. As she dropped her arms, her robe fell off one shoulder. It was a nice shoulder.

She turned to the mirror over her sofa and made a little kiss at herself. Half-turning, she let her bare shoulder — the one towards me — droop seductively. The robe slid off her breast. She pouted at the mirror.

I took one picture fast and zoomed in just as she put her hand on her naked breast. Her index finger was above her nipple and her third finger below it. They squeezed and palpitated, wobbling the dark cone to tilt up, and then down. I snapped.

Her middle finger was still and stiff, extended between the other two, so that the movement of her nipple, up and down, rubbed its tip across the finger's pad. In a few moments her flesh had engorged and darkened.

I panned up to her mouth. Her lips were slack. Down again, as she abandoned the finger-play and weighed her breast on her palm, jiggling. She lifted it even higher, and bent her neck, bringing her mouth down to her nipple. Her tongue, pointed as a kitten's, lapped out and licked.

I got that shot, as well, *and* the thin strand of spittle that glistened for a fraction of a second, stretched between her nipple and her mouth.

Her palm stroked, wiping the moisture away. She gave the mirror one last lustful look, put her hands to her waist, pulled her robe's tie loose, and let the bulky garment drop into a pool around her high-heeled feet.

Double damn! And I hadn't bothered to go prepare myself

because I'd thought it too early.

Delightfully naked, she bent, and stretched, rotating at her waist. I was impressed. Her body didn't look the least athletic. When a woman has breasts as feminine as hers, and hips that are downright voluptuous, you don't expect her to be able to stand stiff-legged, on towering heels, and push her hands flat to the floor, or do back-bends that take her into a wrestler's bridge.

That was exciting. I had close-ups of her sex, from her 'windows' exploits, but with her thighs splayed in the bridge, her sex looked infinitely accessible. She held that straining position long enough for me to get a series of shots. For the first second or two her sex was just a vertical pucker, but as the moments passed her lips parted, slowly, gradually exposing her pink inner lips.

She bumped her hips up twice, straight at my lens, and then writhed to her feet, turned her back to my camera, spread her feet, and bent forwards until her head and upper torso appeared, dangling between the 'v' of her thighs. Her hands grasped her ankles. She pulled, bobbing. Her upside-down breasts bounced and quivered. They had to be very firm, despite their size. Most women's breasts would have flopped in their faces in that position, but hers just vibrated, as if they were packed bursting-tight.

When she paused in that position I zoomed in, tight-tight focus. There just couldn't *be* a better shot of the tender undersides of breasts. My lens could see every pale blue vein that throbbed beneath her skin. Her breasts dangling weight distorted them just a touch, in a most delightful way. Her oversized nipples pointed back towards me at an angle. As my lens was higher, I got them in perfect profile, dark flesh in crisp focus, in vivid contrast against a background of out-of-focus wheat-coloured carpet.

Even though I was just me, the skin that lined my vagina was crawling. Even my insipid nipples were uncrinkling in response.

She straightened and turned to face me. She must have had lessons in belly dancing at some time, because her next series of movements were hip-rolls, belly rippling, and shoulder rotations. I clicked as fast as I could.

She put her foot up on a stool and curled over to inspect her own sex. Damn! If she masturbated when I wasn't painted or dressed suitably to do the same I'd never forgive myself.

In close-up, I saw that she was still exercising — her sex. Its lips clamped, twitched, sighed apart, and then clamped again. A tucking-roll that rippled up her tummy convinced me she was working on her internal muscles. I felt guilty. I'd been neglecting mine. You tend to forget these things when you are your own only lover, but that was no excuse. It wasn't a sex thing, because I wasn't dressed for sex, but I put my hand down there and two fingers up inside. I was still firm, and my squeezing-muscles still worked, but you can't be too careful. I made a resolution.

The man came back, dressed to go out. He slapped her on the rump and said something. She grinned and replied. After a few more minutes conversation, he left. Perhaps she'd play with herself now he was gone.

No. Still naked, she went to the kitchen, put a kettle on and then hip-rolled to the bathroom.

That gave me a chance — nothing fancy — but fast. I grabbed into my closet at random and got back to my stool. It was funny, really. As *I* rolled stockings up my legs, she was doing the same, sitting in his recliner. She pulled on panties, and so did I. Her skirt was long, but slit high. Mine was short, not slit, but wrap-around. She pulled a shawl-neck sweater over her head... but I had no sweater handy and she was already taking a coat out of her hall closet.

Sod! Still — I made an instant decision that left me no time to spare. I grabbed a coat and a wig and ran into my hall, bare-breasted, bare-faced, pulling the coat on first and then the wig. No one saw me. The elevator came quickly when I wanted it to, for once. I crossed my fingers. *He* was out, and now she was going out. There are stores close to the building. If he'd driven, and if they only had one car, she'd likely walk.

In the lobby I watched the bank of elevators that served the other tower. When a door slid open, I turned my back.

I knew it was her without looking. Five inch heels have a distinctive click. I let her pass me, and followed.

It was a supermarket first. I'd never seen any woman make such a production out of buying fruit and vegetables. She caressed the bananas, almost masturbated a cucumber, and when she picked up a peach she held it so close to her face, her tongue-tip extended, that I thought for a moment she was going to lick its crease.

She weighed avocados in her palm as if they were testicles. Ditto the plums.

In Frozen Goods, she put her hand into the upright cooler and laid her palm on the dry-ice frost on a pack of ice cream. She held it there until her flesh had to be freezing, and then, the slut, she slid that hand inside her coat. I watched the movement of her arm. The way it angled, I know she'd worked her hand inside the shawl neck of her sweater and was cupping her breast.

A really cold hand feels nice on a warm breast, just as a breast that is freshly frigid from a naked roll in the snow feels extra good to a warm palm. I *knew* that, but I'd never have thought to take sexual advantage of a supermarket freezer.

By the time she was done shopping she had a trolley-full and I had a small carton of whipping cream. How was she going to carry all that? She didn't. They had delivery service.

She went to the mall. 'Sluts', the sex shop, has a branch there. I waited, hidden behind a fountain, until she came out with two full bags and a parcel under her arm. Either they didn't deliver, or what she'd bought was for immediate use.

Her next stop was a video rental. She went straight for the 'Adult' section, of course.

After three more stores — two clothing and one shoe — I decided I'd be pushing it if I kept trailing her, so I went back home. I had an idea, anyway.

I turned the wrong way in the lobby, deliberately. People do that by accident, sometimes. The towers are identical. You wouldn't find you were in the wrong one until you tried your key in your door. I went up, just as if I was going home, and went to what I hoped was *their* door.

There was a newspaper laying outside. I stooped. The paper boy had pencilled 'Drake' in one corner. *If* I was right, and *if* this was their apartment, I now had a surname.

Just in case, I tried my key in their lock. It didn't work. Back home, I looked through the 'Drake's in the telephone directory. There weren't that many. Only one listing at Crystal Towers North — Hugh and Millicent. Millicent? I didn't like that. I decided I would call her 'Millie'.

VIII

Millie

We were both stiff and drained from the previous evening's gymnastics, so we didn't even indulge in an early morning 'quicky'. Anyway, I had plans for later.

We did our usual weekend thing, lolling and lazing and flirting idly. I still didn't know what was in the mysterious parcel Hugh had bought me, but I could wait.

Sometime after his second mug of Blue Mountain, Hugh told me that there was something for me on the counter. It was an absolutely delectable bra and pants set. Hugh likes me braless, usually, but this one was about as skimpy as it could be, and the fabric was so fine that when I laid the pants on my palm it looked like a dusting of talc, not cloth, at all.

"Shall I put this on for you?" I asked.

"Not yet. Surprise me with it sometime. That is, unless you want to entertain the neighbours?"

"What?"

"We had an uninvited audience last night."

"We what?"

"Opposite. She was sitting in the dark, watching you do those wild things to my poor thumb."

"Who was?"

He shrugged. "How would *I* know? I only saw her for a moment. She lit a cigarette, and I saw her face in the flame."

"Pretty?"

"Of course. Every young woman is pretty when you just catch a quick glance. If I see her again she'll likely be horse-faced and fat."

"And she was watching? The whole time?"

"I'm sure of it. Who could resist? I'd have taken you right here, on the floor, and given her a real show, but I had the bathroom thing planned."

I shivered. The thought having been watched was warming me, in a quivery sort of way. After all, I'd been *really* wild, hadn't I. "Do you think she does it often — spy on us?" I asked.

"How would *I* know? She could be watching us right now, for all we know. You want me to check?"

I glanced out the window. "I can't see anyone. Which window?"

Hugh got up. "Where are the binoculars?"

"Walk-in closet, top shelf, middle hat-box."

He grinned. "Why don't you give her something to hold her attention while I check her out?"

"Hold her attention? How?"

"Do a strip. Do some aerobics — naked. That should hold her."

So he went, and I did. I did more than 'naked aerobics'. I've got a good body, and I like to have people see it. I made a point of showing it off to her, from every possible angle, if she was watching. I hoped that she was.

When Hugh finally came back he was grinning ear-to-ear.

"So — she's cute, is she?" I asked.

"Absolutely gorgeous. Millie, if I didn't have you here to take care of my needs, I'd be swinging over there on a rope right now. *And* she's a horny little slut. I don't know what you did, but it certainly got to her. She was fingering herself while she watched you."

I blushed — with pleasure. It's nice to know you can reach people. "What did she look like? What was she wearing?"

"I couldn't see that well, even with the binoculars. What I *did* see was a pretty little face, very pale, under close-cropped silvery hair, but I only got a quick glance. I got a good look at her legs though. Slim, but very nice indeed — and she wears shoes with proper heels, like yours. Between her legs and her face — well it looked like it was some sort of telescope on a stand she was standing behind, so she was partly hidden. I only knew she was playing with herself by the angle of her arm and the way her thighs parted."

"Telescope? The bitch!"

"Yeah — and getting off from close-up views of your lovely body, my darling."

"So — where are you going?" I asked him.

"Shopping. I've got an idea. What I want may be hard to find. Can you amuse yourself for a few hours?"

"Putting on a show for our peeping neighbour?"

"Not now. We'll do that later if you like, okay?"

So he left. I thought about the coming evening. I'd already wanted to make it special, and now, as we might have an audience, I wanted it more so. Maybe I'm an exhibitionist. There was an outfit I'd seen in the 'Sluts' catalogue that would suit the occasion. We needed groceries, anyway. I dressed and went out.

In the lobby I heard the click of high heels following me. It couldn't be, of course, but I checked behind me in the glass door, and the woman was definitely slim, and pale.

There was likely more than one slim pale pretty woman who wore five inch heels in the building. Or was there? Slim, pretty, and pale, maybe. Those heels though? They're rare enough on the street to turn heads. Perhaps?

I went to the supermarket first, and she followed. She liked a show, did she? Okay — I made my shopping as sexy as I could. She watched, though I wasn't supposed to know it. Then she followed me to Sluts, and the video store, and waited outside the stores while I tried on shoes and dresses.

Then I lost her.

I *think* I saw her again, from the back, on our floor, getting into an elevator as I got out of the one opposite. It was definitely the same coat, same shoes, and the same calves. I glowed. I've been followed before, often. Usually it has been by old men in dirty raincoats. That was no fun, but to be stalked by a *very* attractive, sexy woman... I hadn't had a woman in a long time. It wasn't that Hugh objected to my bisexuality, the reverse, but we'd got so wrapped up in each other we'd had little time for socialising.

There are those that say a woman turns bi because another woman's touch is so much more knowledgeable than a man's. Not true, in Hugh's case. His fingers, and his tongue, were as clever as any woman's I'd had. Still, it'd be nice to taste a woman again, just for the fun of it. Hugh has everything I need, except a...

A 'pussy' we'd called it, back when I was running with the old crowd. 'Pussy'. It's a nice soft purring sort of a word. I'd have to use it more often.

Hugh came back with another parcel.

"For me?"

"For us." He unwrapped. "Better binoculars. They're for night-viewing, with light amplifiers. These were expensive, so I hope she's as pretty as I think. If we are going to turn the tables, and watch our watcher — watch her play with herself, maybe. It'll be more fun if she's worth watching."

"Oh, she is."

"You've seen her?"

I told him all about my shopping trip, without the details of what I'd bought, and about her trailing me. "*And* she's got nice breasts," I told him. "Not as big as mine, but nice."

"Huh? How?"

"In the supermarket. I was spying on her, spying on me. I turned on her once, quickly. She bent to a bottom shelf, ducking me. Her coat gaped. She had absolutely nothing on beneath it."

"Christ!" Hugh picked up the phone.

"Who are you calling?"

"The front desk. I want to know Miss Slim-nice-legs-goes-topless' name."

I did things in the blender while he talked.

"Petra," he told me. "Petra — no last name. Some sort of artist, George thinks."

"I'm surprised he told you. Isn't that against the building's regulations?"

"A man who tips well, asking about a pretty woman? That comes under the man-to-man regulations, which outrank this building's."

"And?"

"And what?"

"Does he agree? That she's attractive?"

"Most definitely, yes. Just talking about her made him drool. So — what sort of a show shall we put on for 'Petra' tonight?"

"Here." I handed him a parcel. "Shave, shower, and put this on. I'll use the other bathroom to get ready in and join you here. Remember I promised you three hours as your sex-slave? Well, get ready, Master. Your slave will be serving you supper, and much more, in exactly one hour."

IX

Petra

They were going to make love that night. I *knew* they were going to make love. The woman, 'Millie', had come back from that sex shop loaded. Whether she'd bought clothes or toys, she wasn't going to be able to resist trying them out on — on 'Hugh'. I know that if I'd been her, I wouldn't have been able to wait.

What to wear? If only I'd known what she'd bought...

Why not?

I'd just taken my coat off and made coffee, but I left the coffee to go cold and put my coat back on. I drove this time. When I asked the girl what Mrs Drake had bought, because we were going to the same party, she gave me a very strange look, but she told me anyway. Her look was even stranger when I bought much the same outfit, but a sale is a sale, right?

I gave myself black eyes, mascara'd to simulate kohl as well as I could. The same olive tint I'd used for the toreador was fine, from head-to-toe though, and with paler nipples this time. Not much make-up, apart from the eyes. The wig I chose was long enough for me to sit on, and midnight black.

My top — pink where Millie's was pale blue — had long leg-o'-mutton sleeves, tight at my wrist. Apart from the tiny flowers embroidered on it, it was transparent. There was quite a cleavage. It fastened with Velcro — *not* authentic — in a band that was snug beneath my breasts.

There was a skirt, also on a Velcroed band, that wrapped low around my hips, and draped down to the floor. It too, was transparent, gauzy, and embroidered, with a front slit to the band.

Dressed, I was naked but lightly veiled, just like my darling Millie would be.

The final piece, an aquamarine where Millie's gem was an emerald, had to be spirit-gummed into my navel.

I raided my jewel box, hanging a dozen gold chains around my neck and loading my wrists and ankles with bangles. Would Millie have the same thought? Well, I'd soon find out.

Neither the barber's chair nor the stool seemed right. I made a pile of silk pillows and satin cushions, and lowered my camera on its tripod until it was a foot from the floor.

To drink? A Caliph's slave-girl wouldn't drink. It'd be against her religion. Still, you can carry authenticity too far. I made myself a milkshake, with peach ice cream, and mixed it half-and-half with Cointreau.

I was ready. All I needed was for the curtain to rise.

X

Millie

Hugh rapped on the bathroom door.

I called, "Stay out. I'm not ready."

"*She* is."

"What?"

"Our own personal pet voyeur. She's in her peeping position and waiting for us to put on a show. I peeped *her* through the bedroom blinds, and you *really* ought to see her."

"Why?"

"Her outfit. I can't make out colours very well with these binoculars, but she's in some sort of harem-girl costume and wearing a long black wig."

"The bitch!"

"Why do you say that?" I could hear the snigger in his voice. He knew *exactly* why I'd called her a bitch.

I finished my third layer of lipstick — I intended to leave kiss marks all over his body. Taking my sweet time, I poured perfume into my palms and smoothed it through my hair. I didn't want to perfume anywhere his tongue might go, and that was the only place I could think of.

When I finally opened the bathroom door Hugh's reaction to the way I looked was *most* satisfactory. He sucked breath. The black satin pants I'd bought him tented before my very eyes.

"You knew she was copying me, didn't you," I said. "She's spoiled my surprise."

"Well, these pasha-passion-pants you bought me and the cushions all over the floor gave me a clue. The surprise isn't spoiled, O nymph of the endlessly-long gorgeous legs. I love your outfit, Delectable One."

He held me at arm's length. His eyes made a slow tour of my body. As he looked down at my legs, I went on tip-toe and flexed the muscles in my thighs. His gaze lifted to my sex. I pushed my mound forward. He licked his lips. Hugh caressed my belly with his eyes. I rippled it, winking the stone in my navel at him. When his eyes reached my breasts I pulled my shoulders back, and shimmied them.

"Everything I see pleases me." His voice was croaking. "My pleasure, O Infinitely Edible, should be obvious."

He took my hand and drew it to the bulge that distorted his satin pants. I closed my fist around it and stroked satin up and down his stem.

Hugh pulled me closer, inhaled the scent of my hair, and whispered, "Two more minutes of what you're doing now and I'll come. Do you want that, or shall we torture me until I can't stand the agony of wanting you any more?"

I squeezed and released. "I am but your slave, Master, but we have an audience waiting. Was it not your Magnificence's intention to drive *two* women wild with lust, this evening?"

He pressed the back of his hand to his forehead. "Oh — the

responsibility of it all! Uneasy lies the head that wears the crown! Okay, Edible One, we'll drag it out. Know then, Little Tease, that your Master will return your torture upon you, yea, a thousand fold."

I liked the sound of that. He led me to the living room where the cushions were, under lots of light, for our Peeper's sake as much as ours, and the bowls of dip were laid out.

"No chips?" Hugh asked. "No raw veggies? I see dips, but nothing to dip them with."

I bobbed a curtsey. "As your slave, my Master, *I* am your dip, if it pleases your Infinite Horniness?"

"How about *you*? Not hungry?"

I ran the backs of my fingers over the front of his pants. "If it please your growing-even-biggerness, I'll find something to suck some dip off, if I search hard, I'm sure."

He was throbbing.

I sat him on the pile of pillows and pulled the low leather stool over. Lifting the sweet raspberry-and-cream dip, I draped myself backwards over the stool and set the dish on my bare midriff. Its base was cold. My bare legs spread wide, parting a flimsy skirt that wasn't hiding anything, anyway.

"If this view doesn't please your hard-and-longness, the stool is on castors. Spin me, babe."

Hugh leaned over and turned me until my parted thighs were open directly towards the window. "I hope she likes what she sees as much as I do."

"Perhaps you'd rather have *her*, spread before you, Master?"

"Prefer? No — you are my first choice, O delight to mine eye, but if it was *both* of you, now..."

I took a deep breath, arching my back and lifting my breasts towards him. "You know — I wouldn't mind that, at all. Do you want to ask her over? After all, she's dressed for the occasion."

"Another night, maybe. I think you, my love, will more than suffice for this night. I wonder what she's doing though. Is she playing with herself, do you think?"

"Like this, Master? If the sight of a woman playing with herself is your desire?" I reached down and parted my lips.

"You're going to spill that dip," Hugh warned, just like a man.

I took the bowl and writhed to my feet. "Then we must consume it. Master?" I pulled my top apart without undoing the band beneath my breasts. It became a sling, supporting me and squeezing my breasts together slightly. I dipped a finger into raspberry cream, and smeared my nipple. Squatting astride his lap, I put my breast to his lips. He gave my nipple one of those special strong sucks of his. It was so powerful it felt as if blood was being drawn through my pores. I can go weak inside from one of those.

"Keep that up," I told him, "and my pussy is going to start dripping on your new satin pants."

"The other one," he commanded.

"Certainly, Master. Tonight, I am yours to use, or abuse, in any way you wish."

He sucked my second nipple until it was throbbing as hard as the first. As he sucked, Hugh's hand found one of the gold chains that looped my neck and dangled between my breasts. He stretched a length between two fingers and used it to flicker over my other nipple.

"Mine to use?" he said. "Absolutely?"

I bowed my head. "It is Araby, Master, and I am yours to command."

"Very well, I notice that you have the magic device for controlling pictures to hand." He picked up the remote control.

"Why?"

"Press, and see, mighty one."

He hit the two 'ons' and 'play'. The video, *A Thousand and One Erotic Nights*, started.

"Appropriate," he said, "but there is other entertainment at hand, that delights my eye more. Perform for me, Slave."

"In what ways, O Master?"

He rearranged the cushions and laid on his back with one beneath his head. "Bestride me, kneeling, my sloe-eyed houri of the desert."

I knew exactly what he wanted. It was one of his favourite things. I knelt with a knee on either side of his head, my sex spread wide a few inches above his face. There were table lamps on the floor, so I was brightly lit. I leaned back, arched, onto one hand. My other hand caressed my pussy's lips, teasing them further apart.

"Do it, bitch!"

I felt inside. I was slick and hot. My fingers spread against elastic resistance so that Hugh would be able to see deep inside me.

Was that woman's telescope aimed into the same glistening pinkness? Was she playing with herself, roused by watching as *I* played with myself?

"Make yourself *very* wet," Hugh said. "I thirst for you. I want you to flow until your nectar drips into my mouth."

When I was a kid my mother made me take dancing lessons. Some instinct must have guided me even back then, because I chose 'acro'. I never became a professional dancer, but the flexibility and abdominal strength that I gained prepared me for my avocation, sex. Even now, at my age, I can still do the splits and I can still cross my ankles behind my neck.

And back-bends.

I let my sex alone for a moment and gripped my thighs, just above my knees. Pushing my hips high, I pulled on my legs. I folded back at my waist. The back of my head dragged up over Hugh's erection. Most of my weight was on my knees as I turned my face sideways. Holding myself in position with just one hand, I started to play with my sex again, and could nibble at Hugh's stem at the same time.

"Oh yes!" he groaned. He took his satin-covered shaft in one hand and steered my head with the other. I opened wide for him, took his glans into my mouth, and held it there, sucking and licking through thin slick fabric.

"That feels good," he told me. "Now be a bad girl and come on my face, sweetheart."

A slave has to do as she's told, right? I parted my pussy's lips again. I was sticky-wet enough that I could open wide and my lips would stay spread. That gave him his view and left my fingers free to work on my clit's shaft, and then its head.

"You're *so* pretty inside," he said. "I can see pink all the way deep up into you. Make it twitch for me, sweetness."

So I did. I writhed those internal muscles as the ball of my finger rotated me close, and contracted them when the urgency got real bad and my finger pressed down hard and *shivered* on my clit, driving it and driving it and driving...

"*Very* nice," he said as I slumped off him. "Did you want to take a break now, or..."

"As my Master wishes."

"Then let's eat and watch the lesser entertainment for a while."

The woman on the TV was trying to work two penises between her thick lips at the same time. Her nipples had been pierced. Big gold rings dangled from them. I made a mental note.

As we watched I fed Hugh dip off the tips of my fingers. From time to time I touched him through the satin, just to keep him at his peak. The woman was servicing three men now, one in each orifice. That's something I fantasise about, sometimes, but I wasn't sure I'd actually try it, in real life. I didn't see Hugh sharing me like that, anyway. Him and me and another woman, though?

I've done most everything there is to do, I guess, but I've never had a threesome. I wondered what it would be like to watch Hugh make love to another woman. Would I be jealous, or would it really turn me on?

I decided it would turn me on — a lot.

"I'm thirsty," Hugh said.

"You want me to come in your mouth again?"

"No — what else have we got to drink?"

I'd prepared vodka and cranberry juice. As I went to fetch it Hugh called after me, "And extra ice, please. Lots of it."

I filled a bowl from the ice-maker and brought it back on a tray with two tall glasses of the drink. Hugh was flat on his back again.

"I don't want a glass," he said. "Tonight I drink only from your luscious lips."

I knelt beside him, filled my mouth, and bent over him. Liquid poured from my mouth into his. My tongue followed. We kissed and drank and drank and kissed. Hugh fondled the nipples of my dangling breasts, smoothed his hand up under my flimsy skirt and over my bum, and laid there, a Pasha in all his glory.

"I'm horny again," I told him.

"Does my slave desire another orgasm?"

"Does it please you, Master?"

"Then an orgasm you shall have, eventually." He stood up. "On your back, wench, across the stool."

I draped myself. Hugh sat on the sofa, the bowl of ice

beside him. "You are overheated, little passion-flower. Let me cool you."

"Aren't you out of character?" I asked. "'Wench', and now 'Passion-flower'."

In reply, he took a cube of ice and rubbed it over my left nipple.

I shivered. "That's cold!"

"Then I'll warm you again." He bent over me and sucked my nipple into the heat of his mouth. It tingled. When he'd sucked it aching-hard, he put the ice back. My belly convulsed from the shock.

"And now..." He trailed the ice down across my midriff, over my belly, along the crease of my groin, to my sex. The lips of my pussy went numb. He thumbed the half-melted cube inside me.

"That's cold," I complained again.

"Shut up and suffer!"

Hugh used both hands. One fistful of ice rubbed all over my breasts. The other hand cupped a handful of ice over my sex. It was strange, but the numbness felt good. I reached sideways, found the elastic waistband of his pants, and dragged down.

I love that viewpoint, being below him, when his erection looms over me. He's big, but looking up at him makes him seem enormous. "Ice?" I asked.

He moved the bowl closer. I scooped ice and rubbed his erection with it.

"You'll make it go down," he warned.

"In which case..." I wiped my hand, found a bowl of dip, and smeared his shaft with it. Before I could get my mouth to work, Hugh pushed me down flat across the stool. Using my breast as his handle, he turned me until my face was at his lap. I pulled his shaft to my lips, opened wide, and slid his frigid dip-coated length into my mouth.

"Oh yes," he said. "But keep perfectly still."

He shimmied forwards. His hands took my breasts, nipples between his thumbs and forefingers, but with my soft flesh crushed in his palms. He pulled. The stool, with me, was dragged closer. His shaft slid deeper into my mouth, almost to my throat.

He pushed the stool, and me, away. And pulled. And pushed.

"And now," he said, "my slave will serve me, even as she rests from her labours."

He knelt down, span me round, and took my ankles in his big hands. Lifting them high, and spreading my legs, he put the head of his penis to my sex. "I think..." He rested my calves on his shoulders, steered himself into me, where I was still dripping ice-water, gripped my upraised thighs, and pulled.

He slithered into me. A still-chilled rigid penis into an icy vagina. I could feel it, and I couldn't. What I felt mainly was the distending.

His hands left my thighs and took my breasts again. His hips didn't move. *I* didn't have to move at all. He simply pushed and pulled on my breasts, pulling me on to him, pushing me off, faster and faster until we were warm, and then hot and until...

"May I?" I gasped, putting my hand over my mound.

"By... all... means." Speech was getting difficult for him.

I did my clit, fast and furious. He pumped me backwards and forwards on that stool, *using me*. It was as if I was one of those plastic love-dolls, and Hugh was using me to masturbate with. I was just his sex-toy, a hot tight sleeve being worked on his hardness. My finger was stiff and vibrating on my clit, but the rest of me just lolled, flopping with each rocking motion.

I was getting very close when a thought came to me.

I lifted my head. "I — she — *we* want to see you come. On my face — on my breasts. We'd like that. Both of us would."

Hugh glanced at the window. "Okay." He pushed me further back, letting his erection slap up out of me, glistening and purple-headed, against his belly. Taking it in his fist he knelt over me, bracketing my waist with his knees. I cupped his scrotum. The hairs tickled my palm.

"You want it? You want cream? Then here it comes."

His fist blurred on his sex. *My* finger blurred on mine. He threw his head back. His shaft was directly above my breasts. I watched its head vibrate in his fist, licking my lips in anticipation.

"Give it to me, Hugh! Give it to me hot and wet!"

And he did. His balls tightened. He jerked. A great wet gout of cream arced into the air and flopped down, between my breasts, on my neck, my chin, my parted lips. That was enough to tip me over the edge.

I clawed his behind while I was still shuddering with aftershocks and dragged him down. I know it's agony for a man to have his cream sucked out of him when he's just come, but it's a delicious agony. He was sobbing before I'd done, but I was merciless. I didn't release him till he was dry and softening.

XI

Petra

I woke still laying on the pile of cushions. I'd had at least half a dozen orgasms and eight ounces of liquor. By then, getting from the floor to my bed was simply too much effort.

But, fresh from a deep sleep, I was horny again already. My mind played pictures of Hugh and Millie, particularly that bit when he'd been playing push-pull with the ottoman. And then there'd been that delicious episode when she'd knelt over his face and done a back-bend. Her hips had lifted high, as if a big hook had been inserted into her vagina and behind her pubic bone, and she was being pulled up by it.

I showered and dressed. My make-up was quick and simple. My wig was chestnut, with bunches. I had to be ready for them, just in case. It was Sunday, after all, the traditional day for a couple to sex it up. *If* they had the energy.

I stepped, bare-legged, into a pair of calf-high glossy black boots, and pulled an old baggy sweater over my head. The outfit wasn't fancy, but my being bare from my navel to my boot-tops made it sexy enough that I'd be able to make love to myself, if the right visual stimulus came my way.

I developed and printed my roll of film and fed it to my computer. Back in my mini-studio, I took a few hip-shot snaps of myself, front and back, hand on hip, sweater tucked up one side, some of me sucking my thumb and looking coy, and then half a roll on my hands and knees. Those ones were the main point. I looked good in that position. Even though my breasts were hidden, the soft curve of my belly was exposed when the sweater sagged down. It looked very caressable.

Once those shots were in my computer's memory, I married one of me on all fours with one of Hugh kneeling, when he was making love to Millie on the ottoman. The poses matched perfectly. A few minor edits, and on my screen he was holding my hips and it was *me* he was pistoning into, but from behind now.

It looked so good I masturbated, just a quick little one, there and then.

Back at the window, with a reloaded camera, I focused into their room again.

He was laying on the sofa, in a pair of bikini pants. She was naked except for her heels, clearing up the remains of their mini-orgy.

I clicked away, with two more rolls of film handy, just in case they got into it again. I used a full roll on him, just sprawled there, reading, and her, bending, stretching, swaying.

He was horny again. I could tell, by his erection and by the dark wet spot where the fabric of his bikini stretched over its head. He said something, perhaps telling her he was ready. She bent over him for a quick kiss, patted his bulge, and got on with her chores.

She went to the kitchen and came back after a while with a plate of sandwiches. That reminded me that I hadn't eaten. When I got back, with a plate of water biscuits, ripe brie and black grapes, he was gone, and she was laying backwards over the arm of the sofa, pulling her nipples up towards the ceiling and rolling them.

I shot six quick ones. It occurred to me that *he* would have enjoyed watching her as much as I was. Where was he? I glanced at their bedroom window. The curtains had been pulled. They must have been skimped in the making, because they'd been drawn tight and smooth to make them meet.

When he came back she stopped her play and they talked for a while, her sitting and him stretched out. Her hand was on his thigh. She could do that. Anytime she liked, she had a male body handy, always within reach. I felt a sudden pang that could have been jealousy if it wasn't that I knew better.

My lens zoomed in close enough to see that she was scratching him gently with sharply-pointed nails. I captured the scratching on film, because it's details like that than can make a composition.

My hand smoothed my belly, its finger-tips savouring both texture and contour. Perhaps her scratching would lead to...

But she went back to chores, and he to his book.

It got dark with me still bent over my camera. I stood straight and stretched. Their lights went off. Damn!

I raced into my den. A dim light came on in their bedroom, but with those sheers drawn, I didn't stand a chance.

The light moved. It shone straight at the window, likely from the other side of their bed. It cast a larger-than-life shadow —

him — standing and stretching, with a perfect silhouette of his up-curved erect penis jutting out in front of him.

The contrast of black shadow on white fabric wasn't sharp enough, or bright enough, for my camera. It was plenty sharp enough for my eyes, though. How lucky I was that the way he stood gave me a profile. From either front or back, the effect would have been wasted.

A second shadow joined his. *Her.* In silhouette, the outlines of a body are emphasised. Those two — my eyes caressed the shape of her breast, sharp peaked at the junction of two complimentary curves. The upper curve was shallower, the lower one more dramatic as it arced down and under to her ribcage.

They were face to face. Her arm bridged the gap, reaching down to his penis. Perhaps she tugged, because the two shadows moved together, blending into one. Were they kissing? They had to be.

The shadows moved apart. Bending at her waist, she stooped until her back was horizontal and her head-shadow eclipsed the tip of his penis-shadow.

She was sucking on him, the bitch, gobbling on his head. And my camera couldn't see it!

His back arched. His spine was an 's', pushing his hips forward and leaning back. My fingers itched to claw down the long sinuous curve of his back and pinch his hard buns. Or jab a stiff finger deep into the dry dragging heat of his anus.

The sensuous shock of it would jerk his hips, wouldn't it, driving his penis deeper between her lips?

Hugh was rocking now, in and out of her mouth. She lifted her hand to hold his shaft, perhaps controlling the depth of his thrust? But she stood. Her hands took her breasts and held them up. It was his turn to bend. He took the shadow-nipple between his lips and sucked, drawing back, elongating her breast.

As he sucked, she knelt, drawing him down with her. She pulled her breast free, and bent backwards, arching away from him. Their shadows merged at floor level. Either he was kneeling between her thighs, or she between his. The first, I thought. Yes. His arm stretched out to her upthrust pubic mound. She pumped her hips up at it.

I imagined — I was *sure* that he had his fingers inside her, and she was driving up onto them.

With her hips still rocking at him, her hands found her nipples, just as they had when she'd draped herself over the sofa's arm. Her body was a bow, strung tight.

Watching her, and fondling inside her, must have got to him. He moved forward on his knees, between her thighs. She didn't rise to meet him. She just laid back in that lovely curve, touching him at one point only, as he too leaned back, and pumped slowly, and faster, and furiously. The queue at the back of his head bobbed.

I had to hurry. I spread wide and opened myself with one hand. My other hand folded into a dagger and stabbed into my own scalding heat.

But I was too late. They toppled into a shapeless heap. After a few frustrating moments, the light went out.

XII

Millie & Petra

Millie

Our apartment has a washer and a drier built into a closet. It's very handy, but they're both quite small. Even with just the two of us, it takes half a dozen loads to do a week's wash.

Just in case — hoping — *she* was watching, I'd made-up and dressed in the bathroom, so that I could make an 'entrance'.

It wouldn't have looked natural to be wearing stockings to do laundry, so I was bare-foot and bare-legged in my mules, and simply tied a towel low around my hips, sarong-style. At first, I knotted it the way I usually do, over my right hip, but then I thought about Petra, and that she'd be mainly seeing me from my left, so I reknotted it, lower on that side. That way the gaping slit would be towards her, if she was watching.

I always do whites first, and start with our robes. I'd loaded, and was just about to add the Tide, when I paused. Those old robes were still good, and very comfortable to lounge around in, but what did they look like, to *her*?

Glamorous? No!

I fetched a garbage bag, and dumped them. Once I'd reloaded the washer it just had room left for the towel I was wearing. Not pulling it off, I sucked in and shimmied so that the knot came loose and let the towel slither down my thighs.

I picked it up bending from my hips, stiff-legged, bum towards the window and dropped it in.

Would she trail me again? To give her a chance, I took my time dressing, making a show of it — a kind of reverse-strip.

The nicest undies I had was that new set that Hugh had just bought me — the bra and panties that looked like a dusting of talc once they were on — that you had to touch to be sure they were real. I took my time adjusting the panties, making sure that the gossamer fabric was smooth over my pubes and bum, while facing the window, and then turned sideways to it to bend over and droop my breasts into the cups of the bra.

That had to be smoothed and adjusted, as well, and my nipples had to be fondled through the gauzy cloth, both for my own pleasure, and that of my hoped-for watcher.

It was a strange feeling. I'm naturally sensual, all the time. I take the time to enjoy textures, and I *do* tend to touch myself a lot, even when Hugh isn't around to enjoy the show, but now I was a tad confused. Was I caressing myself more than usual, because of *her*, or was I just carrying on as normal, but more *aware* of it, because I was likely on display?

And did it matter, provided I enjoyed it?

Whichever, I took my sweet time rolling my hose up my legs, and posed with one toe pointed, and let my fingers trail the insides of my thighs before *and* after, I knotted my garters.

I finished with a coat-dress, navy blue with white piping, three button, and almost knee-length. *If* she was watching me, and *if* she wanted to follow, I'd given her ample time to get ready.

My shopping took two hours, including the time spent lingering over coffee and scanning the mall to see if I could spot her. Most of the time was spent choosing new robes for Hugh and me. Mine was pale blue silk, thin, and an inch below groin-length. Hugh's was also silk, slub silk from Thailand, dark blue, heavier, and slightly longer.

The other shopping, at Sluts' Sex Shop, took very little time. I knew exactly what I wanted. There were a few pieces of costume jewellery that I'd been thinking about trying, and that video had made up my mind for me. The other items hadn't really appealed to me — before Petra. Now they seemed ideal. I took all of the edible fluorescent body paint that they had in those two colours — blue and pale green.

*****

Petra

I got to my camera just in time to see her apartment door close behind her. Well, I had things to do. She'd be back.

The private galleries that sell my paintings, and the publishers of my photographs, both know my finished work, but none of them are aware of the *process* by which I achieve my effects.

There are just three people in the whole world, one man and two women, who are privy to my secrets. There is Velvet Knight — her professional name — who is tall, thin, black, and boasts of being the world's highest-paid stripper. She claims to enjoy at least three orgasms each time she performs. Off-stage, she gives the impression of being a total 'I'll-do-anything' slut, but she is, in fact, still technically a virgin at thirty-three. The only hands that ever touch Velvet are her own.

The other woman is Sybil. She is a strict lesbian and an author of feminist books. Sybil devours three or four pretty little secretaries a year, discarding each one as soon as the girl becomes totally debauched.

The one man is 'Caz' — Castelmain de la Croix. I've thought, from time to time, that it would be interesting to have an affair with Caz. He is dominant, and very much into bondage, but the trouble with Caz is that he always becomes obsessed with pleasing his current 'victim'. When a woman lets herself be bound by his strong hands, she, strangely enough, acquires him as a slave. I just don't need that intensity in a sexual relationship, so he is the one man who I have known well who has remained completely platonic — my choice, not his. It's a shame, because he is *most* inventive.

Those three — my only real 'friends' — all send me erotic photographs from time to time. Most of them are unsuitable for my work, but Sybil had sent me a set from Manilla that I was using for a composition. I worked on it in off moments, much as some people work on jigsaw puzzles. Perhaps that was what it would turn out to be, if I found a way to market it — an 'impossible' jigsaw.

The pictures Sybil had sent me were of a unique erotic night club act. There were two girls, oriental, both contortionists, and twins. It was looking at those two identical faces and figures, intricately entwined, that had given me the inspiration for the composite.

I'd started with an overhead shot of them laying on their

sides, head-to-toe, sex-to-sex, each one's legs parted to bracket the body of the other, grinding their cores together. Then I'd added a fourth and fifth image, these two squatting above the faces of the originals, enjoying oral attention from below. The fifth was bent over and kissing one 'squatter', while her identical 'sextuplet', made love to her from behind with a strap-on dildo. The seventh was performing anilingus on the sixth, and so on.

I was up to seventeen or eighteen of them. The bodies were so entangled it was hard to tell. That morning I added the eighteenth or nineteenth, in a Millie-inspired back-bend, sucking on a breast that I had to reshape to fit, and spread wide enough that I'd be able to insert the next one's head between her thighs. It was quite an exercise — in both pre-planning and in perspective. I had to be able to fit in the next body, you see, and at the same time let the sexual activity be clearly visible, while not distorting any of the bodies into unreal proportions.

By the time I'd redrawn my model's long black hair to hang properly, my body was making insistent demands on me. I 'saved', and left my screen to pace my apartment.

Half of me demanded an orgasm, *now*, while the other half was determined to save my lust for my next 'viewing' of Millie and Hugh. I decided to compromise with just one, small, climax. That meant getting myself ready.

What mood was I in? Silly question! I hadn't had time to reach my orgasm when watching their shadow-play. I was randy. I was 'in heat'. I was downright bloody desperate. I was in that mood where the thought of being gang-banged by half a dozen large sweaty men becomes downright appealing.

It can be quite exquisite, feeling like that, 'crazy-randy', if you are in the hands of a skilful lover. You can be a violin string, tightened to a higher and higher pitch with each expert caress, until the music of it becomes shrill, almost inaudible, and then you snap, and the clear clean joy of it suspends you in a sort of crystalline eternity — an echoing note that needs no instrument, before you finally plunge back to find your body sweat-soaked and string-limp, and sated.

I couldn't let myself have that. I owed Millie and Hugh all the lust I could bring to my watching of them.

But I needed *something*.

Control — that was what I needed. I had to show my body that my mind and will were still in charge. It demanded? I'd show it!

I chose a platinum-blonde wig, long and straight, and did my face innocent-but-pretty. My barber's chair was still in front of the tall mirror. I adjusted the glass's angle and laid out what I needed on the side table.

Seated well-back in the chair, I took a leather strap and buckled my right thigh, just above the knee, to one arm, and then my left leg to the other. Three straps went right around the chair, and me, to hold me very tight, one just beneath my breasts, another over their upper slopes, and the third around my waist.

In the mirror, I looked the perfect captive for some sex-crazed mad scientist, spread-thighed and helpless. My hands and arms were free to move, but from my shoulders down I was clamped into position, immobile.

I started with my nipples, pinching and tugging on them until they were fully rigid. Once they were really hard and sensitive, I reached for a strip of velvet. With it stretched between my hands, I dragged the wrong way of the nap up over the very tip of one nipple.

God, it felt good. If my legs hadn't been strapped apart

they'd have clamped together with the exquisite shock of it.

I repeated with my other nipple, and back to the first, teasing and teasing until my hands convulsed and squeezed my flesh of their own volition.

Once my breasts were compressed in my hands, I kneaded and coaxed, milking their blood towards their tips. I hadn't coloured my nipples, but even so, they became quite a dark shade of pink — for me.

I flicked one with my nail, and almost cried out with the pleasure/pain.

My eyes were pleading in the mirror, but their begging was ambiguous. Did they want the torture to end, or did they need it, and more?

I — the part of me that was the torturer — was merciless.

I laid the strip of velvet across my belly, a silent threat — or promise? My fingers stroked my inner thighs, up high, close to the crease of my groin. My nipples were crying out for more attention, but I ignored them. The sharp tips of my fingernails trailed lower, beneath my sex, and smoothed over what Caz calls my "taint". "It ain't pussy, and it ain't ass."

The pad of one finger found my rosebud-sphincter. I lifted my hand to my mouth, sucked my finger wet, and returned it to rim the sensitive pucker. Once it was twitching, I switched to velvet again, making gentle circles at first, and then tucking a corner inside, clamping on it with the constrictor muscles of my anus, and tugging it out, then poking it back in, over and over.

By that time my buttocks were clenching and my belly was rippling. My breasts were heavy weights, and my nipples were marbles, imbedded in my flesh. Each deep panting breath I took creaked the straps that encircled my ribcage.

My body was screaming for release, but I wasn't done.

I have a silk whisk — a souvenir of Nepal. It is meant to be used in the purification ritual of some obscure religion, but I put it to better use.

My position, and the stimulation, had parted the lips of my sex. My clit had crept from its sheath to throb pink and wet, fully exposed to the air. I flicked my whisk, once gently, across my open sex and across the most tender flesh of my body — my clit's naked head. The second stroke stung — just. That was the force I needed. Again, and again. The tips of the soft fronds became damp with my juices. As they clung together, into tiny wet whips, the sensation of each blow became more intense. It soon reached the stage that, had I not been anaesthetised by my lust, it would have been painful.

In the mirror, I saw that my skin was reddening. The lips of my sex had become puffy and purple with their engorgement. I told my reflection, 'Take it, you slut — you whore — you bitch-in-heat — you painted perverted harlot — you, you, youyouyouyou...'

And then my 'you's turned into a yodelling scream as I came.

I had fresh Smyrna figs and clotted cream for my mid-afternoon snack, followed by three cups of sinful Turkish coffee, laced with Napoleon brandy. I showered and massaged away the grooves that the straps had cut into my skin. Evening was coming. Hugh would be coming home from wherever he went for his working day. Millie was likely already preparing herself for whatever she had planned.

As I'd been both a vicious bitch and an innocent victim for my earlier pleasure I felt the need to be something that was at neither extreme of the sexual spectrum, for my evening.

That's much harder to do than either 'harlot' or 'virgin'. If you aren't careful, it can come out ordinary, which is something I never want to be. I thought about going oriental, but my kimonos are either very short, or high-slit, and my saris are all virtually transparent. In any case, whenever I see a beautiful Oriental woman, whatever part of the East she comes from, I always get the feeling that she is well versed in a number of mystic sexual practises. It's my prejudice showing, I guess.

Perhaps 'flirtatious and playful'? A cheerleader costume seemed a possibility, but I'd done 'schoolgirl' recently, and 'cheerleader' seemed too close. The same went for 'Daisy-May from Dogpatch'.

I finally settled on 'executive'. That can be sexy. It has overtones of dominatrix, but doesn't go that far, unless you are my friend Sybil.

I had a dark wig that was severe, with a bun. That was a start. I made my face fortyish, with large luminous eyes but thin-lipped. Lady executives are reputed to wear the tiniest bikini undies, perhaps to remind themselves of their femininity, but I chose a pair of wide-legged blue silk French knickers. Their elastic came up to my waist, but the legs were wide enough and loose enough that when I stood over a mirror I could catch glimpses of my still-flushed sex.

The pose had possibilities. I laid a camera on its back and took a couple of shots, both before I added gunmetal hose, and after.

My 'executive' suit was grey flannel with chalk stripes. Its skirt came almost to my knees, and fitted very tightly, but it had a high slit that was sealed by Velcro, so I could adjust the exposure to suit my mood.

The jacket was double-breasted. I tried it over four different blouses before deciding it looked better without one. With all three buttons fastened, it was quite demure, provided I didn't lean forward. Undone, hanging loose, it made me look as if I was well advanced in the process of seducing my male secretary.

Satisfied, I prepared myself an 'executive' supper of tiny crustless lox-and-cream cheese sandwiches, plus a pitcher of absolutely arid martinis, and took up my position by my camera.

They were already sitting at their dining table, eating supper. He was in a dark blue robe, and she was in a lighter blue one, very short. That, in combination with her hose, made her look like the principal boy in an English pantomime — maybe Aladdin.

They seemed about done with their meal. He got up, walked around to her, and eased her robe down her shoulders. I hitched myself onto my stool and parted the Velcro of my skirt, to be ready. They kissed, long and slow. He caressed one of her breasts but she pulled away and made a sign towards the bedroom. He nodded and went through.

Damn!

I hopped off my stool and made a quick dash through to the camera in my den. I was in time to see him opening the blinds and sheers. That was okay then. I ran back for my sandwiches and martinis.

When I'd got settled their bedroom was in total darkness, but I could just make out a crack of light around their bathroom door. I crossed my fingers that they weren't going to make love in there, and waited.

I was dabbing crumbs with a wet finger when the crack of light disappeared. I held my breath, waiting for a bedside light to come on, at least. They certainly weren't the type to make love in the dark.

Then, suddenly, there was no real light, but two surreal

glowing figures appeared, one light green and one an eerie blue. It took a moment for my eyes, and my brain, to adjust, but then I realised that the figures were Hugh and Millie, somehow made fluorescent. Of course — glow-in-the-dark paint, and ultra-violet, "black" lights!

I adjusted my exposure in the hope that I could capture a few shots under conditions I'd never tried before, and unzipped my skirt to let it fall.

It was like a dream sequence in an avant-garde porno movie. They stood on their bed, or so I assumed, because the bed was invisible. The light-sources had to be low. Their bodies, underlit, were even more fantastical, and beautiful.

He sank down, in a smooth lithe movement, to kneel at her feet. The undersides of her breasts, glistening green, were perfect half-moons above him. She, Millie, bestrode his upturned face. He nuzzled deep between her ethereal thighs.

She flung her head back, lifting her breasts. The two of them — man and woman — were elementals — fantasy figures — primordial. Her belly rippled and heaved, and each quiver was a dance of green light and shade. Only her navel, a deep shadow, remained unilluminated.

His hands were kneading her buttocks, blue on green, vivid.

He pulled her closer, bending her knees and spreading her thighs even wider, to burrow his face into her softest, sweetest flesh. Millie arched back in that special way of hers, doing her own part in giving him the deepest access to her female secrets.

I started to slide my hand under the waistband of my knickers, but changed my mind. Instead, I fondled the smoothness of my mound through slippery silk, finding the ridge, and then the head of my clit. My fingernail scratched lightly through the fabric. That caress would have been painful had the silk not blunted it, but through the silk... I shivered. Oh yes! I was running wet already.

I took three quick shots so that they were done with, and my other hand would be free.

At that moment she drew him up, turned away from him, and leaned forward to brace herself with her palms on the wall. He took her hips in his hands and drew her onto him, impaling her. I took one last shot.

My second hand found the gusset between my thighs. I made my fingers into a blade, and pushed silk-covered fingers into my sopping sex.

They *were* standing on the bed. Hugh flexed, and bounced. The vibration, transmitted through the bed and their feet, bounced Millie. Hugh bounced again. In the intervals between, neither of them were moving. They simply let the undulation beneath their feet raise and lower them, each one propelling *him*, and his penis, up, and *her*, and her sex, down.

One simple flex was enough to keep the movement going for long delicious seconds.

My fingers stuffed more and more folds of silk up inside me. My knickers were being dragged down from by waist, my belly, my hips, and being thrust in a slippery bunched-up wad into my vagina. At last, no more would stretch. In desperation, I released my clit from its torture and my sex from its impalement, took hold of first one side of my knickers and then the other, and tore them.

My two hands were stuffing my sex with silk as Hugh's bouncing became faster, and more urgent. His head was tossing and his hips were bucking as my fingers found my clit once more.

His back was an arch of lust. His thighs were rigid and straining. I took my shaft between finger and thumb and worked it furiously as two fingers of my other hand hooked into the fabric that was distending my...

He pulled back, and out, fisted his penis, and jetted over Millie's quivering buttocks. And I — I hit my peak. I was still convulsing inside as I dragged the tatters of my knickers out of my body, one delirious twitching inch at a time.

It wasn't until I was curled up in my bed that I began to wonder. That silhouette show on the blinds might have been a fortunate coincidence. The black-light show might have been presented to my eyes by luck — but both — one immediately after the other? Could it be..?

I dismissed the thought and went to sleep.

XIII

Millie

Whatever the store said, that fluorescent paint comes off on sheets. I had to change them and do an extra wash.

While the washer did its thing, I cleared away, feeling a bit guilty. Suppose Petra had started watching early? What would she think of me, leaving the supper things on the table all night?

I made a resolution that from then on we'd wait for our loving until the things were in the kitchen, at least.

Tidying took me longer than usual, and I almost forgot to pose prettily in my frilly apron and heels as I worked. You don't realise what a slob you've become until you get an unexpected guest, do you? Hugh had his paper and his current book both laying on a side table, and the cushions on the couch were rumpled, and a picture on the wall had somehow got uneven, and so on.

And it was that Petra who was putting me through this

guilt trip, right? The bitch!

Once I had the bed remade, with immaculately squared corners, I drew the blinds and sheers, and got Hugh's binoculars. There was no sign of her at her windows, thank goodness, so she hadn't seen the mess we'd left.

One thing I *did* notice, though, in the daylight. Hugh had been wrong about Petra's telescope. It wasn't a telescope at all — but a camera with a long lens.

Our damned 'peeper' had been taking pictures of us!

I got really mad, and then giggly, as I saw the funny side. I wondered whether she'd have the courtesy to offer us prints?

"I'll take two eight-by-ten glossies of me gobbling Hugh's knob, and four wallet-size of him screwing me on the ottoman, please."

Still, funny or not, I was due some revenge.

I put on a pair of black hose and changed my shoes for a pair of bright orange ones that were almost impossible to walk in. The silly little apron stayed on.

First I arranged my bait.

Tottering on my heels, I carried the contents of our 'toybox' into the living room. It made quite a display, laid out on the sidetable. Hugh had brought some toys from his life 'before me' into our relationship. I'd owned a few, and since then we'd, in the two years we'd been together, acquired a dozen or so more dildos and vibrators, in a variety of sizes, from the pencil-slim flexible one with the knob on the end, to the 'big boy', that was as thick as my arm, and with a bulbous end the size and shape of a small fist.

We had two 'tongues', one 'Joni's Butterfly', four sets of ben-wa, three 'ladders-to-paradise', two soft funnels, and finally, one 'Ultimate Dilator'.

I'd thought to bring out the bondage stuff as well, but there was no more room. In any case, there were enough sex-gadgets on that table to open a store with, without bringing out the kinky stuff.

Being careful not to sneak any looks out of the window, I disinfected and polished and changed batteries for the next hour. By then she *had* to have spied on what I was doing, and, having spied, *had* to have been trapped. How could she have torn herself away?

I made a quick dash into the bedroom and to the window, where the binoculars were. Yes! I saw her quite clearly, for the first time. She was wearing a red wig with masses of bobbing ringlets, and a wide-mesh black lace micro-mini dress. Her eyes were glued to the viewfinder of her telescopic camera and she had the remote trigger clutched in her fist with her thumb on the button.

Ready for me to 'pose' for her, was she? Okay, bitch!

Back in the living room, I lingered over my collection, stroking a dildo, sucking on the tip of a 'tongue', running anal beads through my fingers. Finally, I picked up an eighteen-inch novelty dildo, 'The Golf Widow'. It was shaped to look like a stack of golf balls, and was quite flexible.

Sometimes the simplest ideas can be the most effective.

Controlling my giggles, I plopped myself into Hugh's recliner, *and swivelled round so that its back was towards the window.*

Photograph *that*, you peeping Petra-bitch!

I pulled off my apron and tossed it over the back of the chair. I hung one black-hosed and orange-shod leg over the right arm, and one over the left. She'd be able to see my legs from the knees down, and have to *imagine* what I looked like from in front.

The game was to tease her, but there I was, spread wide, lolling back, with a dildo in my fist, so...

I humped forward a touch, to get my bum on the very edge.

She'd be able to work that out from the way my feet moved. I reached out to the table and took a bottle of oil — the one with eucalyptus. That one doesn't taste very nice, but it does leave a nice tingle, and Hugh wasn't there to taste me.

I oiled my pussy-lips, and my toy, parted myself with two fingers, and started to feed the dildo into me. It's the first two 'balls' that are the hardest. I had to squirm some to work them in, and I made sure my legs semaphored what I was doing.

Once those two balls are in, with the first one dilating your vaginal walls, it's just a matter of applying steady pressure and working the thing around. Pretty soon I had six or seven imitation golf balls inside me. I made a fist around the dildo's base, and started pumping.

When I was done, I withdrew the oily plastic, swung to the table for just long enough to give Petra a glimpse of my naked profile, and picked up a triple-pronged vibrator before swinging back.

Hidden from Petra, and her camera, I reversed myself in the chair so that my legs showed above its back, my heels pointing straight up. I just relaxed for a few minutes, and then started my legs trembling and scissoring, finally giving a few little kicks, before I tossed the vibrator aside, and reached for another.

Over the following hour and a half I pretended to go through half of my collection. The lower halves of my legs protruded both over one arm, over the top and an arm, and in every combination I could think of. I flailed them, and bounced hard enough to jiggle the heavy chair, and shook it, and swung it up from recline and back to 'sit', slow and fast.

If I'd really been using all my toys, I'd have been exhausted, so, when I figured Petra had been frustrated and teased enough for the day, I slithered bonelessly to the floor, and crawled all the way to my bedroom.

Through the binoculars, I saw that she was still glued to that camera of hers. Did she expect a repeat performance? That was kind of flattering.

XIV

Millie

While I was clearing away the supper things and loading the dishwasher Hugh asked me, "So you got a really good view of her?"

"Pretty good."

"What was that she wearing, again?"

"A very short dress, black lace."

"When you say 'short' — how short?"

"She was leaning forward over that camera of hers. The hem of her dress touched her thighs, in front, but I could see half-moons of bum behind."

"And you could see through the dress?"

"It was lace, I told you. She has very white skin. It showed through."

"I like *you* in see-through," he said as he got up from the table and followed me into the kitchen.

I bent over the sink. I felt him come behind me and his

hands smooth up the backs of my thighs.

"Was her dress as short as this wrap of yours?" He was caressing the cheeks of my bum.

"Shorter." I gave a little wriggle.

"Really? Not the sort of thing you'd wear on the street then?"

"Not unless you're for sale."

"Did she masturbate?"

"Not that I saw. I doubt it. I just teased her — she didn't actually get to *see* anything."

Hugh chuckled. His fingers were stroking the lips of my pussy, very gently, from behind. "I wish I'd been here, to watch."

"Me — or her?"

"Both. It's frustrating, isn't it?" One of his fingers wormed into me, just between my lips, no further.

"What is?"

"Knowing that she's watching us all the time, and masturbating when she sees us making love, and we don't get to watch her playing with herself." The finger was sliding up and down now, still shallow, spreading my lubrication over the inner surfaces of my lips.

"Do you want to give her a show right now?" I asked. His finger was getting to me.

"Do you think she's watching us?"

"Very likely. She could only see our top halves, though, through the pass-through."

"Let's keep it that way. We haven't done it in the kitchen for ages."

"You want to tease her some more, don't you?"

"And you?" His robe brushed the backs of my thighs as he parted it. The curly hairs on the fronts of his thighs tickled the smooth backs of mine.

"You're really getting off on having her watch us, aren't you?" I accused. Something hard and hot and wet nudged the lips of my pussy apart. "Here — give her something to watch, then." I pulled my robe open at the front, reached behind to grab his hands, and dragged them to my breasts.

"You're enjoying it as much as I am," he said, kneading.

"Mmmmm." I wriggled back at him. "Don't you wish you could watch her watching, though?"

He slid his full length into me.

"It might be fun," he allowed, "but how can we? We get glimpses of her, but she only gets really interesting when we're making love."

"By 'interesting', you mean that's when she plays with her pussy, like this." I put a hand down between my legs so that I could cup his gently swaying balls and thumb my own clit.

"You think she uses a vibrator?" he asked, with a swivel of his hips. "Do you think she might be watching us right now, getting off on it, ramming some over-size dildo right up her..."

"She is! She is!" I bucked back at him.

"No — slow down, Millie. I want to talk as we do it."

I stopped moving and clamped my internal muscles on his glans. "You want to talk about *her*, right?"

"Jealous?"

I thought for a moment. "No. You know what would be fun?"

"What?" His penis twitched inside me. I squeezed back.

"Us making love, maybe masturbating each other, while we watched her — Petra — play with herself."

"Yeah." He started rocking again, still slow and easy. "It's a shame she doesn't have another couple to spy on. If she did, we could spy on her while she spied on them."

"Do my clit — the slow way," I told him. He reached around, pinched my shaft between finger and thumb, and started working its sheath.

"We could always offer another couple the use of our living room and watch her from the bedroom," I suggested.

"I don't know. That could lead to a foursome, and, my dear, I'm afraid I'm just too straight for that."

"Not too straight to get off on having some strange woman watch us, though," I teased. "Not too straight for a threesome, either, from the fantasies you've told me."

"A threesome? What are you getting at, Millie, my little sex-cat?"

"If I was making it with another woman, in the living room, you'd be able to watch Petra from the bedroom, right?"

"I think I'd be more interested in watching you and the other woman."

"That too. And I could take a turn, watching Petra while you made it with the other woman."

"You'd *do* that?"

"Make love to a woman, or watch Petra?"

"I meant, let me make love to another woman."

"Would you?"

"I wouldn't cheat on you, you lovely harlot, but..."

"It wouldn't be 'cheating' if I was there — participating, would it? And you know about my past. It wouldn't be as if I'd never made-out with a woman before."

"Do you miss that?"

"Hugh, you are all the man I ever want, but I admit that I wouldn't mind having a pussy that isn't my own to play with, once in a while, if you didn't object."

"But not some stranger, right?"

"It wouldn't have to be. Hugh — do it to make me come, lover."

His fingertip found my clit's head. "If we had another woman here right now she could be licking on this," he vibrated my clit, "as I screwed you."

"And when you came, she could suck your come out of me." My voice was husky.

"And I could watch the two of you play with each other's nipples, and clits, and..." He was working deeper into me and tensing.

"Slow down," I said. "Let's talk this through while we are still making love."

"Ah — okay." He went back to a slow controlled grind.

"Let's be clear about this," I said. "What we are talking about is getting another woman up here, for both of us to make love to, and we take the opportunity to sneak peeks at our Petra at the same time. Is that it?"

"Well, yes, I guess. No stranger though, and I don't intend to go hire some whore for the occasion, so where would we find a suitable — bisexual — woman?"

I did a little shimmy back against him. "She has to be 'bi', does she? You wouldn't be content with a lesbian? You'd still have the chance to watch how I do it with another woman — *and* the opportunity to watch your darling Petra."

"You wouldn't deny me the chance to fulfil every man's fantasy, would you? Two beautiful women at once?"

"And a third gorgeous one watching?" I humped back at him.

"No, pet. You shall have your fantasy, I promise."

His fingers tugged at my nipples, drawing them out in front of me until it almost hurt. "You wouldn't tease your poor husband, would you," he threatened.

"Can you reach the phone?"

Still in me, still slow-grinding, he leaned over and grabbed the cordless from its cradle.

"And my book?" I asked.

"You're going to call someone now?"

"I have just the girl in mind, darling. Now, keep on doing what you're doing while I ask an old friend to come visit us for dinner, and…"

"Dinner 'and'?"

"From how I remember Nadine, 'and' for a damned good time. If we are going to give that peeper of ours a show, we'll make it a spectacular one!"

I didn't explain anything to Nadine. There was no need. She remembered the old days, just like me. An invitation to spend an evening would only have one meaning. I didn't even tell her that my husband, Hugh, would be there. That'd be my surprise. Hugh, the bastard, made me come while I was still on the phone to her. I think Nadine thought I was masturbating at the thought of seeing her again. To tell the truth, if Hugh hadn't been taking care of me very nicely, and I'd been alone, I would have been.

That night I dreamed about the taste of pussy.

XV

Petra

Never, in my entire life, have I spent such a frustrating day. First there was that dildo-marathon of Millie's, where I could imagine everything, but neither see nor photograph a damned thing, and then the two of them decide to make love in their kitchen, where I at least got to watch Hugh's big strong hands maul Millie's lovely breasts, but from the waist down, nothing!

What was it with those two? Especially Millie? Any other woman, after stuffing herself with so much assorted plastic, would have been content for a week! But no! Clear the damned table and let's get it on! And she even makes phone calls while they do it!

It just wasn't fair! I didn't get a wink of sleep that night, and when I got up, I couldn't work. They were ruining my life with their endless sexual gymnastics. I'd been horny as a rhino the day before, after the glow-in-the-dark episode, but that was mild compared to the state they'd got me in.

Well, I didn't waste any time. I needed orgasms, lots of them, big ones. Millie wasn't the only one who had plastic toys to play with.

It had to be special.

I didn't have the collection of toys that Millie had, but my bottom drawer wasn't completely empty. My electrical device of choice was my Lady Phillips massager. Its vibrating heads are excellent for clitoral stimulation, but Millie and her dildos had given me a yen for penetration — the deeper and more dilating the better. I was in the mood to be totally ravished. I wanted to be stretched to my capacity, and beyond.

First, I rummaged through my work-box for a camera-clamp, and screwed it to the edge of my desk. The biggest dildo I had, a mere one foot of plain chromed plastic, fitted into the adjustable-angle jaws. I tightened it in at an upwards slant of thirty degrees from horizontal. When I stood up to it, the end prodded my belly just above my pubic mound.

I swivelled my monitor around so that I'd be able to see the screen, and called up the animation of Hugh's tongue on Millie's oversized clit. From where I'd be standing, I'd be able to watch the screen, and also to see myself in the wall-to-wall mirror.

Okay — that was ready. Me next.

I took a long bubble bath, patted dry, and made-up. This time I wanted a 'fantasy me'. My wig was a riot of tinsel. My contacts were metallic silver mirrors. I used silver paint on my eyes, my lips, and my nipples, leaving the rest of me naked and white. When I was done I fancied myself some sort of futuristic android, created from flesh and plastic to be sold as a living sex toy, or perhaps made to entertain horny astronauts on long lonely trips to distant planets.

Sex — that's all I was — a sex-thing. I'd been built to serve the perverted lusts of whoever bought me. I was programmed to be in a constant state of highly-tuned lust, and now, with my needs having been neglected, my program was running wild.

As a machine, I'd need oiling from time to time, wouldn't I? I took a squeeze-bottle of body-oil, spread my legs over my toilet, in case I dripped, and worked the end of the bottle into my sex.

The oil was cold going in, but my body-heat soon warmed it.

Some dribbled out, running down the insides of my thighs. I didn't wipe it away, but simply took a few steps with my thighs rubbing together. It felt good.

A woman-machine like that would likely masturbate, right?

That wasn't what I wanted. Masturbation was too simple — too natural. So — why wouldn't I..? I knew. My hands were confined, so that I couldn't use them on myself.

There was some bondage gear in my props case, left over from a photo-shoot. I chose a vinyl sleeve. It was wide enough — just — to fit over two arms at once, and it had a zipper. I slipped the ring of the cord I'd used to get into my bullfighter pants over one of the brass scrolls at the foot of my bed. It was quite awkward, getting my arms into the open end of the sleeve, behind my back, but I made it, and then wriggled around on the bed until I got the hook into the ring on the zipper. Once that was done, simply standing up did the zipper up, and my arms were clamped tightly together.

It suited me. When your arms are sheathed together from wrist to elbow, behind you, it pulls your shoulders back hard, and lifts and separates your breasts. You look totally helpless, and completely available. For a brief moment I wished that there was someone there with me, to admire the effect, and to take advantage of me.

With oil still oozing from my sex, I elbowed my bedroom

door open and went back to my studio.

Hugh was still lapping at Millie, on the screen. My mechanical lover was waiting for me, a foot long, steel-hard, and tilted upwards.

Damn! How was I going to switch it on? I wanted cold hardness inside me, but I wanted that purring sensation as well.

It was the base of the dildo that was held in the clamp. Turning it would turn the motor on. I knelt, very carefully because my arms were confined, and took my robot-lover's penis into my mouth. My teeth gripped. I turned my head, and the vibration started.

It tickled my tongue and lips, but my lover wanted to use my mouth, so that's what I gave him. I bobbed a few times, watching the effect in the mirror. It was incredibly obscene.

If I turned my head sideways, the tip of the dildo bulged my cheek. I took a deep breath through my nose, and pushed. My gag-reflex was still well under control, even if I hadn't had a real man in my mouth for — God — it had to be eighteen months! Was there something the matter with me? Had I turned into some sort of recluse?

Anyway, I was still able to force the plastic penis all the way back, just like Cynthia had taught me with a candle when we'd been experimenting back in our schooldays, and got the tip of it into the actual opening of my throat.

I did that 'swallowing' thing, that'll massage a man's glans, just to be sure I could still do it, and then went back to bobbing and licking.

The mirror showed me the whole obscene thing — a woman so obsessed by lust that she'd give head to a plastic penis, and enjoy it. What kind of nympho-slut was she?

I made saliva — lots of it. Oil is slippery, but oil plus water is even slipperier. I wanted to dildo to slide in nice and easy.

With one last long noisy slurp, I released the dildo and writhed to my feet. The dildo was slick with my spit. I spread my legs and went up on tip-toe. Plastic that my mouth had warmed, and wetted, nudged at the lips of my sex. I wriggled so that it parted me. My hips did a little jiggle, with just the tip inside me. I manoeuvred it deeper, past my lips, until the round head was at the mouth of my vagina, where the flesh is convoluted and funnels into a constricted passage.

A stiff penis will force those folds apart, and straighten that intricate passage. Hard plastic will do the same. I lunged my hips forward and down.

I almost screamed. It was dilating me deep — deeper than anything had entered me for a year and a half. I'd almost forgotten the divine pleasure that being stretched apart and *entered* can bring.

Maybe I hadn't thought it through when I'd set the thing's angle. A penis usually curves up, and so does a vagina. The dildo didn't. I had to lean back at an angle to get it in deep, but that was okay — the more awkward it was, the harder I'd have to work for my pleasure. I was a total tramp. It was right that I'd have to struggle to reach my orgasm.

I took a little half-step forwards, driving the spike into me so far it nudged the mouth of my womb. Nothing touched my clit, but when I bore down hard, the dildo pressed against the back of my pubic bone, where the 'g' spot is, and the vibrations were transmitted through bone and flesh, quivering my hard little nub.

I lifted myself on my toes, withdrawing from my impaler an inch, and then slammed down on it again. Up, and down! Up, and down! The lips of my pussy were stretched like rubber bands by the thickness of the dildo's base. I wriggled, and rotated, revelling in the sensations as the thing's head prodded my insides, front, back, to either side. I was *reaming* my vagina with it. My vagina was a sleeve over its hardness. My juices flowed. Despite the lubrication, on the downstroke the lips of my sex were inverted, tucking up inside me. On the outstroke, the inside lips were being pulled out of me, slurping the plastic, reluctant to let it go.

My hands, locked behind me, kneaded my buttocks, urging me to drive harder, just as a lover's might. In the mirror, my breasts, firm as they are, were wobbling with my efforts. Sweat ran from beneath my wig. My breasts were beaded with it. God — I hadn't sweated from sex for so long! It felt wonderful. I'd almost forgotten what it was like to give yourself totally to the sheer *sensations* of sex — to be nothing but a ravenous animal — to be *consumed* by lust.

I was gyrating, attacking my inanimate lover from every angle, skewering myself down on him and bucking back off him and... and I came.

XVI

Millie

I told Hugh, "Don't use the towels in the other bathroom, please. I've straightened the ones in the en suite."

"Did I mess them up? Sorry. How do I look? Should I wear a tie?"

"Not if you don't want to, darling. You look very handsome just the way you are." And he did. I'd bought him a new pair of pants, in grey silk, with a shirt that was just a couple of shades lighter, and a dark green velvet evening jacket.

"How about me?" I asked, turning for him.

"Very sexy — but a bit severe, isn't it?"

I was in black and white. Black pumps, with really vicious five and a half inch heels, silky black stay-up hose from the Victoria's Secret catalogue, a plain black long skirt that hugged my thighs, a broad black-patent belt, and a sheer white tailored blouse that you could see my nipples through.

"Sexy — but severe? That's ideal for Nadine, Hugh. She

likes a woman to look something of a disciplinarian."

"Oh? Well, in that case, perhaps I should change into something in black leather."

I adjusted the collar of his jacket for him. "Maybe next time, dear. You'll do as you are for now. Are you nervous dear, about tonight?"

He rubbed his chin. "Well, it's been a while since I seduced anyone, Millie, and I've never actually had my wife watch while I did it."

"Leave it to me, darling. Nadine and I are old friends. You just be your own sweet self, and let things develop."

"Suppose she doesn't want to... you know."

"Nadine? Not want to? Hugh — the girl is sex-mad. In the old days I just had to snap my fingers. One of her big 'things' is making it with a man and a woman at once — though she and I never got around to that. And Hugh, darling..."

"Yes?"

"One look at you and she'll be drooling, I promise you."

He preened a little and took a quick glance into the mirror. Men!

"How about — er — Petra?" he asked.

"Her too. The drapes are wide and there's lots of light. Once she sees that there are three of us, she'll be glued to her camera, and with the action she's going to see, she'll wear her trigger finger out — both of them. Hugh," I went close enough that my nipples nudged his jacket, "there will be action, I promise. Let's not rush it though, okay? Why do you think I made you take a nap this afternoon? Nadine will still be here come breakfast, and the chances are, one of us will be it."

"I'll see to the wine then."

Nadine was prompt at eight. I watched Hugh's eyes as he took her coat and her small overnight bag. It would have spoiled everything if he hadn't found her pleasing, but his eyes twinkled at me over her shoulder, and he winked, so that wasn't going to be a problem.

Not everyone finds Nadine attractive. She isn't pretty, in the conventional sense. She's slender to the point of being skinny, for a start, with virtually no breasts. I thought that would make a change for Hugh. I'm — well — 'well endowed' is the usual phrase. It'd be a different experience for Hugh to handle flesh that was so much nearer the bone.

Nadine hadn't changed in the three years since I'd seen her. She still favoured black.

Her make-up was still too thick, and too dark, with so much mascara she looked like a racoon, and livid lips that were almost orange. Her hair was still in an out-of-date urchin cut, and dyed black.

Nadine's face was redeemed by her high cheek bones and unusual, almost startling, eyes. They had pale grey irises, streaked and rimmed with yellow, like a wolf's. Apart from that, her nose was too snubbed and her mouth too wide for her to be pretty. Even her lips were imperfect in an incredibly erotic way. She had a slight overbite, so that twin pearls of teeth always showed between her lips, and those lips didn't match. The upper one was cruelly thin. The lower was very full, almost drooping, the sort of lip that makes you want to sink your teeth into it deeply enough to draw blood.

She still dressed the same, as well, black-on-black. Her feet were in ballet-style flats. Instead of black opaque hose, she now wore those over-the-knee socks, but that wasn't much of a difference. From the tops of her socks almost to her groin she was bare — just two long slender thighs. Her lower torso was coated in black satin — abbreviated shorts that moulded her flesh closely enough to divide the puffiness of her pubes.

From just below her navel to immediately under her tiny breasts she was naked. Her belly was flat, almost hollowed. Hugh could have circled her waist with his hands. Every chiselled bone in her ribcage was clearly outlined.

The cropped top that she wore was skinny-fit black ribbed cotton, and buttoned at the front. A black velvet choker circled her slender throat. Long drops of black jet dangled from her lobes.

And she still had the same effect on me. I never knew, on first seeing her, whether I should feed her straight away, or do something obscene to her body first, and feed her later.

I gave her the seat of honour, at the head of the table, facing directly towards the window, and towards Petra's camera. Hugh was at her right, and I was at her left.

We started with an avocado and watercress soup, laced with sherry, smooth as the skin on a young girl's thigh, but with a tangy aftertaste.

"So, Nadine," I asked, "how's your love-life?"

"Much the same. No dramatic changes — unlike yours." She made a little pout, as if she didn't approve of my having married.

"You didn't expect me to settle down? Married life has its compensations."

"I'm sure it has — especially marriage to a gorgeous hunk like your Hugh here, but you were always so..."

"Wild? Playing the field? Don't worry about what you say, Nadine. Hugh knows all about my lurid past."

"Even about..?"

"You and me? Gretchen and Harry? Viola and her sister — what was her name?"

"Stephie. So he knows you were bi?"

"Was — and still am. I haven't indulged for some time, but

the old appetites are still strong, as you'll doubtless discover, later."

Nadine sighed. "Well, that's a relief. When I came in and found you'd become a married woman, for one dreadful moment I thought that this was going to be just a social visit."

I sipped my wine. "Social, friendly, and later — who knows? You mustn't think that just because Hugh and I are married and in love, we're dead. Even married people have sex-lives, you know."

"But boring ones, usually."

"Well, ours certainly isn't. Why, we even have our own tame voyeur."

"Tame voyeur?"

"Don't look, but there's a woman in the apartment opposite who most likely has a telescopic lens trained on you right now."

Her eyes flicked to the window. "You're joking!"

"No I'm not. Hugh, why don't you go check?"

Hugh went to the bedroom, where the blinds were drawn and the binoculars were ready.

Nadine asked me, "You mean she watches you all the time? Like — when you make love?"

"Yup, and that means every day, for hours on end."

"So you're still just as horny as ever?"

"Still a slut, and Hugh is randy enough to keep up with me."

Hugh came back with a grin on his face. "Yes, she's there all right."

Nadine asked, "Watching us? Right now? What's she like? Some dried-up old maid?"

"Young, and lovely," I assured her. "Hugh'd take her to bed any day, wouldn't you Hugh?"

"How can I even think about a woman who's fifty feet away, when I have two such lovely creatures so close?"

"Thank you darling, but apart from the flattery?"

"I wouldn't say no."

I turned to Nadine. "And nor would I, Nadine. I doubt you would, either."

Hugh poured more wine, blushing, the dear. Idle chat with a new woman, one whose body he'd been promised but who he didn't know, was embarrassing him.

I said, "I told Hugh that you possess the three qualities that he most admires in a woman."

Nadine smiled. "And those are?"

"Depravity, depravity, and depravity."

She giggled. Hugh looked at his empty soup bowl and said, "I thought you were going to quote me on other feminine qualities, those I looked for, and found in you, darling."

"Okay, I'll bite," Nadine said. "What qualities were you looking for in a wife, Hugh? That'd be a secret most women would like to learn."

"That she be a SEA wife — Seductive before, Enthusiastic during, and Appreciative after."

"Well, I'm sure that Millie qualifies. She's certainly the most seductive woman I've ever met. I've missed her." She stretched over and patted my hand.

I cleared away the soup things and brought the finger foods — mussels that had been steamed in Sauterne, whitebait fried to a crisp, chunks of lobster meat on sticks, devilled crab on toast, and raw sea urchins that had been peeled and dribbled with vodka and lime.

As I laid the dishes out Hugh mixed cocktails of his own concoctions — clam juice, tequila and lime, with a brandy float, in glasses that were rimmed with sugar and salt.

"I made these in your honour," he lied to Nadine. "I'll call them 'Essence of Nadine'."

She sipped and raised one plucked brow. "How did you know..?"

"The right flavour? I experimented until Millie told me I'd got it right."

I think that if Nadine had been capable of blushing, she would have. She certainly looked pleased. "Your wife has quite a memory then. It's been years."

"We can confirm its accuracy later," I said, with a leer, "but right now I'm concerned about Petra, our 'peeper'."

"How come?"

"She might get the idea that this is strictly a social visit, and get bored. We don't want her to lose interest."

"Oh?" Nadine's eyes brightened. "So we are going to give her a show, are we?"

"You don't mind?" Hugh asked.

"Oh no. I think it'll make it more fun. Mmmmm." She made a slurping production out of sucking at the raw flesh of a sea urchin, broke it part way, and slithered her tongue sensuously along the slit she'd made.

"That'll help," I allowed, "but how about..." I reached across and popped the top three buttons of her top, slowly, one at a time.

"That won't give her much to look at," Nadine said. "*You're* the one with the boobs, Millie."

"She's seen them. She hasn't seen yours, yet."

"Not much to see," Nadine admitted.

"Small can be nice," I said. I reached out once more and stroked down the fabric of her top with the tips of my fingers, just letting her feel my nails. Although Nadine's breasts are very small, they make up for their lack of size with their sensitivity. She arched her back and almost purred.

"How about some fruit for dessert?" I suggested. I fetched the bowl and put it down carefully, where it wouldn't block Petra's view. Nadine and I both chose bananas. In unison, we peeled slowly, raised the naked fruits to our mouths, and slid the creamy spikes between our lips. All the time we both kept our eyes on Hugh, making it obvious that the suggestive display was for his benefit.

Hugh retaliated with a peach, lapping at its crease with the tip of his tongue, then taking a cherry and balancing it at the tip of the same crease before sucking it into his mouth.

"Have you seen this trick?" he asked Nadine. He broke the stem off a cherry, popped it into his mouth, puffed and worked his cheeks, and then spat the stem onto his palm, in a knot. It's a trick, of course. He'd put a knotted stem into his mouth beforehand. I'm sure Nadine knew that one, but she oohed and aahed and giggled anyway, humouring him.

"I think we should turn up the heat," I said, standing. I crossed to stand behind Nadine. My hands took hers and pulled them behind her, behind the upright back of her chair. "Hold the bar," I told her, "just as if you were tied to it."

"You could always tie me for real," she offered. "I'd like that."

"Later, perhaps." I reached over her narrow shoulders and flipped the last two buttons of her top open. It parted. I laid the tips of my fingers on her collar bones, lightly.

Nadine's breasts are just gentle swellings on her rib-cage, almost boyish, and her nipples are pale, barely defined. They look more like bee-stings than nipples, always slightly puffy, and incredibly tender, with next-to-no spikes rising from her haloes, just tiny buttons. Those small nodules hardened in anticipation of my touch.

I looked at Hugh. He was staring at Nadine's chest, as eager as she was for my next move.

"She likes them to be treated the way I like you to do my clit," I told him. "Sucked hard, and flicked with a tongue-tip."

"Do it for me, Millie," Nadine gasped, her head squirming back against my midriff. Her eyes, gazing up at me, were pleading.

My fingers pressed hard on the upper slopes of her chest, and then raked down to her ribs beneath her breasts. She spasmed and arched as if my touch had been electric. Her eyes hooded and glazed.

"She's eager, isn't she," I said, still to Hugh, "but I want a nice kiss hello first."

Holding her delicate ribcage in my palms, I stooped over her. Nadine's mouth was open, waiting for me, her tongue already extended. With our heads reversed like that, I stuck out my own tongue and gave hers a long slithery wet lick, flat-to-flat. My eyes were still on Hugh. I could see by his eyes that we were getting to him, and hoped that we were having the same effect on Petra.

"Nadine wants to suck my nipple," I told him. My hands moved higher on Nadine's flat chest so that my fingertips could play on the incredible smoothness of her haloes. "Can you help me?"

Hugh stood and reached over Nadine's head to undo the buttons of my blouse. He held it apart, took my left breast in his hand, and steered my nipple down to Nadine's waiting mouth.

My nipples are as large, and dark, as Nadine's are small, and pale. Her lips closed over my nipple's very tip, and then parted as she sucked the entire pulsating strawberry-sized cone of it into the heat of her mouth. She made little happy grunting noises as she increased the suction and slid the flat of her tongue over its point. Her head shook from side to side, worrying at my flesh and wobbling my breast.

"Get our tops off, Hugh," I said.

He went behind me and tugged Nadine's top off her shoulders and down her arms. I released Nadine briefly as he did the same for me. His arms encircled me to hold the weight of the breast that Nadine was suckling and to tweak my other nipple.

"Tip her chair."

"No," he said. "Let's get more comfortable — nearer the window."

I cupped Nadine's cheeks and tugged my nipple from her mouth. She nuzzled up and back, but I stood away and let Hugh scoop her up from her chair in his strong arms and carry her, with me following and stroking her face, to Hugh's recliner, by the window. He draped her across the seat with her head hanging over one arm and her legs over the other.

Hugh looked at her for a second, and then adjusted her position so that her back was arched over the black leather and her ribcage spread like a fan.

"Thank you, darling," I told him. "That's exactly how I wanted her." I leaned over Nadine, drooping my breast to her mouth, and bent low enough to get my lips on the tiny button of her left breast.

She sucked. I sucked. Hugh watched for a moment and then said, "I'm just going to change. I won't be a moment."

We'd both switched breasts by the time Hugh got back in his new short robe. I released Nadine's flesh for long enough to ask him, "Is she still watching? Is she enjoying it?"

"You wouldn't believe! She's all done up like some Indian squaw, in a buckskin mini and a feather in her hair, except the mini is rucked up around her waist now. She's taking photos with one hand and diddling herself with the other. By the look on her face I'd guess she's come once or twice already."

"That's not fair," Nadine sulked up at the undersides of my breasts. "Nadine want a nice come, too."

She gets quite babyish when she's in deep lust.

"You're the guest, Nadine," I told her. "You get the first orgasm, and the lion's share of the attention, this time. Do something nice to her, Hugh, while I go and get out of this skirt."

Hugh's report had been accurate. When I looked through the binoculars Petra had abandoned her photography, though. That buckskin mini of hers laced up from the waist with thongs. She'd pulled it open so that she could manipulate a breast with one hand as she played with her pussy with the other. I saw her judder and her knees give for a moment, so I guessed I'd caught her at her climax, but she just reached out, triggered her camera, and started caressing herself again.

I got out of my skirt fast, and had a quick fondle of the shaft of my clit, just sliding the loose skin a few times, while watching her, before returning to the party in the other room.

Hugh had obviously overcome his shyness. He'd got Nadine out of those tight little satin pants and shed his robe. Naked, he'd locked the recliner upright, and was just lifting Nadine by her hips to sit on the top of the chair's back, facing away from the seat. He held her thighs as she bent backwards until her head was cushioned by the leather seat.

I grabbed our half-empty glasses of Hugh's cocktail from the dinning table in passing, and joined them.

Nadine made a nice picture, bent back at her hips like that. I put the glasses down and scratched gently at the stretched crease of her groin. Hugh parted her thighs and bent his head to her pussy. Her position had parted her lips, exposing their melon-pink, oozing wet, insides. Hugh extended his tongue and took a long lap, from the base of her slot to the tip of her clit.

"So? Is the flavour the same as your cocktail?" I asked.

Hugh lifted his head. "You try."

I stooped to put my face next to my darling husband's. He sucked her left pussy-lip into his mouth as I sampled the right. Our tongues met, between her lips, tickled each other, and returned to savouring her juices.

Nadine stretched up to wobble a fingertip on the head of her clit, but I pushed her hand away.

"Be patient," I told her. "We'll get to it."

"Why don't you kneel up on the arms?" Hugh suggested.

It seemed like an excellent idea. I straddled the chair's seat, and Nadine's head, and then split wide, dipping my sex down to within her mouth's reach. Nadine responded. Her hands gripped my splayed thighs and pulled her head up. I felt her face nuzzle at my puckered lips, teasing them apart, and then her tongue slide into me.

"Is she eating you, darling?" Hugh asked me.

"Mmmm. And it feels good."

"Then why don't we..." He took my nipple between his thumb and fingers, and tugged it down to Nadine's clit. "I've always wanted to do this," he said, rubbing my engorged cone over Nadine's pink pearl, "and this." He lowered his face until he could lap the flat of his tongue across both the tip of my nipple and the head of Nadine's clit.

Nadine moaned into my pussy.

"How about a 'taste test'", I giggled. I picked up a glass and tilted it on the slope of my breast. Liquor trickled down, over my nipple and Nadine's clit. Hugh sucked it off both at once.

He twitched his fingers, and my nipple between them. It frotted Nadine's clit-head. Nadine dug her nails into my thighs and burrowed her face deeper. Her cheeks spread my lips as she delved and lapped.

"You try some of this," Hugh suggested. He took the glass from me and urged my head down as he poured more cold liquid over the two sensitive polyps of flesh.

I'd never tried that — nibbling a woman's clit and my own nipple at once. It was — interesting.

Hugh poured more, so that it ran down between Nadine's open lips, and followed it with his tongue. He lapped. I licked. Nadine began to groan.

"She's going to come if we don't stop," I warned Hugh.

"Then we'll make her wait — and earn it. Nadine, I want you to stick your tongue up my wife's ass. Do it well, and we'll let you come."

Nadine obeyed instantly. Her hands found my cheeks and spread them. She hitched her body, slid her tongue from the base of my pussy to my ass, and squirmed it into my rectum.

Hugh pulled my head up and kissed me. He tasted of Nadine's spending, and I guess I did too. His finger pressed my nipple onto the head of Nadine's clit and wobbled, just enough to keep her on the brink, but not fast enough to take her over it.

As our mouths parted, Hugh asked, "Is she doing it right?"

"Oh yes," I sighed. "Hugh — this is *so* obscene, isn't it? You sucking a woman's come off my tongue while she licks my ass? And my nipple on her clit? What next, darling? Think of some way to make it even lewder."

Hugh looked at me thoughtfully. "You two really are depraved, aren't you? Very well, how much of your lovely breast do you think you could cram into Nadine's pussy?"

Before I could answer, he lifted Nadine's thighs high and wide, pointing her toes towards the ceiling and tilting her gaping sex at me. Her legs, slim or not, looked beautiful. The contrast between those black over-the-knees, and the white skin of her naked thighs was incredibly erotic.

I took my breast in both hands, compressed it, and started to stuff my creamy flesh into her wet pink sex. As I screwed and worked it in, Hugh dipped his head again, to lick between the cheeks of Nadine's bum. Nadine gave a little squeal and worked the harder at mine. It felt to me as if a hot little worm was wriggling deeper and deeper inside me, right up my rectum.

"Yes, Nadine, my sweet slut," I cried. "Now do my clit, just like this, and we'll both have a lovely come."

Her hair tickled the insides of my thighs as she pulled back, found the head of my oversized clit with her mouth, and sucked it in. In return, I pulled my breast, dripping with Nadine's juices, from her pussy, and clamped my mouth to her button. My folded lips protected it from my teeth. My tongue found its tip, stiffened, and flickered. She did the same to me.

Hugh stretched Nadine's legs wide apart — so wide the tendons on the insides of her thighs felt like wires under my fingers. He slobbered as he delved into her anus with his tongue. Nadine, still working my clit, squirmed a probing finger into my ass.

It was so decadently beautiful I couldn't hold back. My hips juddered, driving my elongated clit into Nadine's mouth as if it was a pussy and I was a man.

Nadine and I both convulsed and grunted at the same time. Nadine slithered limp down the chair and out from under me. Hugh, his mouth now free, gave me a long loving kiss.

Laying panting on the floor, Nadine interrupted us with, "How about you, Hugh? We've both come, but you haven't."

"Nadine's the guest," he said. "Her choice."

"Well," she mused, "I've tasted Millie's come tonight, and both of you have tasted mine. It only seems fair that I get a taste of you, Hugh."

"Hugh likes to jerk off into my mouth sometimes," I told Nadine. "Would that suit you?"

"That sounds yummy, but what will you do, Millie? Play with yourself as you watch?'

"No — I can wait for my next one, for a while. I've got an idea. Wait for me a moment."

I ran to my dresser drawer and came back with a length of white silk cord. We always keep some handy for bondage games. I made a loop and secured Hugh's wrists behind him.

"How am I supposed to masturbate like this?" he asked.

"You aren't. Just stand there, with your legs spread, and leave everything to us girls. Nadine — I want you to kneel at Hugh's feet. You can play with yourself, if you like. Your mouth is the cup. Keep it wide open, and in position. Make sure that when he comes you catch every last delicious drop, okay?"

"And if I spill some?"

"There'll be a forfeit."

With Nadine in position, her mouth open wide and tilted up just beneath Hugh's gleaming glans, I knelt behind my man, parted the cheeks if his bum with the fingers of one hand, rimmed him some, to persuade his knot to relax, squirmed my tongue into his rectum, reached around him, and began pumping. I'd figured that he liked to masturbate into a woman's mouth, and he liked me to jerk him off, and he liked to have his ass licked, so if I gave him all three at once, which I couldn't have managed solo, it'd be a special treat for him.

It must have felt good, because his body started to quiver almost at once, and he kept saying, 'Yes,' over and over. When he *did* squirt, Nadine caught most of it, but some of the foam splashed across her cheeks and chin, so I had to make her pay a forfeit. She didn't seem to mind.

At breakfast, Nadine asked us, "Do you think that peeper of yours saw everything we did?"

"I'm sure of it," Hugh said. "I checked a couple of times, and she seemed to be matching us orgasm for orgasm. That minidress of hers was soaked in sweat by then, and she seemed to be hanging on her tripod, just to stay on her feet."

"I'd love copies of the photos she took," Nadine said. "What a shame she wasn't with us, to get some real tight close-ups." She leered at Hugh and squeezed my thigh. "I'd love some really intimate pictures of you two, to frame and stand beside my bed."

"She's always *very* careful to stay hidden," Hugh explained. "I think she's shy to participate. It seems she just likes to watch."

"Well, if *I* was you two, I'd ask her over. She can only say, 'no'."

"But she might be embarrassed, and not peep any more. We enjoy her watching us," I objected. "I'd hate to scare her off."

"Do you have a video camera?"

"Yes — why? You want us to tape the action next time you visit?"

"I'd love it, but I was thinking of a way you could persuade your peeper to visit — an invitation she couldn't refuse."

XVII

Petra

the concierge buzzed me that I had two parcels waiting downstairs. I wasn't expecting anything, and it
was too early for the mail, so I was curious. I dressed
myself up as a housewife, and went down for them.

The packages hadn't come through the mail. They were just
plainly wrapped, tied with string, and sealed with pink sealing wax. One was oblong, like a shoe box, but bigger, and the
other was the size and shape of a book. I cut the string and
opened the long one first. There was no card or letter. When
I opened the box I found an oversized vibrator inside — one
of those massive ones that plug into the mains.

It had three shafts. The central column was only about
eight inches long, nowhere near the length of some of the
monsters I'd seen Millie polishing, but incredibly thick, and
with a sheath of soft plastic that was knobbled like a ping-
pong paddle, except at the head, which was hard, and shiny,

and smooth, with a little dimple in the centre.

The second 'branch' was shorter, and much slimmer, smooth all over, slightly curved, and with a small round knob at the end. It was sprung, so that its knob pressed lightly against the central column.

The third piece was shaped like an oversized tongue, also sprung, smooth, but with ripples across its inner face.

The way you were supposed to use it was pretty obvious. If a woman could somehow force the thick column inside her vagina, all the way up, she'd also have to work the slim prong into her anus. The tongue-flap would cover her mound. Curious, I plugged it in. There were three little buttons. I pressed them all at once.

The thing quivered as it came alive in my hand. The soft-surfaced tongue-thing quivered and wagged an inch to either side. The hard ball on the end of the thin shaft trembled. The main bulky body of the thing was telescopic inside its sheath. It extended another four inches, like a hydraulic piston, to a full foot, then retracted, and extended again, in a slow steady rhythm. As it stretched, its body narrowed. As it shrank, its body thickened. It would probe incredibly far, forcing its way deeper into the woman's body, but letting her vagina contract, a little. As it retreated, and thickened, it would dilate its victim, stretching her vaginal walls outwards once again.

I felt my internal muscles knot. My thighs clamped together protectively. If a woman could stand it, the effect would most likely be devastating. It wouldn't just invade her body, it would take her body over.

I searched again for a note, but there was nothing, so I unwrapped the other parcel. It wasn't a book. It was a video tape. I don't own a TV, but I *do* have a VCR, that hooks onto my small computer. Trembling inside my tummy for some reason, I popped the tape in. The screen of my monitor flickered, ran dark for a few seconds, and then I got a picture.

It was *them!*

Hugh and Millie were sitting side by side on that leather couch, in their new short robes, his arm around her shoulders. He spoke. "Petra, please don't be alarmed. We know what you've been doing, but we aren't the least bit angry."

Millie leaned towards the camera and said, "Petra, we really quite enjoy having you watch us. Now, don't take this the wrong way, and we aren't trying to get you into a sexual threesome or anything, but wouldn't it be nice if your camera was closer? We'd be very happy for you to take close-ups of us, and we'd even like prints. Why don't you give us a call at..."

I snapped it off and sat with my arms wrapped around my body, quivering. They'd known all along! They'd likely been laughing at me — the strange woman who can only get her kicks by peeping at the sex lives of normal people! I was furious. I was humiliated. I was ashamed, and disgusted, and..!

I stormed around my apartment, kicking things, beating my hands on the walls, swearing and sobbing and screaming. The *swines!* Who in hell's name did they think they were! Did they think they were so irresistible? There were dozens of people I could watch, if I wanted. They should feel privileged that I'd devoted so much of my precious time to them!

Then I went to bed, pulled the covers over my head, and stayed there for the rest of the day.

The trouble with sleeping during the day is that you can't sleep properly when night comes. You just doze, and dream, wake up, and doze and dream again. I dreamt that night. I dreamt of close-ups of *his* glans, so tight in that when its eye oozed a single clear drop of seminal fluid, it was like a gigantic crystal ball, trembling.

When I zoomed in even closer, right inside that fluid crystal, there was the pink arrow-head of Millie's clitoral head, throbbing at me, becoming a drum-beat, and the drum was saying, 'Close-up, close-up, close-up.' And then there was a glistening pink maw beneath me, Millie's sex, wide open, and I fell into it, slithering and sliding into her vagina, and its walls were a drum also, and they beat the same words into my brain, 'Close-up, close-up, close-up.'

I reached the opening to her womb, and I knew that if I fell inside it would be dark, and hot, and stifling, and there would be no escape, ever. I clung onto slippery oozing flesh, bracing myself between the soft pink-and-purple walls, but they were too slick, and when they convulsed and I heard Millie scream, "I'm coming, Hugh", I fell into the maelstrom of her orgasm, became part of it, and dissolved.

For breakfast I made a large pot of thick dark Turkish coffee, laced with Greek brandy.

Nothing beats Petra. Nothing ever has — not even back when I was plain 'Patricia'. Okay — I live alone — and some people think I'm hiding from the real world by living a vicarious life through my craft, but that isn't true. I'm not hiding. I live the way I do because that's the way I like it. It's better to be alone, really. If you get involved with people they always want to own you, eventually. They call it 'love', but it isn't that at all. They simply want to get inside your head, and make you think the way they do, and use guilt to manipulate you. Why do people think that their loving you puts you under some sort of obligation?

My relationship, my long-distance, one-way, clean-and-simple relationship with Hugh and Millie, had been just about perfect, for me, and now they'd spoiled it. It'd serve them right if I *did* answer their invitation, and let them get to know me, and then I'd remodel myself, the way I always did, into someone they couldn't help but love.

And then I'd spit in their silly faces and dump them!

Or was it possible that the way they felt about each other would be strong enough to protect them from me? That'd be nice.

What would it feel like to have friends who were near, and available whenever you wanted, for sex, or just for company, but who didn't put you under any sort of obligation?

My three friends, my only friends, were far away. That, and their having their own sexual peculiarities, was what made the continuing friendships possible.

Was it possible that Hugh and Millie..?

Just out of curiosity, nothing more, I booted my computer and started the tape again.

Millie gave me their phone number, and then Hugh took over again. "Petra," he said, "we wouldn't want you to have sex with us, either of us, unless that was what you really wanted. Millie and I don't need anyone else, though we tried a threesome the other night, as you well know, and thoroughly enjoyed it. It just seems that we could have fun, you and us. You are obviously a voyeur, and Millie and I have found out, thanks to you, that we enjoy being watched. What could be a nicer, less complicated, relationship? One voyeur, and two exhibitionists? One watcher, two watched?

"Look, Petra, if you'd rather stay over there and get your kicks from long distance, that's fine with us, and we'll make sure you get plenty to watch."

Millie interrupted, "But we won't promise not to tease you once in a while."

Hugh continued, "It's up to you, Petra, but even if you don't want to meet us, we'd get a real thrill if you'd watch the rest of this tape, and use our other gift as you do so. If you like it — the tape — and still don't want to get any closer, we'll even make more tapes for you. What could be fairer than that?"

Millie again. "Petra, when we promise 'no touch', we mean it. I've discussed it with Hugh, and he agrees. We could set things up so that you could be here, and we wouldn't even be able to see you while you watch us. We'd even pose for you. Wouldn't that be nice?

"Now, I'm going to apologise in advance for the quality of this tape. We aren't experts at photography, like you. Still, what we lack in expert camera work, I hope we make up for in content. Our friend, Nadine, who you 'met' the other night, is going to put the camera down now, just to say 'hi'."

The elfin waif who I'd so enjoyed adding to my photo-files came from behind the camera, out of focus and then in, her childish body naked apart from a skimpy thong. She waved at me, blew me a kiss, and disappeared again.

She was an interesting model. The contrast between her elfin body and vulpine, almost vicious face, with those startling eyes, plus the way she threw herself into sex like a shark in a feeding frenzy, was something I found incredibly erotic.

I could base an entire picture book, or even two, on her. One could be portraits of urchin-whores, like those dreadful velvet paintings of children with over-sized eyes, but eroticised.

The other could have text, perhaps a retelling of Peter Pan. She'd make a delightful 'Tinker-Bell trollop', getting it on with Pan and Wendy; an orgy with the Lost Boys, in their animal costumes, and perhaps being captured by Captain Hook and ravished by his entire crew — and enjoying every minute of it.

I'd include a portfolio of close-ups; whip-weals on the taut skin of a boyish but silky buttock; finger-bruises around the pale nipple of an almost-breast; bite marks on a delicate shoulder; the hook's claw marks on the tender inside skin of a too-thin thigh.

Perhaps the final picture would be of her sex, its lips spread, enpurpled, and puffy, as if fresh from some incredibly obscene violation.

I shook myself. My thoughts were seducing me. It wasn't *my* fault. She was one of those child-women who invite, or even demand, cruelty from their lovers, because sexual abuse is what they crave most.

The camera swung again, and refocussed on Hugh and Millie. Hugh said, 'Petra, we want to be completely honest with you. We've watched you, watching us, and we both find you very attractive, but Millie and I are complete, together. We are Ying and Yang, if you like. We don't *need* anyone else — sorry Nadine, not even you.

"Petra — if it happened that you and the two of us, or even the three of us, had some sort of relationship, sexual or whatever, we think it would be fun, exciting, thrilling even, but like a ride on a roller coaster, when it was over, it'd be over. Nice memories, but no regrets. With that understood, we'd love to get to know you, on your own terms, okay? If you want to join us for the fun of the ride, no complications, just let us know."

Millie took over. "Petra, this tape is for you, as a 'thank you' for the extra spice you've added to our love-life." "Okay, Hugh, let's do it. Please, Petra, relax." She giggled like a naughty schoolgirl. "So, make yourself comfortable, plug one end of that present we've given you into a socket, and the other end you-know-where, they're both three-prong, after all, and enjoy."

I switched the tape off.

They were very persuasive, and I hate to be persuaded. I think for myself and make my own decisions. For the first time since I'd moved in, I closed all the blinds, sealing myself away from the outside world and all its messy, uncertain, temptations.

I went to my dressing table to draw someone new on me, someone who'd be immune. There was no particular character in my mind. I simply started with a thick layer of pancake make up, like an artist might cover a bad picture with a coat of Chinese white before reusing the canvas.

There was a set of double-thickness, extra-long, false eye-lashes in my kit, that I'd never used. I glued them in place, and chose pale blue contacts to deliberately *not* go with them. Smeary layers of dark blue and silver eye-shadow completed the effect — the eyes of a cheap over-painted whore.

I drew a line with my lip pencil, beyond the natural lines of my lips, and filled it in with a purplish 'blush rose' before covering it with too much gloss. Instead of subtly highlighting my cheekbones, I rouged them into crude ruddy blotches.

Yes, the new me looked cheap, nasty, well-used, and tough enough to screw a jack-hammer, if the price was right, or for free, if she was horny.

Once I had the image, the costume was obvious. I laced myself into a scarlet satin Victorian corset that had rigid stays and black lace quarter-cups that were padded, to lift my breasts — no — my tits — high enough that my nipples showed. Then I carmined them. An old pair of opera hose, with a snag in one, plus pom-pom mules completed the picture.

Working myself into the mood of a nineteenth century Madam, the hard-bitten owner of a mining-town cat-house, I lit a rare cigarette and poured myself a straight shot of vodka. Rye would have been more appropriate, but I didn't have any. What the hell! The sort of tramp I was now would have drunk melted boot polish if that's all there was.

I took three quick shots with muslin over my lens, to give the pictures a grainy texture, but my heart wasn't in it. My work comes easy, when I feel sexy. For once, I didn't. It showed in my eyes and in the way I posed.

It was that damned couple, Millie and Hugh. Rejecting them, it was almost as if I'd rejected sex. Very well, I'd exorcise them. I'd use that bloody great dildo they'd had the cheek to send me, and watch their stupid home-made tape, and by the time I'd had a few cheap-thrill orgasms they'd be flushed out of my system forever.

First, I poured another half a tumbler of vodka. That damned dildo was a bit scary.

I oiled up lavishly — both it, and myself. Two slippery fingers prepared my rectum. I'd almost forgotten what I felt like, in there. The walls were incredibly smooth, and very strong. I experimented, squeezing and relaxing on my fingers. The important thing was to be able to relax the muscles at will. A sphincter will open quite wide, if it doesn't clamp up by reflex. Relaxed, it will accept a variety of large foreign objects, without any pain. I'd been taught that years before, about the same time that I'd learned to control my gag-reflex.

Strange — he'd been a good teacher, and I'd been an avid pupil, but now I couldn't even remember his name. My mind could summon detailed pictures of his penis, both at rest, and erect, but not his name. Isn't that weird?

I held a towel between my legs, and spread another on the seat of my office chair. I'd slathered so much oil that I was dripping.

The base of the vibrator was wide enough for it to stand upright. I set it down, turned, braced with one hand on my chair's arm, and lowered myself backwards.

The smooth dome went into my sex without too much trouble. I simply parted my lips, arranged them spread over its glistening surface like lips slurping an orange, and wriggled down.

I paused, awkward, half-sitting. It seemed obvious, at that moment. That was as far as I was going to get. The body of the damned thing was just too bloody thick, and knobbled. How was I going to force it any deeper, into where I was narrow and convoluted? It would dilate me, straighten my intricate folds, and, despite the oil, those bumps would drag on my skin.

Petra doesn't surrender! I bumped down hard, driving two inches into my tight funnel. A grunt bubbled up from deep inside me, out through my throat. I bit my lip, and transferred part of my weight from my feet to my invader, sitting on it. My hips squirmed. The walls of my vagina could feel the knobbles forcing, sliding, slowly... Yes! Another two inches. I had a full four inches of the stupid thing crammed up inside me!

That was the hardest part, right? All I had to do then was keep bearing down and inch by dragging inch...

Whoops. Pause for a moment. The smaller prong, with the little round knob, was nudging between the cheeks of my bum.

With my weight on the balls of my feet, and on that distending column, gripping it with my internal muscles despite their forced dilation, I groped behind, found the small slick ball, and steered it to my anus.

"Relax your knot, Petra," I told myself. "Relax, and..."

With a judder, I forced myself down another inch. The tiny globule popped through, past the clench of my sphincter, into the tight rubber tube of my rectum.

Determined, I braced myself on both arms of my chair, and lifted my feet from the floor. Like a one-inch rubber sleeve on a two-inch piston, I slid slowly, juddering down until my sex's lips were spread on the plastic base.

It was in!

I was *impaled.* I felt totally helpless, unable to move, but it was *in!*

My toes found the floor. Poised like that, I commanded my muscles, one at a time, to relax. Once I felt secure that I wouldn't topple, I let go of one chair arm and adjusted the spring-loaded plastic tongue until it pressed firmly, but not uncomfortably, against my hairless pubic mound. The ordeal that I had forced myself through hadn't been without its pleasure, and my body had responded. The oily plastic was cold on the exposed head of my clit.

I wasn't ready to touch any of the three buttons yet. It would be better to let my insides get used to their plastic invaders, first. It would be easier if I were more relaxed, too. Watching Hugh and Millie should take care of that. Hugh and Millie, and... I reached out, very carefully, and retrieved my glass of vodka, for a long swallow.

On screen, Millie said, "...and enjoy." She and Hugh stood, shrugging out of their robes. The camera panned down, jerkily, as Millie knelt at Hugh's feet. "I love my man — adore him — from his toes..."

She bent low, and kissed his naked instep. The camera zoomed in to show me Millie lifting a foot to her mouth, and sucking on its toes, one at a time. Her mouth made love to the big toe, slurping its length as if it was a penis. Her tongue extended to slither between that toe and the next, and then flattened to glide wetly under Hugh's arch, his heel, up his ankle, and his calf. Small white teeth nibbled his knee, and then she mumbled higher, up the muscular inside of his thigh, to nuzzle beneath the full hairy sac of his testicles.

Her mouth turned up, opened wide, to make a cup, and engulfed one dangling ball. I heard a muffled humming. Hugh's penis, already thickening, lolled against her cheek. Like a tree growing in a fast-motion movie, it lifted, smoothing its slow way over Millie's face, until it reared above her curls, vibrant and triumphant.

The waif behind the camera said, "Wouldn't you like to get your hands on that, Petra? I've had that pleasure. I've had it inside me, as well. He's really good, Petra. And look at the size of Millie's nipples! Like walnuts, they are, but hot, and rubbery between your fingers. Suck on one of those, Petra, while that great pole skewers you, and it's like you died and went to humping-heaven, believe me."

The stupid little slut should have been paying more attention to her camera-work. She'd lost focus. As if she'd heard my thoughts, the picture became sharp again.

Millie stood, dragging the points of her nipples up Hugh's body. He took her in his arms and stooped to kiss her. Their lips didn't touch. With their mouths half an inch apart, his tongue stretched out to lick between her lips with darting little stabs. As it withdrew, hers followed, to give his mouth a similar treat. Both tongues extended, to meet in mid air, fencing with each other. Millie and Hugh kept their eyes open, each feasting on the lust in the others.

I could envy them that, if I let myself. I must inspire lust in thousands of people, right around the world, through my work, but I never get to *see* it. Looking into someone's eyes, and seeing the desire there — desire that I'd created? It would be very satisfying.

Hugh scooped Millie up in his arms and sat her on the couch. She slumped back. Her thighs fell apart. Hugh's broad hands urged them wider, exposing her sex to the camera's eye. It zoomed in for a close shot of glistening pink, and then drew back as Hugh dipped his head.

The camera panned up. Millie's mouth was slack with her need. Her cheek twitched a response as Hugh found some sensitive spot. Her eyes hooded.

Perhaps the waif moved the microphone closer, or else the sounds were very loud, because I could hear lapping and gobbling noises. Hugh had no inhibitions. He was slobbering over the sweet wet flesh he was mumbling on.

My finger fumbled beneath me, and found a button. I pressed. The ball that was clamping the thin membrane between my rectum and my vagina against the cylinder that dilated me, purred into life. I'd have squirmed if I hadn't been so thoroughly impaled.

I pressed another button. The plastic tongue quivered and wagged, rippling over the exposed head of my clit. Slick with oil, it metronomed, each slow stroke pumping my clit, coaxing it to engorge even harder.

Millie drew Hugh up and swung herself round to stretch the length of the seat with one leg lolling off. Hugh's face was glistening with her juices. With him poised above her, she reached down and steered the head of his penis between her thighs.

As he entered her, I pressed the third button. The thing inside me quivered, and grew. I was almost lifted up on it, but I bore down bravely, feeling it open and penetrate my secret flesh, wider and deeper than I could ever remember being opened before. It was almost as if I was losing my virginity all over again. Each elongation and contraction was like a gigantic pulse, an internal wave of overwhelming sensations. My vaginal walls were too tight around it for it to slide easily. Each upstroke stretched my skin. Each outstroke dragged on it, as if to turn me inside out.

Whether it was that, or the tingling in my rear, or the slow lascivious licks of the mechanical tongue, I came.

It didn't matter. The *thing* didn't care. It just kept going. My limbs flopped. I felt like a wet rag. I was being sexually consumed, from within, and I had no choice but to ride out the throbs of my orgasm, helpless, until the great massaging engine rekindled my lust and I started the long slow climb back up towards my next cataclysmic convulsion.

Hugh was still a bridge over Millie's lush body, braced on straight arms and stiff legs, just his hips slow-grinding down at her, and withdrawing his glistening length just as slowly. Their eyes still held each other.

The waif, in the background, was urging them on. The excitement of what she was watching was obviously getting to her, for she was babbling obscenities.

Her words got to me, in turn. My pictures have no sound.

Without either a word or a signal, Millie and Hugh moved. They didn't break contact. They just rolled, so that she was kneeling on top now, ridding his shaft in the same slow controlled rhythm as he'd been grinding into her. His hands lifted. His fingers gripped her nipples. Millie leaned back, and shook her shoulders, wobbling her breasts, tugging her strawberry-cones into tortured pears.

She ground down harder. The camera zoomed in to their juncture. That enormous clitoris of hers — now the size of a baby-boy's penis, was rubbing its exposed head into the curly hairs of Hugh's hard pubic mound.

Her hips swivelled, jerked, gyrated, attacking Hugh with an arrowhead of sensitive flesh.

Somehow — somehow I managed a small twitch of my own hips, urging my pink pearl harder against the rippled surface of the wagging plastic tongue.

Millie went into spasms, from her waist down. Her head tossed. Whips of sweat-soaked hair flicked her shoulders.

"I. Love. You. You. Sexy. Bastard!" Each word was a gut-deep grunt. On 'bastard', a judder rippled up through her body. She sobbed incoherently for a few seconds, frozen, suspended above Hugh, paralysed by the intensity of her orgasm.

He bucked into her for the first time since she'd assumed the superior position. She swung one leg up to put its foot flat beside his hips, lifted herself, and let his long glistening column of engorged flesh flop free. Her fist grabbed his shaft, and jerked it into an orgasm that fountained up at her open sex, splashing it, and the insides of her thighs, with thick creamy foam.

The camera swung wildly. When it steadied, Millie had flopped onto her back, her legs bracketing Hugh's, her sex wide, and saturated, drooling her man's spending.

The waif came from behind the camera, threw herself face-down on top of the pair of entwined lovers, and tried, in frantic lust, to simultaneously lap Hugh's spending off, and out of, Millie and to cram his still-hard penis into her mouth.

I came again, for the fourth or fifth time, as the screen went black.

XVIII
Millie

I'd finished all my housework. There wasn't a speck of dust, not a cushion out of place, nor a book on the bookshelf that wasn't erect, spine out, and lined up in size order. Petra could peep all she liked, and find nothing to fault me on. In fact, the President could have walked through my door, with the Queen of England on one arm and the Pope on the other, and all I've had to worry about would have been the way I was dressed.

All I'd worn was the bottom half of a skimpy bikini, and my heels, in the hope that the sight of my body might encourage Petra to call.

At eleven, it hadn't. I decided to escalate. I fetched a hand mirror from the bedroom, and the binoculars, and one piece of the jewellery that I'd bought from the sex shop. Taking my time, I pulled Hugh's chair, and a side table, into the triangle of windows. With my profile towards Petra's window, I sat on the chair's arm, and leaned my breasts over the mirror. My nipples were already semi-hard. I didn't dare play with them, because if they were fully engorged what I wanted to try might have been impossible.

It looked a lot like an earring, with a pendant gold ring. The clip, though, was larger, and longer, than the clip on a clip-on earring, and it was padded between its jaws. I experimented, squeezing the jaws open as far as they would go. Each jaw was slightly curved. With them fully open, I could get a finger between them. When I let go, they held, quite firmly. They didn't hurt my finger, but the flesh they were intended to grip was much more sensitive than a finger.

I took a deep breath. There was no point in putting it off. If I was going to do it — do it!

My fingers pinched the tip and about half the length of my left nipple, compressing my flesh as flat as I could — enough to make me wince. With my other hand, I slid the jaws of the pendant over where my nipple was thinnest, and let go.

It held. It held, pinching me, but not as hard as Hugh pinches, sometimes, when I'm in the mood for a little pain. When I hooked a finger into the ring and tugged, it still held. I pulled harder, drawing my flesh out strongly enough that I could feel it to the roots of my nipple.

Looking down, into the mirror, and at the underside of my breast, the view was obscenely erotic. Hugh would really get a kick out of this, when I showed him.

With my finger still hooked, maintaining the tension, I picked up the binoculars and checked Petra's window.

She was there!

She was watching me. Dressed in just a floor-length, low-on-the-hip black skirt, she was looking through her camera and plucking at one of her own nipples, mimicking me.

I waved. Her arm lifted, paused half-way, and then decided to wave back.

I almost danced with glee. I pointed to my cordless phone, there handy. She nodded, and disappeared, returning in a moment with her own phone in her hand. My phone rang.

"Did you get a picture of that?" I asked.

She cleared her throat. "Er — yes. A good one, I think. Would you like a print?"

"Only if it's part of a set."

"A set?"

"I bought a number of pieces, similar in function to this one." I gave my nipple-ring a twitch. "I think," I continued, "that it would make an interesting montage — the various parts of my body that the pieces are designed for. Don't you agree?"

"What — er — what sort of..."

"You'll see for yourself, if you visit us, Petra. If you are shy of my husband, Hugh, we could have a daytime photo-session, just the two of us."

"I — um — I think perhaps I should meet you both. You meant what you said? Your promise? You two would pose for me, no complications?"

"Petra, you have my solemn oath that neither Hugh nor I will so much as touch your fingertips, until — unless you ask us to."

"And — and I could be concealed? Almost as if you didn't know I was there?"

"If that's what you'd like, certainly. We'd have a quiet little dinner, and then you could..."

"No," she interrupted me. "No dinner. Nothing 'social'. Just you two, making love, and me, where you can't see me, with a camera."

"You want us to leave the door unlocked, so you can just sneak in?"

Her voice was colder. "It won't be necessary to go quite that far, thank you. Just — just nothing social, okay? You two are just bodies to me, nothing more. Beautiful bodies, I'll allow, but just bodies — models — photographic subjects."

"Very well. So, when would you like to see these bodies? Tonight?"

"Tonight? Oh — er — I hadn't thought... How about tomorrow? About eight?"

"That'll be fine. Tomorrow night at eight it is. Well, Petra, I'll just go and return this," I gave my nipple another tug, "to the rest of the set. We'll see you tomorrow, then."

"Millie?"

"Yes?"

"Will you be wearing — that jewellery."

I grinned to myself. "On our first date? I don't think so, Petra, but there'll be lots of lewd shots for your camera to enjoy, I promise. Ciao!"

I took the phone with me into the bedroom, so I could bring Hugh up to date, but I didn't tell him about the jewellery. I was saving that, for a surprise. In any case, fulfilling our fantasy of having Petra visit would be enough of a treat for him, for one occasion. I never 'shoot my bolt'. Finding new ways to please Hugh was getting harder and harder, as the years went by. For a while though — with Nadine first, now Petra, and the jewellery yet to come, there'd be enough variety in Hugh's love-life to keep any man happy.

He came home that night lugging two oriental screens. They were nothing fancy, just black wooden frames with horizontal split-bamboo slats. He opened one's three sections between the dining table and the couch.

"There! She should feel quite private, behind that, and she can poke her lens through the slats."

"Why two screens?" I asked.

"Aha! Just watch." He opened the other screen across the pass-through from the kitchen.

"So?"

"I'm not done." He fetched the video camera. "I put this on the counter, like this, and make a little hole, like this, and..."

I put my arms around him. "You clever devil," I exclaimed. "You're going to make a movie of her — watching us!"

"Exactly. There's a delay timer on this camera, to let the user get 'in shot'. I think, if I tinker with it, I can make it wait ten minutes, instead of just fifteen seconds. Once she's in, one of us will go into the kitchen, and hit the button. It'll tape away quite merrily by tself for up to two hours. Do you think that'll be long enough?"

"For a 'quicky', sure. Darling, you're a genius!"

We abstained from sex that night. Neither of us said anything, but we both knew we were saving ourselves for Petra's sex-show.

I spent the morning in the beauty-parlour, hair, facial, nails, body-wrap, leg-and-bikini-line wax, the works. In the afternoon I visited Sluts, and 'Muscle Bitch', the gay body-builder's store. I bought Hugh a posing pouch, some bronzer, and a bottle of the oil that they use on their bodies before posing. It was fun. I enjoy preening myself for my Hugh, and this time I had the pleasure of preparing my man for display, as well as myself.

Hugh brought cartons of Taiwanese home with him, so we could eat quickly and get it over with. He rearranged the furniture and the lights while I filled a bowl with salty nuts, and prepared a plate of extra spicy hors d'oeuvres for Petra —

including anchovy-wrapped curried scampi and 'suicide' chicken wings.

I showered while he mixed a pitcher of zombies. We didn't know what, or if, she drank, but most people will go for a fruity, innocent-looking, zombie, especially if their mouths are burning the way Petra's would be after she'd sampled my snacks.

The way Hugh mixed zombies, they were far from innocent.

He used grenadine and concentrated orange and pineapple juices, for the colours and flavours, but the finished drink was eighty percent rum. The dark and amber were just ninety-proof, but the light was one-fifty. If drink could loosen Petra's inhibitions, one glass of Hugh's special would have her stark naked, screwing the bananas from the fruit bowl, and begging *us* to take the pictures. And she *would* drink. The extra salt in the nuts and the spices in the hors d'oeuvres would make sure of that.

I trimmed the hair on my pubes while Hugh bronzed himself, and then we oiled ourselves until our bodies gleamed. Hugh had problems getting himself into the posing pouch. Perhaps gay body-builders have small balls, or maybe they know some way to suck them up. Then Hugh had to bend his soft penis to get it into the leather pouch. I'd have given him a hand, but he claimed that one touch from my fingers and the job would have become impossible.

My own costume matched his, pretty well. It was just a black silk thong, small enough that my pubes bulged from its sides, and the head of my clit was covered, and half the ridge of its shaft, but no more. Once it was on, I poked it with a finger, making a fold between my pussy's lips. I love the feel of silk.

Hugh saw me tuck the fabric into my crease. He had to clutch himself to hold his penis from unfurling right out of its pouch, so I guess I looked fairly sexy.

I'd bought us matching black silk kimonos. We put them on, and we were ready.

Petra was prompt, at eight. If I hadn't been expecting her, I wouldn't have recognised her. She was in scuffed Reeboks and a powder-blue baggy track suit. Her face was covered with pancake make-up. She was wearing oversized sunglasses, with pink lenses. A green figured scarf covered her head. The Adidas bag held her photographic equipment, I guessed.

"Come on in," I invited, unsure whether I should shake her hand or not.

She nodded, and brushed by me.

"Are the arrangements satisfactory?" Hugh asked.

She looked at the screen, sideways-on to our kitchen, facing the sofa, and the food and drink I'd laid out handy to where she'd sit, on a straight-backed dining chair. I'd have asked Hugh to move his recliner, but it was big enough that she could have been hidden from the video camera by it.

She nodded, cleared her throat, and said, "Fine. You didn't have to — er — go to so much trouble." Her hand waved over the dishes.

"No trouble," I told her. "Even inanimate bodies can be hospitable."

"I — er — didn't mean to offend you — er..."

"Millie. And Hugh. And we intend to call you 'Petra'. We aren't offended, Petra. It's quite flattering to have an artist consider us worthy of immortalisation. It's just that we lack your impersonal viewpoint. After all, we could be cold marble, for all you care. It isn't as if you'd ever feel anything personal about mere 'models', is it?" I almost added some snide remark about her masturbating when she spied on us, but she was nervous enough as it was. I didn't want to frighten her away.

"I've taken one slat out of the screen," Hugh said. "If your lens is close, it should give you a good field of vision. Can I give you a hand setting your equipment up?"

"Setting..? No, I'm fine, thanks." She took a camera with a fancy lens and a collapsible tripod from her bag. Baggy as her pants were, they were soft wool. Wool clings. When she bent over I could see that she had quite a shapely bum. I nudged Hugh, but he'd already noticed.

"If you're ready," Hugh said, once she'd settled into the chair and checked through her viewfinder, "we'll drink a toast, and get on with the show."

"A toast?" Petra asked, but Hugh was already in the kitchen, getting us glasses, and switching on the video camera.

He poured short drinks for us and a long one for her. "Here's to... to 'pretty pictures'! 'Pretty exciting ones', I mean. Okay, darling, ready?"

I slipped out of my robe, and Hugh dropped his. He looked magnificent — good enough to eat. I hoped I looked the same. Petra blinked behind her tinted lenses, but kept a very composed face as she bent her eye to her camera, ready for our 'performance'.

I hoped that the perfume I'd sprayed on the bamboo slats that were six inches from her nose still lingered. Smells can be very evocative.

Hugh and I stood, side by side, almost naked, facing the screen. "Is there anything in particular you'd like us to do, Petra?" he asked. "Some pose you'd prefer?"

"Just — just make love. Forget I'm here."

"Okay," he lied. "You don't exist. Millie, my love?"

I turned into his arms for a nice long kiss, my back to the

screen. As our tongues played, Hugh stroked down my body to cup my buns in his big strong hands. They pressed hard, urging me towards his body, rotating their palms, one on each buttock. I felt my cheeks being pulled apart, and then squeezed together. The string on my thong was supposed to be invisible, in my bum's crease, but the way Hugh was manipulating my ass, Petra must have been able to see it.

I kneaded Hugh's ass, in return, but Petra couldn't see that. My foot lifted, to stroke its sole up Hugh's calf. The smooth inside of my thigh caressed the outside of his hard and hairy one.

Hugh whispered in my ear, "Backbend?"

Supported by my leg, hooked around Hugh's, and by the pressure of his hands on my bum, I let myself fall back, bending at my waist, until my head was upside down, looking back at the screen. My hair brushed the floor. Hugh seems to find me irresistible in that position. Perhaps Petra would, as well.

His left hand moved to cover both my buns, and tightened. His right deserted my ass, to pluck at my nipples alternately, drawing each one up towards the ceiling and wobbling my breast with it, before repeating with the other. I think I might have mewed, softly, with the pleasure/pain.

Hugh's groin moved against my belly, not in a sexual way, more like he was uncomfortable. I swung myself erect, and to one side, pulling him around a half-turn, so that his back was towards Petra. "Flex those nice hard buns of yours," I told him, softly. "Make 'em dance for the camera."

I dropped to my knees. Sure enough, his poor penis was being strangled by that tight pouch. I tugged the bow at Hugh's hip free, and released him. It sprang up immediately, slapping his nice flat muscular belly.

"Mmmm!" I said, "Very tasty. You horny goat, Hugh, you're

leaking already." Nuzzling his balls, I wrapped my arms around his hips and kneaded his buns, feeling their hard muscles flex in my palms.

I stroked down, hard, and then cupped, and parted. "Wink at the nice lady," I told him. My hands squeezed their hardest, and then my fingers stroked, trailing, barely touching his skin. I hooked my fingers, and dragged my nails down over his buttocks, digging deep enough to leave weals. Hugh jerked forwards, wagging his column over my head.

"I'm going to play with your ass," I told him. "Turn a bit, so the camera gets a profile."

It's different — making love for an audience. You have to be more theatrical about it, broadcasting your next move, and making sure that what you do is visible.

I let my mouth slide, open wide, up the curved underside of Hugh's stem. As my lips slithered, I made a production out of my hand's gestures, flattening my palm and straightening all of my fingers except one. With a flourish, I parted his cheeks with my other hand.

My lips reached his glans, where he was deliciously wet. Planting a kiss on the knot beneath the dome, I whispered, "Try to keep still. Follow my cues."

The tip of my extended finger circled his sphincter. I whispered, "Open wide."

As his knot relaxed, I wormed my finger into rubbery heat, high enough that I could feel the walnut of his prostrate.

"Bitch!" he gasped.

I just managed an affirmative "mmmm", because that was when I took his glans into my mouth. I bore down, pulling my lover's beautiful penis with me, until it was jutting straight out from his body.

It must have made a lovely picture. My head, his body, and

the gap between them bridged by the white bar of his straining penis.

The flat of my hand, on his bum, and the spike of my finger, urged him towards me. His glans glided between my
tongue and my palate, to butt against the back of my throat.

I hooked my finger slightly, and drew him back, drawing his
column of hot flesh through my slurping lips. I paused, to
worm at his glans' eye with the tip of my tongue, and then
drew him to me again, deep into the warm wetness of my
mouth.

Out, and in. Out, and in. Totally under my control, my darling was slowly screwing my mouth.

Hugh was perfect. I could tell that I was getting to him,
because his thighs were knotting, but he restrained himself.

"Millie!" Petra called from behind the screen.

I paused, and took Hugh from my mouth. "What is it?"

"Your hair. It's in the way. I can't get a good shot of your
face."

"Sorry. Hugh, can you help? I need both hands."

Hugh brushed my curls up from my cheek and held them
to the side of my head. His legs were trembling. I knew exactly what the poor darling wanted to do, right then. He wanted to hold my head between both of his hands, and pump
into my mouth, hard and fast, until he came.

Well, he couldn't. It was too early in the game. If we'd been
alone, I'd have let him. Then he'd have eaten me, long and
slow, while I played with his penis until it got hard again. We
do that sometimes, *soixante-neuf* for hours, with each of us
making the other come, alternately, until we finally fall asleep,
each pillowed on the other's thigh.

It wouldn't make a very interesting show, though, would it?

I stood up, deserting his poor penis, for the moment. "Do

my clit," I suggested. "You know — like a man jerking off."

"Like this?" He turned me to face the screen and cuddled me from behind. His fingers twitched the bows on my thong loose, and tossed it aside. One of his big hands cupped my right breast, offering my nipple to the camera. His other hand smoothed down my ribcage, across the soft mound of my belly, to take a finger and thumb grip on my clit's shaft.

He had to be half crouched, because his penis slithered up between the cheeks of my bum, and stayed there, a hard bar in the cleft of two soft cushions, twitching. His fingers drew back on the hood of my clit, baring more than its head, and then pushed down, covering it.

His other hand gripped the rubbery spike of my nipple, twitching it from side to side. It was so hard that it felt to me like a pebble, imbedded in my flesh.

Hugh pumped, and twisted my nipple, and pumped, and frotted my nipple's tip, and pumped, and tugged my breast away from my ribcage.

He crouched even lower, dragging his hard wet glans across the twitching little mouth of my anus. His legs bent. His hips manoeuvred. His penis glided between my thighs, silk on silk, to project from between the gaping lips of my pussy.

To Petra, it must have looked as if I'd suddenly grown a penis.

I lifted myself on tip-toe and reached down between my thighs. My hand guided Hugh in an upwards curve, so that his glans glided over the head of my clit. My other hand brushed Hugh's — the one that was masturbating me so delightfully — aside, and took over, so that I was masturbating us both, rubbing the head of my clit with his glans. I leaned forward, and yes! I was able to get my clit to the eye of his penis, and, with tiny jerks of my hips, I screwed it!

Oh! I'm *so* glad my clit is so big! There was a time, in my teens, when I'd been ashamed of it, thinking it looked unnatural. Nowadays I appreciate it. There are things I can do that no other woman I've known can manage.

"Hugh," I panted. "Bend over the arm of the couch for me."

He must have been puzzled, because what I had in mind was something we'd never tried, but the darling released me, and obeyed.

I massaged his buns for a while, careful to stand to one side so that the camera could see. "Relax your ass," I told him. "This is going to be tricky."

He let his muscles go limp. I snuggled up behind him, his bum in my lap, and spread his cheeks as wide as I could. His sphincter opened for me. "Hold your buns apart for me," I asked. "I need both hands."

He did as I requested, spreading himself wider than I'd been able to. I found my clit's shaft, and worked it, dragging its sheath back as far as I could, until I had perhaps half an inch of tender flesh exposed.

I didn't know whether Petra could get what I was doing in focus, and at that point I didn't give a damn. I had something new to try. That's what was important.

I opened my thighs as wide as I could, and bore down on Hugh's bum. My tail tucked under. I pressed, and strained, and... ...and got the head of my clit to Hugh's pucker. One last jerk, and I got the tip inside. Just the tip, but that was enough. I was actually buggering my husband! I doubt he could hardly feel it, the penetration was so shallow, but the thought of what I was doing, and the friction of that wrinkled little hole on my most tender flesh...

I came. I think perhaps I yelled, or something.

Petra's voice said, "Did I see right? Did you actually..?"

I turned my head just in time to see her duck down from above the screen. She'd been standing on the chair, to get an overhead shot!

When my voice came back, I told her, "You saw right, Petra. You just witnessed a woman sodomising a man, without using a dildo. How's *that* for a show? And now, you can watch and learn how a real woman gives head."

Hugh perked up at that. He perked, and stood up, to sit down again on the edge of the couch's arm, his legs straight and spread. "Okay, bitch-slut," he told me. "Enough chat. Put your mouth where it belongs. Make it do what it does best."

Mindful of the camera, I bent from my hips, with my rear in quarter profile. That way, the lens would be able to wander from my thighs, with the doughnut of my sex squished between them, to my dangling breasts, to my face.

I opened my mouth to its widest 'o', targeted Hugh's glans, and swooped. In one deep stroke I rammed his head against the back of my mouth, and deeper, into my throat, so that I could nuzzle into his pubic curls. My lips closed around his shaft. I drew back, very slowly, slurping my way up his pole to its head.

Hugh remembered to hold my hair aside, the sweet man.

I took his shaft in my hand, opened my mouth again, and wobbled his glans in circles inside the loose ring of my lips, gurgling in my throat as I did so.

Hugh's free hand reached beneath me, to fondle a breast.

I drew back another half-inch. His dome fitted between my lips like an egg in and oversized, soft egg cup. I made circles, lapping all the while, pumping on his shaft. It was hard for me to speak coherently, but I managed, "Gi' i' to me, lo'er. Come in my mou'. Gi' me you' swee' cream, baby!"

I felt the pulse in Hugh's staff throbbing in my palm. His

fingers tightened on my nipple. The hand that was holding my hair aside moved to cup the back of my neck. His thighs tensed.

"Yes! Bitch!" he bellowed.

I dragged him in deeper, hollowed my cheeks, and sucked with all of my might. My mouth filled with foaming cream. I swallowed, but more came, and more. I drew on him as if I wanted to suck his balls flat.

Eventually, he pulled my head up. "Enough — I'm drained."

I stood, pulling him with me. Turning to our invisible audience, I licked my lips slowly, and said, "That's all folks! Hope you enjoyed the show."

XIX

Millie

We put our robes back on to see Petra out. She didn't say much, apart from "thank you", but her face was flushed beneath her make-up, and her track suit was crumpled.

She'd not eaten much, but she'd finished her tall glass, and half a second one.

"Come on then," I told Hugh. "Get the tape. Let's see it."

"You don't want to wait until tomorrow?"

I punched his arm, not that he felt it. "Go get it. We'll relax and finish off Petra's leavings."

While Hugh unloaded the camera and rewound the tape in our VCR, I moved the booze and hors d'oeuvres into the living room, handy for us to sip and nibble while we watched.

"That was quite some trick you pulled," Hugh said. "Perhaps we should call the Guinness Book of Records. 'Woman buggers man?' It sure beats, 'Man bites dog'."

"How was it for you?" I asked him. "Did it feel good?"

He shrugged. "Sorry, darling. I hardly felt it. I still prefer your nice squirmy tongue up there. Still, the *idea* of it was exciting. I think I'd like to watch you do it to someone else. Maybe Nadine? She'll try anything."

"How about Petra?"

"Do you think she'll be back?"

"Ask me again after we've watched the tape. I'll make a bet with you. If she played with herself, and I'm sure she did, she won't be able to resist a return visit."

"Just as a watcher, or as a participant?"

"Here." I passed him a drink. "Shut up and watch the tape."

The first few minutes were boring. Petra sat on the chair, enveloped in that ugly track suit, hunched forward with her eye glued to the camera. I tried to work out what we'd been doing at that point, but it's hard to judge 'boring' time against 'exciting' time.

Then her free hand moved. It fumbled at her waist, and slipped up inside the top of her track suit. I figured that would be about when I was bent over backwards, and Hugh was stretching my breasts towards the sky. Hugh must have agreed with me, because he grinned, and reached sideways to grope under my robe and give my nipple a tweak.

"Are you horny again *already*, you randy old goat?"

"Not 'horny' exactly, but..." He twitched his robe open and stretched his legs out. His penis was still limp, but it gave a little jerk where it lay along his thigh. I reached out and took it in my fingers. I love that feeling, as it thickens in my hand, and then rears up.

On the screen, Petra worked her top up under her armpits, and plucked at a nipple.

"Ummm. Nice little bod, what we can see of it," Hugh

commented. "Not as big in the boob as you, my love, but quite edible, wouldn't you say?"

"You'd like a piece of that slut, wouldn't you?" I said, deliberately referring to Petra in degrading terms. It's funny, we don't think of ourselves as sexist, racist, or any other 'ist', but when we're horny, it's 'bitch' and 'bastard' more often than not. My calling Petra a 'slut' was including her in our 'circle of lust', in a way.

Hugh said, "Yes, I admit it. There's something icy about our Petra, that makes me want to hear her beg for it."

"On her hands and knees," I added.

"And drooling with lust."

"What would you do to her?"

"After she'd begged? Maybe I'd bugger her."

"Yeah — me too."

He laughed at that.

My hand tightened around his shaft. Petra's hand had left her breast. She picked up her drink, took a long swallow, and swivelled on her chair so that she had room to stick her legs out straight. Her flat palm slid under the elastic at her waist.

"Take it off, damn you," Hugh growled.

She didn't, but her wrist dragged her pants low enough to expose the soft white curve of her belly. The cloth at her groin bunched and bulged, betraying where her fingers were working.

"She's going to get off with her hand hidden down there," Hugh grumbled. "We aren't going to see a damn thing."

I stroked the satiny skin of his shaft, comfortingly. "She stands up on the chair, later. I spotted the top of her head."

"Oh? Really? Well, in that case..." He folded my hand around his stem, inside his own, and began slow-pumping.

"Give me your fingers," I said. My leg lifted over his, companionably. I took two of his fingers, laid them alongside my shaft, hooked their tips between my lips, covered them with two of my own, and worked them up and down in the same rhythm as he was sliding my hand on his shaft. "This is nice and cosy, isn't it," I remarked.

"Mmmm." He stretched and slumped down deeper in the couch, only to sit up sharply.

Petra had stood. She jerked her pants down her thighs, to her knees, and sat again.

"No underwear," Hugh commented. "The little bitch came prepared, didn't she?"

"Wouldn't you like to get your face between those nice smooth thighs?" I asked. "You could watch her play for a while, close up, and then maybe move her hand out of the way and get your tongue into her."

He licked his lips. "Mmmm. Millie, remind me, if this happens again, to switch the mike on. I'll bet her pussy's sloppy wet by now. The speed her hand's moving, I'm surprised we didn't hear it splashing."

"We were otherwise engaged, remember? I think this is about when you were poking out between my legs, and I was rubbing you on my clit."

"Yeah — that was nice. That was right after my penis slid between your silky soft buns, sweetheart. Do you know how close you came to getting buggered, right then?"

"Why didn't you?"

"Remember what you told me, the day we met in the park? 'I don't do anal sex on a first date.'?"

"That was just to make sure you asked me out again."

"Well, anyway, I didn't think we should do it for her, on the 'first date', as it were."

"You're so sweet." I gave him a squeeze, and humped up at

his fingers.

"Now, *that's* better," he said.

Petra had stood again. It had to be about when I had Hugh bend over. She'd need a higher viewpoint to see much.

Very awkwardly, with her pants around her shins, she clambered up onto the chair. Squatting there, peering over the top with her camera, she spread her legs as wide as she could, and reached back between her thighs to finger between them.

Hugh pumped my hand harder on his shaft. I push-pulled his fingers on my clit's shaft and into my slopping heat.

Petra, looking anything but elegant with her pants down and her bum up, was fondling the lips of her sex, tugging on them, twiddling them between her fingers, drawing them apart, and then pinching them together.

By then, she had to have been watching my initial assault on Hugh's bum, because she abandoned her sex's lips, leaving them swollen and purple, to massage her own bum's cheek, squeezing at first, but then pulling it sideways to part the crease.

Her anus winked at us, a tiny pink rosebud, parting and closing its tightly furled petals.

"It's a shame we didn't have a remote-control zoom," Hugh said.

"Maybe next time we'll get Nadine to work the camera. Hugh, do you realise it's been at least a week since I had your tongue up my ass?"

"Sorry, sweetheart. Do you want to roll over?"

"Not now — maybe later. This must be where I was working my clit into you, you tight-assed bastard."

Petra had leaned over sideways, to lay her camera aside, on our table. That gave her two hands free. One folded into a spear, to stab upwards between her thighs, into her sex, while the other parted her bum's cheeks, with one finger probing into her anus. Her knees were flexing, bobbing her up and down.

I squeezed on Hugh's shaft. My other hand urged his to move faster, harder, deeper, frotting my clit and rubbing against my pubic bone, from inside me. "Let's do it, Hugh," I panted. "She's on the brink. This is where I was just about to come, from buggering your sweet ass. Let's... Uh, uh, uh!"

Hugh's hips, and mine, jerked. I felt myself flood, squirting between and over our linked fingers. Warm wet flopped onto my other hand as Hugh fountained straight into the air.

"Ahhh. That was nice," he sighed. "You spilled me though. That means a forfeit."

I lifted our still-linked fingers to my mouth, to suck off my salt-lemon juices. "Are you up to 'a forfeit'?" I asked.

He slithered my other hand up his now-loose foreskin. "Not right now, I'm not, but you wanted my tongue, right? Ten minutes of servicing your cute little bum, with my tongue, and I think a really clever woman would be able to squeeze one more orgasm out of me."

"That sounds like a challenge, darling. Okay — let's go to bed and leave the mess for once. This is one night when we can be pretty sure Petra won't be peeking into our home. That last climax of hers nearly knocked her off the chair."

XX

Petra

There was just one package. I knew it was another video tape, without having to open, so I got myself prepared first.

I didn't bother with anything elaborate. There was no need to. The visual stimulation that I need for my sexual fulfilment would come from the video, not from me. All I had to do was make myself over into someone who would be able to respond. Anyone would do — anyone except the 'natural' me.

I turned myself into a blue-eyed blonde. The wig was straight, slightly turned under at the ends, and just short of shoulder-length. It was designed to be combed forward and flop in a silky skein, half-veiling my left eye. It gave me the sort of look that Hollywood would pose lounging on a chaise, sophisticated, cool, but with a of hint glowing embers just beneath the surface, waiting for the hero to fan them into flame. Fire under ice.

I dressed in ice-blue silk pyjamas, but then decided that the hero and heroine in *my* movie had advanced beyond that, and took off the pants. In any case, women's pyjamas aren't made with those nice handy slits in front, like men's. That's a shame. There's something very sexy about those.

I had a momentary vision of a man and a woman, laying side-by-side, each with a hand inside the slit of the other's pyjamas, fondling idly while they chatted about other, totally non-erotic, things. The picture warmed me strangely, in a sexy-romantic way, which is a combination of feelings that I hadn't experienced in years. I had a pang of yearning, very brief, like an ageing woman's flash-back memory of a long-forgotten childhood doll.

I punched up the diary program in my small computer, the 386, went to 'costume', the file where I keep notes of things to order from Peggy, my seamstress. At the bottom of the list I added 'pjs' in the 'general' field, 'silk' in 'fabric' and 'slit-fly' in 'detail'. There was no need to mouse-pencil a sketch. She wouldn't have to make them, just shop for them.

I paused for a moment. That warm feeling was still with me, and those two, Hugh and Millie, had really gone out of their way to keep to our bargain, and to give me interesting poses to photograph. Under General Notes, I added, 'Three pairs. My size, a man's extra large, and a woman's, measurements to follow, likely small pants, thirty-sixish inch hip, and a medi-um-to-large top, perhaps a thirty-eight.'

I paused, and decided to delete the 'measurements to follow, likely small'. Pyjamas don't have to fit, exactly. In fact, a poor fit can look more erotic, sometimes. I changed Millie's pants order to 'extra slender, petite'.

Tight around her buns, and almost gaping at the fly, would suit her just fine. This last addition filled my page, so I zapped it modem-to-modem. I love modern technology. My order would be on Peggy, my seamstress' screen, already. She'd be selecting fabrics by noon. As I hadn't starred any items, she'd complete the order before sending anything. The full delivery of costumes, the raw materials for twenty more 'me's, would arrive in about a week.

They'd look good in silk pyjamas, Hugh and Millie. She'd most likely leave the top completely undone, or with just one button fastened, to show of those lovely breasts. I could just see her, sitting on that leather sofa, beside her husband, with her hand inside his fly.

My fingers curled by themselves. I knew why. They'd been thinking about what Millie's fingers would have been feeling, and doing, under those circumstances. It'd be kind of fun to share that, wouldn't it? Two women with their hands in Hugh's fly? Their fingers interlaced, perhaps, and curled around his hot smooth shaft, together?

Not my fingers, of course! No, certainly not! That fox-faced waif though? And then his penis would grow, and straighten up through the slit, wouldn't it. And they could masturbate him, together, in sisterly lo... *affection*. That was the word I was looking for.

As he got close, from the two-handed pumping, they'd likely bend over his lap, with parted lips, so that when he squirted they could share the liquid bounty, and then perhaps kiss? I saw their lips moving apart, with drooping strands of creamy semen stretching from mouth to mouth, and then licking their lips, lasciviously. Their own lips? Each others? Both?

Perhaps I should order a fourth pair of pyjamas, child-sized, for the woman-brat?

It'd make a lovely photo-sequence. All I'd need to do was change the faces a little — a few tiny touches — to make them unrecognisable, and *Depravité du Monde* would snap it up.

The video was waiting. I was moist already, either from my mental pictures or from anticipation. I popped the cassette in the slot, booted my computer, and hit 'play'.

There was another of their 'introductory leaders'. They were on the couch again, stark naked this time, turned into each others arms and kissing passionately. I pushed my chair back, lifted my heels up onto my desk, legs open wide, my pyjama top spread in a reverse cleavage from its single fastened button, hands loose in my lap, and settled down to enjoy the show.

Their kiss ended. Hugh bent to nuzzle at Millie's breast as she turned to face the camera.

"Hi Petra!" she started. "We hope you enjoyed our little performance, the other night. This tape is something special, for you. I'd like you to know that Hugh and I think it's the sexiest video we've seen in ages, and we watch a lot of blue movies.

"You've spent hours watching us, Petra, and all we'd had was brief glimpses of you. We thought we'd even things up, some. We can't understand why you hide that lovely body of yours, Petra. You've got nothing to be ashamed of. Both Hugh and I think that you are absolutely beautiful."

Hugh lifted his head, for a moment. Even with no zoom I could see how engorged the nipple he'd been sucking had become.

"You're an inspiration, Petra. We two had a *lot* of fun, watching you."

I thought, "Watching me?"

Millie pushed Hugh's head back down, to her other breast. "Petra — we love looking at you. Why deny us that pleasure? If you still want to stay hidden, next time, we'll accept that, and we won't cheat again, without your permission, we promise, but what we'd like is to put on another performance for you. Next time, though, we'd love it if you were where we could see you. If you decided to play with yourself while you watched us, well, we'd take it as applause, and you know that actors perform better when they're appreciated."

Hugh pulled Millie's naked thigh up across his lap, without stopping his nipple-sucking. His fingers parted the lips of her sex.

"Petra," Millie went on, "Think about it, please? As you'll see, we've seen you at your most unguarded, intimate, moments. Your position might have been ungainly, but it was still a wonderful sight, in our eyes. Now that we've watched you once, what have you got to hide? Watch the tape, and give us a call, okay? We didn't actually break our word, and we wouldn't. We just promised not to *touch* you, without your permission. Well, we didn't touch, did we? No one made any promises about not *watching*.

"Petra, I hope you enjoy the rest of this tape as much as we have."

There were a few seconds of black, and then *I* was on the screen, in that ugly track suit, behind their screen.

The bastards!

Still, what was done, was done. My sex-life, these days, was mainly me watching myself, in mirrors or in photographs, and masturbating. It'd be interesting to look at myself when I'd been unaware of the camera, for once, not deliberately posing. And, even though I'd made myself into an unattractive person that night, it wasn't as if they'd seen me as *me*, was it? All they'd spied on, and taped, was one of my creations.

I just had one minor orgasm, watching my screen-self masturbating and masturbating as I did so. Good grief! If they found me so thrilling when I was made-up deliberately ugly, what would they do if they saw me made-up to be someone glamorous? They'd likely have orgasms on the spot!

Okay — they wanted to pay games, did they? Very well, I'd show them a game or two. I would take great pleasure in rousing their lust for me to fever-pitch, stretching it out with unspoken promises, and then denying it. I'd get my kicks out of teasing them, and at the same time, I'd fill my files with more lovely pictures of their sexual gymnastics.

There'd be no danger of any emotional involvement, on my part, because the relationship would be strictly sexual. They'd be in no position to make demands on me, because the rules would be preset, and clear-cut. They'd get to see me, and I'd get to see them. That was it, finito!

I patted my naked, still damp, still flushed, sex. "You'll see this, but only I get to touch," I told Hugh and Millie, in my mind. "I'll be in your wet dreams, but never in your bed, so *suffer*, damn you!"

I picked up the phone, and punched their number.

It took me almost half a day to prepare for my appointment with them. I wanted to create the most seductive female I could, the easier to rouse their lust. Usually, that would mean tops that were 'off-the-shoulder', and almost, 'off-the-nipple', or deeply plunging necklines, matched with long skirts with high slits, or fabrics that would puzzle the eye — 'is this see-through or not?'

On the other hand, they'd accused me of being shy to show my body. Perhaps that was true — of *my* body, but when I was being one of my creations, the creature I'd created wasn't shy at all. To prove them utterly wrong, I wanted to be someone blatantly sexual, 'in-your-face' erotic.

The latter consideration won, not that blatant can't also be seductive.

I started with a long hot soaking bath, with lots of perfumed oil. I used my hairdryer to dry myself. Skin is softer when it's dried that way, not that anyone was going to get the chance to touch me, of course.

Still in the bathroom, I laid out all my equipment on the vanity. The first tasks were the trickiest. Spread-legged over a hand mirror on the toilet seat, I opened my sex wide. With a sponge first, then a dry cloth, and finally the hairdryer, I made sure that no trace of moisture remained on the skin of my inner lips.

I dipped a medium camel hair brush into a pot of livid crimson vegetable dye, and began to paint myself, inside. Once I'd completed one coat, I dried it with my hairdryer, on the 'cool' side of 'warm', and applied a second.

When I was done, and my sex's lips were relaxed into a vertical pucker, no trace of colour showed. The moment my lips parted, I displayed a gash of deepest, mouth-watering, pomegranate. The skin inside me had been a matte finish, when it had dried, but my natural moisture soon coated it, making it glisten.

Phase two. I coaxed the head of my clit from under its hood. It too, was dried three times, and then painted, dried, and painted again, but with the finest brush I owned.

By the time I'd finished, my fingers were quivering. A camel-hair brush can feel *really* nice, applied in the right places. My sex was oozing, as well, but the dye didn't run.

From then on, it was easy. I powdered myself from hair-line to feet, stark white. My eyebrows became thin, slightly demonic, black lines. I did my eyelids with black mascara, touched at their centres with the slightest smudges of silver grey, just to give them some shape. Black contacts. Black nipples, done with liquorice-flavoured balm, as if the flavour mattered. Red lips, full and lush, in a shade as close as I could match to the inner lips of my sex.

My next step was to make sure that my pubes drew their eyes, so that when my lips parted, they wouldn't miss the effect.

I rouged my hairless mound, subtly, merging the soft pink into the surrounding white. Then I drew two darker pink lines, one on each side of my clitoral ridge, and blended them into the paler pink. The final touch was a fine white line, vertically along the crest, also smudged. When I was done, my pubes, and especially my clitoris, were emphasised nicely, almost glowing against the flat whiteness of the surrounding skin.

I glued on artificial nails, painted them glossy black, and trimmed them to dangerous points. My wig was short, almost a pelt, like my real hair, but jet black. I dabbed perfume, one of the 'Sluts' line — 'Use Me', if I remember rightly — behind my ears and on the pulse-points of my wrists.

In the mirror, I saw a naked succubus, cold, eerie, totally unnatural, but incredibly erotic. Just one part of her was human, and warm — her sex. The red gash of her mouth didn't soften or humanise her, it just made her look vampiric.

Perhaps what I'd created this time was an accurate representation of the 'real' me. After all, didn't I feed off other people's sexual energy, without giving anything back?

I pushed those thoughts away. They had a bitter taste.

Just to check the effect, I popped my clit's head. Its deep crimson was downright *startling*. Well, if *that* didn't stir them with the desire to touch, and taste, nothing would.

Maybe they'd beg me. Maybe I'd let them grovel, hoping, desperate, before I denied them and stalked out of their apartment.

The boots I chose were the black skin-fit PVC ones that clung to my legs to half-way up my thighs. I covered my naked body with a tightly-belted black plastic raincoat that was just long enough to expose two inches of white skin between its hem and the tops of my boots, and I was ready.

Hugh opened their door. His eyes widened when he saw me, even though I had my raincoat on. He was wearing plain dark blue cashmere pants and a buttonless pale blue cambric shirt, open to his waist. I licked my lips. He looked quite edible.

"Come in," he said. "What can I get you to drink? One of those like I made you before?"

"Can you do a really dry martini, Bombay Sapphire gin, or Tanqueray?"

"I'll try. Sorry — may I take your coat? Millie will be with us in a few moments. She just had a few finishing touches..."

"I'll keep it for now, thanks."

He shrugged, and ushered me into their living room. The ugly screens had disappeared. The centre of attraction, in a brilliant pool of light, was his recliner. There was a sidetable next to it, with something that was covered by a cloth. At either side, nearer the window and beside the sofa, were two video cameras on tripods.

"I hope you don't object," he said when he saw me looking at them. "We'd like to make another movie, but missing none of the angles, this time."

I smiled at him. "Not at all. We can trade after — your videos for my photographs."

I unpacked the two cameras I'd brought, one with a manual zoom and the other with a fixed-focus lens with an eight-inch depth of field. They had their own clip-on floodlights. I found an outlet and plugged in.

Behind me, Millie's voice said, "Good evening, Petra. We're *so* glad you decided to come."

I turned. She was posed in a standard, 'whore in the bedroom' outfit, heels, hose, and a choker. It was trite, but effective. She certainly had the body for it. If her waist and hips hadn't been so slender, she'd have been Rubinesque. Her breasts were so spectacular that I'd have suspected silicone, but I'd inspected them, visually, in great detail, and was sure they were completely natural.

Her garters were cruelly tight ribbons, which was a nice touch. Seeing how they nipped into the softness of her thighs, you knew they'd leave deep marks when they were untied, and you automatically thought about kissing those grooves away.

I stepped back, so that I could watch both of their faces, untied my belt, shucked my raincoat, and posed.

Their reaction was quite satisfying. Hugh sucked a deep breath. His brows lifted. Millie bit her lower lip, and swayed her hips towards me, just an inch or so.

"You wanted to see me," I purred at them. "You see — I'm not so shy, after all. Will I do? Is this about what you expected?"

Hugh cleared his throat. "More. Better. A nice surprise, thank you, Petra."

"You're absolutely gorgeous, Petra," Millie croaked. Without taking her eyes off me, she added, "Hugh, I'd like a drink, please."

As he poured, Millie swayed to their CD. I waited, hoping that her choice of music wouldn't break the mood. A deep contralto thrummed from the speakers, followed by a trill that sounded an octave higher than soprano.

"Do you like Yma Sumac?" Millie asked me.

A cascade of clean crystal-pure notes punched precise little holes in the air.

"I'm not familiar," I admitted.

"The last track is 'The Virgin of the Sun God'. It has a part that gives Hugh an instant erection, and makes me feel as if someone is drawing velvet across the back of my neck."

"I'll listen for it."

"Not everyone reacts the same way. Our friend Nadine says it makes her feel like she's being buggered by an icicle."

I grinned. Millie was good. I can recognise verbal seduction when I hear it. I could also smell the musky perfume that Millie had poured over the bulbs of her lamps. She and Hugh were sparing nothing in their efforts to seduce me. It was a shame, almost, that I wouldn't let them succeed.

"I take it," I said, "that your friend means that as a compliment? She's the sort that would enjoy the sensation of ice sliding slowly up her rectum?"

"Nadine? Oh, she enjoys *everything*. You'll have to meet her, in person, in the flesh, sometime. She's totally depraved. No inhibitions at all. I admire that, in either sex, don't you?"

"In others," I said. "As for myself, I pick and chose which depravities I indulge in."

"But not which ones you photograph? Tell me, Petra..."

She was interrupted by Hugh, with a tray of giant-sized martinis and a refill pitcher.

They drank. I sipped. Getting a slight buzz first had become part of my sex-ritual. If I allowed myself enough alcohol to take the edge off my inhibitions, I could easily slip, which was exactly what they planned, of course.

"If you don't mind, Petra," Millie said, "I'd like to get started. We've been planning the show all day, and it's made me horny. I can't wait to feel Hugh's tongue on me, with you watching, from close-up. Come to that, I'm hoping that you'll feel free to diddle yourself some, even if you don't want to join in. Watching you play with yourself, while Hugh works his magic on my body, would be a real thrill. You *won't* feel too inhibited, I hope?"

Keeping my face straight, and my voice cool, I said, "That'll depend on the quality of the performance."

Millie grinned. "Then we'll just have to do our best, won't we Hugh? Shirt off, please."

Hugh stripped to his waist. Those slabby muscles of his seemed much sexier when they were in touching-range. I got a better sense of the texture of his skin.

"Would you like him to take his pants off as well?" Millie asked me, in much the same tone as she might have asked how many sugars I wanted in my coffee.

"Just carry on as you would if I wasn't here," I said. "I presume he'll become naked, one way or another, at some point in the proceedings?"

"Usually," she assured me. "The first part, though, is devoted entirely to *my* pleasure, tonight."

"And *your* pleasure is my pleasure, my love," Hugh said.

He scooped her up, and deposited her on the recliner. Laying, pale, on the black leather, she looked for all the world like some sort of human sacrifice. Perhaps she was — a sacrifice on the altar of Eros.

Hugh pushed the back of the chair down, until his wife was almost horizontal, and twitched the cloth off the tray. I looked at it, curious. There was a pumice stone, a length of feathery stuff that looked as if it had been cut from a feather boa, some face-cloths, a bottle of baby-oil, and another bottle, plastic, with a narrow spout. The last was filled with amber liquid.

Hugh picked it up and stood looming over Millie's head, behind her. "This is Millie's own concoction," he told me. "She lets vanilla and mint soak in liquid honey. After about a week, she mixes in lemon juice, and brandy, and then strains it. The way she makes it, it's quite liquid, but still sticky enough to stay where you pour it." He passed Millie the bottle. "The game, Petra, is that she squeezes it wherever she likes, and I have to lick it off. It's always her choice, and I'm not supposed to use my hands unless she tells me to. Millie?"

She stuck her tongue out, as far as it would stretch. Raising the bottle, she squeezed out a line of the liquid, lengthwise, on her tongue. Hugh leaned over her, braced on the chairback, and licked, flat-tongued. As his tongue slavered hers, his pony-tail bobbed at the nape of his neck. It occurred to me that a woman could get a grip on that short queue and use it to steer his head, guiding his mouth to wherever she wanted to feel his tongue lap, or the heat of his breath.

When the honey mixture was consumed, Millie lifted the bottle once more, but this time she squirted it *under* her tongue. Hugh bent again. *My* mouth watered, in sympathy, so Millie's had to be doing the same. The lemon juice in it had to bite, didn't it? Despite the sweetness?

Hugh was lapping up a mixture of the potion and Millie's saliva. Even without tasting, I knew it would be delicious. Just to wash the ghost-taste away, I took a drink from my martini glass.

I moved in closer, with my fixed-lens. They accommodated me by twisting sideways, and opening their mouths even wider. I took three quick shots that I could never have got through my telescopic lens. They'd been right, I *was* benefiting by being there, in person.

Hugh pulled back. I fully expected the natural progression — that Millie would target her nipples next. Instead, she turned her head, and poured a little pool in the hollow of her neck. When both sides had received that treatment — the liquid, and its lapping, she drew a line that traced the contours of a lower rib. Hugh moved to her side, and licked some more.

Then it was her navel. The dimple was deep enough to take a

teaspoonful, or more, before Hugh was allowed to follow it with the tip of his questing tongue, and lap it like a dog at a puddle.

After her navel, a vertical line from it to the root of her clitoral ridge, just short of the trim patch of fur that decorated it. As he licked that, she drew sticky lines in the creases that ran from the jut of her hipbones into her groin. Hugh's mouth was so close to her sex, I was sure he'd be tempted to stray. Few men could have resisted the temptation, but Hugh did. He was so careful that even though his chin came to within a hair's breadth of her pouting lips, and brushed her inner thigh, his tongue obeyed the game's rules, meticulously.

It was then that Millie took him away from her sex's temptations, by dabbing a single amber droplet on the very tip of each of her nipples.

I triggered my camera, quickly. Those trembling dewdrops made Millie look like a goddess, lactating ambrosia. How Hugh kept himself from suckling, I don't know, but only the tip of his tongue touched, a dozen stabbing little laps to each nipple.

I was moistening. It would have been so easy to snatch that bottle away, and squirt the stuff into my own sex. I had no doubt at all what would follow. No one had said anything — no one had to. The rules of our agreement were obvious. They wouldn't lay a finger on me, no matter what I did to *myself*, but if I gave either of them the slightest caress, I would have voided the contract. I would no longer be just an 'observer', but a full participant.

After the second application to her nipples, Millie took her breasts in her own hands, squeezing and manipulating them as Hugh licked, flicking them away from his questing, so that he had to dart his tongue after them.

I was moved to aid him — to hold her breast still for him

— but I resisted the urge, and took a deep swallow from my glass. It was obviously early in their game, but I could feel that the membranes that lined my vagina were swollen already, oozing out their nectar.

I clamped my thighs together, in case I dribbled.

Millie said, "Take me to the brink, now Hugh, but don't push me over, whatever. Not even if I beg, okay?"

He nodded, and stood, waiting. Millie squeezed the tiniest dab onto the head of her clit. As Hugh touched his tongue to the sweetness, Millie turned to me and said, "I learned this trick from an old school friend, Petra — uh — uh." She applied another drop. "My friend," she continued through gritted teeth, "had a cat — a beautiful Siamese — that was — uh — uh — addicted, to, uh..." Another droplet. "To — con — condensed milk. Oh! Uh — Hugh! No more, darling. I'm too close. Do the other thing now, okay?"

Hugh raised an eyebrow. Millie grimaced, getting a grip of herself, nodded, and rolled over. "Make me so I'll feel it," she told him.

Flat on her belly, she lifted her hips a few inches, presenting her ass. Hugh took up the baby-oil and the pumice. Apparently her words gave him permission to use his hands, for he poured the oil onto the pad of muscle at the base of her spine, and massaged it in.

It was as if they knew. I *love* that caress, and it's one that is very awkward to do to yourself. Even if you do, it somehow doesn't feel the same as when someone does it for you.

When the firm mound was glistening, he used the pumice, rubbing her skin in small tight circles. I took another drink, cleared my throat, and asked, "Er — er — what? What's that for?"

Millie turned her head to me. "He's exfoliating me. Taking

the top layer of skin off. Sometimes he uses a facial scrub to do me all over. When he's done, there'll be a fresh layer of new skin exposed. Hugh's an expert. I won't be sore, but that area will be left incredibly sensitive."

"Oh!" My thighs clamped again. Soft little explosions tingled inside me, as if I'd been filled with a string of silent firecrackers. My fingers strayed to my breasts. They were growing heavier as they engorged. My mouth was drying. When I picked up my glass, it was empty, so I refilled it from Hugh's beaded pitcher. The coolness felt so good in my fingers that I held my glass to my breast. Somehow, my nipple flipped the edge, almost buckling my knees with the sweet shock.

"Are you going to play with yourself?" Millie asked, calmly, as Hugh patted the last traces of oil from her rear.

They both looked at me, expectantly.

Okay — they were so clever, so sexually sophisticated, were they? I'd show them something they'd never seen before!

I forked my fingers along the ridge of my clitoris, and pulled its hood back. They both gasped as my bright scarlet pea popped out.

"Oh — lovely!" Millie exclaimed. "Thank you so much, Petra, for taking the trouble."

"You like that?" I asked, feeling incredibly brazen all of a sudden. "Then how about this?"

I put one boot heel up on the arm of the recliner, turned my thigh out to display my sex more, and opened its lips.

"Absolutely gorgeous," Hugh said. "You must tell Millie what you use. I'd love the chance to get my tongue into a pussy that looked as delicious as yours does right now, Petra."

Millie stared up into my scarlet sex with lust clouding her eyes. "Stay just like that, please Petra," she begged. "Stay like that, with your lovely pussy nice and close, and play with it, please, while Hugh does his thing. It'll drive me crazy with lust, and I simply *love* to be driven wild. Hugh, take your pants off. I might need you in me, quickly."

I toyed with myself, slowly and gently, more for Millie's pleasure than my own, I think. I was so intent that I almost forgot to get a shot of the look of desire in her eyes.

Hugh hung his pants over a chair and hooked a thumb into the band of his blue bikini. "These too?"

Millie dragged her eyes from my finger-play for a second. "Better, darling. You'll strangle yourself if you don't."

Stark naked, his beautiful penis wagging its heavy head like a cobra preparing to strike, Hugh bent over his wife's rear once more. His eyes darted between the new pink skin at the base of her spine, to my core, where my fingers were everting my sex's lips, and rubbing them, as if he didn't know which was more exciting.

I admit it, I took it as a challenge. My response was to lay my camera aside, take a quick drink, and pull back on my clit's sheath again, exposing its unnaturally-tinted head, and using the moist ball of my thumb to coax it into twitching life.

Hugh swallowed, hard. His eyes stared at me, but his fingers tested the smoothness of Millie's new skin, fumbled for the strip of feathers, and drew it gently up between her bum's cheeks, and across that gentle swelling.

Millie yelped. She curled backwards, lifting her upper torso and her thighs from the leather. The muscles in her back rippled. Her buttocks knotted. Her legs spread wide. The tendons that ran their insides stood out in ridges, hollowing the shadowed softnesses that bracketed her sex. Leaning sideways, being careful not to take my sex out of her line of vision, I saw the lips of her vulva flutter.

She couldn't be faking it. The feathers' caress really had

given her that much pleasure. She gasped at me, "The bottle!"

I passed it to her. Arched like the figurehead on a wooden ship, she squirted the amber liquid lavishly, onto one nipple, first, and then the other. It coated her breasts with layers of amber sweetness, like toffee on candy-apples.

With her entire weight grinding down on her pubes, on the leather seat, she grabbed both of her own breasts, and pulled them up as her neck craned down. With the two succulent globes squished together, she drew both nipples into her mouth at once, and sucked until her cheeks hollowed.

Hugh snatched up the bottle from where she had dropped it, and began to draw spirals on the patch of new, hypersensitive, skin.

Millie sobbed around her nipples. Her teeth were worrying at them. Sticky liquid smeared her lips. Her whole body juddered as Hugh bent once more, to trace the spirals that he had drawn, with the tip of his tongue.

"Now in my ass," Millie screamed between slobbering over her own nipples. "I won't be able to stand it. Do it, you horny bastard!"

My own fingers frotted wildly, savaging my sex. I'd forgotten my cameras. My eyes were feasting, sucking in what they saw. They'd never enjoyed such a rabid display of unbridled lust, ever.

Hugh parted the cheeks of Millie's ass. The bottle nuzzled. He squeezed hard. I couldn't see it, but the nectar had to be squirting deep into her rectum, perhaps tickling as it trickled down inside the uptilted passage. As he pushed his face into the crease between her luscious cheeks, the bottle fell.

I snatched it up, put it to my mouth, and jetted a stream of the same sweet fluid that Hugh was tonguing out from deep in his wife's ass, between my lips.

Millie's eyes, maelstroms of sucking lust, drew me. Perhaps that was the moment that Yma what-ever-her-name-was' voice hit those magic notes, because I felt as if my spine had split open, and an electric breeze was blowing the length of the exposed nerve.

Before I knew it, my face was close enough that I could feel Millie's breath on my cheek. I could taste the air she panted out, sweet, spiced, brandy-rich.

She released her nipples. Her mouth was slack, soft-lipped, infinitely vulnerable, incredibly desirable. I dropped the bottle, and, with my fingers still flickering across the straining head of my clit, I kissed her.

As our lips touched, I knew that I had violated our agreement. That one kiss changed everything.

And I didn't give a damn!

My tongue stabbed deep. There was enough honey in both of our mouths to make the kiss deliciously sticky. I sucked her tongue. She sucked mine. My nails, deliberately cruel, raked down her sides.

The chair moved beneath me as Hugh straightened it up. I toppled, into Millie's open arms, half beneath her. Trapped, I lay there, helpless to resist, the chair's arm under the small of my back, my legs scissoring in the air.

Millie devoured me — my mouth, then wet slithery kisses down my neck, to feast on my breasts. She heaved herself up, dragging me further under her with unexpected strength. Her hands pinned my shoulders as one lush thigh lifted over my waist, and pulled me down until it was I who was laying on the chair, and her soft weight was crushing down on me.

She reared up once more, gazed down on me with a look in her eyes like a canary who'd just swallowed a cat, and braced herself on one arm. Her free hand found my breast, and drew it up as hers descended. Nipple-to-nipple, she shook her shoulders, flicking her stiff over-sized cone on my smaller, but no less rigid spike. There was enough honey still clinging to her peaks that each touch dragged, just a little.

Her fingers clamped, as cruel on her own flesh as on mine, and rolled the two nubs together. "Hugh," she husked, "do our clits. Get your fingers working, damn you! I want to spend right into Petra's pussy."

I felt a hand insinuate itself between our pubes. Strong fingers gripped my clit — and Millie's. Just as our nipples were being pressed and wobbled together, so were our clits.

"Come, you bitch," Millie growled down at me. "Let it flow, you slut! I want your juices to run. Let it flow, baby. Let's make wet together. Don't hold back — *do it!*"

And I did. It jagged through me, from clit to nipple and back again. An umbrella of fire opened inside me. I remained whole, externally, but inside, I was shattered into a million delirious pieces.

She didn't let me up, even after I stopped sobbing. She held me, while Hugh cleaned our spillings with his educated tongue. That, and her softly nibbling kisses, roused me again.

That night I learned their flavours, both of them, and they both learned mine. By dawn, I thought myself past all desire, but then Hugh did his pumice trick on my naked pubes, and Millie showed me what her short-trimmed tuft of pubic hair could do, on my sensitised mound, and to my crimson-hued clit. It was fully light when I finally fell into a happily exhausted sleep, and noon when the two of them woke me. I felt something cool pour over my toes.

I blinked my eyes open, to see the two of them, lifting one of my feet each. It was the last of the honey mixture. Hugh sucked it off my left big toe. Millie slithered her tongue between the toes of my right foot. She saw my eyes, or maybe heard my soft groan. "There's just time," she told me, "for one last, *au revoir* orgasm, each, before Hugh has to go."

XXI

Petra

I did some electronic shopping. Raoul used to say that the reason I was always moved to give gifts to anyone who'd pleased me was because I felt that a material repayment cancelled any emotional debt. Perhaps he was right. Raoul had more insight than most shrinks do. Sometimes it was as if he could read my soul. That's why I dumped him.

I clicked my cursor on the 'send' icon. My requests flashed through wires, were translated into radio, bounced off satellites, and were at their destinations, Bangkok and Copenhagen, before my hand released my mouse.

Then I voice-mailed my seamstress, Peggy, to hurry my order up. There were going to be more meetings between Hugh, Millie, and me. That was obvious. They were hooked on me now, and I wasn't tired of playing with their magnificent bodies, just yet. I calculated it would take three or four more sweaty, straining, flesh-on-flesh sessions to work them out of my system.

For two hours I reran their video tapes, taking out stills for my computer files. When they gave me the tapes of our triple-bodied sex, I'd have a lot more editing to do. I didn't want a backlog.

My phone was at hand. Millie would be calling me, to thank me for the pleasure I'd given her and her husband, and perhaps to beg for another appointment, if I was willing. I'd already decided on my response. I'd put them off for a few days, just to show them I wasn't over-eager. By then, my parcels would have arrived. It only takes three days, maximum, to courier a small package from anywhere in the world, if you're willing to pay the extra charges. Then I wouldn't have to visit them empty-handed.

The phone hadn't rung yet, so I sorted some files for another hour. The phone still didn't ring. It just sat there, a useless lump, not ringing.

When I happened to glance out of my window, just by accident, I couldn't see any movement in their apartment.

And the phone still didn't ring.

It was still connected. The jack of its station was secure in the wall. The little green light was glowing. I got a dialling tone when I thumbed 'on'.

There were left-overs in the fridge. I sliced Portuguese sausage onto a plate, added some limp asparagus spears, drizzled them with mornay that had gone lumpy, poured a glass of Chablis, and took my snack to my desk, where the phone was.

When it got dark, I went to bed.

The phone rang at eleven the next morning. It was an adenoidal girl who wanted to sell me and my husband side-by-side burial plots. I was quite rude.

I don't remember what I ate that day. Perhaps nothing. I went to bed with a bottle of vodka, just in case I had trouble sleeping.

My packages arrived five days later, all within a few hours. I unpacked my new costumes and hung them to let the creases drop out. The pyjamas were laid out on a table in my bedroom. I didn't know for sure whether I'd still be giving Hugh and Millie theirs. The other two parcels — from Bangkok and Copenhagen — were definitely to be gifts, though, even if I ended up mailing them. I unwrapped, and was satisfied. The one from Copenhagen had an instruction booklet. I studied it, but I didn't try either of the implements out. They were for Millie. When she called. If she called.

Gustav had included some magazines, for packing. There were two copies of *Climax*, one of *Lesbo-raunch-orama*, and three of *Depravité du Monde*. I leafed through. You never know where you'll come across new ideas. I didn't find anything to inspire my work, but there were colour photo-sequences, like cartoons in a comic book, of two women and a man, in two copies of *Depravité*. I tore them out, and used them for gift-wrap. It seemed like a nice touch.

I set the two parcels next to my phone. All three were equally silent.

When you have a gift for someone, it puts pressure on you.

You've invested time and trouble, looking forward to seeing the unwrapping, and, one hopes, squeals of delight. Those parcels itched at me for the rest of the day. In the morning, I made my decision. I'd deliver them. Either Millie would throw her arms around me, or she'd be cool. Either way, the suspense would be over.

I did my face and nipples, put on a curly carrot-toned wig, and went to my closet. It was hard to make a choice. If I went as a 'frump', she might think I wasn't interested in continuing our physical relationship. If I dressed too obviously sexy, I'd be throwing myself at her.

Shorts seemed safe. A woman could wear shorts for house-work, or shopping, and not be deliberately showing off her legs — just dressing comfortably. With shorts, it's all in how you stand, and carry yourself. They can say, "I'm going for a nice brisk walk," or they can signal, "Look at these legs. Wouldn't you love to touch them?"

Plain white linen shorts — a little wide in the leg — wide enough to tempt a lover's hand — but otherwise totally neutral. I added a short-sleeved angora sweater, because nipples don't show through fluffy angora, no matter how hard they get. It was cropped enough to show two inches of midriff, no more, no navel, and scooped at the neck to display just a hint of cleavage, unless I shrugged it off one shoulder. If I did, it was transformed into something that you'd want to drag down on until a breast popped out.

No hose, no socks. Even knee-length socks make shorts erotic, for some reason. Plain spaghetti-strap sandals, beige, to match the sweater, with heels that were only four inches — the shortest I had. Perhaps flats, or even running shoes, would have been more appropriate, but I couldn't bring myself to sink that low.

My mirror told me, "Yes — I'd turn a few heads, on the street, but I didn't look as if I was advertising."

Gathering my parcels, and my courage, I left my apartment, rode the elevator down, crossed the lobby, and rode up again.

Millie opened her door with her face bare of make-up, and wearing a black silk teddy under a short, matching, open, robe.

"Why, Petra! How nice! I was just thinking about you." Her fingertips strayed to her breast, unconsciously. My eyes noted the pout of her nipple, prodding through the silk. Was that what thinking about me did to her? That was nice.

"Come on in," she invited. "I was just making coffee."

Well, she hadn't grabbed me, but she hadn't sent me packing, either. I followed her into her kitchen. Her legs were as bare as mine. They slithered together as she walked, as if her thighs were in love with each other. Her heels were higher than mine. They made her buttocks knot and relax, with each rolling step.

I put my parcels on her kitchen table.

Millie adjusted the folds in a cloth that hung beside the fridge before turning to face me. Her eyes lit up. "Oh — for me?"

"Just a small token — a thank-you for your hospitality. I know that you're a collector."

"A collector? What of, I wonder?"

But she knew what sort of present I'd brought her. I could see it in her eyes. "Open and see," I suggested.

She delayed, deliberately teasing me, I was sure. She poured coffee, and removed the wrapping carefully. "What interesting paper," she giggled. "Is it any indication of the contents?"

I just waited. She smoothed the paper out, raised her eyebrow at some of the pictures, and lifted the lid of the box. It was the gift that had come from Bangkok, and a work of art.

"How *lovely!*" She lifted it out, tenderly, in two palms. "It's supposed to be a dragon, isn't it?"

"You don't have one like it, I hope?"

"A dragon-dildo? No way, Petra. It's gorgeous!"

Her fingers stroked the golden length. It was formed into an arc, about a third of a circle. Straight, it would have been about a foot long. Delicate scales had been engraved from head to tail. The head itself was bluntly arrow-shaped, but with smooth lines. The tip of the tail was a handle. Between head and tail, a double ridge of tiny gold balls ran the length of the dragon's back, along the inside curve.

"You use it like this," I said in a matter-of-fact voice, taking it from her. "You hold the tail like a dagger." I made a stab-bing motion, downwards. "It's curved enough that the rows of balls can run each side of your clitoris. You can imagine the effect." I demonstrated the curving path that the dragon would make, its head driving deep into its user's sex, the balls rippling over her clit's head. "I imagine it's quite effective."

"Oh yes, it would be. Haven't you tried it?"

"Me? Of course not. I bought it for you. Would you like to give it a trial run?"

"Now? Here? With you watching?"

I kept quiet.

"Petra — I'd love to test it, but..."

"But?"

"Don't you understand? I'm faithful to Hugh. Sex with you was wonderful, please believe me, but if we were to — er — *do* anything, behind Hugh's back, that'd be cheating."

"I quite understand," I said, standing. "You might want to unwrap the other gift later, in private, or with your husband."

She laid her naked fingers on my bare arm. "No Petra, don't go. There *is* a way. Wait a moment."

She picked up her phone and hit the speed-dial. "Hugh? Hi Darling! Guess who's come to visit me. Yes — Petra." She looked at me and said, "Hugh says 'hello'." Back into the phone, she continued, "She's brought me some lovely gifts, Hugh. One is a beautiful dildo, oriental, and rare, I'd imag-ine. Hugh, darling, how would you feel..?"

He must have interrupted, because she was quiet for a while, just nodding, with the occasional smile and glance at me. When she hung up, she said, "Hugh says it's okay for us to play girl-girl, on one condition."

"Condition? What sort of condition?"

She grinned. "That you stay over, until he gets home, and that we both save some for him. He said it's every man's fantasy, to walk in on two incredibly beautiful and delightfully sexy women who are making passionate love to each other, and be asked to join them."

I smiled back at her. "Could we manage that? Saving some loving for Hugh?"

Her hand reached out and smoothed my sweater off my bare shoulder. "I think so. I've got plenty of loving to give. How about you?"

"Let's take it slow and easy then, okay?"

"Wonderful! Let's make a day of it. If it's okay by you, we'll save this dragon for later. Why don't we just chat, and whatever, and see what develops. We hardly know each other. There are all sorts of things I'd like to learn about you, Petra." She perched her rump on the table. The smoothness of her thigh radiated heat at my arm. The two limbs weren't an inch apart.

"You want my life story?" I asked.

"Life story? No, I don't give a damn about the puppy you had when you were six, or your disappointing tenth birthday party. I wouldn't mind hearing about the first time you were seduced, perhaps, or who taught you to give head, but I had more important things, immediate things, in mind."

"Such as?"

"Oh — would you choose thickness over length, in a man? Or whether you prefer to have your nipples rolled, or tugged? What style you use, to diddle your clit, when you're alone? How you feel about anal sex. Things like that."

"Oh — *that* sort of thing! Me too. I mean, I'm curious

about you too, Millie. I've noticed that you are very limber, double-jointed, almost, for instance. Just how supple are you? Could you..." I tried to think of an example.

"Get my tongue to my own pussy, for instance? Yes, I can, and have. I can do a pretty mean splits, as well. You'll see demonstrations of all my talents, in due course, I promise. What else did you want to know?"

"Well, I'm a clothes-freak, as you'll have noticed. I'd love to see what lingerie you have. Do you ever dress up, just for your own pleasure, even when Hugh isn't around?"

She stood and arched her back. The silk robe slithered from her shoulders. She caressed herself with her fingertips, just inside her French-cut teddy's legs. "Hugh isn't here now, is he?" she asked me. "And I didn't know that you were coming to call. I'm dressed like this just for me. Let me just open that other parcel, and I'll be happy to show you some of my things. I'll even model for you, if you like."

"I'd like." I laid my hand on the package. "Why don't we leave this until later," I suggested. "Once we're both hot, we can explore my presents, together."

Her eyes narrowed. "You're teasing me, aren't you, Petra?" she accused. "I like that. Okay — to the bedroom, first, but we'll take these with us, to be handy."

Their bed was larger than it looked through a telephoto lens. It had to be custom-made. The bedhead was brass, like mine, but had rails where mine was scrolled. Brass beds are so handy when you get into bondage games, but their one had no foot, which limits what you can do. Perhaps that wasn't part of their repertoire.

One thing that I hadn't even glimpsed through my camera was the mirror, set in the ceiling above the bed.

"Make yourself comfortable," Millie told me. "I'll just slip into something less comfortable."

I sat on her bed and waited while she swayed into her walk-in, mirror-doored closet. She came out wearing another teddy, of sorts. Perhaps it was supposed to be a one-piece swimsuit. It was lime-green, and glossy, like some sort of smooth Spandex. The legs were cut up in 'v's almost to her waist on the sides, with just enough crotch to cover her slit but let her pubes bulge out either side. She spun on her stiletto heels, to show me the back. From behind, it was a thong, leaving her delightfully bare-buttocked. She had the sort of peachy bum that makes your mouth water.

"Turn back," I asked. "I hadn't finished looking at the front."

There was a built-in bra to support her ample breasts. It would have been almost modest, except that a key-hole shape, reversed, had been cut in each cup. The 'v' of each hole was like a plunging neckline, but over each breast, instead of between them. The round holes fitted around her nipples perfectly. Volcanic cones, dark brown, slightly crinkled, protruded from green backgrounds.

"You like?" she asked me, her fingers lightly stroking the fleshy tips.

I cleared my throat. "It was made for you, wasn't it? It wouldn't look as good on anyone else. Most women's nipples wouldn't fill the holes, the way yours do."

"Hugh's very fond of my nipples," she said. "I try to find different ways to present them to him."

"I know. I have pictures of you — trying on that nipple-jewellery, remember?"

She chuckled, deep in her throat. "So you have! Did you like the effect? I have more pieces, similar, to match, some for my breasts, and some for, er, other places."

"Does Hugh like them?"

"I haven't shown him, yet. I was waiting for a special occasion."

"Can I see them? On you?"

She paused. "Maybe — maybe next time. The effect is a bit — a bit extreme. Let's not rush things, okay?"

"Now who's teasing?"

She crossed to where I sat and put her knees on the edge of the bed, straddling my legs without touching them. Her nipples were inches from my face, and mouth. Her sex was six inches above my bare knees. I fancied they could feel its heat.

"Teasing? Of course. Be honest, Petra, that's what we're doing, isn't it? Teasing each other? You'd love to be sucking this..." She took her breast in her hand and squeezed her nipple towards my mouth. "And have your fingers inside my pussy, soaking in the wet heat, wriggling in deep, perhaps pumping, or squirming. You want that, and I want it just as much. Just as I'd love to have my tongue on your clit, right now, whipping it into a frenzy. We both want those things, Petra, but we're making each other, and ourselves, wait for it. Isn't that right?"

My tongue flicked out at her nipple, close but not touching. "Of course you're right, Millie. I'm wet inside from thinking about it." My fingertips traced the hollow high inside her thigh. She froze for a moment, letting my fingers wander until my nails scratched gently at the thin strip of fabric that was stretched taut over her mound. I was just about to move it aside when she jumped up, and back.

"Let me find something for you to try on," she said. "I'll change in the bathroom. You change out here."

She went into her closet. A few moments later, she returned, tossed me a bundle, and disappeared again, into the bathroom. I pulled my sweater over my head and stepped out of my shorts. I hadn't lied. I *was* damp between my legs.

What she'd thrown me could have been called a bikini. At least, it was a bra, of sorts, and there was something to wear lower, but the set would have been illegal, even on a nude beach. In it, a woman was barer than nude.

I heard water running.

"The belt on the bottom half has to go exactly around your waist," Millie called from the bathroom. "It should fit you, but both belts adjust if it doesn't."

Two hard leather belts, black, each about two and a half inches wide, was about all there was. I strapped one around my ribs, just beneath my breasts. There were two stiff pieces, shaped like petals, with notches at their tips. I flipped one up and settled my breast — not *in* it, more *on* it. The petal tapered from three inches at its widest, the base. My nipple fitted into the notch, with just its tip poking through, nipped between leather prongs. On Millie, with her more generous proportions, the notch would have simply decorated her pale brown halo, if it came that high.

It gave firm support, lifting my breast so that it pointed straight out from my body. If it had the same effect on Millie, her nipples would have constituted a hazard, spikes of flesh that would precede her by a good six inches.

Once I'd settled both breasts onto their petals, and both nipples into the notches, I buckled on the other part. Like the top, the leather was shaped to conform to body contours. I had to suck in to fasten it.

I felt a momentary pang of jealousy. Millie's bust had to be bigger than mine by three inches, and her hips by two, yet her waist was a good inch smaller.

A ribbon hung down my back, from the belt. Just a ribbon,

perhaps half an inch wide, made from some slippery material.

I reached between my legs, snagged it, and pulled it up over my belly.

It wouldn't reach the snap fastener under the buckle. I tugged, hard. It was elastic. It stretched, sinking deep into the crease between my bum-cheeks. The metal tag on the end was still a couple of inches short — half way between my navel and my waist. I opened my legs wide, and tugged on it again. The ribbon cut into the left side of my vulva. I twitched. It slipped, slotting neatly between my sex's lips.

There was no other way to wear it. I adjusted my lips, one to either side, and admired the obscene effect in Millie's mirror. The ribbon fitted my sex the way a bit fits a horse's mouth. The 'bra' offered my breasts, without covering a thing. Stiff leather petals, black, contrasted dramatically with the white skin of my breasts. The leather belts divided my body into three distinct erotic zones, each to be admired, and used, individually.

If I'd known what I was going to be trying on, I'd have come to Millie's made up the same as the last time, black-haired and black-nippled. The combined effect would have been devastating.

I heard the bathroom door open and turned. Millie took my breath away.

She'd applied a little make-up, just lips and eyes. All that she'd changed into was a simple white shift with narrow straps over her shoulders, and just long enough to cover her sex. I couldn't tell what fabric it was made of, because she'd soaked it with water. It was transparent, where it clung, and watered milk in the few places that it didn't. At ten feet, I could see that the chill had turned her nipples to cones of brown crystal. The location of her navel was revealed by an opaque patch, punctuating the pink skin of her softly-curved belly. Her tiny thatch of pubic hair had curled.

Before I could recover my voice, she'd crossed to me, and squatted by my side. Her breath warmed my hip as she said, "This needs a tiny adjustment, Petra, and it'll be perfect." Cold fingers slipped under the ribbon, at my belly and at the small of my back. They tugged the narrow strip forward, and back, and forward, and back. Each slither dragged the ribbon between my sex's lips, and across the head of my clit.

The flesh inside my thighs trembled. Someone squirted oil into the joints of my knees. I bit my lower lip. "Millie," I said, "I need an orgasm, *now!*"

"Then an orgasm you shall have," she assured me. Her curly head snuggled against my lower belly, tickling my skin. Her fingers folded my mound, sandwiching the strip of fabric between its lips. She worked her hand, up, and down. Ribbon slithered over my clit's head.

"Open your legs wider," she ordered.

I obeyed. Still working my pubes around the cloth, she probed between my bum's cheeks with her other hand. A fingernail found the ribbon, where it was tight across my clenched sphincter. It scratched, gently. I could hardly feel it, yet what I felt was heavenly.

Millie nibbled at the undercurve of my belly, and then lower, taking the bulging side of my mound between her sharp little teeth, and nipping the skin. "Come for me now, baby," she hissed. "Do it for me. Make wet, sweet pussy." She shook her shoulders, slapping my thigh with her wet breasts.

Her mouth, open-lipped, slithered across my skin, to cover my pubes entirely, replacing her fingers. It closed on me, pinching my sex, squeezing my lips on the frotting ribbon. Her right hand, now free, tickled the edges of my hanging lips as she shook her head, violently, performing the service that her hand had been devoted to, with her mouth. Her breath scalded me.

I gripped both of my nipples, hard, and tugged. My hips jerked at Millie's face. "Yes," I sighed. The knot in my vagina unravelled. Something inside me unplugged. My juices were released. I let them flow in one long, slow, sweet juddery orgasm.

Millie tumbled me sideways, onto the bed, or perhaps I simply fell. She knelt, spread my legs wide, and slobbered at the juncture of my thighs, greedily. Her fingers found the ribbon's fastening, at my waist, and unclipped it. I felt a sudden release, as the cruel strip relaxed. Millie dragged the saturated strip from between my lips, and nuzzled deep, lapping out every drop of my spending.

When I'd recovered enough to notice how clammy her shaft was between her body and my thighs, I said, "Get out of that wet thing, Millie, and I'll do you now."

She sat up and pulled the garment off over her head. "No rush, Petra, dear. I'd like to open my other present now, if you don't mind."

I'd deliberately left the instructions back in my apartment. I wanted to be the 'expert', instructing her, and perhaps demonstrating.

There was a black metal box, quite plain, for the batteries and the controls. A lead ran from it, to the half-globe base. Two chrome rods ran up, jointed to swing together or apart, each with a smooth but irregular, copper-coloured, egg-sized, knob.

Millie looked puzzled. "Thank you, Petra, but how does it work? What does it do?"

"It's electric, but quite safe," I told her. "It delivers an electric current to the knobs, at about three seconds intervals. The current runs from one knob to the other, through — through whatever part of you happens to be between them. Give me your arm, and I'll show you. It won't hurt, I promise."

Nervously, she held out her arm. I adjusted the power to 'low', touched the two knobs to her forearm, about five inches apart, and switched on. For a moment, nothing happened. Then the muscle in her arm flexed, and relaxed.

Millie squealed. "Oh! That feels funny. It made my arm tingle, but nice." She paused as her muscle bunched again.

I switched off. "That's why the knobs are a funny shape," I explained. "There are dimples, here and here..."

"For nipples! Or your clit?"

"Yes. Or the flat sides could press anywhere, pretty well. The knobs are smooth though, so you could put one..."

"Up my pussy — and the other in my ass? It'd be a tight fit, up my rear."

"Or both in your pussy. The rods are telescopic. If you part them a little, so they didn't touch each other, it'd be like an exercise machine. It'd make the walls of your vagina clench, and relax, and clench..." I let my fingers trail across her wet belly.

"What would it do if you put the flat ends one on either side of your clit?"

"Shall we try?"

"In a bit. Do my nipples first, please Petra." She lay back on the bed, a breast in each hand, pointing her nipples at the ceiling.

I switched on and leaned over her. "Are you ready?"

She nodded.

I laid a flat surface either side of her left nipple. We waited, and then Millie's legs rose up and her belly writhed. Perhaps it was my imagination, but it looked as if the flesh of her breast contracted, shrinking into a knot, for a moment.

"Oh yes," she said. "Oh yes, that was *very* good. Do both nipples now, please Petra."

I switched off, fitted the dimples over Millie's nipples, and switched on again.

She gurgled a scream. "Oh — wow. Leave it there. Leave it there."

"You hold it," I suggested. "It's time little Millie had a nice hard come, and I know just the way to give it to her."

She gripped the chrome rods, pressing the knobs to her breasts. Every three seconds, her body convulsed. I found lubricant on her bedside table, and oiled the dragon-dildo. The lips of her pussy were already slightly parted, even before I nuzzled them with the dragon's head. They opened easily. Millie's hips bucked as another shock tingled from one nipple to the other. I made a fist around the dragon's tail, and probed. She jerked at it, impaling herself to half its length.

"Don't screw around," she gasped. "Get it in deep, and work the damned thing! My pussy is about ready to blow."

I obeyed. My hand steered, pressing the inner curve's double row of beads, one to each side of her gigantic clit. Its head, dark pink and glistening, fitted perfectly. With a curving motion, I stabbed, and withdrew, hard but slow, timing my thrusts to match the pulsating current that was thrilling Millie's nipples. The beads rippled her clit's head. Millie's behind lifted off the bed, her legs straining, her belly palpitating.

"My mouth," she demanded. "My mouth, my ass, I need something..." Her voice rose into a shriek, and then gurgled. "Damn! Too bloody late. Never mind." She laid the chrome rods aside. "You can stop now, thank you Petra. I came three times. That last one was a killer. I need a break. Shall I use this gadget on you, now?"

After my second orgasm, we broke for a snack. I repaired my sweat-streaked make-up while Millie cleared away. I was just in time. The real Petra was beginning to show through the paint.

Afterwards, we just toyed around. There was the occasional kiss, or gentle caress, as we tried on more of her wardrobe, but nothing that led anywhere. She had an extensive collection of 'for foreplay' wear, sexy outer garments with Velcro fastenings, for quick removal, and dozens of sets of seductive loungewear, mainly in stretch lace or fine net. She favoured black and green, to show off her pale skin and tutti-frutti hair. As I was a redhead, for the day, they suited me, as well.

Eventually, we fell asleep with me sprawled out and her curled beside me, one thigh across my legs, her arm over my waist. By then she was wearing just a silk scarf, a Hermes, I think, knotted over one hip. My costume was even less concealing — three narrow leather belts, one tight around the top of my left thigh and two snug around my waist, one high and one low.

I was woken either by the feel of Millie's fingers, softly smoothing over my mound, or by the noise of ice. Her husband, Hugh, said, "Did you girls leave something for me, or are you too exhausted?"

XXII

Millie

Hugh's voice said, "Did you girls leave something for me, or are you too exhausted? Don't try to tell me you just napped all day. I could taste your musk in the air while I was still in the elevator."

I sat up. "Sorry, darling. I was just about to wake Petra and start over, so you could walk in and 'surprise' us with our heads between each other's thighs, or something. You're home early, aren't you?"

"Of course. I've been home for ten minutes, already. Didn't you expect me early, considering what I was looking forward to coming home to? I've had time to shower and change while you babies slept, *and* I've started the champagne."

He must have been very quiet. It was true, he was in his short robe, and magnums were cooling in both of our ice-buckets, the good silver one and the old cheap plastic one.

"Sorry, love," I apologised again. "We'll let you catch us

being naughty girls next time, I promise. Not to worry, though. We've got lots of energy left." I let my fingers curl over Petra's smooth bare mound, finding her ridge. "You want me to show you how *much* energy?"

"What did you have in mind?"

I trapped the edge of the scarf I was wearing under my knee, and knelt up. The knot at my hip pulled loose, leaving me naked. I paused there, posing on the bed, swaying my hips a little, my fingernail denting my lower lip.

Hugh loves that 'little girl' pose. I guess the 'sweet and pure' look suits me, as my body is so blatantly sexy. There's something about an angel/slut that gets to most men, I find.

A woman with fewer curves and a more innocent face than I've got can achieve the same sort of effect by dressing like a whore and coming on like a vixen in heat. It's the contrast that does it, I think.

Still, I've got the advantage. I can get the same sort of contrast by using 'naive' body-language and putting on a virginal expression. On the other hand, when *I* show what a ravenous nymph I can be, Hugh says I could straighten the Leaning Tower of Pisa.

I held my position, pretending to think about what I was going to do to demonstrate my energy level, but I already had it planned. The pause was deliberate, to fake spontaneity, and to focus Hugh's attention on *me*.

It wasn't that I was jealous of Petra. Hugh is mine, and no woman could change that, no matter how exotic, or depraved. I just wanted to rub it in, to both of them, that when it comes to sex, I'm the queen, number one, the best.

Three-in-a-bed is fun, but I wanted to let Petra know that she'd better not think about competing with me, for her own sake. That way I'd stop any rivalry developing between us, before it started. The sooner she realised that she was there as an accessory, like that dragon-dildo, to be used, enjoyed, and then set aside, the better.

My eyes sent Hugh my 'erotic challenge' look. "Petra..." My fingertips trailed over her tummy and up her ribs. "...was wondering about how limber I am. *You* want to know about my energy level. Let me show you both, okay?" I slid off the bed and beckoned to Petra to follow me. "You know this one, Hugh," I said, reinforcing the bond between us. "Bend your legs, and brace."

I tugged his robe loose. His lovely long penis was thick already, but not stiff yet. "Petra," I said. "Help me get him nice and hard, will you?" That was to show her I wasn't hogging him — and I didn't need to.

"Hand or mouth?" she asked, with a pretty potent 'sexual challenge' in her own eyes.

I thought. "Neither, for now. Hugh wanted to surprise us, making lezzy-love, so let's give him what he wants, for starters. Hugh would love to watch you playing with my pussy. He's very 'visual'."

I knelt on the edge of the bed, legs wide, my pussy pointing straight back at Hugh. "Get your fingers nice and oily, Petra, and work me up. Get me really slippery, and wide open, please."

I felt her fingers part me, and then her hand cupped my pussy. She poured oil into her palm, and massaged round and round, splaying and squishing my lips, pressing hard. I had to brace my arms so as not to fall on my face.

"Um," I said. "Yes, now fingers inside please, and your other hand can work on my ass, if you don't mind. Are you watching, Hugh? Can you see those two — no — three fingers, working into your wife's pussy? Is it getting to you, darling? Oh yes! How high are your fingers, Petra dear?"

She told me, "To my knuckles, and it's four fingers now. I've just got the tip of one in your ass. Relax, Millie, and I'll work it deeper. Yes, that's right. How deep do you want my fingers in your sex, Millie? Shall I try for a whole hand? You want me to fist you?"

I gritted, "No — not now, anyway. Keep your palm flat. Don't stretch me too wide. I want to be tight for Hugh. Hugh, darling? Are you hard yet?"

"With this obscene exhibition to look at? Like a rock. I'm ready when you are."

"Then excuse us a moment, Petra. Hugh, you know the position. Hands behind your back, now."

Petra moved aside. I felt Hugh take a step closer. His glans nudged my lips.

"Okay! You two can suck tongue if you like, or whatever takes Petra's fancy, but Hugh is to keep perfectly still, and keep his hands off me. Ready, set, go!"

I lunged back, taking the entire length of his penis into me in one go. My hips went into overdrive, twisting, jerking, juddering, thrusting, tucking under and arching up, all at top speed. I impaled myself onto him from every possible angle, rotated, ground back, withdrew until only his head was trapped, and swivelled on it, before lurching back for full impalement and a hard circular grind.

"What are you up to, Petra?" I panted. "I hope my Hugh isn't neglecting you."

"I have to keep my hands behind me, right," Hugh responded, a wicked chuckle in his voice. "That's where she is, sitting on the dressing table with her legs spread. Right now, my love, I'm diddling her nice little clit. She's raked my back with her nails until I'm sure I'm scarred for life, but that's okay. Her tongue is doing wonderful things to my wounds. I told you she was a vampire."

"Screw you, Hugh," I gasped. "I'm dripping sweat from all this effort. Take that! And that!"

I jerked back hard, twice, slapping my butt into his belly. "Petra and I will lick every drop off your lovely bod, my love," he told me. "But first things first."

I can get him off in about five minutes of that frenzied attack, as a rule, but he was holding back. The wonderful man knew exactly what I had in mind. I was showing my own erotic abilities off to Petra, but also demonstrating his.

"Phase two," I announced, still gyrating my hips and undulating my belly. "You can move now, Hugh. My turn to hold still. You know what to do."

He took the undersides of my thighs in his palms, and lifted my rear. I swung my left leg from under me, and then my right, to point them straight ahead on the bed. My entire weight was on my heels, Hugh's hands, and his lovely hard column of burning flesh.

"You should watch closely, Petra," Hugh said. "Millie is very talented."

I waited until I heard her drop down from the dressing table. I bent forwards, over my knees, stretched my arms out, grabbed my ankles, and pulled down. Legs stiff, in a perfectly straight line from my heels on the bed to my rear in Hugh's hands, I folded myself. My breasts squished on my knees. My head went down between my feet, until my forehead rested on the bed. I was a closed jack-knife, rigid as a board, a human lever.

Hugh lifted my hips, raising them on his hands, letting his penis slither back down through my vagina, and drew me back, bodily, so that my rear end projected over the edge of the bed. He lowered me. His stalk skewered into my heat. Raise, lower, raise, lower. Slide in, slide out. I did nothing but keep absolutely stiff, and let him use me. His body was as still as mine. Just his hands moved, lifting and lowering.

"Damn!" Petra said. "I don't have a camera with me."

"We'll give you a repeat performance, someday," Hugh promised. "This is what we do next."

He held me still, suspended in the air above his penis, and jerked his hips up. I was still motionless, being used by my magnificent man, merely a soft wet receptacle for his penis to enjoy. His strokes were fast, and then slow, and then fast again.

"You want to come?" he asked me.

"Yes please, lover."

He leaned back, to sharpen his angle. His feet moved him closer. The undercurve of his shaft pressed against the head of my clit. My true love's body juddered up at me, faster and faster, driving sweet sensations through my clitoris and my vagina. His motion became furious, a pounding that had one object only – my climax.

I couldn't resist any longer. My insides melted. I let myself flow, spilling around the spike that stretched and plugged me.

As I went limp, Hugh heaved me aside, letting his penis spring free.

"You didn't come," Petra told him. "Would you like me to suck you until you do?"

"Not just now, thanks. It's early yet."

Petra dropped onto the bed beside me. "That's a remarkable man you've got. I noticed his stamina last time, as well. What's his secret?"

Hugh answered. He knows I can't speak for a few minutes after a good one.

"No big deal," he said. "It's just that I've got everything going for me. I'm old enough that I can't make it six or eight times an hour, like in my youth, but I *can* control myself. That's an advantage of age. I've passed the stage when a man prides himself in how many orgasms he has. Now I measure myself by how many I *give*."

"Sure," Petra agreed, "but you still get it up again pretty fast, after the ones you *do* have."

"I can't take the credit for that, Petra. Once a man has come, there are four things that will bring him up again, quickly. An expert mouth; a different orifice with the same woman; a fresh woman; or watching two lovely women make love. How can I fail, when I've got all four going for me?"

"Oh — and there's a fifth. If a man knows that the woman he is with is really horny for him, that'll revive him pretty quickly, too."

"Petra's horny for you, darling," I told him. "Isn't that right, Petra."

She caressed my breast with one hand, and Hugh's flank with the other. "For both of you, you beautiful people."

"I'll drink to that," Hugh said. "To 'beautiful and horny', the perfect combination."

"Don't forget 'depraved'," I said.

"That goes without saying. Champagne, you two?"

Petra said, "I don't see any glasses. Shall I fetch some?"

I giggled, knowing what Hugh had in mind.

He said, "No need, if you don't mind sharing with me?"

"No, but..?"

"Millie, are you recovered?"

In reply, I moved to the head of the bed and did a hand-stand against the wall. Hugh popped a cork, my signal to let my legs fall to either side, into a 'splits'.

"This is the *only* way to drink champagne," Hugh told Petra. "Will you join me?"

Kneeling on the bed, he put his thumb over the neck of the bottle, upended it, and slid it into my sex as he took his thumb away.

Icy champagne foamed into me. I felt it gush, frigid, rinsing into every last fold and recess, chilling my insides numb. Hugh's mouth covered my pussy. He sucked, and lapped.

"There's more," he told Petra. "Your turn."

As I felt her lips spread on my vulva, I squeezed my internal muscles, pumping champagne up from my depths and into her sucking mouth.

"Mmmmm. Warm, but delicious," Petra said to Hugh. "How about Millie? Doesn't *she* want some?"

I dropped back to the bed. "Of course I do, Petra. Can you do a handstand?"

By the time both magnums were empty, the first drunk from we women's pussies, the second passed from mouth to mouth, lapped from navels, or slurped off Hugh's still-rigid penis, we were all a touch tipsy.

"I think Hugh should come now," Petra giggled. "Champagne always makes me thirsty."

"You want him to come in your mouth?" I asked. "Okay — so he shall then. We won't give him any choice, no matter how self-controlled he is, right Petra, my lovely? Hugh, you're our love slave. We women are going to use your lovely male body, any way we damn well like, right?"

He bowed to us. "I am but your slave, ladies. Do with me as you will."

"There are cords in the top drawer," I told Petra. "Hugh — to the top of the bed, kneeling, facing us, hands behind your back."

Within seconds, we had him trussed up, but not too uncomfortably, of course. *I* like a little gentle discomfort with my bondage. Hugh doesn't.

His wrists were bound together behind him, and to the bed-head. His ankles were crossed, tied, and hitched to the lower rail. Once he was secure, Petra and I teased him with our mouths and hands. We licked his belly, brushing his wagging staff with our cheeks. We toyed with his testicles, scratching lightly beneath them. Our nipples traced lines on his skin. Our mouths sucked his nipples, nibbling, and with the occasional sharp little nip, to make him jerk. Petra and I kissed, in front of his face, but just out of his tongue's reach.

"He's supposed to come in my mouth," Petra reminded me.

"And so he shall — the first time. I hope you're *really* thirsty, Petra. The poor man hasn't had an orgasm since last night, and now all this teasing? These," I jiggled his balls, "will be pretty full. Lay on your back, Petra, with your head between his knees. Good. Here's our pet dragon. Use it, with your legs spread, so he can see everything. Now I'm going to make him kneel forward some, so his penis is right over your mouth, Petra. I'm oiling my finger, and now... "He's a real slut, Petra. No resistance at all, when I slip my greasy finger up his bum. That's it! Look up, Petra. Watch him carefully.

"Hugh, watch Petra screw herself with that dragon. See how the balls frip over her clit. That feels *so* good, Hugh. I tried it myself, earlier, so I know.

"Okay — my hand is nice and oily. I'm going to stroke you, Hugh. I'm going to pump your hose for you, and wiggle this finger in your bum, like this, and pump harder..."

"He's going to come on my breasts, not my mouth," Petra objected.

"No he won't. Leave it to me. Just keep your mouth wide open and keep that dragon busy. I'll take care of the rest."

"You're not going to..?" Hugh gasped.

"Yes I am." As I slithered my greasy palm up and down his shaft, and over his naked purple glans, I bent lower, so that I could alternately lap at him, and into Petra's gaping mouth, darting my head up and down, from one to the other.

Petra juddered an orgasm, but kept stroking the dragon into her pussy, like a good girl. Pretty soon she was panting again. Her belly heaved, signalling that another climax was close.

Hugh's balls tightened.

"Ready for it, Petra," I warned. "Here, it..." I pushed my finger deeper into Hugh's rectum, driving his hips forward. My still-pumping hand bore down on his shaft, forcing it from its natural upwards angle, straining it down, to Petra's open mouth. Its head slapped on her lips. Her tongue flickered out. Her hips lifted high, tilting her head backwards, so that I could direct Hugh's penis straight between her waiting lips.

"Do it!" I ordered him, and he did. A great gush of semen squirted from his tiny hole, directly on its target — Petra's tongue. I kept pumping, milking out every last drop, until he had no more to give.

"That was yummy," Petra said as she rolled onto her belly, "but he's going limp now. How do we get him up again?"

"Remember what he told us? Another orifice, another woman, or watching two beautiful women make love? Let's start there, Petra. Come play with my breasts for a while. Get that other gadget, the electronic one. After my breasts, I want to see what it'll do if one end is in each of our pussies, and our clits touch. Maybe we'll make sparks. By then, Hugh will be hard again, I promise. How would you like to back onto him then, on all fours, while I'm beneath you, and we're eating each other? How's that for a menu, for appetisers, anyway?

"Look Petra, even thinking about it is having an effect on him. He's twitching already."

XXIII
Petra

It's strange, isn't it, what other people's expectations do to you? You meet someone, at a charity auction, perhaps, just when you happen to be feeling in a good mood, and are bidding like crazy for some piece of junk. That person gets the idea that you are generous and charitable. From then on, you feel under some sort of obligation, when that person's around, to *be* generous. You can't pass the most disgusting crusty-lipped panhandler, without forking out five bucks, even though your natural self would do the 'averted eyes' thing.

The way Hugh and Millie had come to know me, they saw me as an incredibly exotic sex-toy — a live 'anatomically complete' Barbie doll, that came in a kit with an infinite range of erotic 'dress-up-and-play' costumes.

Wasn't that nice? Not only *could* I conceal the real Petra behind makeup, leather, and lace, but I was *expected* to. I never had to 'come out from behind'. Even stark naked, I was still in disguise, provided my face was properly painted. For me, it was the perfect sex-life. I knew the real them, but they never got to see the real inadequate me. Even when our three bodies were sweatily tangled, I was able to remain the voyeur, the hidden observer, peeping out at them from inside the safety of my false persona.

All I had to do, to maintain this delicious situation, was keep coming up with exotically erotic females to *be*. That's what I do anyway, right?

It was perfect. By pretending to be *their* sex-toy, I made them both *mine*.

It kept Peggy, my pet seamstress, busy. I spent my early mornings browsing through magazines, looking for inspiration. After ten o'clock coffee, I sketched, on-screen with my mouse-pen, of course, and then transmitted my new order. I learned that you can do more 'in real life' with just varying fabrics, colours, and textures, than you can for photographs.

For instance, I came across an old pin-up, in the style of Vargas, of a coffee-skinned farm-girl. She was wearing overalls that fitted her legs and buns as if she'd been wading through liquid denim. The bib was just big enough to stretch from boob-tip-to-boob-tip. One strap was dangling to her elbow, letting a corner of the bib droop. Her exposed nipple was like a mouth-watering chocolate-covered cherry.

I sketched those skimpy overalls, and ordered pairs in orange slub silk, gauzy white chiffon, tight black leather, shiny black PVC, and matte-finish dark blue rubber. That gave me five different looks — 'cheeky-playful', 'submissive-accessible', 'butch-dominant', 'kicky-kinky-slut', and 'clinically-depraved'. And that was before I accessorised them.

After a few moments of contemplation, I added a pair in a

cheap denim-look cotton, specifying that the seams should be basted, not properly sewn, so that they would rip easily.

I can be all things, from coldly dominant, to avidly submissive, and it was the latter that suited my current mood. I had visions of Hugh and Millie ripping my clothes off and raping me — him rampant, pounding my bruised sex until it was pulpy, her strapped into a dildo harness, reaming my poor over-dilated rectum. I'd be totally helpless, incredibly stretched, crammed full, feeding on their insatiable lust for my body, sucking it in through my avid orifices.

And if there were three of them? I'm equipped to endure three simultaneous assaults, after all, like all women. Hugh pistoning my mouth, my body sandwiched between Millie and that other girl?

I shook off my submissive 'use me' mood, and adjusted my mind-set for 'exotic-playful'. That was to suit the costume I had ready, for that night. I'd picked it with a purpose. Millie fancied herself as the sexual expert, the one of us who knew all the little tricks. Well, I had a trick of my own in mind, and the liquor store had delivered exactly what I needed to show Millie that I could give her Hugh some oral attention like he'd never enjoyed before.

Humming 'Au pres de ma blonde', I ran a bath and laced the steaming water with French perfume — lots of it.

XXIV

Millie

"**H**ow do you think she'll come tonight?" I asked Hugh, over breakfast. "Or should that be, 'who will she come as'?"

"Who knows? In six weeks we haven't seen the same 'Petra' twice. What was that they said about Lon Chaney? 'Don't step on a bug, it could be him'?"

"I liked that cat-woman outfit."

"Me too. That 'biker-bitch-from-hell' wasn't bad, either — all those wash-off tattoos in intimate places, the cropped leather jacket, the leather thong and the boots! When she handcuffed and screwed me, I could just imagine I was being gang-banged by the first in a long line of teenage nymphos. She really gets into her parts, doesn't she?"

"Not the ballerina, though," I commented. "I don't find tu-tus sexy, somehow, even if she was bare above, except for her frilly pasties. Come to that, the outfit that was all clear plastic didn't do a lot for me either."

"Would *you* like some fancy-dress outfits?" Hugh asked me.

"And compete with her? No, I don't think so. I don't feel I need to compete, do I?"

"How could you? You're the champ, and she's just a novice. She needs all the accessories. All you need is your gorgeous body, and a lustful look in your eyes. Anything else is just 'gilding the lily'."

"Thank you, sir," I said. "A pretty compliment like that deserves a reward." I opened my robe to show him my breasts. "Will these do? Should I wrap them to go or will you eat them here?"

"Bitch! You know I have to go to the office. Now I'll have to drive with a hard-on."

"I could always come with you, and give you a blow-job as you drive."

"In the rush-hour? I'd have an accident. Can I take a rain-check?"

"Of course. Hugh?"

"Yes, sluttling-mine?"

"I really *am* curious about Petra — what the real one looks like."

"Me too. Why don't we find out?"

"Find out? How? You know her — one smudge of her make-up, and she's got to fix it, even in the middle of making love."

"Well, we've had her in the bedroom, and the living room, and the den. We've used about every piece of furniture we've got. How about we get her into the bathroom tonight, for a change?"

"And?"

"There's water there. And the shower? You like it in the

shower. Good clean sex?"

"She wouldn't go for it."

"Wouldn't she? Not if we were *very* persuasive? Let's think about it, shall we? I'm sure that one of us can come up with a plan."

By 'one of us' he meant me, of course. Once Hugh leaves the apartment, he's a different person. He forgets all about sex, I'm sure, unless I phone to remind him. I'm not complaining. He thinks I'm crazy, but I'm sure that his secretary, and half the women he works with, are desperate to get his pants off him. Fat chance! I make sure I keep his balls drained, and his interest focused on *me*, except when there's two of us women, sexing him together, of course. I don't count that as infidelity. He can come in, or on, any face, pussy, or ass he likes, provided I'm there to supervise, but his heart has to be true to me, *or else!* That's what I like about Petra, and Nadine, come to that. There are no emotion overtones with them, just unadulterated sex.

I trust pure lust. It's her evil sister, love, I'm wary of.

It was Friday, one of Petra's regular days to visit. She came over in the week sometimes, to see me, but Hugh has to work, and once the three of us got together, it was always a long session. It had become a routine, Fridays and Saturdays, so we could all sleep in the next morning. She never slept over, though. Afraid she might wake with her wig and her make-up gone, I suppose.

She was always prompt at eight, so we ate early. At five to the hour Hugh taped an envelope to our front door, with a note for her. The door was unlocked. She was asked to join us in the bedroom.

We dressed in the pyjamas Petra had given us. You do that, don't you, with gifts? To show you like them? Hugh wore the pants to his, and I wore the top to mine, with heels and hose, in matching pale blue.

At a minute to eight, Hugh lifted me up, with one strong swing, from the floor to the bedhead, and stood me perched precariously on the top rail, with my heels hooked over it. Propping me with one flat hand on my pubes, he climbed up, held my hips as I spread my legs wider, and nuzzled his face into my pussy.

I was just beginning to feel good, when the bedroom door swung open. Petra danced in, wearing a French Maid's outfit, and singing 'Voulez-vous couché avec moi?'.

A tiny white cap perched on top of a riot of dark brown curls. Her false lashes had to be two and a half inches long. Her mouth was a pouting rosebud.

The uniform she wore was exaggerated, even for a French farce. The neckline scooped under her breasts, presenting them for our approval. She'd done her nipples a dark reddish brown, quite like mine in colour, but smaller, of course. I took it as a compliment.

The waist of her dress was cinched tightly by a broad belt. Her skirts flared over a dozen layers of frilly white petticoats. It was short enough to just skim the rosetted garters that held her glossy black hose. Her shoes, as usual, had five-inch spike heels.

She was carrying a tray, with two bottles. One was créme de menthe, the other a chocolate liqueur.

She trilled, in an atrocious accent, "Room service pour M'sieu et Madame! 'Ow can I be of the serveece? 'Ow you like for me to do for to you, please?" She put her tray down and opened the chocolate. "You like theese flavour, maybe perhaps?" Her finger smeared the liqueur on one nipple. She lifted that breast, and sucked it off, smacking her lips. "Ver' nice,

I promise."

I bumped my pubes at Hugh's face. So — Petra was in a playful mood, was she? *And* she'd brought sweet sticky drinks. That made my plan much easier.

"Kick your shoes off and join us up here," I told her. "When m'sieu is done eating, I'm sure he'd like a drink."

"Is Madame not about to give him one?" she asked.

I spread my thighs even wider, leaned back against the wall, grabbed the back of Hugh's head, pulled hard, and ground my sex on his mouth. "Any — minute — now," I gritted. "Hold tight, Hugh. I'm going to screw your face."

Hugh, the darling, gripped my clit with lip-padded teeth. I juddered down at him, hard and fast, bringing myself off quickly.

Jumping down onto the bed, I picked up the créme de menthe. "Okay, French tart, let's see what a French pussy tastes like, when it's all liquored up!"

"What I had in mind," she said, forgetting her accent, "was a treat for Hugh. Did you ever get a long slow blow, Hugh, from a mouth that's full of ice-cold créme de menthe? I'm told it's something special."

"Why don't you demonstrate then?" I offered. "Kneel on the bed, Hugh, and let Petra do her thing. I'll find something to amuse myself with, I'm sure."

And I did. Petra bent to her task, standing beside the bed, stiff-legged, just as I expected. As her mouth worked on Hugh's penis, I found the fastenings for her costume and stripped her down to just heels and hose. I tipped the chocolate bottle over the small of her back, poured a small pool onto white skin, and lapped. Then again, lower, so that the thick liquid trickled between her bum's cheeks. When I'd licked that all away, I went lower again, with the neck of the bottle into her pussy, the way Hugh likes to do with champagne.

It didn't fizz, of course, but I managed to get a good glassfull into her, and smear a good deal more of it over the backs of her legs, and my cheeks.

Hugh was doing his bit, as well. Petra's proud of her ability to let a man piston into her mouth, deep, without gagging. Hugh was doing just that, and each thrust had to be pumping créme de menthe down her throat. Every few minutes he'd pause, and demand, "More!" so that Petra would refill her mouth.

By the time Hugh rinsed the last mouthful down on the gush of his orgasm, a third of the bottle was gone. At my end, I'd smeared about the same quantity of the chocolate over Petra's rump and thighs, with yet more finger-painted on her pubes and breasts.

"My God!" Hugh said. "You two look a mess!"

I knelt to remove Petra's shoes and hose, disguising what I was doing with caresses. Standing, I did the same to myself, and said, "Well, I'm for a shower. Coming Petra? You want to watch, Hugh?"

Hugh said, "I wouldn't miss it. Come on Petra, Millie in the shower an exhibition by itself."

She drew back. "I — I don't think... No, no shower for me, thanks."

Hugh grabbed her wrist. "Never mind. Come and watch then. I'll clean you off with a nice warm wash-cloth."

When Hugh tugs you, you go. He's a very gentle man, but inexorable, when he uses part of his strength. Petra stumbled after him, into our bathroom.

The quarter-circle shower stall has a sliding glass door. I left it open. Water was going to splash out onto the floor, but it's tiled, and it was in a good cause.

Hugh stood Petra in the opening, where she could watch me easily. I turned on both showers, the wall-mounted one and the hand-held, wet and soaked a wash-cloth, and passed it out to them.

I can make a big production out of a shower, when I've got an audience. I started with a foamy sponge, all over, but particularly on my breasts. Next came the loofah-strip. I held it between my legs, one hand in front and the other behind, and slithered it hard on my pussy, first holding still and letting my hands do the work, and then holding it still and jerking my hips.

It folded between my lips, of course. The surface of a loofah is quite rough, but when it's soapy, what it does to my inner lips and my clit is just heaven.

Hugh was being true to his word, just wiping Petra down from behind.

"There's a lot of that chocolate stuff inside her," I reminded him.

"Pass me the other loofah then," he asked, "the long stiff one."

I soaped it, and passed it. He knelt behind her, urged her thighs further apart, and began to work the sea-cucumber skeleton into her pussy. He does that to me, sometimes. It looks impossible, with the loofah being so big, but it compresses. Getting it inside is nice, but the best part is when he rotates it, and all the roughness scours the sensitive parts inside you.

As he rotated, and Petra clung to the sides of the doorway, I switched to the hand-held shower. I adjusted it to 'jet', and 'pulse', and held it two inches from my clit.

Petra was squirming back at Hugh's hand. My clit was

throbbing in time to the hot water's pulse. When I saw Petra's eyes start to glaze, I quickly lathered my pubes and mouthed, "Now!" at Hugh.

He pushed. Petra stumbled into the shower, on her knees. I grabbed behind her head and ground her face into my belly, pretending to be overcome by lust, but slyly plucking clips from her curly wig.

My pubes spread lather over Petra's face. I rinsed it with the shower head, and smeared more on.

She must have realised that she was losing her precious mask. She stood up, leaving her wig in my hands, and tried to back out. Hugh was in her way. I sprayed her, from toe to face, dissolving every last trace of makeup.

"No!" she sobbed.

Hugh let her push past him, and then wrapped her in his strong arms, from behind. She wriggled and screamed and kicked, trying to cover her head and face, but Hugh had her trapped. He walked her to the vanity and pressed her against the counter. I'm sure that he enjoyed every wriggle of her soapy wet bottom against his rigid penis.

"Look at yourself!" he demanded.

Her eyes had been screwed tight, but when Hugh uses that tone of voice, you do what he says. He doesn't threaten. He doesn't have to. Her pale eyes, teary, blinked at her own reflection.

Hugh changed his grip, holding her face in one hand and trapping her wrists behind her with the other. "What is it with you, Petra? What are you hiding from? What don't you like about the way you look?"

"My hair — my eyes — my skin — my nipples... so pale, so colourless, so, so..."

"Do you know what we see, when we look at the real you,

Petra? We look at your hair, and think that someone has poured liquid diamonds into a cotton-candy machine. Your hair isn't colourless, Petra, it sparkles, with every colour.

"Your eyes? What we see is a morning mist, laying in the hollows of a lush lawn. They're pale, Petra, beautifully pale, with just a hint of green, deep beneath their surfaces.

"Your skin? We love it! It's a field of fresh snow, carved by the wind to form shoulders, piled into drifts, for your breasts. You know what fresh snow does to you, Petra? It makes you want to walk on it. It urges you to defile it. It's so pristine pure and white, you can't help but want to leave marks on it, like this."

He bent his mouth to the junction of her neck and shoulder. His teeth savaged her.

Perhaps it's in our genes. Perhaps primitive women, feeling dominant males' teeth on their necks, knew they had a clear choice, sexual surrender or death. Maybe they knew they had just a few moments to decide, and signal their compliance to their masters.

Dogs expose their throats to other dogs, as signals of submission. Foxes take the slack skin at vixen's napes between their teeth. As soon as the vixens feel that threatening grip, their hormones take over. They arch their tails, and their rears. Their vulvas moisten. It's the same pattern throughout the mammalian kingdom. A male's teeth, gripping, triggers an intense sexual response in the female.

I know it works for me. One nip from Hugh, at my nape, or his teeth worrying the hollow of my shoulder, and the nerves that radiate from those spots seem to cringe deliciously. The thrill of it crackles through my body, to my nipples and my pussy, and I'm in instant heat.

Petra fought her natural response. She squirmed, desperate

at first, but as his mouth worked, her struggles turned into an arching writhe.

When he released her flesh, the shape of his mouth was livid on her skin. Twin arcs showed where his teeth had been. She was panting. There was lust in her eyes. Even if she wasn't willing to admit it yet, he'd reached something primordial inside her.

"Your nipples?" he continued. "Pale? Of course they are, exotically so. You know the delicate icicles that come from an ice-storm, turning the countryside into a fairy-land? That's what your nipples are, spikes of ice, with the dawn tinting them. You know what people do to those tempting icicles? Show her, Millie."

He half-turned her, so that I could get my mouth to one bloodless nipple, and suckle greedily. I was determined to *make* it redden, if I had to suck for an hour.

"You see, Petra? The real you is gorgeous. There's no reason to hide from us."

"But — I can't *feel* when I'm like this," she sobbed. "My body just doesn't respond."

"Nonsense!" he told her. "Millie, sit up on the counter. Petra, watch yourself in the mirror. Watch your eyes. Look at the lust we are going to bring to them."

He pulled her back. I hitched up onto the counter and bracketed her thighs with my own.

Hugh whispered into Petra's ear. "Millie wants you, don't you Millie?"

I laid a finger on my clit's shaft and eased its hood back. "Of course I do. You're lovely, Petra. See what you do to me?"

She looked down at my pink pearl, glistening above the parted lips of my cleft. "But..."

My fingers found *her* clit, exposed it, and drew it to mine.

"You see? They want each other, just as my mouth wants your nipple." I wobbled our clits together, bent my head, and nibbled at the tip of her nipple, giving sharp little sucks to the very point.

"I'm going to make love to you, Petra, to the real you," Hugh said. "Try to resist all you want, but I'm going to be inside you, deep inside. Deny it if you like, but your body won't lie."

He released her face and fumbled behind her. I saw a brief shock twist her face before it became stubbornly impassive. Hugh's arm, a solid bar across her waist, folded her forward. Her hips lifted between my thighs with a soft hiss, silk gliding over silk, as Hugh impaled her, very slowly, from behind. I pinched her nipple with one hand, still sliding our clits together with the other. My mouth caressed her shoulders and her neck, nuzzling where Hugh had bitten.

Hugh's body curved over her back. His tongue traced her spine. I winked at him, over her shoulder.

She kept stiff for a long time. She didn't move when I tweaked her nipple, nor when my tongue squirmed into her ear. I let my mouth trail across her cheek, to her mouth. Her lips were sealed tight.

Hugh moved her though. His hips surged, strong as a slowly rolling sea, lifting her onto her toes, and letting her settle back again.

Her lips softened under mine. My tongue probed. I plucked on her nipple, drew it to mine, and rolled the two nubs together.

"Look," I said. "See how lovely they look together? My dark cone, your icy spike?"

She groaned, softly. Her hips twitched, not moved by Hugh, but of their own accord.

"We want you, Petra," he said. "Both of us. We love your body. We want it bad. Millie is going to climax soon, I can see it in her eyes. It's you who is doing that to her, Petra, the real naked you. Me too. I love the feel of my thighs against the backs of yours. I love the softness of your bottom against my belly. My penis — it's begging me to pound into you, Petra, but I'm holding back. You're so tight, and hot, and wet, in there. I can feel your muscles, Petra. They're squeezing on me. They want it. Tell me when, Petra. It's up to you. Tell me..."

"Do me, you bastard!" she screamed. "Do me deep! Come, both of you. Scald me with your come, damn you!"

Her belly juddered, driving her clit against mine and thrusting back on Hugh. We both froze, and let her. She was sandwiched between our rigid bodies, writhing and bucking. Her tongue lashed my mouth. She ground her lips on mine and sucked my tongue until its roots ached. Her shoulders shook, slapping her breasts on mine. Petra had become a flash-flood, released on us suddenly, punishing and overwhelming everything she touched.

She broke into a fevered sweat. Her eyes glared with hate, love, lust, desperation. She was ferocious, a demoness of desire, released from an imprisoning bottle after centuries of frustration. She sobbed, she keened, she bellowed hard and deep enough to rupture her throat.

Finally, she jerked three times, her eyes staring into mine, intense beacons of desire, her mouth twisted into a twitching rictus grin.

She slumped, and would have fallen had we not held her.

"Carry her to the bed, Hugh," I said. "We haven't finished with Petra, the real Petra, yet."

XXV

Petra

illie taught me how to go shopping again. I don't mean, 'how to buy things'. When 'Patricia' became 'Petra', she didn't stop buying, she bought more, in fact. 'Petra' had ample money, where 'Patricia' had never had enough.

I guess what Millie taught me was how to go shopping, with nothing particular to buy, in the company of another woman, and have fun doing it. For the ten years before Millie and Hugh, I'd sent myself, in other guises, to get whatever I needed, or I used catalogues — paper ones at first, and then most often electronic.

Once I'd established my relationships with my seamstress, my wig-maker, and my cosmetician, I just had to fax or e-mail, to get supplies. Hairdressers get personal, which was one reason I kept my hair cropped, and did it myself.

I'd cocooned myself. My work was solitary, and secret. My money wrapped me in thick warm layers. Human contact had dwindled, until the only people I could claim as friends were those whose quirks shifted them *sideways* from the normal human spectrum. Even those, I could only tolerate in small doses, preferably at a distance.

With so little human contact I hadn't been exposed to people's coughs and sneezes, nor their envy of my success, or their disapproval of how I'd achieved it.

They'd been protected from me, as well. People are attracted by surface appearances. In my youth, I'd learned to win approval by being a chameleon, showing people whatever 'me' I thought they'd be charmed by. That had proved dangerous. I was too good at it. Men, and women, fell for the seductive illusions I showed them. Then I was under obligation, wasn't I? If I stopped pretending, they'd be hurt.

My self-imposed quarantine worked two ways. It protected me, and it protected the rest of the world.

Hugh and Millie called me 'Ice-Queen'. They were right, I had been, in every way, not just in my frosty appearance. I'd lived on one side of a pane of ice, observing the world through bleary smears, untouchable, unable to touch. My new friends, Millie and Hugh, had melted that barrier. They were teaching me the joys of warm human contact, all over again.

It was risky. I knew that. I had to have faith in the strength of Hugh and Millie's mutual emotional bonding, to protect them from me. Me from them?

Despite the dangers, the rewards were too enticing for me to resist. It wasn't just the sex. I had — Patricia had — cuddled people, once.

I slithered my bum across the booth's bench seat and nudged Millie with it. My arm circled her narrow waist. I gave her a squeeze.

"What was that for?"

"Just because I felt like it."

"Uninhibited, are you?"

"You betcha! Didn't I demonstrate, in the last store?"

It'd been our favourite, 'Sluts'. I don't know if the girl had recognised us, even though we were regular customers. I'd pinned Millie's riotous hair down flat, and fitted her with a wig that matched mine, waist-long, straight, and blonde. With the same make-up, the same big black picture hats, the same black and white polka dot blouses and matching wrap-around skirts, and identical skyscraper-heeled pumps, we could have passed for twins, despite the difference in our shapes.

The giggling fits had started even earlier than Sluts. Millie had been outrageous in the lingerie department of Lord and Taylor's, insisting that we call each other 'Blondie', to confuse the sales staff, walking out of the changing room to ask my opinion of the see-through hostess gown that was all she had on, and finally dragging me into the cubicle after her, for a quick kiss and a fondle, leaving the door wide open.

She hadn't done it because she'd been overcome by lust. She did it just to shock — to be 'naughty'. Maybe it had been a test? To see if I'd go along? If it had been, I'd passed.

We'd been close to hysterics by the time we'd got to Sluts. You know the mood? When a smudge on someone's nose can make you dissolve into uncontrollable laughter?

It was the wrong mood, or maybe the right one, to take into a sex-store. If we hadn't been buying so much, they'd likely have thrown us out. Most of Sluts' customers treat the place like a shrine — hushed voices, averted eyes, tippy-toe creeping about, carefully avoiding any human contact.

We two, by contrast, commented loudly on every toy, every gadget, and every garment. Between us, we virtually emptied the exotic end of the dildo display. We sneered at the hairy plastic pussies and inflatable love-dolls, suggested that the eighteen-inch knitted 'cock-warmers' were designed to fit under-equipped castrato midgets, and complained to the teenage assistant that some of her vibrators that we'd bought on a prior visit had died after only fifty or sixty hours of continuous use.

After that, we needed a drink and a sit down, which took us to 'Sombrero Jack's', a Chicago-style 'meeting, eating and drinking' place. The 'eating' meant gigantic greasy burgers, herbed fries, tiny limp salads, chicken wings in a 'heat' range from 'warm lips' to 'blister-tongue', and a five-item 'Tex-Mex' insert in the menu.

The 'meeting' meant shadowy booths, on multi-split levels, so that bosses could grope their secretaries without being seen.

Their drinks list reinforced the 'meeting' message, with names like 'Between the Sheets', 'Long Slow Screwdriver' and 'Bottoms Up'. Still, they were all a full three ounces, which made up for a lot.

Millie sipped her 'Randy Rooster', and slipped a hand under the wrap of my skirt. 'Petra,' she said, 'how do you feel about S&M, D&S, Bondage, and that sort of thing?' Her fingers pinched the bare skin inside my thigh, just above my stocking top.

I flinched. "How — how exactly do you mean?"

"I mean — have you tried that scene, and did you like it?"

"On which side of the fence?"

"Either. With your extraordinary versatility, you could fit into most roles, couldn't you?" Her fingers patted my mound through the wisp of silk that almost covered it.

It sounded like a challenge. I had to think about that.

"You claim to be totally uninhibited, after all," she added.

"What did you have in mind?" I asked.

She picked up one of the glossy pink plastic 'Sluts' bags and her purse and put them both on the table. "Somewhere in here..." She pulled a package of double-A batteries from her purse. "Here," she said, setting the batteries and the 'Handy-Dandy, Use Anywhere' vibrator that she'd bought, side-by-side. "Load it, please, Petra."

She signalled to a waitress for another round of drinks. I unscrewed the base of the four-inch black cylinder and was just thumbing a battery into it when the girl brought another 'Randy Rooster' and a fresh 'Hot Mexican'. She turned red, and stuttered over her ritual, "Enjoy", when she saw what I was doing.

"How was that?" I asked, when the girl was gone.

"Now use it," Millie said.

"Here? Now?"

"It's supposed to be 'Use Anywhere', isn't it?"

"But..?"

"Do it, Petra. Do it, knowing that the girl knows that you're doing it."

"She won't be able to see anything."

"No — but she'll know." Millie glanced down and to the side, at the bar two levels lower. "She's pretending not to, but she's watching this booth. Do it now, Petra, unless you're chicken."

I shrugged, to show I didn't care, and moved the vibrator to my lap. Millie helped. Her hand, still inside my skirt, fingered the crotch of my panties to one side, and parted my lips for me.

"I want to feel the buzzing," she said.

I slid the plastic between the 'v' of Millie's fingers, and into my sex. A twist of the base started it humming. "There," I said. "Is that what you wanted me to do?"

"Work it. I want you to get off on it."

I turned my head to look into her eyes. "You're a bitch, aren't you, Millie?"

"Yes. Now do it." The heel of her palm moulded my mound, squeezing and pressing down. Her fingers pinched my sex's lips tight around the toy. A high-pitched drone filled my sex. She had to be able to feel the vibration. She had to be able to hear it. If there was anyone in the next booth, they had to be able to hear it as well.

"It'll take a long while," I complained. "It's not that big. You're really supposed to use it on directly your clit. The feeling isn't intense enough to..."

"You want to swap it, for a bigger one?"

"No — no. I'll get there, I promise."

"Good girl. As you're so willing, I'll help you."

Her finger found my clit's head and pressed down hard, compressing it between the ball of her finger and the vibrator, doubling the intensity of the sensations it was beginning to enjoy.

"Tell me when you're ready," she said.

"Soon. Very soon. Very very... I'm..."

Millie twisted on her seat. Her free hand took the nape of my neck and turned my face to hers. Just as the short sharp spasms hit me, her mouth covered mine, demanding and avaricious. It was as if she was sucking my climax from me.

"Satisfactory," she said as she released me. "We'll continue this later, but for now..." She dropped a fifty on the table. "The girl deserves a good tip, don't you think? Let's go."

My legs were wobbly all the way to my car.

Millie checked her watch. "Hurry up, Petra. Hugh will be home at five today. We have to get ourselves ready for him."

"Lots of time," I said. "It's only just gone three."

"This time it'll be special. You're still a voyeur, aren't you?" She squeezed my thigh. "And you've been dying to see me wearing my 'special' jewellery? Now's your chance. I'm going to dress up fancy for my Hugh, and give him a nice surprise."

"Should we stop off at my place first? What would you like me to wear?"

"That's all taken care of, Petra dear. You just leave everything to your Auntie Millie. I've got it all planned."

There was no one else in the world I'd have surrendered control to, but Millie had taken charge before, hadn't she? That evening, in the bathroom? It had worked out for the best, hadn't it? I comforted myself with the memory, but I still had a queasy feeling in my stomach.

The first thing she did in her apartment was pour us long strong drinks. "Drink it down," she said. "You'll need it."

Still a touch nervous, but excited at the same time, I obeyed, finishing it in one long swallow. "Now what?" I asked.

"Turn around."

I turned my back to her. She took the hat from my head and pulled my arms behind me. I felt cord loop my wrists.

"Bondage games?"

"That's right. Hold still."

She had to have had everything ready. A strip of black cloth looped over my head, blindfolding me. She knotted it tight. I shivered. There's a big difference between being restrained when you can see what is going on — what is being done to you — and being both helpless and blind.

"What are you going to do to me?" I asked.

"Nothing painful. Don't worry. It's going to be a treat for you as well as for Hugh. Come with me."

She steered me, to the living room I guessed, and sat me down on a straight chair. My arms were lifted over to hang down the back. I felt her thread another cord through the one that bound my wrists, pull down on it, and anchor it somewhere low.

"You're going to be what we call a 'captive audience'," she said.

"I won't see much, will I? Or does the blindfold come off?"

"Later, perhaps." Her fingers fumbled at the waist of my skirt. "Lift your bum."

I did. She tugged the skirt from under me.

"Again."

My panties were pulled down my legs, and off. The chair had a cut-velvet seat. The pile prickled my naked skin. It felt good under my sex.

"The heels and stockings can stay," she said. "They'll make a nice touch."

"How about the blouse?" I had to say it. Making the suggestion gave me some small illusion that I retained a measure of control over what happened to me.

"Just a minute."

I heard the snipping sound of scissors cutting air. A chill trickled down my spine. Cold hard steel pressed against the base of my throat. I held my breath. The blades snipped once more, and again, severing cloth. The steel was between my quivering breasts. Snip. Snip. I felt my blouse fall apart down the front. The scissors touched my nape. The shock of frigid steel, so terribly *close* to my spine, paralysed me.

"Lean forward."

She glided the blades in one long slithery cut, from my neck to the small of my back. Two more quick cuts to each side slit my sleeves. Fabric tugged, and I was naked, except for heels, hose, and blindfold.

"Are you done?" I asked, in what I hoped was a brave voice.

"No. Not yet."

She bound my ankles to the chair's legs. A cord circled my left thigh, just above my knee, was drawn under the chair, and tied around my right one, binding me to the seat again, and holding my thighs apart. She did it again, higher, above my stocking tops, close to my groin.

Millie adjusted the bonds, drawing them tight, tighter. They cut grooves into my flesh, not deep enough to stop my circulation, but deep enough to mark.

"I guess I'm helpless."

"Yes you are, totally, but I'm still not done."

The next one went around my waist and the centre slat of the chair's back, tight again. One immediately beneath my breasts, and then one above them, compressing their soft flesh. All tight. All very tight.

The final two cords passed over my shoulders and crossed between my breasts.

The people at the Janus club, who'd let me photograph their games, once, would have referred to it as 'mild', 'vanilla', or 'cosmetic' bondage. I had to agree. There was no real discomfort, if I didn't struggle. There was just that feeling of total helplessness that is inevitable when you can't move, at all, and you can't see, either.

I felt Millie's lips move on mine, soft and loving. That's often the way, I'm told. Bond-masters, or mistresses, are often filled with warm affection towards someone they've just tied up. I hoped the surge of fond emotion wasn't *too* strong. I've also been told, 'The stronger the love, the tighter the knots'. With some people, 'You always hurt the one you love' isn't a way of apologising for a carelessly cruel word. It's a way of life.

Millie knelt before me. Her fingers caressed my cheek, softly. "You know that this could stop, right now, don't you? It's up to you, Petra. One word, while you still can, and I'll release you. No hard feelings, either way. Do you want me to untie you?"

"No," I said. "I'm helpless, but I trust you. Do to me whatever you are going to do, Millie."

"Are you sure? Really sure? I could do anything to you — anything at all." The tips of her fingers rested on the points of my nipples, barely touching them.

"I'm sure, Millie."

"Very well." She stood up. "Open your mouth, wide."

It was exactly what I'd been dreading from the moment she'd offered me the chance to ask for my release, "while you still can".

I stretched my mouth. A hard rubber ball forced it even wider. I'd seen them, in specialised stores, and other places. A rod, usually chromed, that spiked through a ball of hard rubber, usually black. There'd be straps running from the ends of the rod, to fasten behind my head.

Millie lifted the long hair of my wig up, drew the strap tight, fastened it, and let the hair fall back over it. I could feel the metal rod, pulling back on the corners of my mouth. My jaws started to ache, and it had only been a moment.

"You couldn't even scream now, could you, if I was to hurt you?" Her fingers touched my nipples again in a gentle threat.

I shook my head.

"You can't see, either. I could be preparing — implements — couldn't I? You wouldn't know, until you felt them."

I felt a tiny prick on the soft underside of my breast. It had to be just the point of her nail. I knew that this was part of the S&M bondage game, just a ritual, nothing to be taken seriously, but the skin on my belly crawled. My anus knotted.

"Now you must wait," she said. "Now that *you* are prepared, I must ready myself for *my* master."

Then there was just an echoing silence.

My mind calculated. It had been gone three o'clock when she'd checked the time, in the car. Say three-twenty, when we got to the apartment. A few minutes to pour drinks and down them. Two more to bind my wrists and cover my eyes. Say I sat down on the chair at twenty-five after the hour.

Okay — stripping me, cutting off my blouse, the rest of the

tying? Ten more minutes? Say eight, to be sure. The kiss, the gag, the gloating and teasing? Another six minutes, minimum. That made it about ten to four. She expected Hugh at five. I had an hour and ten minutes to wait.

When Hugh got home, something would happen. It might be more bondage, or something else entirely. It didn't matter to me what it was, provided it was *something*. I'd been bound, blindfolded, and gagged, for just a few minutes, but it seemed like a numb eternity already.

It wasn't sensory-deprivation. Not really. I could still hear, if there had been any noise. I could still wriggle, and feel the cords cut deeper. It was just sight that I was being denied — sight — and freedom of movement.

I could stand that, for seventy more minutes, or perhaps sixty-five, by then. My mouth was incredibly dry already. How much time had passed? A moment of panic swamped me, and then I did all I could do.

Sixty-five minutes is three thousand nine hundred seconds — call it four thousand. I started counting. A thousand and one, a thousand and two...

"Welcome home, darling!" Millie's voice shocked me from somewhere about two feet in front of me. How long had she been there, just looking at me in silence?

Hugh's voice chuckled. "A present? For me? Gift wrapped? Thank you, Millie darling."

I felt a large warm hand on my naked shoulder.

"There's something quick for you in the kitchen," Millie said. "Eat and get changed, darling. Poor Petra has been waiting patiently for such a long time."

The hand left my shoulder, leaving it bitterly lonely. How long would he take, to eat and change? Ten minutes?

One thousand and one, one thousand and two...

Hugh's voice asked, "What are you hiding, Millie, under

that ugly kaftan?"

"A surprise I've been keeping for you for a long time, waiting for an extra special moment. Do you want to see?"

"Of course, but what about Petra? Isn't she supposed to see your surprise?"

I nodded violently, even though I didn't know whether either of them was looking at me.

"You're too kind, sometimes Hugh," Millie said. "Okay — uncover her eyes and take the gag out of her mouth, if you like. I'll fetch drinks. She'll be quite thirsty by now."

Light — blessed bright light. Then fingers at the back of my head, and the rubber ball was eased from my aching mouth. My eyes blinked. I worked my jaw. I couldn't speak. My tongue felt as if someone would have to prise it from the roof of my mouth first.

Strong fingers pressed the hinges of my jaws, massaging them to life. Cold glass pressed against my lower lip. I let my mouth sag open. Water flowed in. It felt as if my tongue expanded as it soaked up water. My throat remembered how to swallow.

"Thank you," I managed to croak.

"You are very beautiful, bound like this," Hugh said. "Tight cords compliment the tender purity of your soft white skin."

I was swamped with gratitude at his kind words. I knew that an irrational emotional fixation is a common response to a 'captive situation', particularly when some sensory deprivation is involved, but I couldn't help it. At that moment I loved them both, with all my heart.

"Are you okay now?" Millie asked.

"Fine, thanks, thanks very much."

"Something more to drink, stronger?"

"More water, first, if it isn't too much trouble."

She gave me more water, and then poured vodka and lime

between my lips.

"Thank you."

My eyes focused. Millie had discarded the blonde wig I'd given her. Her hair was its own tousled self again. Her make-up was theatrical, a 'witch-queen' creation that I had taught her. I felt a glow of pride that she had been willing to learn from me, and use what she'd learned.

The golden cascade earrings that she wore descended from her delicate lobes to brush her shoulders.

"Don't keep us in suspense, Millie," Hugh said. "Get rid of the damned kaftan, darling. Unveil."

"Very well." She stood straight. Her fingers undid the volu-minous robe's fastenings. She let it drop.

Millie was a barbarian empress straight out of some x-rated Swords and Sorcery fantasy. A dozen gold chains of various weights and lengths hung around her neck, forming a mail collar. Each of her wrists were weighed down by bracelets. Gold bands circled her biceps. Her ankles were heavy with gold. Her body...

She'd done incredible things to her breasts. Somehow she'd forced her over-sized nipples through golden rings that were a fraction less in circumference than her halos. Those soft, cof-fee-toned aureoles had followed, so that the rings gripped them, puffing them into swollen prominence.

She'd used smaller rings, tiny ones, to trap the tips of her nipples. A chain ran from each, up, around the back of her neck. Her nipples were tugged upwards. The divine heaviness of her breasts was suspended from them, giving her an 'uplift', not from beneath, but from her breasts' tips. Each move she made, each step she took, every slightest sway of her body, had to tug on those sensitive spikes of reddish-brown flesh.

I swallowed, hard.

Lower, running in a line from just below her cleavage to the paste jewel in her navel, was a row of tiny diamanté studs, each mounted on a minute, skin-pinching, clip. A golden chain cinched her narrow waist. Two more chains strained down from that one, following the lines of her groin, to disappear beneath a brief gold satin skirt that draped low on her hips. Its fringes brushed her thighs as she swayed there, posing, sucking up our lustful admiration.

And I didn't have a camera. I wouldn't have been able to use it, if I'd had one.

"Millie," Hugh sighed. "You are totally magnificent!"

"I am but your slave, my master," she said. "And your slave lives only to please you." She turned to me. "Petra, my love, you have spent hours watching Hugh and me, in secret, haven't you?"

I nodded.

"And playing with yourself as you watched?"

I nodded again.

"And that is what you are going to do now. I am going to make love to my man, and you are going to watch us. You'd like that, wouldn't you?"

Once more, all I could do was nod.

"This time, though, you are going to have to work for your pleasure. Your orgasms won't come cheap."

"How..?" I croaked, turning my bound wrists to show that I had no way to reach my sex with my fingers.

"First," Millie said as she produced two more items of jewellery, "these, for your nipples."

I cringed. What she showed me could have been earrings, but I knew it wasn't my lobes that were going to feel their clips' sharp bite.

My nipples were already erect, but Millie's fingers coaxed them to a more vibrant length. She clipped the jewellery to them. Silver pendants tugged my peaks cruelly. Thin chains hung from each viciously nipping clasp. At the end of each chain dangled a silver ball, half the size of an egg, but unnaturally heavy.

"They're filled with mercury," Millie explained. "That's almost as heavy as lead, but it's liquid, right?"

Her finger moved one ball, swaying it. As it swung like a pendulum, it dragged my nipple to one side, and then the other. The mercury jiggled inside the ball, so that no movement was smooth, but bounced around in an irregular, unpredictable motion, sometimes bobbing, sometimes spinning.

"You see, Petra?" Millie gloated. "You may be bound, but you can still twitch. Flex your muscles, Petra, and see how the balls dance. *Do it!*"

I flexed. The balls flopped and flipped and jigged. Each motion pulled at my nipples, not always both at once, but alternately, in no regular rhythm, a random movement. There was no way I could brace myself in preparation for the next twitching torture.

"But you couldn't climax from just that, could you?" she said. "You might not manage an orgasm, anyway, but I am going to give you a chance to work towards one."

I felt myself tense. She knelt between my thighs. Her hand held a third silver ball, twice the size of the other two. Its clip was longer. The chains were strings of silver balls, two of them, fastened one to either side of the clip.

Millie's fingers stroked the hood of my clit back. What I had seen, what had been done to my poor nipples, had already prepared me. My clit's head popped out, glistening, swollen. The clip bracketed my shaft behind the soft pea at its head, tight, but not painful. Now there was no way for my clit's tender bud to retract into its protective hood. It was pinned out — exposed — with no possible retreat.

Millie arranged the two strings of silver balls, one to each side of my clit-head, and let the big ball swing free. It jiggled as if it were alive. The tiny balls caressed my clit with each sway.

"Some lubricant would be kind," Millie mused. She squirted oil from a plastic bottle, gushing it over my clit's head.

"Yes." Her fingers moved the chains. They flipped over my exposed nub.

I bit my lip and jerked my hips, desperate for more of that cold impersonal caress.

"Wobble on your bum," Millie advised me. "That'll keep the ball swaying. Who knows, perhaps you'll manage to come? You can only try, right?"

"What torment did you have in mind for me, my love?" Hugh asked.

"Torment? Oh no, my master. For you — only pleasure. If my master would disrobe, and seat himself upon the couch?"

Hugh obeyed. Millie knelt at his feet. He was already fully erect, his column wagging, his glans bare and swollen to purple ripeness.

She poured oil over it, and into her palm. "If my master will just relax? Don't move, please, my darling. Let your slave serve you."

Hugh grunted and leaned back, stabbing air with his straining penis. Millie anointed it with yet more oil, until its full length glistened and ran. Her hand circled it, and stroked slowly upwards. Her palm smoothed over its head, cupped and rotated, before slithering back down its stem.

She poured again, slathering him from dome to dangling testicles. Her hand pumped faster, whipping oil into a creamy lather. Two hands, stroking, kneading, polishing. Hugh's grin spread wide and tight. The muscles in his thighs bunched. Sinews stood out on his neck. Muscles twitched and jumped.

I squirmed, sending three torturing balls into teasing

motion. My nipples were *demanding* more. The twin chains flipped over my clit, and back, all too gently, even though I managed to raise my hips a fraction and buck as they swung. Hugh grunted again, deep in his chest. His penis had been fully engorged at the beginning, and yet it grew still longer under Millie's slippery ministrations. The long ridge that ran its underside pulsed. His glans was an overripe plum, dripping oil, ready to burst from internal pressure.

Through a straining throat, he squeezed, "If you plan to make me come this way, you wonderful slut-bitch, I'm very close."

"No," she said, slowing her strokes. "I want you *in* me. I want to feel your hot cream spurt."

"Then get that damned skirt off!"

"Very well." She stood and turned sideways to him, half towards me. "Pull it off yourself, then."

He tugged. The scrap of golden fabric fell away. Hugh and I both stared.

The two chains that ran down from her golden belt, outlining the soft swell of Millie's lovely belly, ended at her clit. The clip that gripped her ridge was similar to the one that held my hood back. Like mine, her clit's head was exposed, unable to retract. Her sheath had been forcibly withdrawn even more harshly than mine had, for the chains strained it upwards.

"My God!" Hugh exclaimed. "Isn't that uncomfortable?"

"No," she replied, "It feels rather nice, but *this* is."

Her thighs parted. She thrust her pubes up and forward, tucking her rear under, showing us her sex. There was a line of clips, little golden clips, running the full length of her pucker, clamping its lips tightly together. Her vulva had engorged since she'd applied that self-torture. The indentations were deep, biting puffy flesh. When they were removed, they'd leave dents, like teeth marks, that would need massaging, or kissing, away. My mouth watered.

"Get them off!" Hugh barked. "I want into you!"

"No — master! In me, yes, but not that way. I want you in my ass, please? Bugger me? Sodomise me, my love? Ream my tight little hole? Be merciless. Take me as a master takes a worthless slave."

She knelt on the edge of the couch's seat, her back hollowed and her rump tilted upwards. "Do it, please Hugh! Use me! Take me!"

Millie buried her head in a cushion. One hand parted her own cheeks. Two fingers of her other hand forced their greasy way into her anus, at first just their tips, then one joint of each, and then two.

The fingers parted, spreading her flesh, straining her sphincter open wide.

"Do it! Do it now!"

Hugh took his position behind her, looming over her, looking twice her size. Twice her breadth. Four times her strength. With a rampant weapon that was infinitely thicker than its intended sheath's capacity.

What he intended, what she had invited, was an act of love — cruel love. That's the most intense kind, isn't it?

He laid the glistening column the length of her crease. His fingers plucked hers out of his way. His glans nudged at her tiny 'o'. He leaned closer. His hard dome dimpled Millie's softness. Oil ran down the slope of his column, pooled in the indentation his pressure made, overflowed it, and trickled down the backs of Millie's thighs.

Hugh pressed.

Like a greedy little mouth opening to engulf an orange whole, her anus parted. It was Millie's turn to grunt, but she didn't flinch. She pushed back at him, slowly impaling herself. His glans sank in to half its depth, more, more. The rubbery mouth closed on his stem, trapping the hard egg-plant purple globe that capped it.

His hips pressed. His hands pulled her thighs. Inch by inch, the thick column was forced deeper, and deeper, until, at last, his pubes pressed against the base of her spine.

"Now do it!" she sobbed. "Do me hard — no mercy — use me!"

Her hands stretched back to him, imploring. He grabbed her wrists, and tugged, probing one more impossible inch, flattening her rump on his hard thighs. Her arms were stiff. He pushed. She moved forwards.

I watched in awed fascination as the monstrous piston withdrew an inch, three, six, and more, until his glans was stretching her sphincter once more, from the inside. Hugh paused.

And he thrust. As he yanked back on her arms, he lunged forward with his hips, lancing her rectum.

Millie squealed. Sounds came from her throat, deep, inhuman, animal sounds. She slobbered and gurgled. Grunts of joy distorted her mouth. Her chest heaved, sucking air. Her belly rippled. Her hips twitched.

As she arched her back, the strain on the chains that ran from her neck to her nipples distorted and lifted her breasts. Her spasmodic jerking had to be working the clip on her clitoral ridge, masturbating her in its metal grip. I could only imagine what the stretch and strain on her skin was doing to the lips of her tight-clipped sex.

As Hugh pounded his wife, I gyrated on my seat, rubbing my own sex's lips, spreading them on velvet nap. My panting tugged at my tethered nipples. The weight that dangled between my legs swung wildly. Metal balls flipped across my clit's desperate head. I reached my brink, and *willed* myself to climax, but, even though I hovered there in desperate need, I just *couldn't* drive myself over the edge.

"Yes!" Millie screamed. She fell forwards, onto her belly, dragging her rectum from Hugh's stalk.

He'd climaxed. She'd come. It must have been the scalding flood, deep inside her, that had finished her. Liquid white trickled from her anus. More hung in sticky strands from the eye of Hugh's penis.

"Me!" I shouted. "Me, me, me!"

Millie rolled onto her back and looked at me speculatively.

"What would you do for it, Petra? What would you do, for an orgasm, for release?"

"Anything," I sobbed. "Let me come, for God's sake."

She stood in one lithe flowing movement. "Anything? Anything at all? You'll serve us, in any way we demand? Very well, Petra, we'll put you to the test."

I left their apartment at three that morning, wearing a cloak that Millie lent me over my naked body. I was sore, weary to the marrow of my bones. The lips of my sex were so swollen and bruised I walked bow-legged. My legs tottered. My nipples were so tender that the silk lining of Millie's cloak chaffed them. My breasts felt as if they had been permanently distorted into new shapes. My mouth was tired. My lips felt twice their normal size. My tongue ached to its roots. I had never been so sated, nor so tired, in my entire life.

I didn't go straight to my bed, though. There were marks on my body, interesting marks, weals, scratches, bruises, cord-burns, that my camera had to record before their obscene beauty faded.

XXVI

Millie

I was intoxicated with Petra. I was drunk on my power over her. We'd *peeled* the Ice-Queen's false frigid skin, that night, in the bathroom. Beneath it, we'd found the real quivering raw flesh.

She was putty. I'd exposed her, and could mould her, but that wasn't enough for me. Petra had been living a lie — a series of lies, for a long long time. Even now, now that she was able to really feel, I still didn't think my task was done. What was she like — really like — deep in her psyche?

She'd acted for so long. Was she still acting? Were there more layers to peel away, before the true Petra emerged?

It'd be for her own good — therapy. Any pleasure that Hugh and I might feel during the process was entirely incidental.

I'd tried her as a submissive, and she'd responded nicely, but was that still yet another role for her to play? Perhaps the real

Petra was dominant, sadistic, even? Submissive is the flip side of dominant, isn't it?

I'd seen her as a voyeur, at the beginning, and then as an exhibitionist. Her performances in the mall, in Sluts and in Sombrero Jack's, had been genuine. I was sure of that.

She had opened her girl-loving side to me from the first. After all, her peeping had been focused on me more often than on Hugh, so I knew that was a true aspect of her personality. What else was she? How many layers did the Petra-onion have? How many facets on the gem? I was determined to find out.

I can be very patient. It'd been weeks between my buying the special jewellery and my first display of it. I keep clothes and toys in a locked chest, against the day I decide the time is ripe to use them. I could be just as patient with Petra. She had potential — lots of it. She could be a mine of new erotic experiences, for me and for my Hugh, as well as for herself. I'd dig slow. I'd dig deep.

For my first step I called Petra and Nadine and asked them both to visit.

Petra arrived first. I'd told her three o'clock. Nadine was due at three-thirty. Half an hour gave me time to get some booze down Petra, her pink jean-jacket spread open, and her panties down, loose around one ankle. My mouth was on her breast and my hand was tickling her mound when the doorbell went. She sat up, straightened her pink skirt, and made to zip her jacket. I pushed her back onto the sofa, bent backwards over the arm, opened her jacket wide again, and flipped her skirt to the tops of her slender white thighs.

"Stay exactly like that," I told her, without explanation. It was a tribute to my control over her that she asked for none.

Nadine was in her usual dead-black, a turtle-neck and a

flared felt micro-skirt, plus opaque black hose and ballerina slippers. I gave her a peck, lead her into the living room, and put a drink in her tiny hand.

She raised one finely plucked brow when she saw Petra on the sofa, sprawled, dishevelled, and with her naked tooth-marked breasts pointed at the ceiling, but just said, "Hi", and plopped into Hugh's recliner.

"You two know each other," I grinned, "but from a distance only. You have a relationship, of sorts — watcher," I nodded to Petra, "and watched." I indicated Nadine.

Nadine licked her lips. "So — is it to be a party? Girl-girl-girl? Or is Petra here just to take pictures?"

Petra's hand strayed to the revere of her jacket, but my frown froze her hand before she could cover up.

"I want you two to get to know each other," I said. "You are my best female friends."

Mischief danced in Nadine's eyes. "Oh — I'm sure we'll become acquainted — intimately acquainted, quite quickly — the sooner the better, by me. Your 'peeper' friend is lovely, Millie."

"I think she's feeling awkward, being exposed when we're not," I said. "Are you, Petra?"

Before Petra could find an answer, Nadine was on her feet and her skirt had fallen. She wasn't wearing any underwear. "Does that make you feel better?" she asked Petra.

"Nadine is very bold," I said, as if it wasn't obvious.

I was wearing a peignoir, emerald green, lace above my waist, satin below, with a plunging 'v' and a soaring side-slit. I shrugged one side off my shoulder, exposing a breast. "There. Now we're equals."

Nadine sat back down, spread her legs, and caressed her own mound. "Do we start now, Millie, or do we waste time socialising first? When do I get a taste of your friend?" She licked her lips and leered.

"Patience," I said. "I asked you two together for a special reason. I need a favour. I made a promise to Hugh, and broke it. I have to make it up to him."

"What promise?" Nadine asked.

"It was a while back. I had Petra over, for the afternoon, and promised Hugh that he'd walk in on us, making love. Well, we got sort of carried away. When he got home we were sound asleep."

"I'll bet he woke you up though," Nadine said. "He'd be good at that."

"Yes, and we all had a good time, but it wasn't the same. I told him there'd be another occasion, but I haven't delivered on my promise yet. I wanted to do it with 'interest'."

"So," Nadine guessed, "the idea is for him to walk in on the three of us, all nicely naked and tangled, right?"

"Exactly. What do you say, Petra?"

She looked at her toes. "I — er — I don't know. I don't know Nadine, do I?"

"You will," I said. "We have plenty of time to break the ice before Hugh gets here. Nadine's game, aren't you Nadine?"

"Try me — and I mean that literally."

It was hard to read Petra's eyes through her pale blue contacts, but I think they showed interest.

"Where were we, before Nadine arrived," I said as I swayed towards Petra. "My hand was here, I believe." I slid my palm up Petra's skirt, to her pubes. "And you were just about to suck on my nipple, right?" I dragged her head to my exposed breast.

"Watching is nice, and enough for some," Nadine said, "but I like to get in on the action. Millie?"

Half astride Petra, feeding my breast to her mouth, I pulled her skirt to her waist. "Get your tongue into this," I told Nadine. "She's reluctant now, but once we've worked on her for a while, she'll show us what a nasty little slut she really is, I promise."

Nadine knelt on the floor between Petra's thighs. Petra made to close them, but Nadine's hands spread her knees. Petra moved under me, as if to get up. I pushed my breast onto her face, forcing her back down. Before five minutes were up, she was mewing on my nipple and bucking her hips at Nadine's mouth.

We kept her pinned through two orgasms.

"Nadine's turn," I announced. "Come on up, Nadine. Kneel up on the arm, over Petra's face. I'll work on your tight little bum while Petra eats your pretty little pussy. Will that suit you?"

It did. Nadine was up and writhing her hips, pressing her pussy forward onto Petra's mouth, and back onto my squirmy tongue, before Petra had time to think about what was happening. When Petra wriggled around beneath us a few minutes later, it was to remove her skirt, not to escape. My peignoir fell to my waist, somehow. I lifted one of Petra's hands to my breast and closed it crushing-tight on my soft flesh, signalling the sort of caresses I wanted.

Nadine stretched as she pulled her sweater over her head. As Petra and I serviced Nadine's ass and pussy with our greedy mouths, we all three groped. Nadine reached back to one of my breasts and down to one of Petra's. Petra milked at one of my voluptuous ones, and stretched up to Nadine's little-girl swelling. My fingers found Nadine's other little bud, and one of Petra's crisply pointed ones. We toyed and twisted and plucked until Nadine juddered and sagged.

"I want my nipples thoroughly sucked now," I pouted. "Bring your mouths here, both of you."

I sat, bare to my waist, in the middle of the sofa, with both of them laying on their backs, their heads resting on my satin-sheathed thighs. I leaned over them, dangling my nipples into their mouths. Reaching out to either side, I played finger-games with two pussies, one bald, the other covered with wispy little soft black hairs.

I didn't make them come. I didn't demand an orgasm for myself. The ice was thoroughly broken. I wanted all three of us to be as horny as we could get, for my Hugh's arrival.

Five minutes before he was due, I plucked my swollen nipples from their sucking mouths.

"I want to arrange us," I told them. "Hugh will be here in a minute. I want us posed, when he walks through the door."

"Like this isn't sexy?" Nadine said. "Okay — what did you have in mind?"

"Nadine, would you lay over the back of that arm of the sofa, please, face up, head on the seat? Petra — the other arm? Face up, but kneeling on the seat with your thighs spread and your head hanging back?"

Giggling, both of them followed my directions, leaving just enough room between them for me. Mine was the difficult part, demanding the most flexibility. I knelt over Nadine's head and then inched back, pulling on my knees with my hands, folding myself backwards at my hips until my sex dipped down to Nadine's mouth. Leaning back even further, my hair brushed between Petra's thighs, and down, until the back of my head was on a cushion, directly beneath her pussy.

"Let's eat, shall we girls?" I suggested.

My mouth nuzzled up between Petra's parted lips. I felt Nadine's tongue curl up into mine. And that was how Hugh found us, a three woman face-up back-bend pussy-gobbling daisy-chain.

His reaction to our little tableau was *most* satisfactory.

The next morning, once I'd done my housework and opened the blinds, I called Nadine. I thanked her for her enthusiastic co-operation. When she assured me, "Any time", I asked her how she'd feel about being thoroughly used, viciously abused, and being forced to suffer endless unbearable sexual torments.

She said she thought it sounded like fun.

XXVII

Petra

I was determined to get some work done, for once. There was an idea I'd been toying with, for some weeks. It would be a big canvas, about four feet by six. The concept was that the rock wall between the Nordic, cold Hell, and the Christian, hot one, had collapsed. The ice-demonesses and the fire-demons were having an orgy. The idea of fire and ice, entwined in frenzied acts of debauchery, desperate for their lusts' consummation before the one type melted or the other's fire was doused, really appealed to me. My work is usually driven by lust. This one would have lust, and more. I felt a strange emotional commitment to it.

Perhaps Freud was right. Perhaps a climax *was* a 'little death'.

I'd just taken the dust-cover off my big computer, when the phone rang. Millie wanted me to go over the next Tuesday, at eleven in the morning — an ungodly hour, for her. She rarely drew her blinds before eleven-thirty.

"Will Nadine be there?" I asked.

"Nice, isn't she? Yes, it'll be the three of us again, but it'll be different from last time. I have something special in mind. Petra, would you come as a Dominatrix, please? Complete with some sort of mask?"

Black leather is so obvious, isn't it? As soon as I hung up I called my seamstress, with a rush order. Then I sipped tea and wondered about what it was that Millie had planned. That time, after the shopping trip, she'd been dominant, and I'd been her willing victim. It couldn't be a repeat, not with the way she'd asked me to dress. Perhaps she wanted *me* to tie *her* up? I thought about that. Millie — naked — spread-eagled on a web of tautly stretched ropes, or tightly restrained, in some obscene position, by a dozen leather straps, totally at my mercy. Chains? Indenting her soft flesh?

But then, she'd said Nadine would be there, too. Two of them, grovelling at my booted feet?

My thoughts led to other things, and I didn't even have to dress-up before I pleasured myself. Seeing myself through Hugh and Millie's eyes had enabled me to appreciate my natural looks. After a couple of nice little finger-induced orgasms, I took a nap.

When I woke, I was horny again.

One way and another, I didn't get any work done, that day. I was up at six-thirty, on Tuesday, before the alarm had a chance to waken me. I showered and dried, and prepared myself.

No hose. My new outfit was all in glossy orange vinyl, with matching mid-thigh boots, on heels that were extreme, even for me. They had tiny platforms under their toes, so that I could walk on six inch spikes.

I stalked into my bathroom, and did my face golden and vicious, with metallic eyelids and orange lips. My wig was medium length, and ash-blonde. I tried styling it into a pony tail, and then decided on a severe bun, high on my head.

I had to talc my hips to get the skirt on. It was just a stretch-vinyl tube, under fourteen inches long, shaped to conform to my hips and tapered to constrict my thighs so tightly that my legs had to glide round each other, when I walked. The effects excited me, the smooth texture, the restricting rubbery confinement, and the way it looked.

I took a couple of shots of myself, like that, before struggling into the top.

My seamstress, Peggy, had included a note, explaining how she'd achieved what she'd done, bragging, I guess. She had a body-form of me, taken from a plaster mould she'd made of my naked body, three years before. The plastic she'd used for my garment was a heat-shrink plastic. She'd "built it" as she put it, as close to my measurements as she could, dressed the form in it, and then played a hair drier over it, until it contracted, again, to fit me "maybe a bit better than your skin".

It was a brief jacket, fastening with a band snug around my rib-cage, just beneath my breasts. It had elbow-length sleeves. The front was a wide 'v', that showed most of the inner curves of my breasts. The cups were an exact negative of me, right down to dimples inside, where my nipples fitted. When I finally got myself into the jacket and fastened the strap, it looked as if I'd been painted with high-gloss orange paint. In my mirror, I could see the shapes of my ribs through their plastic coating, delicate arches between my breasts and my arms. As my arms moved against my sides, plastic squeaked. My breathing opened and closed my cleavage.

Peggy had made me a matching mask, a domino, with stiff wings. My gloves were almost as tight as my jacket, just overlapping its sleeves at my elbows.

I took some more pictures of myself — the fiery dominatrix — looking impossibly slim and tall. It was my first real work in along while. Then it was time. I covered myself with Millie's evening cloak, pulled the hood up over my head, and left for my appointment.

Millie opened the door wearing a more conventional dominatrix outfit — high black boots, a glossy black leather thong, a bra with cups that were just flesh-pinching triangles of straps around the bases of her naked breasts, a choker with four-inch curved spikes, and a black domino. We admired each other for a moment, both of us salivating in anticipation, even though *I* didn't know what the plans were.

"A quick drink before our victim arrives?" she asked.

I nodded and took the glass she handed me. "Any special instructions?"

"Just follow my lead. She'll be here shortly. You open the door."

We'd barely finished our drinks when the bell rang. Millie took a position behind it and nodded to me. I opened it. Nadine was wearing nothing special — a black vest with silver embroidery, over bare skin, and a long button-through black skirt.

She goggled at me and said, "Wow!"

I backed up, to let her in. No sooner was she inside than Millie looped black silk over her head and knotted it. Millie's hands circled Nadine's slender body, snatched her vest, ripped it back so violently that the buttons popped, and skinned it down her arms.

Nadine's mouth gaped, uncertain, not understanding what was going on. Before she recovered, Millie had her wrists in chain-linked leather manacles. Seconds later there was a stiff leather collar around Nadine's neck. Millie spun the girl and pushed her face-forward against the wall. She ran a chain from the manacles to a ring at the back of Nadine's neck and pulled.

And pulled.

Millie set her knee in the small of Nadine's back, and dragged on the rattling chain. Nadine's wrists rose higher. Her back hollowed. Her head strained back.

"The lock," Millie said.

I found it, on the hall chair, and forced the hasp through two links. It snapped closed. Nadine was held firmly, her wrists doubled up between her shoulder blades, her neck bent back so that she stared blindly at the ceiling.

"What are you doing to me?" Nadine mewed, her voice quavering.

"Shut up!" Millie ordered. To me, she said, "Get the slut's skirt off."

I couldn't kneel in that outfit. The boots kept my legs stiff and the skirt made bending impossible. I undid buttons from Nadine's waist down to her groin, pushed the skirt over her skinny hips, and let gravity take over.

Millie wrapped the loose end of Nadine's chain around her fist and propelled the helpless girl into the living room.

A sturdy mahogany coffee table, about two feet by six, stood before the sofa. Millie marched Nadine to it, and said, "Kneel. Now lean forward. Take your weight on it. Good."

Nadine lay crosswise, her head, shoulders, and tiny breasts over the far edge, her rump and hips over the other.

Millie knelt behind Nadine, took hold of her right ankle, and wrapped it in a leather strap. Then the left ankle. She secured a cord to each, stretched them out, then attatched them around the table's legs, and pulled. Nadine's legs parted sideways. Millie kept pulling, dragging Nadine's ankles until they were a full six feet apart, in a forced 'splits', before tying the cords to the table's legs.

"Isn't that pretty?" Millie asked me.

Nadine was balanced on her skinny hips, the hard wood pinching flesh against bone. Her legs were straining. Their muscles each showed, distinctly, pulled to their longest. Only the touch of her toes on the carpet kept her from toppling backwards.

Her sex — her bum, both were open to our gaze. Her ass cheeks and her sex's lips had been tugged wide apart by the strain on her ankles.

"She's — available? Would you say that was the right word?" Millie asked.

I swallowed and croaked, "Yes — available. Very."

"Every orifice," Millie continued. "She's totally helpless, completely at our mercy. We can use her any way we like, right?"

I nodded. "Did you want to gag her?" I asked. After all, *I'd* been forced to endure that hard rubber ball, hadn't I?

"No," Millie said, "We have other uses for her nasty little mouth, don't we? Petra — get that skirt of yours out of the way. Pull it up, or down, whatever."

'Up' was impossible. It was smaller around my thighs than around my hips. I squirmed and tugged, and squirmed some more, until the orange vinyl was a pool at my booted feet.

"On the couch," Millie said. "You get first go at her mouth. Sit down, in the middle, and spread your legs wide with your heels up on the table."

I obeyed, bracketing Nadine's straining head with my thighs. Millie took Nadine by her leather collar and steered her face into my groin. As soon as our captive felt my sex on her mouth, her lips parted, her tongue probed.

"You can either lay back and let the slut do all the work," Millie said, "or you can hump her face. It's up to you, Petra.

She's going to get you off, though, because I'm going to be doing *this*, until she does."

On *this*, the flat of Millie's hand slapped down on Nadine's rump.

"Let me know if she slacks off," Millie told me. "While she works well, it'll just be my hand. If she gets lazy, I've a cane that'll encourage her."

Nadine's tongue slithered between my sex's lips. As my pucker parted, she stabbed deep. Millie's hand came down again.

"Is she doing it right?" Millie asked. "Let me know what drives her best. I can do it like *this*..." Her hand slapped Nadine's left buttock. "...or like *this*." Millie stepped back, to one side, and swung up, underarm. Her palm cracked flat between Nadine's thighs, exactly on the parted lips of her sex.

Nadine jerked. Her chain rattled. Her face nuzzled me higher, searching blindly for my clit.

Cruel lust possessed me. "Yes," I said. "Like that! That makes her work better. Hit her sex, Millie. Slap it hard."

Millie rained blows. Nadine didn't cry out, her mouth was too busy, but a single tear trickled from beneath her blindfold and rolled down her cheek.

Nadine's lips and tongue were frenzied on me, gobbling and lapping and squirming into me. My eyes darted from her frantic mouth, to the sharp valley between her uptilted buttocks, to Millie's lust-flushed face, to her leather-strangled full ripe breasts, jiggling with each jolting blow.

My hips bucked, flipping my clit across Nadine's lips. My hands wrapped the back of her head and dragged her even closer into my crotch, so that I could hump her face.

Nadine slobbered and grunted. Her tongue flattened, to give me a wet cushion on which to friction my clit's head. Her hips rose higher, as if her tortured sex was eager for more punishment.

Millie slapped, and slapped, and slapped. The crack of flesh on flesh changed into more of a 'splat'. It was the sound of wetness. It was then that I first realised that Nadine had to be oozing sex-juice. The little whore was actually getting off on her pain!

I came. I didn't just 'come' — I gushed. Sweet nectar flowed from deep inside me, soaking Nadine's mouth, and cheeks until it dripped from the point of her sharp little chin.

I wriggled harder against her. My hands steered her face, using it to wipe myself.

Millie paused. "My arm aches," she complained.

"Shall we swap?" I asked. "Do you want her mouth for a while, Millie? I can take over the spanking, if you like?"

"Not yet. Come here, though. I need you to give me a hand with something."

I lifted my stiff leg over Nadine's head and stood. "What did you want me to do?"

"Remember this?" Millie picked up the electronic sex toy I'd given her — the two copper eggs on brass rods. "We've had fun with this, haven't we? I love it on my nipples. I can get off with it, eventually, when I put it to either side of my clit. I've tried it with one ball inside me, and the other on my mound. That's good, too. There's one way I've never used it, though. It's going to be Nadine's privilege to try that way out, first."

"How? What way?"

"First — watch."

I bent beside her, between Nadine's straining thighs. The girl's rump was blotched. The backs of her slender thighs showed livid hand-prints. Her sex was dark, and swollen, with puffy glistening lips.

Millie picked up a bottle of oil, and anointed one copper ball. "This one," she said, "goes in here." She pressed the copper egg to Nadine's sex, between her lips. They parted easily. One hard push and the ball disappeared. Holding the rod, Millie urged the intruder higher, deep into Nadine's vagina.

"You do the other one," Millie told me.

"What? Where? On her clit?"

"I told you — I've done that. No — here." Her fingertip probed the soft crater of our captive's anal pucker.

"I don't think..? It won't fit, Millie."

"She's taken Hugh up her ass. She'll take this, if we force it."

"I don't know."

"Then we'll just have to find out, won't we?" Millie put the nozzle of the plastic bottle to Nadine's slightly-open anus, wriggled it in, and squeezed. A dew-drop of oil overflowed, trickled down, and disappeared between Nadine's sex-lips.

"Now oil the ball, and do it," Millie ordered.

My own anus twitched and clamped tight in sympathy, but I did as I'd been told. The thing was as big as a hen's egg. There was no way it was going into a hole a pea would have blocked.

When the ball was dripping oil, I put it between Nadine's wide-spread cheeks, nestling it against her crinkled rosebud.

"Push!" Millie said.

I pushed, as a token of obedience, *knowing* it was impossible. I'd watched as Hugh's great knob had forced its way into Millie, plundering her tightest depths, but Millie was a voluptuous woman, with a shapely, rounded, full-fleshed bottom. Nadine was built like a boy, with the hips of a half-starved alley cat.

I felt a measure of elastic give. The girl's anus had to be opening, some, relaxing before the smooth copper invader, but even so...

I pressed harder — felt more give. It was impossible, but...

I leaned into my cruel task, certain that I would hear a scream at any moment. Peering closely, I saw a rubber egg cup of flesh, expanding slowly, stretching to fit around a too-big metal egg.

"The other ball!" I said. "It'll be distending her, inside. Won't it block..?"

"It's higher," Millie assured me. "I made sure it was in deep. Keep pushing."

So I did. My hand gripped the rod and eased it gently, but firmly. The flange of flesh dilated, stretching impossibly. Perhaps Nadine sucked a sharp breath. I couldn't be sure.

Millie shoved my elbow.

Nadine grunted. I released the rod and straightened. My eyes widened. The egg had been inserted past its widest diameter. Like a python swallowing a calf, the mouth of Nadine's anus slowly closed, contracting on the egg, *pulling* it in.

It disappeared. Just the obscene chrome rod projected from Nadine's anus — two rods — one from her anus and the other from her sex.

"Well done!" Millie exclaimed. "Now — I'll just switch it on..."

Nadine juddered from her waist down as the current pulsed from her cruelly distended rectum, up into the depths of her egg-dilated vagina.

"...and we can get comfortable on the sofa, Petra." She stood and plucked off her leather thong. "How about a nice long slow 'sixty-nine' while we leave Nadine to her electronic pleasure?"

XXVIII

Petra

Millie called me and relayed Nadine's thanks for "a wonderful day".

"She's okay?" I asked. "No after-effects?"

"None. After you left I took her to my shower and gave her a Water-pic enema. She loved it, the little slut. We finished off clit-to-clit, with the Water-pic doing all the work. She was stiff-legged, but still eager. Nadine's insatiable, bless her. You're a pretty avid little harlot yourself, come to that."

"Thanks, I guess."

"I mean it as a compliment, I assure you. Okay, Petra, you're the 'artist'. What next?"

"How do you mean?"

"I wrote that script — directed that scene. Now it's your turn. You can't expect me to do *all* the work."

"My turn?"

"To be creative. Pick a cast, write a story, we'll follow your direction. I'm interested to see what you come up with."

"You want me to script a sex-scene? Who for, exactly?"

"You — or you could just direct. It's up to you. Cast me, Nadine, Hugh — any combination you like. If it's for just two or three of the four of us, the ones left out can be your audience. Total control, Petra. You pick the costumes, the 'circumstances', and who does what to who."

"When for?"

"Friday nights and Saturdays are best, or early Sundays, if Hugh's in your cast."

I thought for a moment. "Saturday then, at noon. I'll have a scene ready for then, and then it has to be someone else in charge, Hugh or Nadine, the same time Sunday."

"That'll make a tiring weekend, delicious, but tiring."

"We're both fit, and Nadine, as you said, is insatiable. I'll make it easy for Hugh, so he'll have something left for Sunday."

"Don't worry about my Hugh. His hair may be going grey, but his balls are working just fine."

"Could you give me Nadine's number, please?"

"What for?"

"She'll be in my cast, if she's available. I may need to give her some instructions, beforehand."

As soon as I hung up I called Nadine. She was free for the whole weekend, and had no problem with my ideas.

"You want me to come to your place sometime?" she asked me. "A rehearsal, perhaps?"

The thought was tempting, but I made excuses. After all, I had work to do, didn't I?

Not much got done, though. My work is driven by my sexual energy. The less sex you get, the more you fantasise. It was erotic fantasies, translated into pictures, that formed my 'art'.

My energy was being used up, either in *doing* sex, or in planning ways to do it. There wasn't much left over for my work.

Still, I consoled myself that I was gathering material. When I tired of Millie and her games, I'd have lots of memories to draw on. I'd catch up.

Setting thoughts of work aside, I concentrated on planning for Saturday. I guess I have a spiteful side, or perhaps Millie just brought that out in me. She thought herself the 'sexpert', did she? Millie had always been 'in charge' — of me, of Nadine, and, from when I'd watched her with Hugh, she did most of the 'directing' in their sex. Okay — for once, Millie was going to be passive, and a 'victim'. It was 'Petra-in-charge' time!

On Saturday morning I made myself into a 'School-marm'. My hair was severe, in a bun. My ice-floe eyes were partly hidden behind the plain-glass lenses of heavy horn-rims. I tucked a tailored white broad-cloth shirt into a wide leather belt. My black serge skirt was mid-calf, and straight. Only my shoes — five-inch ankle-strap patent pumps, denied my image as 'Miss Grummidge, terror of grade six'.

I met Nadine in the lobby. She opened her coat wide for me to approve her costume. It was the first time I'd seen her in anything but black.

She had flat buckled shoes on her feet, white socks, knee-high, and a plain white button-through dress, gauze, with a pink sash. 'Alice-in-Erotic-Wonderland' was the effect I'd asked for, and she'd done beautifully. I was young boy's wet-dream of a teacher, and she was his lurid fantasy of the girl in the desk next to his.

I let my 'pupil' carry my bag of equipment up in the elevator. Hugh and Millie met us exactly as I'd instructed, both stark naked, even barefoot. That put them at more of a psychological disadvantage than shedding robes later would have done.

Millie gave us drinks, as usual. I was sure that one day she'd greet the devil, and hand him a two-olive martini.

"What's the script?" she asked me. "What are your instructions, 'directrice' Petra?"

"I'm a teacher. Nadine here, is my pupil. It's a school-for-sex. I have to instruct her in the finer points, so that she can graduate and serve the Lord and Lady, properly."

"And I suppose that Hugh and I play the 'Lord and Lady'?"

"By no means." I poked a dimple just below her navel with the point of my fingernail. "You two..." I dragged my nail down her naked belly, to her pubic mound, leaving a thin red line. "...are merely 'equipment'. You are slaves, given to me by our Lord and Master, to serve for instructional purposes. You are 'anatomically complete' human toys, that's all."

All she could say was a very small, "Oh".

"Male dummy," I said to Hugh, "move that table aside. Pull that leather chair over, so it faces the pass-through to the kitchen. You, female dummy, more drinks for me and my pupil, please, while we wait."

Millie fell into her part. She did a little curtsey before scurrying to the kitchen for our refills.

When I was satisfied with the arrangement of the furniture, I told Millie, "Back to the pass-through, now. Nadine, my bag!"

Millie stood dutifully at attention. I buckled tight leather cuffs on her arms, just below her elbows, threaded cords through their brass rings, and tossed the ends through the opening in the wall.

"Follow and watch," I told Nadine. "You may be expected to restrain someone, some day."

In the kitchen, I pulled the cords taut, dragging Millie's arms back through the gap, and tied off to the taps over the sinks. A pair of leather manacles secured her wrists together, and they too were anchored by short lengths of cord, to the taps.

Without her heels, Millie is quite short. The edge of the counter pressed just under her shoulder blades. The tension tilted her a touch, arching her back and lifting her breasts nicely.

Back in the living room I directed Hugh into his recliner and secured him with straps that ran from bicep to bicep, behind the chair. He really had very nice muscles. I had to let the arm-bands out, twice, to get them around his arms.

"We'll start with the female subject," I said to Nadine. "Note the unusual nipples." I tapped one's tip. "These ones are perfect cones, and much larger than most. The halos are also over-sized. If the subject had smaller, more normal, breasts, halos like these would cover half their area. You will also observe the colour difference, between halo and nipple. In this case the halos are relatively pale, almost fawn. The nipple itself is much darker, but not yet at its darkest. Engorgement will deepen the tint quite dramatically. Suck on this one, and let's see how deep a colour you can get it."

Nadine leaned over Millie and took a nipple into her mouth.

"Harder!" I said. "Work at it, girl. Worry it some. Let your teeth scrape the slopes of it. Use your tongue on its tip. Very well, enough. Not bad, for a first attempt. Next time, though, I expect to see tooth marks."

"Yes, Miss — tooth marks."

"Let me demonstrate." I took Millie's other nipple into my mouth. My cheeks hollowed as I sucked, drawing on it until my tongue felt its shape change, elongating. Maintaining the suction, I clamped hard with my teeth. Millie winced. My tongue found her nipple's tip, and flickered on it for a few moments before I released her.

"You see the marks?" I asked Nadine. "And this one is darker, right? Darker, longer, and harder."

"I see, Miss. Shall I try again?"

"Not now. We have a lot of ground to cover in this lesson. Bring that footstool over. Right — up on it. Now lean over the subject's face. I want you to kiss her. Remember, when you kiss someone, for the amusement of our Lord and Lady, they are going to want to see what you are doing. If your mouth presses too close, the action is hidden. This kiss can start lip-to-lip, but then draw the subject's tongue out — that's right. Extend your own tongue. I want to see two tongues, please, active ones. Very good. Get down now, and show me what you've learned."

She descended, and we kissed. Our mouths weren't six inches from Millie's face. She strained her own tongue out, but it couldn't reach to join the kiss.

"That was good. You've earned some marks already. Keep it up, and you'll graduate with honours."

Nadine looked at the floor and swayed her girlish hips. "Thank you, Miss."

"Our next topic," I announced, "is women's sex. This is a clitoris. Again, with this subject, it is oversized. She was chosen for her rare dimensions, as ideal for demonstration purposes. Kneel, child, and watch closely. There will be a test."

"An 'oral' one?" Nadine asked with a giggle.

"Of course. This is a practical lesson. Now, you will note that the subject's sex is closed. Her lips are puckered together. We are going to part them, without touching them. How do you suppose we shall achieve that?"

"By clitoral stimulation, Miss?"

"Very good. Now, the most sensitive part, the head of the clitoris, is hidden at the moment, inside its hood. Our first task is to expose it. I want you to take a two-finger grip on the subject's shaft, just behind the head. Good. Now ease the skin up, and back. Very good! Note how the head pops out."

"Do I lick it now, Miss?"

"In a moment. First, I want you to learn a different technique. Slide that sheath of loose skin back, high on the shaft, and then forwards, until it covers the head again. Excellent! Repeat, until the shaft thickens and the head swells so that the hood will no longer cover it.

Good! You will see that the vulval lips are already unpursing, as they swell. Your stimulation of the subject's clitoris is bringing blood to the area, engorging and reddening it. The mound is flushed, right? So, to open those lips further, without touching, what do you suggest?"

"Direct stimulation to the clitoral head, Miss?"

"Very good. And how would you apply that stimulation?"

"With my tongue?"

"Right! Do it, with just the tip. Nice technique, girl. You're learning fast. Keep licking, but listen closely as you work. What you are doing now is 'type one' oral-clitoral stimulation. You use this method when you are being observed, by the Lord or Lady. It is more visual, but less tactile."

Nadine paused. "Please, Miss, what's 'tactile' mean?"

"I mean that this method *looks* good, but there is another way, that *feels* better. I want you to grip the subject's clitoris, now, with your teeth, but fold your lips over them first. Good. Now suck the clitoris hard, drawing it into your mouth. Got it?"

She nodded, without releasing Millie's clit. Millie sighed.

"Now the tip of your tongue. Flick it hard and fast, over the clitoris' head. Be careful. This treatment will bring most women to climax, very quickly. I'll teach you the methods that will warn you when the subject's orgasm is close, later, but for now, remember that when she reaches her brink, you pause, and change the style of your licking. If you were working vertically, hard and fast, you might switch to a side-to-side motion, soft and slow. This way you can hold a subject at the edge of her climax for as long as you wish. If you are doing it to our Mistress, that means until she instructs you to take her to completion. In other cases, my own preference is to keep switching until my subject begs me to give her release. Very well, stop."

Nadine took one last long flat-tongued slurp, and sat back.

"Now," I said, "observe the lips of her sex. If you look closely, you will see that they have parted by at least a quarter of an inch. There is a trace of that deeper pink showing between them."

"They're wet, as well, Miss."

"Because you did well. That's ten bonus marks."

"Thank you, Miss."

Millie said, "Tell her to do it some more."

I snapped, "Shut up! Be a quiet dummy, or we'll have to start over."

I asked Nadine, "Are your nails trimmed?"

She showed me that they were.

"Good. Now — the 'G' spot. This is a circular area, inside the vagina, just behind the pubic bone. Insert one finger, please. Hook it, so that the pad of your finger presses the front wall of her vagina. Good. Feel around. It's between the size of a dime and a quarter in most women, but in this one it's more like a half dollar. It serves two purposes. With some women, it is very sensitive. Stimulating it can bring them to orgasm. With other women, there is no more feeling there than anywhere else, internally, but its stimulation still affects them. It causes certain vaginal glands to secrete, lubricating the passage. In extreme cases, the lubrication can be so copious that the woman 'comes' like a man. That is not the case with this subject, although she does get quite wet. It's about the only way that this one is sexually 'normal'. Very well, massage her 'G' spot if you've found it."

Nadine probed, and rubbed. Her extended finger stabbed into Millie's sex. I watched until I saw her folded knuckles glisten with Millie's seepings.

"Enough," I said. "You have it right. We must proceed to the next lesson."

Millie glared at me. She'd been close, three times. Each time I'd stopped Nadine before Millie had come. She was being a good 'subject', but she was getting desperate.

I opened my bag. "Our next topic is 'toys'."

"Dildos?" Nadine asked.

"That's another class. These are 'love-beads'. As you see, they come in two sizes. As a general rule, this size is for vaginal insertion, and this one for anal. Some bad girls," I grinned at her, "use the larger beads for anal, or even bigger ones."

Nadine licked her lips. "In *this* case? The 'subject' looks like a 'bad' girl to me."

"Let's start at the beginning, shall we? Oil this string of beads, and insert them into the subject's anus, one at a time, please. Do it slowly. The pleasure, for the subject, is in the 'plopping' sensation as each bead is forced though her sphincter."

Nadine took her time. It was a full five minutes before just the cord with its ring was dangling from Millie's anus. By that time, Millie was breathing hard, and wriggling.

"Now the larger balls, please, in the subject's vagina. Don't take so long this time. The entrance isn't so tight. With anal beads, there is equal pleasure for the subject when the balls are inserted, as when they are withdrawn. With vaginal, the greatest part of the pleasure is in the withdrawal. Wait for her climax, and tug sharply upwards, so that the balls run swiftly over her clitoris. This will extend and intensify the orgasm."

"And the anal?"

"At the same time, preferably. Double the pleasure, twice the fun."

"What next?" Nadine asked, when she was done cramming Millie's sex with small plastic balls.

"This particular female boasts about the strength of her internal muscles, and her control over them. As you can see, she is lubricating copiously. There is a danger she might expel the beads, before we wish it."

I took a strap, and clamped Millie's knees together with it. A second compressed her thighs.

"Now the beads are safely lodged. There are numerous other vaginal and anal toys, but now I'm going to transfer your area of instruction to the male subject."

Millie slapped her butt back at the wall, tossed her head, and groaned, but she didn't speak, so I had no reason to reprimand her. Leaving her dangling, two clit-licks short of an orgasm, was punishment enough.

"Men are very visual," I said. "You will observe that this one has attained an almost complete erection just from watching what you did to the female. Watch his penis closely, while I do this."

I unbuttoned the top buttons of Nadine's dress and spread it wide. The gentle swellings of her breasts were flushed, but her nipples were still smooth. Bending, I kissed her halo, licking tight circles around its centre, and then sucked sharply. Nadine's nipples never get large, like Millie's, or long and sharp, like mine, but I managed to raise hard a hard little nodule, like an orange pip.

"He's getting harder," she said.

"Watching a woman make love to another woman will do that for most men. Now you suck mine."

I unbuttoned my blouse and bared one breast. Her lips tugged at me. "Perhaps," I said, "*this* as well?" I turned her a little, and wrapped an arm around her slight form, and pulled her dress up at the back. My finger probed her rear crease, sliding round the rim of her sphincter. Nadine really is an anal-slut. No sooner did her anus feel my touch, than it opened to welcome me. I probed, just enough to acknowledge the invitation, and said, "He's fully hard now. Time for the next lesson."

She released my nipple. It quivered in the cool air.

"We'll take our clothes off, now," I said. "But what I want you to learn is another powerful stimulus, for males. They like to watch, and they also need to know that a woman or girl is responsive — sexually speaking. There are three main qualities that a man likes in a woman."

"And they are?" she asked as she tossed her flimsy dress aside.

I skinned my skirt down my hips and stepped out, naked except for my heels and hose. "Depravity, depravity, and depravity."

Nadine giggled. "So *that's* why the men like me so much!"

"Exactly. You're fortunate. You *look* depraved, all the time. With some girls, it's not so obvious. Now, show me lust, on your face."

Her eyes hooded. She licked her bottom lip.

"Very good. Now give him the same look. Right, well done. Now we are going to try a depraved kiss."

I led her behind Hugh's chair. My hand pressed on its back, tilting him. "Male subject, tongue out, fully extended, please."

Hugh obeyed.

"Bend over him from behind," I told Nadine, "and slather the flat of your tongue over his. Good. Pant a little, to show how much you enjoy it. Excellent! Pinch his nipples, but gently. Okay — now rake your nails down his chest, just hard enough to let him feel your claws. Bob your head! Good. Now close your mouth on his tongue, as if it was a penis and your mouth your sex, and bob some more. Excellent!"

I closed my hand around the base of Hugh's straining penis and wagged it. "As you can see, his foreskin is fully retracted now, his glans is glossy and a deep purple. That's all from a little visual stimulation, and a nice hot wet kiss. At this stage, most men will want to touch your body. The important thing is to show how responsive you are. Men hate to caress a woman and not have her show her pleasure. Come round to the side."

I took Hugh's hand in mine, and steered it to Nadine's delicate breast. Two fingers closed on the tiny nub I'd raised with my sucking.

"Gasp now," I said. "Wiggle your hips. A little sob, perhaps? A heart-felt sigh? Good."

I slid Hugh's palm down Nadine's body, to her sex.

"He's going to slip a finger into you now. Wriggle again. Squirm on it. Pant and thrust? That's good, Nadine."

I drew his finger out and put its wet pad to her clit. "Rub," I told him. "More panting, Nadine. This is heaven for you, right? Don't go overboard, though. We'll try your reactions to his oral caresses, next. That's when you go *really* crazy. Okay, stand up on the two arms of the chair."

I tilted Hugh's chair up again.

"Spread wide, Nadine, hips thrust forward. Male subject, tongue out, as before. Don't move it.

"Nadine, squat until your clit is the on flat of his tongue. Good. Now move it. Jerk your hips. Tight little circles, please. Now squeal. Lots of panting. Glare down into his eyes as if you hate him. Show extreme passion. *Use* his tongue, Nadine. It exists only for your pleasure. Men like that. You may have an orgasm now, if you wish."

Her hips juddered. I stroked her buttocks, encouraging. Muscles danced under my palm, tightened, shivered.

Nadine threw her head back and yodelled a hymn to lust, from somewhere deep in her gut. Her bum knotted tight, and then relaxed under my kneading hand. I knew exactly what she wanted, so I gave it to her. My moistened finger stabbed into her anus just in time for it to feel the contractions that undulated her vagina.

She fell backwards, into my arms.

I lapped between her orgasm-slackened lips as I lowered her to the floor, at Hugh's feet.

"You will note that the male subject is desperate for an orgasm, now." I stroked the underside of Hugh's wagging column with the backs of my fingers. "His glans is running with seminal fluid, and his flesh is taut." I stroked a finger over Hugh's dome, wetting it in his fluids, before putting it to Nadine's mouth.

She sucked.

"Tempting, isn't it? But you must resist, Nadine. The object is to keep him in this desperately aroused condition for as long as possible. Then, when you *do* allow him to climax, he'll be much easier to stimulate to another erection. Remember the rule, 'The longer they wait, the quicker they recover'."

I rose to my feet. "The next lesson is very important. The skills I am about to teach you will shorten a male's recovery time by a half, at least."

I tilted Hugh's chair back again, dragged him forward on it, and heaved his legs, one after the other, over the arms.

Kneeling again, I lifted Hugh's stalk with one hand, and his balls with the other.

"Come here and watch closely," I told Nadine. "This spot..." I dabbed the tip of my tongue at the stretched skin between Hugh's anus and scrotum, "is very sensitive. Lick it with the tip of your tongue, or scratch it gently, with your fingernails." I demonstrated both techniques before moving aside to let Nadine try.

"Very good. See how his testes shrink? You can lick there, as well, just a tantalising touch is best. Excellent! Now work down, over the lower area, and to his anus. Men love to feel women's tongues in their bums. It feels good for them, just like it does for us, but it is also a sure demonstration of your..." I paused.

"Depravity!" Nadine said.

"Good girl. Now — work your tongue in. It helps if you slobber a little. The spit running down will tickle him nicely. Are you getting him wet inside?"

She nodded without withdrawing her tongue.

"Good. Now we are going to taste that lovely big plum of his. Stroke the flat of your tongue up the underside of his shaft, and wiggle just the tip of your little finger into his bum. That's right. Now, lap at that little knot just beneath the head of his penis. That's fine. Open wide now. Let him see what you intend to do. Now — flat of tongue again, please, right across the head. Keep that finger wiggling. Good. Now you are going to show off. Mouth open as wide as you can, pause for a second to let him feel your hot breath, and *down*. Good work, Nadine. Work your lips. Mumble slowly down his shaft. That's right. Face right into his pubic hair, please, nuzzle — nuzzle — and a long slow slurp, all the way back up."

She really was good. Just to encourage her, I reached between her squatting thighs and toyed with the lips of her sex.

"Now a sucking little kiss, right on his penis' eye, Nadine. Make it noisy, now."

She moaned onto Hugh's flesh, quite delightfully. I gave her sex's lip a tiny tug.

"Can you try the tip of your tongue in his glans' hole? It won't go in, but he'll enjoy seeing you try. Fine, now a nice slack-lipped mouth please, wide open. I want you to make a loose ring, and wobble it around his head. Don't forget those noises now, and a little drool, please. Whoops!"

I reached out, under Nadine's chin, and squeezed the base of Hugh's penis.

"We almost had a little accident, then. You're doing very well, but be careful. Another second and you'd have had a mouthful of come."

"I wouldn't have minded," she said. "Not one little bit."

I patted her shoulder. "Of course you wouldn't, dear, but sucking a man's balls dry is another lesson, for another day. Right now, I want you to screw him. Up on the chair, Nadine."

She scrambled up, sitting herself astride him, hips high.

"Lower," I told her.

My hands steered Hugh's shaft into Nadine's sex. "Lower,

slowly. Rotate a few times on just his glans, and now lower, and lower, and... Good — all the way in. Hands on his shoulders, Nadine. Look him straight in the eyes. One long squirmy hip rotation, lift a little, and hard down! Excellent! Can you keep that up, Nadine? A rotation pressing down, a slow lift, another rotation when he's *almost* out of you, and then down again. Rotate *up*, and rotate *down*. Keep doing that, Nadine, until you feel you can't stand it any longer, and then just let yourself go wild, okay?"

Nadine managed that very well. She was able to retain control for a good five minutes, before her lust overcame her.

I helped, of course, by pressing on the base of Hugh's penis every time I saw he was about to come. When Nadine, sweaty and breathless, finally collapsed on top of him, I plucked his penis from her and masturbated it, vigorously, making sure that its head rubbed between the cheeks of Nadine's bum. Five strong strokes, and he jetted.

"Come on down," I told Nadine. "There are two tests to finish your lesson. I'm going to time you while you use the oral techniques you've just learned to get him hard again, starting, *now.*"

It took her four minutes and twelve seconds of scrotum and under-scrotum licking, anus tickling, and glans gobbling. I helped, some, by nestling a breast into Hugh's hand.

"Okay — he's hard. Do you remember the other stimulus, to get him desperate?"

"Visual? Two women?"

"Very good. Come and give teacher a nice big kiss."

We knelt up on the chair's arms, our bodies a bridge over Hugh's lap, and kissed and fondled for a while. Poor Hugh tied to hump up at us, or grope between us, but all his confined arms would allow was a little bum squeezing.

I released Nadine and climbed down.

"The final test — have you managed to get him desperate again? I think so, but we must make sure. Release his straps, Nadine, and then join me on the couch. I'm going to take some pictures."

The straps fell away. Millie mewed at Hugh, voiceless with lust, but her message clear. She'd endured a lot of visual stimulation, and the pleasure-balls inside her had likely had their effect.

Hugh leapt out of his chair, dashed across the room, and thrust a hand between Millie's tight-clamped thighs.

"Unbuckle me!" she demanded, but Hugh hadn't time for that. He dragged the string of balls from her sex, squatted in front of her, low enough to be able to force his rigid flesh between her thighs, gyrated his hips, and lifted her as he impaled.

Straddling her thighs, Hugh screwed in a frenzy. She must have been incredibly tight on him, with her legs strapped close, and that must have felt good for her, because she came almost instantly.

I took my pictures, sitting on the sofa, with Nadine's fingers busy on my sex. Hugh humped and grunted and heaved, shaking his wife like a rag doll.

I smiled at Nadine, and said, "Put your tongue where your fingers are, and I'll give you an A plus."

XXIX

Millie

I called my bridge partner, Penny, and apologised once more that I couldn't make it for a game. You have to set priorities, don't you? No matter how much you miss something? I had more important things to think about than finesses and squeeze-plays.

I had intricate sexual relationships to think about — and plan.

I decided Petra had done very well. She was certainly learning from me. There'd been a number of nice touches — getting my Hugh off once before letting him have me — having my legs confined, and my rectum stuffed with beads. The net results had been that I'd been incredibly tight, and Hugh had lasted for a very long time. That's a great combination, for both partners.

I'd been through four orgasms before he reached his. Even having my arms strained back like that had been a good touch. It'd done nice things to the appearance of my breasts, so that Hugh'd been moved to use his mouth on them, and more savagely than usual, because of his frenzy.

I was proud of what I'd created out of the original Petra. I was even prouder of my Hugh, and the ingenious script he came up with, on the Sunday.

He had the three of us in just heels, hose, and chokers, nothing original, but visually pleasing. We all got to appreciate the picture we made, thanks to Hugh. He dragged the sofa into the middle of the room, and arranged mirrors on both walls, so that we could watch the full scene, front and back.

He started us kneeling up on the sofa, side by side, facing over its back. We were instructed to fondle each others bums, while he moved along the line, behind the sofa, kissing mouths and playing with breasts.

Next, we had to sit down, spread our legs until our thighs overlapped, and fondle pussies, for a change, while he stayed at the back, leaning over our shoulders to caress breasts and plant kisses on our upturned mouths.

I got off, once, during that stage. I suppose it was because I was in the middle, with both Nadine's and Petra's hands working on me. Four fingers of the same hand, inside you, is nice, but when the four fingers are two pairs that belong to two different people, it's much nicer. There's more variety in the movements, I guess, or perhaps it's all in the head. Having two people play with your pussy, at once, is more 'forbidden'. That makes it more fun.

Hugh's third scene showed his imagination, and his consideration of other people's needs. He gave each of us girls the position that would appeal to her the most.

He produced, and lubricated, two double-ended dildos — the long and bendable kind, designed for girl-girl love. He must have searched hard for one of them, because it had a thick end, and a thin end. Perhaps he'd had it specially made. I think we own part of a plastics company.

Hugh sat me up on the back of the sofa, with my bum protruding back over the edge. Hugh had the others watch as he knelt between my thighs and performed cunnilingus on me, got me close, stopped, and then worked the end of the normal dildo into me. Then he beckoned Nadine up onto the sofa. She stood facing him, thighs spread. Pumping me gently with one hand, he put his face to Nadine's groin, and started lapping into her. His free hand played with her anus as it pulled her belly harder against his face.

When she, in turn, got close to a climax, Hugh took his face away and eased the other end of my dildo into her, which was about what we expected, but then he surprised us.

The darling man *knows* how anal Nadine is. She was absolutely delighted when he knelt behind her, relaxed her sphincter with his tongue and fingers, and then drove the thinner end of the second dildo high up into her bum, leaving the thick end protruding, like her ass had grown a plastic penis.

Then it was Petra's turn.

If ever there is an Olympic event for marathon pussy-eating, Hugh will be a gold medallist. His tongue seems tireless. He'd brought two women to the brink, performed anilingus on one, and was starting on his third bout of pussy-and-clit, without so much as a moment's rest. Come to think of it, Hugh's pretty good in a sprint, as well.

Once again, Hugh was being thoughtful. Petra had displayed a nice sadistic streak, so after Hugh had driven *her* to the edge of a climax, she was only too glad to work herself onto the other end of that imitation penis. Hugh was giving her the chance to do something that few women have done —

sodomise another woman.

When we were all arranged, Hugh stood up on a stool, behind me, and parted my cheeks. I felt his tongue, his finger, a squirt of oil, and then the nudge of his glans. I held my breath. I'd taken Hugh anally before, often, but this time my vagina was distended around that long thick dildo. It was going to be like having two big men use me at once.

That's always been a fantasy of mine, two men, or three. Darling Hugh was indulging me again, but I was worried he wouldn't be able to get in.

"Be patient, girls," he told the others. "This is going to be a tight squeeze."

His glans rotated in my crease, opening me. It pressed. I pressed back and commanded my sphincter to relax. Hugh's hands gripped my hips. He pushed, hard. I felt that delightful 'plop', and he was in me.

"Damn, but you're tight, Millie."

"Ram me harder, darling. I can take it."

He did, and I did. All the way.

It was almost a disaster. Four people, all standing, all humping at each other, is quite a trick. We almost fell a couple of times, but we got into a rhythm eventually. Hugh buggered me, crushing one of my breasts in his right hand and stroking Nadine's tiny one with his left, as he did humped. I was being buggered, was screwed by Nadine, and screwed her, all at once. Nadine was sandwiched, just like me, with one dildo in each lower orifice, and our tongues avid together.

Petra was both sodomiser, and being screwed herself, by every backwards lunge of Nadine's ass.

As we four learned to synchronise, it was as if Hugh was making love to us all. His thrusts into my rectum drove my dildo into Nadine, and her reaction stabbed *her* anal invader into Petra's pussy. Petra, on the rebound, as it were, thrust back, sending a shock wave undulating through Nadine, and me, impaling me backwards onto Hugh's penis.

We four made multiple love, a snake's progress of screwing. I think Nadine came first, and me second, but we couldn't drop out, or rest, we were trapped.

Hugh was next. I felt his teeth on my nape and the scalding flood in my rectum, but he didn't stop thrusting, the darling man.

The sounds and scents of sex filled the air. My belly slapped Nadine's. My bum slapped Hugh. Mouths fed on mouths, and necks and shoulders, whatever they could reach. Hands groped forward and back.

Petra screamed, juddered, and resumed her anal assault on Nadine's anus with barely a pause. We were all drunk on it — the obscenity and the *togetherness*.

It seemed to last forever. How could any of us stop? You can't leave a partner close to his or her orgasm, can you? And if, inevitably, in driving that partner to climax, you start your own climb, you aren't going to stop then, either, are you?

Eventually, though, we slowed. The rhythm faltered. At last, it stopped. Between the four of us — I guess we'd shared at least a dozen orgasms. Stiff-legged, weary, we disengaged, withdrew our impalers, and sank to our knees, or sprawled.

My Hugh had performed wonders, both in his performance, and in the planning. I wasn't surprised. In the old days, before Petra and Nadine, he'd come up with special erotic treats for me, regularly. Much as I loved our new sex-lives, I kind of missed that, but you can't have everything, can you? I missed the constant flirtation we'd used to enjoy, but that seemed to have died, as well.

You have to make sacrifices, don't you? I didn't *really* mind getting up every morning at five, to get the apartment looking as if I was expecting a floral-shirted photographer from House Beautiful at any moment.

I didn't mind not cooking so much, either. Take-out can be good, if you know the right places. I still added my own special little touches, anyway, like toasting and grinding my own almonds for the carton-packaged sweet-potato soup, and adding sherry to the instant pea.

Hugh didn't mind, either. He never complained, anyway. He didn't always finish his meals any more, but he never complained.

Nadine's scripts were predictable. Whenever it was her turn to 'direct' she cast herself as a schoolgirl who was caught masturbating, and had to be spanked, and sodomised, and finally forced to service the three of us, orally, or as a secretary who messed up the files, and had to be spanked — and so on. Sometimes she added 'high-heel' touches, sucking on, or masturbating with, Petra's or my shoes. That was a novelty, the first time.

Petra wrote good ones, heavy on bondage and exotic costumes, but always interesting. Mine were enjoyable for all, I hope. I made sure that Hugh had a good time, anyway.

Hugh's were typically masculine, I guess, very gadget-centred. The 'Y' shaped dildo for three women at once didn't work that well, but the rotating screw-threaded one was a big hit.

I was convinced that I'd given Hugh any normal man's version of Paradise, but then, one day, he brought home a bundle of travel brochures.

"Aruba? Or Cancun? Or how about somewhere new, The Virgin Islands, perhaps?"

"We'll have to check with the others," I said. "They may not be able to take a month off."

He laid his hand on my shoulder. "I was thinking of just the two of us — alone?"

I pretended interest, but my stomach was queasy. Vacations in hot climates are sexual things, aren't they? Bikini beaches to rouse an appetite, and afternoons in bed to sate them? People take off to the Bahamas because their sex lives at home lack something. Hugh obviously wasn't satisfied with what he had — what he was getting.

I was failing him. Somehow I had to come up with something new.

XXX

Petra

technology is wonderful. Someone spent millions to develop computer-optical morphing, for a big-budget movie. It seemed only weeks later that the same special effects were in half the commercials you saw, on TV. Within six months the price of the equipment came down to be within the reach of anyone who was reasonably wealthy, like me.

I had to wait half a year, though. Demand exceeded supply. When it arrived, there were eight pieces to assemble, including a special scanner and a CD ROM that was four times the size of the one I already had. If I'd waited another year, the entire set-up would likely have been reduced to the size of a thick book.

The programming was complex enough that I was reduced to the last resort — reading the manuals. Even so, it took me four or five hours a day for a week before I was ready to roll.

Millie was our 'ring-mistress'. Sure, she'd arranged things so that each of us was 'in charge', alternately. That was the point. She'd *arranged* it. When Hugh, or Nadine, or I, orchestrated the sex, it was by permission of Millie. Millie, naked, tightly tied with yards of thin biting cord, hanging helplessly from a hook, with the three of us tormenting her beautiful body, was still the one who was really in charge. Being spanked by Hugh, and sucking on the heel of my boot, it was Millie who was calling the shots. It all revolved around Millie. If *I* spent an evening as the centre of attraction, being worshipped by three slippery penetrating tongues, the object of their total adoration, it was because Millie had directed it to be so.

That rankled.

Well, with my new computer animation equipment, I could contribute an element to our little orgies that none of the others could have supplied. Come to that, I was likely the best qualified in the whole world, at what I intended to do.

Mocking-up a little scene where Hugh's animated tongue lapped forever at Millie's straining clit was crude, and basic. With my new magic, I could create, on tape, anything I could dream up. I could give Hugh a penis like a Beardsley drawing — big enough that he'd need a wheelbarrow to carry it. I could graft Millie's ripe breasts onto Nadine's slender frame, but bigger. I could extend her nipples, to the length of knitting needles.

When I'd created these new composites, I could put them through sexual gymnastics that no human body could endure. I could...

I loaded Millie first. My computer ate stills of her in a score of positions, taken from a dozen different angles. I added the videos I had of her, erasing any other bodies that were in the scene. That was kind of fun. There was one of Millie on her back, humping up at Hugh. I took Hugh out from between her legs, which left some blanks, of course. A few simple commands had my computer search for other images of Millie, and use parts of them, to fill the empty spaces. Before my very eyes, as they say, the blank area where Millie's far thigh had been covered by Hugh, closed up. Where one of her breasts had been left nippleless, because Hugh's mouth had been sucking on it, a new nipple grew. Within ten minutes, I had Millie whole again, swivelling frantic hips up at the empty air.

Once my electronic aide had digested Millie thoroughly, I commanded it to show me a basic 'model' Millie. She appeared, standing straight, arms by her sides, blank-faced, just like an illustration in a Home Doctor book.

When I clicked on her ankle, and dragged my mouse, her legs parted slowly, following the blip of light, until she was doing the splits. I clicked again, on her hand, and carried it across to her sex. My joy-stick zoomed in on her, expanding her until her hand and vulva filled the screen. I crooked her finger, and twitched it from side to side, wobbling her clit.

On 'replay', Millie did the splits once more, and masturbated. I could stand her, bend her, or turn her upside down, and still that finger did its job, as it would until I commanded it to stop. In some ways, computer-image people were better than the real thing.

I went to 'edit', gave her left nipple a clockwise rotation, and her right a counterclockwise. My clever toy adjusted her breasts to react. I had to adapt her shoulder movements myself. If I'd put tassels on her nipples, she could have been a burlesque star.

My on-screen Millie was a mechanical doll, at that stage — almost a cartoon — but I was just learning. I knew my own skills. In a week, I'd be able to create as many Millies as I liked, doing anything I could think of, and looking totally realistic.

My joystick pulled her head into a close-up. I started to work on her facial expressions.

XXXI
Millie

It was Petra's turn. I was impatient to see what she had in store for us. For three weeks she'd been secretive and constantly dropping unsubtle hints about some special erotic treat she had in store for us. What in hell's name could it be? We'd contorted our four bodies into every position that human forms could assume. My own body, in particular, had made the greatest variety of contributions. Both Petra and Nadine are slimmer than I am, but I'm the one who can tongue her own pussy, or stand and fold backwards until my head touches the backs of my knees.

We'd all played master or mistress, and all been slaves. We'd all bound, and been bound. We'd all spanked, and been spanked — except for my Hugh. He didn't mind spanking us, but being on the receiving end didn't appeal to him at all.

What else could Petra add to our playtimes? Could it just be some extra-exotic costume? I liked Petra's special clothes, but even variety can get boring.

The first clue came by truck. Three men delivered a large screen TV, with a built-in VCR.

"Do you think we are just going to watch movies?" Hugh asked as he plugged it in.

"She's very visual," I mused. "If it *is* to be a movie, I'm sure it will be an extra special one."

"Do we have popcorn?"

"Will Cadbury's Flakes do? Eaten from pussies?"

He slapped my blue-jeaned butt. "Sounds delicious. So — what are we supposed to wear? Do we dress as teenagers, and pretend this is a drive-in?"

"Petra left a message on the machine. We're free to wear whatever we like, just so it's comfortable, and accessible."

"That's nice. Those leather pants she had me in last time were too tight on my bum."

"But it looked so nice in them, sweetheart. Looks before comfort, right?"

Hugh settled for a robe over pyjama pants. I took longer, getting ready. It'd be just like Petra to tell us not to bother fussing with much, and arrive in something totally stunning.

I painted on my whore-face, which Hugh likes so much, and trimmed my pubic hair. I'd learned, for group sex, to wear the hair on my head piled up high, or pulled back. Long hair tumbles around your face, when you lean over. It can block a watcher's view of what your mouth is doing to your partner's body. That's a big part of the pleasure of group sex, being watched, and showing off your skills to your audience.

Hugh got the most benefit from our competitiveness. On one occasion, Nadine had given a virtuoso performance, holding Hugh still, as she bobbed her mouth on his shaft, very rapidly, each stroke going from lips-pursed-on-glans, to deep throat.

Petra and I had applauded, but, having acknowledged Nadine's exceptional skill and control, had both felt compelled to show that we could do the same, but faster, with head shakes, with laps at his testicles on the bottom of the downstroke, and so on. Poor Hugh!

Petra had specified 'simple' for our costumes, so 'simple' was what I wore. I draped a folded length of violet chiffon over my right shoulder and breast, leaving my left side bare, opened the fabric out into a skirt, and tied it at my waist with a thin ribbon. A second piece of the same ribbon nipped my left thigh, about two inches below my groin. I stepped into strappy sandals, and was done.

I'd just finished laying out hors d'oevres, from Exquisite Eats, on Market Street, when Nadine arrived. Her idea of dressing simply and comfortably was opaque black over-the-knees, a black choker, and a broad brimmed black felt hat trimmed with black satin roses. I couldn't help but notice, as I took her coat, that she'd shaved off her thin wisps of pubic hair, to match Petra's style. Okay — I'd watch Hugh's reaction. If bald pubes turned him on especially, I'd just have to go get a waxing. Or get him to shave me? That might be fun, some evening when we had sex all alone, if that sort of evening ever happened again.

Petra surprised me. She obeyed her own rules, pretty well. No boots, no hose, just high-heeled pumps. Her dress was clinging black velvet, ankle length, open at the front from hem to mid-thigh, and with a deep neckline. It was sexy, but the sort of thing that you could wear in public, in the evening. Compared to Nadine and me, she looked over-dressed. Even her make-up, hazel contacts, and feathery fawn wig were glamorous, but not outrageous. Hugh and I thanked her for the TV, and asked her what the program was to be, for the evening.

She passed Hugh a cassette. "I thought we'd make it a restful one," she said. "I want to show you some of the little tricks my computers and I can do with videos. You know the old saying, 'Seeing is believing?' Well, it isn't true, not any more. Now — how shall we arrange the seating? I know! Let's get really cosy. Hugh, in the middle of the sofa, please. Nadine and Millie — sit either side of him, okay? People neck while they watch movies, don't they? If I sit on the ottoman, between Hugh's knees, everyone will be able to neck with everyone, right?"

Everyone would be able to neck with my Hugh, was what she meant. Still, I couldn't complain. I'd have made the same arrangements. She loaded the VCR, sat, and pointed the remote. Hugh draped his arms around Nadine and me, letting his hands settle where they liked, which happened to be on one of each of our breasts. The fifty-two inch screen flickered alive. I reached sideways, into Hugh's pyjama fly, and found that Nadine's hot little hand was already there. That was fine. Hugh is plenty long enough for two small hands, or even three.

"This is a home movie?" Hugh said. "Remarkable, Petra. It looks like a professional Hollywood set."

"Thanks for the compliment, but that's exactly what it is. I lifted it from an old Arabian Nights movie. This is the Sultan's harem from *The Thief of Baghdad*. Her hands pulled her neckline deeper and wider, with that distinctive Velcro sound. The crafty bitch — her dress could open all the way, with just a tug. I put my free hand over the one of Hugh's that was cupping my breast, and squeezed, just to remind him which of the three of us women had the best boobs.

I said, "You should have warned us, Petra. I'd have dressed in my slave-girl outfit."

Hugh's finger and thumb pinched my nipple.

"But you *are* wearing a slave-girl outfit," Petra said. "Watch."

There was a bottle on the screen, laying on a cushion. There was something wrong with its perspective, so I guessed Petra had edited it in, somehow. Its cork popped. A cloud of purple smoke billowed out.

Petra said, "I lifted that from an old Harry Harrihousen movie. Watch the djinni!" She spread her legs and tugged at the slit in her skirt, parting it to her crotch. The sound of Velcro parting always gets to my Hugh. Men are just like Pavlov's dogs, aren't they? I felt his shaft twitch between Nadine's palm and mine.

The cloud of smoke condensed. My mouth dropped. The djinni — the one on the screen — was me! I was in curly-toed slippers, like I'd never owned, gossamer pants, and about twelve pounds of assorted gold bangles.

"How did you do that?" Nadine asked, leaning forward.

"Computer-magic," Petra gloated. She turned between Hugh's splayed thighs, gave the head of his exposed penis a quick peck, and went on, "You are really going to like this next bit, Hugh. This is your dream-come-true, I'd think."

A gigantic slave appeared from behind a drape, lifted his scimitar, and slashed at me-on-the-screen. I was just about to bite Petra's head off, for daring to suggest that Hugh'd enjoy watching that, when the screen-me shimmered, and then there were two of them — me — us.

"You see what I mean — Hugh? Millie? What could be better than having your gorgeous wife, twice over?"

"Am *I* in this movie?" Nadine asked.

Petra patted Nadine's naked bald pubes. "Of course, dear. We all are."

The two of me on the screen were dancing, some sort of

belly-dance. I seemed to recognise a few of the movements as ones I did when I exercised, but those were blended seamlessly into an erotic routine that I'd never performed in my life. It was really nice, watching myself, twice over. My four breasts jiggled nicely, my two waists flexed and bent with equal litheness, both of my shadowy navels winked. I turned, and did two spread-legged handstands, followed by a walk around the pillows and couches on my four hands.

I've done handstands, but usually against a wall or something. I've *never* been strong enough to walk on my hands. It made me quite jealous of myself — selves. Hugh's hand tightened on my breast. The two me were getting to him. That was nice.

"You really are very clever, Petra," Nadine said, "but when do *I* come in?"

Petra ripped her neckline even wider, exposing one breast completely. "Be patient," she said. "Play with this, and maybe I'll fast-forward to your entrance."

"No you won't," Hugh said. "I'm enjoying this part — two of my Millie — too much."

I gave his stem a "thank-you" squeeze. Despite Hugh's words, Nadine's hand found Petra's breast and twitched its nipple.

"This next part might amuse you, Millie," Petra said. "With my computer's help, you can do things you've never even dreamed of doing."

As it turned out, she was wrong. What followed was something I *had* enjoyed masturbation fantasies about, but she'd made a reasonable assumption. Not many women reach my depth of depravity.

The two Millies cartwheeled across the carpeted floor, landing sprawled together on a pile of cushions. They knelt up, embraced, and kissed each other. *I was kissing me!*

"My God that's sexy," Hugh gasped. "If only you had a

twin, Millie."

The Millies on the screen were rubbing their breasts against each other as their tongues tangled. Hugh was right. It was incredibly erotic. I've rubbed breasts with a number of women, but none who had such beautiful ones as mine are. Then they sucked on each other's nipples. I joined in Hugh's wish. If only I had been twins, we could have had an incredible incestuous relationship.

They toppled to the floor, still in each other's arms, and twisted around, head to tail. Their harem pants disappeared, by computer magic. One tucked her head down between the others thighs. The second me threw her head back. The picture zoomed in to catch my ecstatic expression, as I gave myself head. Well, I can do that, but not double-bodied. It turned into a soixant-neuf. If only there had been sound! I bet I was making incredibly sexy gobbling noises — both of me.

Hugh took the nape of my neck and turned my face to his. His tongue parted my lips for a quick stab into my mouth. "I'm going to dream about this," he said. "I can't think of any two people I'd rather watch making love, sluttling, than you and you."

The sound of Velcro interrupted again. Petra had ripped her dress all the way open. She turned on the ottoman, her body a startling white inside the shadowy drape of her black velvet dress, to face the three of us. "I've seen this," she said, "often. Why don't you three watch while I make it good for you?"

She took Nadine and my hands from Hugh's staff, and bent her head to it. Her fingers stretched out to Nadine's puffy bald pubes, and up under the brief gauze of my skirt. That was fine by us. We all three wriggled closer to the edge of the sofa, legs spread, to give her easier access.

Petra sucked, and fingered. Nadine fondled Petra's breast.

Hugh stroked Nadine's flat little tummy, to one side, and cupped my breast, to the other, while I snuggled against him and played spider-fingers over his chest and ribs with the hand that wasn't holding his penis to Petra's slurping mouth.

"Christ!" Hugh said. "Three identical editions of my Millie, plus you two? I think this must be what heaven is like."

Petra's lips released his glans for just long enough to say, "There's better, to come."

"You'd better slow down then," Hugh told her, "or I'll have come before the best part."

Drapes parted, on the screen. Two lines of naked girls filed in, all long-haired slender Orientals, all identical.

"You think that being twins is great, Millie?" Nadine asked. "How do those girls feel, being — whatever having fifty of you is."

"They could make some spectacular daisy-chain," Hugh remarked.

A massive throne rose up through the floor like an organ in an old time theatre, with Hugh seated on it, in a Caliph's jewelled turban, but otherwise handsomely naked.

"Are there going to be two of Hugh, as well?" I asked.

Petra slurped off Hugh's glans, and answered, "Maybe in the next production. How would you like a movie, Millie, with ten versions of Hugh gang-banging two versions of you?"

"How about me?" Nadine complained.

Petra's pussy-probing fingers soothed her.

"Oh — here I come," Nadine squealed.

The two Millies had risen, gone to Caliph Hugh, and seated themselves at his feet. They still fondled each other, stretching across Hugh's thighs to reach breasts, but I noticed that their expressions didn't change, and their caresses became unnaturally repetitive.

Nadine was right. She was making her entrance. Four gargantuan Nubian slaves were carrying her, naked, face down, by her wrists and ankles. Petra deserted Hugh's penis and twisted to the screen, still fondling me and Nadine, though. "Watch this part carefully," she said. "Keep an eye on Nadine's waist. I'm proud of this bit."

The slaves draped Nadine across a trestle.

"That looks uncomfortable," the real Nadine mock-complained.

"You ain't seen nothin' yet," Petra told her.

Another man entered the harem — bigger even than the Nubians. I seemed to recognise him as an actor who had played Hercules in a series of old movies. One of the mass of identical Orientals ran to him, and snatched his loincloth away.

"A man could get a complex," Hugh said.

The man's penis hung to below his knees, thick as a python. Three of the identical Orientals gathered around it, on their knees, kissing and caressing. The python reared, thickened, and lengthened. Soon, it was long enough that it stood higher than his head, and was as thick as his thigh.

"That's impossible, unfortunately," Nadine sighed.

"Not for my computer-magic, it isn't," Petra boasted. "Brace yourself, Nadine."

The silly girl actually stiffened, there on the couch. Two of the Nubians on the screen took screen-Nadine's ankles, lifted them, and spread them. Two Orientals parted the cheeks of her ass.

"I don't know if I can watch this," Nadine giggled.

The dome of the man's penis, bigger than my head, nudged between the screen-Nadine's buns. He lunged.

"Watch this!" Petra shouted.

As the man sank in, impossibly, the screen-Nadine's waist thickened, showing the depth of his progress.

"What a way to die," Nadine gasped.

Petra had cut that sequence short, once she'd done her trick. The man simply reared up, with Nadine skewered on his rod like a kebab, and marched out with her still impaled on it.

"Is that all there is, of me?" Nadine asked.

"I'm working on a sequel," Petra assured her. "You're in it a lot, with all the spanking and whipping your cute little butt could desire."

"Oh? Oh — okay."

Petra said, "There isn't much more. Each minute of tape takes me a hell of a long time to produce. Shall we get serious?" She turned back to Hugh, opening her mouth to engulf him again.

We all knew what she meant by 'get serious'. It was time for orgasms. Although Petra's fingers were working on my sex, Hugh added his own, and did the same for Nadine. Neither Nadine nor I could reach Petra's sex, but we played with her breasts. Petra was 'hosting' this session, anyway, and we could always take care of her after. Hostesses always came last, in our protocol.

Just as I expected, the last of our foursome to appear on the screen was Petra herself. She was unrolled from a rug, at Caliph-Hugh's feet, just like Cleopatra.

On the screen, Hugh was, of course, devastated by Petra's awesome beauty. He had her chains struck off, and lifted her onto his lap. Even the two screen Millies looked up at her in adulation.

She straddled him, and sank onto his rampant penis. As she rose and fell, one me lapped alternately at her ass, and Hugh's stem, while the other me just stood by, masturbating, overcome with the joy of watching Petra make it with my Hugh.

The genuine Hugh, the doll, said, "The real you, playing with yourself, Millie, looks much sexier than that one on the screen." His thumb pressed down on my clit and rubbed, hard.

I felt my love for him whelm up inside me. The feeling was so strong, it overcame my good manners. I could have put up with Hugh getting excited, watching Petra bounce in his lap, on screen. I had often watched her lips gobble on his shaft, in reality. Both at once was too much for me, at that moment. I covered up my jealousy, I hope, by taking Petra by the chin, and lifting her head off Hugh, to kiss her. When my lips left hers, though, they swooped down on Hugh, taking him deep into my mouth, before she had the chance to.

He groaned, "Oh yes!" and humped up at me, butting his dome against the back of my throat. I made a gargling noise, and pushed down harder, trying to swallow him.

Petra took it well. I felt her lift my leg, and then her cheeks smooth against the insides of my bare thighs. Her mouth made a small tight 'O' around the swollen head of my over-sized clit. I retaliated by reaching down to her sex and fingering her, frotting her clit as fast as I could.

Hugh said, "Oh my God — look at that!" but I couldn't look, not with my head buried in his lap.

Nadine was pleasuring herself. I could tell by the way the sofa shook. Whatever was going on, on screen, it had to be quite spectacular.

And then Hugh came, flooding my mouth, and I came, and I think Nadine came. We didn't leave Petra out, though. All three of us attended to her, while we watched the replay.

XXXII

Millie

I t was Nadine's turn to "direct". She'd done her best to inject some variety into her "scenario". This time she'd had all three of us bound, bent over. I suppose she was doing to us as she would like to be done to, but that doesn't always work, does it. To be good at sex, you have to do unto others as *they* like, not as you'd like. That's why sadists and masochists get on so well, right?

It hadn't been bad. She must have worn her tongue out, performing anilingus on three bums, while masturbating us, one after the other. We all got off, but not spectacularly. Not even Hugh did, and when *I* give him that treatment, it usually ends in a scream and a gusher.

Then Hugh had eaten Nadine, as Petra and I spanked her buns. None of us had our hearts in it, though. We none of us seemed inclined to get straight into another scene.

I made drinks, to cover the emptiness.

Petra was sprawled at Hugh's and my feet. "I'm way behind in my work, you know," she said. "I kind of miss watching, and taking pictures."

"Yes," I agreed. "It was a real kick when you were spying on us, and didn't know that we knew."

"That was the good part — when those you watch don't know you're there. It makes it more 'forbidden', somehow."

Nadine picked up the binoculars and wandered naked to the window. "Perhaps there's some action... My God! There is! Come here, everyone."

We all huddled round. There was a young couple in the window of the apartment above Petra's. They were nude, and embracing. Unfortunately, at that angle, all we could see was from their waists up — and then they moved back, out of sight.

"Come on," Petra said. "Get something on quickly. Two floors up is the common room. The window of the pool room will give us a better view."

At that time of night, the common rooms are deserted. We lined up in front of the window, passing the binoculars backward and forward, fondling each other's sexual parts in a rather desultory fashion.

The couple didn't do anything spectacular, just mainstream sex, a caress or two, a little oral, and then doggy-style, but they were *new* bodies, and they didn't *know we were watching them*.

Hugh dragged me out of the line and left Petra and Nadine to share the binoculars.

"Give us a commentary," he said over his shoulder.

He took me on the pool table, hard and fast.

When it was over, we went down again, to get dressed and for "goodnight" drinks.

"Suppose," Petra mused, "we somehow got night-vision binoculars to them, and suppose somehow they found out that there was something exciting to watch, through your window, huh Millie? You're smart, Hugh. Could you make a plan?"

Hugh shrugged. "I guess I could. And the next step, once we got bored with that, would be to invite them over, wouldn't it? And then we'd have to find someone else to spy on, or get to spy on us. Where would it end, Petra? The entire population of Crystal Towers, peeping or being peeped?"

We all sat in silence for a while, thinking. Finally, I got up and fetched Petra and Nadine their coats. I gave each of them a peck and a hug. "Sweethearts," I said. "It's been a wonderful year. I'll never forget it, or you two, but from now on, I'm afraid, my blinds stay drawn, okay?"

They nodded their understanding, gave me another hug, and left Hugh and me alone.

XXXIII

Epilogue

Millie

I t was Sunday night. Hugh and I were lounging in our new fluffy and comfortable robes, almost identical ones to those I'd trashed. The supper things were still on the table, the debris of six exotic courses that had taken me two days to prepare, all congealing nicely. The *New York Sunday Times* was spread across the floor. I was on the sofa, reading the fashion insert. Hugh was doing the crossword in the magazine section, in ink, of course.

"Millie," he said, "how about we try something really new, in our sex lives?"

"I'm game. What did you have in mind?"

"How about we go to bed, under the covers, with the lights off? And then..."

"And then?"

"And then we snuggle up, me against your nice warm back, and we do it 'spoons' style? No foreplay? Just 'do it'."

So we did just 'do it', and it was great.

*****

Petra

My *Twin Hells* sold for a hundred and eighty-three thousand, a record for me. I'd caught up on my magazine commitments. The proofs for the new coffee-table book, *1001 Erotic Nights*, were in the mail.

I was clear to start a new project. First, I browsed though all my 'Millie/Hugh/Nadine/Me' shots. Nothing there inspired me. Those three were beautiful, but I didn't feel that there was any erotic energy there. Flat batteries. All their charges drained.

I have a book of 'famous nude sculptures'. Flicking though, I came to Michelangelo's David. Such a beautiful body! Now, if I gave it an erection? And added myself, worshipping at his feet, bronzed? And some of Rodin's nudes had distinct possibilities. Now, how much metallic body-paint did I have? Order more, anyway?

I loaded a camera, stripped bare, and started by spraying my feet gold. It was a wonderful feeling! I hadn't been so excited in — oh — over a year, anyway. And after I'd taken pictures of the gilded Petra-statue? There was a mirror waiting — and my clever loving fingers.